KNOW THY ENEMY

JEFFERY H. HASKELL

aethonbooks.com

KNOW THY ENEMY
©2023 JEFFERY H. HASKELL

This book is protected under the copyright laws of the United States of America. No part of this publication may be reproduced, stored in a retrieval system, or transmitted, in any form or by any means, without the prior permission in writing of the publisher, nor be otherwise circulated in any form of binding or cover other than that in which it is published and without a similar condition including this condition being imposed on the subsequent purchaser. Any reproduction or unauthorized use of the material or artwork contained herein is prohibited without the express written permission of the authors.

Aethon Books supports the right to free expression and the value of copyright. The purpose of copyright is to encourage writers and artists to produce the creative works that enrich our culture.

The scanning, uploading, and distribution of this book without permission is a theft of the author's intellectual property. If you would like to use material from the book (other than for review purposes), please contact editor@aethonbooks.com. Thank you for your support of the author's rights.

Aethon Books
www.aethonbooks.com

Print and eBook formatting by Steve Beaulieu. Artwork provided by Vivid Covers.

Published by Aethon Books LLC.

Aethon Books is not responsible for websites (or their content) that are not owned by the publisher.

This book is a work of fiction. Names, characters, places, and incidents are the product of the author's imagination or are used fictitiously. Any resemblance to actual events, locales, or persons, living or dead is coincidental.

All rights reserved.

ALSO IN SERIES

AGAINST ALL ODDS
WITH GRIMM RESOLVE
ONE DECISIVE VICTORY
A GRIMM SACRIFICE
KNOW THY ENEMY
A GRIMM DECISION
TRADITIONS OF COURAGE

Check out the entire series here! (tap or scan)

CHAPTER ONE

15JAN2937 HORSEBACK MOUNTAINS, ALEXANDRIA, ALLIANCE SPACE.

Cold seeped into Wit DeBeck's bones from the wind blowing across the mountainside. Despite having his cabin in the woods compromised, he just couldn't bring himself to give it up. For twenty years, the antiquated home served to ground him and keep him centered.

He swung the axe with the never-dull blade, splitting another log for the woodstove. The cabin had all the modern conveniences. He wasn't a troglodyte—he just enjoyed the physical labor and exertion. There was something fulfilling about working with his own sweat and muscles for the wood to fuel the stove.

After his monumental failure to see the spy network in the Alliance, he had rightly lost his position as the head of the Office of Naval Intelligence. If it were up to him, he would have retired and never left his cabin again. It wasn't up to him, though. President Axwell had made that abundantly clear.

Which is why, on a frigid Sunday morning, Wit trudged

through ankle-deep snow, carrying an armload of freshly cut wood to his cabin. Once inside, he dumped the wood in the box next to the stove. After that, he picked up his thermos of Consortium coffee and pressed the hidden button under the counter. The moderate-sized fridge lifted with a quiet whirr, revealing the hidden passage to his crisis center.

It was, Wit admitted, a little childish to have such a room. However, it had proved invaluable in his war against the Caliphate. A war he'd waged for most of his life, with or without the permission of his government.

Once the fridge closed and the electronic security net locked the place down, he sat in his chair and palmed the activation button. Nothing in the room would work if his biometrics weren't present.

Multiple reports waited for him, some good, some bad. Wit let out a long sigh as he sank into his heated leather chair. Three holo-screens popped to life, showing him the most urgent messages.

As he read the first report, he balled his fists in frustration. The Consortium's primary shipyard, Anjō, had come under attack and they'd lost half their production capability—along with a dozen heavy cruisers under construction—in one fell swoop. Wit analyzed each line, reading and re-reading until he understood everything he could, then taking that information and placing it in context with what he already knew.

The Caliphate Navy's tactic became obvious as he analyzed the data. Their FTLC tech had allowed them to coordinate a multipronged attack on Anjō. A feint drew out Anjō's forces, leaving them wide open for the main Caliph fleet to come through the opposite starlane and obliterate the orbital infrastructure.

No one knew of the FTLC but the Alliance. They couldn't share it with their allies until they knew how to duplicate or jam it. It pained Wit that they couldn't counter the tech... yet. With the Consortium ship production halved, their chances of winning the war—hell surviving the next eight months—nose-dived.

"Dammit." His voice echoed in the dark. They needed more time.

The second report filled him in on the research Navy R&D did on the schematics Nadia had stolen from Medial. Appended to the report was a note from the lead engineer asking for a meeting.

Wit activated his secure comms, which immediately encrypted his voice and routed the line through millions of servers.

"Dr. Sterling Iverac. How may I help you?"

"Sterling. I'm reading your less-than-encouraging report. What is going on?"

"I don't have good news, I'm afraid."

Wit frowned at the admission. "Sterling, you're the single most brilliant quantum physicist in the galaxy. You can't tell me something like that."

Sterling chuckled softly from the other end. "Not quite, but thank you. I wish your agent had brought us a unit intact, but I seriously doubt I could have reverse engineered something this complex even then."

"Quantum entanglement is old tech. You're losing me," Wit said.

"Like you said, I'm the expert. I can't tell you how it works, but I can guarantee you it doesn't use quantum entanglement. What ever this is, it isn't like anything I've ever seen or heard of. Nothing in this schematic lines up with what we know about quantum physics. If anything, this looks more like a Higgs-Boson field generator. I have no idea how they could make one small enough, or why it would even help them."

Wit sipped his dark coffee, letting the heat flow to his belly. When Nadia had first brought him the schematics for the FTLC tech, he'd thought they were going to pull it apart and have their own form of "space-telegraph" the way the Caliphate did. It was downright disappointing for it to fail.

Wit switched tracks, not wasting time on wishful thinking. "Who came up with it? Any ideas?"

"Do you know how long they've had it?"

"A few years at least."

Dr. Iverac didn't respond for a moment. Wit could tell he was trying to give a thoughtful answer.

"The scientific community has always tried to supersede the national one. Keep lines of communications alive and all that. Before the Great War, I met a brilliant young physicist at a conference. He regaled me with his theories of faster-than-light communications. If anyone cracked the barrier, I would think he would've."

Wit frowned, wondering why this was the first he heard of this man. "Where is he now?"

"His name was Dr. Hassan Abbasi. I never heard from him, or of him, after Hamid took over the Caliphate. There were a lot of political and religious purges at that time. When I didn't hear from him again, I assumed they killed him, but... this looks like his work."

The name tickled a memory in Wit. A report from one of his civilian contacts who traded in the Caliphate.

"Thank you, Sterling. Keep working on it, but relegate it to tier two."

"Right. I'll put it in the bin for showers and long walks. Goodbye Wit," he said before hanging up the line.

Wit played a dangerous game, and he knew it. As Secretary of the Navy, his responsibilities were to the fleet, but as the former spymaster, he couldn't just let it go. Nor could he turn it all over to his replacement.

The final report caught his eye. His new job as the SECNAV challenged him in ways ONI never had. One of them was the strategy and tactics of long-term naval conflicts. With Noele behind the fleet's strategy, Wit focused on the war. There were two ways to fight a war: weapons and morale. His specialty lay in the latter. He would crush their spirit.

Which was why a fully reformed Task Force Sixteen headed for Medial at that very moment to take the planet from the Caliphate and let them know, in no uncertain terms, that no matter how the war played out, the Alliance would fight tooth and nail to stop the slave trade.

Without their own FTLC, he wouldn't know about the outcome of the battle for weeks. In the meantime, though, he needed to get moving on finding the source of the FTLC. He could turn it over to the new ONI, but that didn't sit right with him. All the men and women he worked with at ONI were outside his reach now... all but one.

A plan bloomed to life in his mind. One that would turn the tide of the war if successful. He typed up several orders and sent them out with *all haste* attached to them. When that was complete, he exited his secret room and headed for his aircar. For his plan to have a chance at success, he needed his top infiltrator. A chuckle escaped his lips as he imagined her surprise when she realized he'd known where she was all along.

CHAPTER TWO

Jacob gripped the armrest hard enough his fingers hurt. Each hit shook the battleship like a rag doll. The holographic display before him repeated the task force's combined sensor data to show him and Admiral Spencer the "picture" of space around them. Naval tactics being what they were, the ships currently slugged it out with an enemy fleet eight hundred thousand klicks off their port beam.

The broadside engagement wasn't Jacob's preferred tactic. They lasted far too long, resulting in too many casualties. Which meant the only people at risk were the crews of the ships. A defensive fight was no way to win a victory.

He held his tongue, though, not wanting to second guess Admiral Spencer. As Jacob had learned, the task force XO was more about paperwork and acting as a sounding board than making any real contribution to the overall strategy.

Still, engaging the enemy with the goal of a stalemate felt wrong. Not only to him, but it felt wrong that the Caliphate Navy would act so passively. He'd fought them several times and he could attest to their aggressiveness.

Jacob manipulated the controls on the holo, expanding the

box ahead of their course. Passive sensors picked up nothing, but Jacob's gut told him something was off. The screen rewound to when they first made contact. As he watched, the enemy ships switched to a defensive formation immediately and changed course.

If Jacob were commanding the *Enterprise,* he would've vectored to shrink the gap and engage with the Long 9s at close range. Instead, they were duking it out at nearly max range. Why?

"Viv," Jacob said over their shared channel, "anything about this strike you as odd?" He asked while gesturing at the replaying battle on his screen.

As *his* XO, she sat beside him, watching the same battle and likely feeling the same helplessness. Tin Can skippers didn't worry about fleet tactics.

"Sir?"

"You've fought them just as much as I have. I don't know. It just doesn't feel right."

To her credit, Lieutenant JG (frocked) Boudreaux examined the situation with thoughtful eyes. One thing Jacob appreciated about her, both as a Corsair pilot and an XO, was that she never jumped headfirst into anything, including answers. Her eyes widened slightly. If he hadn't been looking directly at her, he would have missed it.

"What?"

"Sir, I think they're leading us into a trap."

Jacob switched the holo to a forward view of the Task Force's active radar and lidar. Any ship within ten million klicks would light up like a Christmas tree during a blackout.

"Help me see it?" Jacob wasn't above asking his officers to explain something to him. Especially when the fate of the entire task force loomed in the balance.

"There's a starlane roughly three million klicks ahead. If an enemy force were to come out of the lane at just the right time, we would be decimated."

She wasn't wrong, of course. Starlane exit and entry vectors were well charted. Every ship in existence used gravity detectors to mark them and update their drift every time they went through. However, for a fleet to come through the starlane at just the right time, the Caliphate Navy would have to know exactly when TF16 would be there, and that wasn't possible.

"Viv, I like where your head is at, but that's a starlane, not a planet they can hide behind. There's no way... for... them... what?" He stopped because her expression told him she knew something he didn't. "Spill."

"I take it if I told you they could, you wouldn't be satisfied?"

"If it were just me—yes. Without a doubt. But I must convince Spencer, and my word won't be enough."

Something nagged at her, that was for sure. Her face screwed up as she debated telling him. Every second, though, brought them closer to the lane.

"Okay, but you didn't hear this from me. Got it? Uh, sir."

He nodded, eager for her to tell him.

"When we were here last time on the mission, and after I made my way back to the compound with the survivors from the crash, I went downstairs to find Commander Dagher... well, we thought she was a commander..."

Jacob understood the confusion for sure. Nadia changed identities the way most civilians changed clothes. He stowed how much he missed her, putting that in a box for later.

"Go on."

"She made a discovery there, sir. A VIP, but also a machine. I overheard her call it a *Conundrum Cipher*. I *may* have talked to Chief Redfern about the idea, and he seemed to think it was FTL comms."

Alliance Navy ran on the rumor mill. There were always

stories of both the basic and the fantastical. New technologies were a favorite source of speculations, so there were always whispers of FTLC tech. Viv wasn't telling him a rumor, though. The nature of their mission to Medial precluded them from discussing it even with personnel who were there. No wonder this was the first he was hearing of the possibility.

"Are you sure?"

She shrugged. "As sure as I can be. It fits the situation."

Jacob's mind ran through all the potential factors for what would happen next if she were correct. They could do nothing, and TF16 would die. If they altered course, it would save the fleet, but they would have to retreat. If no fleet appeared, then they would have broken off the engagement for nothing and while no ships were destroyed, the battle would be considered a loss.

If she were right, though, and a fleet was mere moments away from appearing, what could they do? How could they counter it? A plan popped into his mind. It was a little crazy. He wished to God he didn't have to do it, but he couldn't see another way out.

"Admiral Spencer?" Jacob switched his comm over to the direct line.

"A little busy, Grimm." The Admiral's total focus lay on the holo tank as they battled the enemy fleet.

"I know, sir, but you need to hear this. This is a trap." While Jacob didn't know for certain, there was no point in trying to convince Admiral Spencer of a guess.

Spencer's head snapped around. "What?"

"There are ships coming through the starlane ahead of us. When they appear, we will either be forced to surrender or be destroyed."

"Astro, gravity readings?" Spencer barked.

"Nominal."

Spencer glanced at the tank again before looking hard at Jacob.

"There's no way they could coordinate an ambush like that. They would have to know we were coming, and exactly when we would hit the lane."

"The enemy has FTL comms, sir. If that's the case, we can follow this plan here." Jacob pulled up his NavPad and showed it to the admiral. "And lose nothing. Worst case, you took terrible advice from your *former* exec; best case, we ambush the ambushers."

Time ran down while Spencer thought through the implications. Jacob desperately wanted him to listen, but would he? It all came down to if the admiral trusted Commander Jacob T. Grimm. This was the biggest offensive of the war to date, and it would make or break Admiral Spencer's career. Not to mention the thousands of lives wrapped in nano-steel of TF16. All based on something as absurd as the enemy having FTL comms.

"Do it."

Enterprise, her eight heavy cruiser consorts, four light cruisers, and four destroyers, suddenly ceased fire. The enemy fleet continued to pelt them at maximum range with less than effective plasma turret fire. The order went out through the Alliance ships, and it took all of sixty seconds to reconfigure the weapons, open the outer hatches, and prepare the barrage. In that time TF16 moved *one hundred and eighty thousand* kilometers closer to the starlane. That much closer to possible destruction.

Spencer's eyes looked like hardened flint as he stared Jacob down. "You better be right," he muttered. Then, on the TF wide comms, he said one word. "Fire."

One hundred and twenty-six MK XVI advanced torpedoes burst into space, launched at a thousand KPS before their own gravcoil kicked in and they sped away at seven hundred gravities of acceleration. With warheads set to proximity detonation and targeting packages programmed to detect gravity emissions, they would home-in on the hyper-dense gravcoils of enemy ships.

Seconds slipped by as Jacob white-knuckled his chair, hoping he was right but praying he was wrong. The last thing the Alliance needed was an enemy who could talk in real time. The last thing *he* needed was thousands of deaths on his conscience. War didn't care who was right or who was wrong, only who lived and died. Jacob did his duty with all his heart and every ounce of his ability. Killing, though, even when necessary, chipped away at his soul.

When the torpedoes closed in within fifty thousand klicks, Jacob allowed himself hope that no ambush would happen. Surely if ships were going to appear, they would have by now?

"Contact, multiple contacts, bearing three-six-zero relative," the astrogator shouted. "A dozen, no, two dozen, more." The updates came so rapidly, the astrogator had to stop to breathe.

Someone gasped over the open comms. This was no ambush; it was a slaughter. An entire enemy fleet appeared. Two battleships dominated the screen, along with dozens of smaller ships. Numbers flashed by, almost a hundred, including the ships they were already engaged with. They weren't there just to destroy the *Enterprise*. This was their counterattack. A fleet large enough to crush the Alliance and the Consortium and take the wormhole in one massive blow.

"Fire again, keep firing," Admiral Spencer shouted. *Enterprise* shuddered as her multiple Long 9s added to the fire plan. More torpedoes shot out into space. Turrets went into rapid fire, adding their volleys to the mix. They had one chance to destroy the tsunami of ships before them. Just one.

Tactically speaking, starlane travel made battles difficult.

Ships made full stops before entering. They exited the lane with so little base velocity they might as well have had none.

For the Caliphate Fleet, it was an unmitigated disaster. Torpedoes moving at thousands of KPS with plenty of fuel left in their drive dove right for them. Eighteen went for the first battleship, detonating their payload at point-blank range. Tungsten balls accelerated out in a twenty-degree arc with enough energy to turn into miniature stars. They slammed into the ship's forward armor, burning, melting, and exploding their way through until they hit the fusion reactor.

Jacob did not know what ship exploded first. Astro barely had them on the screen when it turned into a giant ball of plasma and thousands of Caliphate spacers were consumed in nuclear fire. Half of *Enterprise's* screens went dark to protect the sensors as waves of radiation lashed out from the exploding fusion reactors.

The second battleship faired only slightly better. Her sistership's explosion forced the torpedoes off course by a degree and their payloads exploded, vaporizing the large ship's gravcoil and her bottom three decks along with four hundred of her crew.

Long 9s hit next, doing their deadly work as nano-reinforced tungsten arrows blasted through heavy armor and struck at the very hearts of dozens of ships.

Ninety more torpedoes homed in on the remaining ships prioritizing the heavy cruisers. By the time the third volley set upon them all the heavy capital ships were nothing but burning husks. After the fourth, not even the light ships escaped destruction.

The enemy fleet surrendered moments later. Task Force Sixteen's victory was complete. Medial, was free.

Jacob watched the chrono tick over to 0500 ship's time. He hadn't slept a wink. The numbers were still coming in, but the rough estimate came closer to ten thousand spacers dead in the black. Killed before they could run their coils hot. He did what he always did: his duty.

"It's not your fault. You didn't start the war," he told himself in the mirror. "Yeah, but you still did it," came his reply. He saved lives, all their lives, not to mention the slaves on Medial the Marine battalion were liberating at that moment.

A soft knock on his hatch alerted him.

"Come," he said. The computer automatically disengaged the lock, letting the hatch slide open.

Chief Warrant Officer Vivian Boudreaux leaned against the door. Jacob frowned on seeing her chief's rank.

"Viv? What happened?"

"OCS denied my application, sir. I'm back to chief for now."

No one had told him and since he was the sponsoring officer, the orders should have routed through him. An alert blared through his NavPad as the Navy anthem played. Jacob groaned inwardly. Some things never changed.

Boudreaux took one tentative step inside toward the dour officer.

"It wasn't your fault, sir. You didn't start the war, and in fact, I seem to recall you doing everything you could to keep it from happening." She knew him well, to know what weighed on him so heavily.

Jacob picked up the pad and read through the official denial of her OCS application. It wasn't based on merit, at least, but that there were no open billets for the next two classes. She could reapply in six months if she wanted to.

"Fault has nothing to do with it. Tell that to the dead spacers. We didn't beat them in a battle, Viv, we slaughtered them."

She nodded. "I know. It was my intel. I just... you can't blame yourself is all."

He gave her a wry smile. "I don't, nor do I blame God. Blame isn't what has my heart broken. It's the need to do it at all. But, if it's my people or them, then there is no contest. I'll be okay and—" he broke off suddenly as new orders appeared on his NavPad.

"What?"

"Recall. The Navy is sending me to Kremlin."

Just then, her NavPad beeped. "Great," she said, rolling her eyes. "Looks like I'm going with you. Is this more secret squirrel stuff?"

"Think of it this way: you get to fly a Corsair again."

That cheered her right up.

CHAPTER THREE

Nadia huddled under her blanket, a steaming cup of tea cradled in her hand. Outside, the wind howled and the snow fell for what felt like days. She didn't mind the winter on Alexandria, or that she slept in Jacob's old room. His family's home felt like her home, and his father made her feel welcome.

Though it shocked her how dissimilar the father and son were. She laughed inwardly that Ben Grimm would have been right at home next to Gunnery Sergeant Jennings. In fact, she would bet money that the older Grimm was more laconic than the Marine, something Nadia hadn't thought possible.

She shifted under the blanket, losing herself in the pattern of falling snow and howling wind. For the umpteenth time, she asked herself if outing the ISB agents in the Alliance was worth her career. Worth her freedom. It was, and she knew it was. But at the end of the day, she sulked on a stuffed chair in the middle of a snowstorm while others fought the good fight.

There simply was no way out for her. Admiral DeBeck wasn't even an option now that he was SECNAV. In order to avoid prison, she would need a presidential pardon, or maybe a signed proclamation from the Department of the Navy that they wouldn't press charges. None of which would happen without some extraordinary mitigating circumstances.

Nadia wasn't an idiot, though. She'd spent most of her adult life as a secret agent under the purview of ONI. In that time, she'd watched agents get burned, dismissed, and disavowed. Step on the wrong toe or betray the wrong person, and suddenly you're a deniable asset. Not that Wit had disavowed her.

She did that all on her own.

It was early, still several hours before sunrise, and Jacob's father would be up soon. She didn't want him to worry about her. He understood how important her hiding was, but if he became too concerned, he might contact Jacob and that could get her caught.

Besides, she decided, she'd stayed long enough. Jacob wouldn't be coming back soon. After a year of hiding out, the heat died down enough she could go off planet, head for her home of Providence. Maybe even see her brother again.

Her leather bag with its numerous straps sat next to the door. Inside it she had cash, fake ID, a gun belt rolled up around her old pistol, and a change of clothes. Everything she owned on Alexandria. Half of everything she owned in the entire galaxy.

"Time to go?" Ben asked.

She glanced over at him. He stood at the entrance to the kitchen, holding a cup of tea. His face betrayed no emotion, no hint of what he thought.

"Yes. If he were coming back soon, I would have heard by now."

"You might want to get going, then. Unless you want to talk to the man standing out in the snow," he said.

Man?

Nadia slung her pack, opening the door carefully to see what the older Grimm had. Sure enough, in the black of night, illuminated only by the barn light, was a tall, broad-shouldered man. Her heart leaped as she thought it was Jacob. But no, it wasn't a uniform but a suit and parka. It wasn't her boyfriend, but former Admiral DeBeck. Nadia let out a long sigh. Had he known all along where she hid?

She dropped the bag and walked out into the snow. The white powder crunched softly under her deft step. Silence and shadows were second nature to her. Even in the snow-covered ground, she could be as silent as needed. A certain level of stealth came with her everyday life. Not unlike the hyper-vigilance she'd seen Marines and some Army do. It was simply impossible to practice their craft as often as they did and just shut it off.

Over the gale, she heard his voice. "Nadia, can we go inside?"

"Are you here to arrest me? Because that's not going to work out the way you think it is," she said. He was her admiral, but he was also a civilian now, a politician. She'd born witness to good men throwing their morals away once they left the uniform behind and started down the path of politics.

"Of course not. Don't be silly. I have a mission for you. A way back in. I won't lie, though, you're not going to like where I need you to go."

Doctor Yusra Abbasi tapped absently on the side of her computer as she ran the numbers for the millionth time. She knew the answer before the computer did.

Negative result. Try again?

The question mark blinked at her, taunting her. Yusra pushed away from her desk, slowly spinning her chair around to take in her lab. There wasn't anything unique about it, nothing a million other labs across the universe didn't have. Other than Yusra herself.

Above the doorway, a light blinked twice, subtle enough only she would see it. She spun back around, focusing on the computer and typing in a new set of calculations.

An alarm sounded, notifying her of the impending entrance to her lab. The doors slid open. A fit, good-looking officer, with a beard to his first button, strode in. He waived his SecPad at her by way of greeting.

"Doctor Abbasi," Malik said with a stiff half-bow. "I'm here for your daily report."

"Of course," she replied formally.

Malik waved to the door and Yusra hopped off her chair and followed him out. As they walked, Malik checked his pad. Yusra couldn't tell if he was really reading information or making a show. It was difficult for her to glean any insight from him, even though she had dealt with ISB agents most of her life.

Even though she was only 167 centimeters tall, they saw eye-to-eye. His short, bulldoggish stature lent him a powerful gravitas. One look at his ripcord taut muscles, and she knew how dangerous the man was. His uniform, from his boots to his meticulously groomed head, was perfect. Since he had taken over as head of security six months before, she'd worked overtime trying to keep him in the dark. Despite her head start and indomitable intellect, the man caught on quick. She knew he knew something wasn't right with her.

But there was no way he could know what. None of them could.

He waved at the window to the outside of Shegeft Angiz as they walked.

"As you can see doctor, my men don't enjoy being here. The world is cursed, as they say. The sooner we can leave the better. So please, show me your progress on the device?"

Yusra noted his politeness, and how he framed the question as more of a defense of his men than his orders. Everything was in layers, and some days she couldn't keep it all straight. This, though, was her area of expertise... or so they thought.

"I, too, do not care for this planet. However, the unique astronomical properties of this region of spacetime cannot be duplicated."

Malik huffed as they continued their walk. Life could survive outside, but with their odd orbital situation, the dark side was always too cold and the light side always too warm. Because of the unequal heat distribution of the planet's atmosphere, Shegeft Angiz, or *Masa* as the locals called it, played merry hell with the weather. Massive storms, tornadoes, hurricanes, everything and anything could sweep up in a moment's notice and engulf the base. For that reason, the scientific outposts existed on a continental divide along the southern continent at the bottom of a giant crevice that stretched hundreds of kilometers. There were, of course, buildings outside. A spaceport and barracks formed a semicircle around the entrance to the main base.

Yusra pushed down a pang of guilt toward the poor men forced to live in the barracks and endure the harsh weather.

After all, none of them would be here if not for her.

"Then it should be simple, Doctor, solve the equation and we can all go home." Malik abruptly stopped, a scowl forming. "Who is responsible for this?" He stormed over to the large, thick, transparent shield that allowed the grand hall to see outside to where the shuttle was parked. With a thick finger, he lanced out at the window and started shouting. A young man with a cloth came rushing up. The poor lad was barely eighteen,

Yusra decided. He didn't even look military. Malik slapped him across the head, yelling more about the smudge he'd seen from across the room.

Here she was, trying to unlock the mysteries of the universe, and Malik only worried about the appearance of the base.

After slapping the young man several more times, Malik left him to scrub the window.

"Now, where were we... ah yes. You were about to tell me you can have the riddle solved in six months. Isn't that right, Doctor?"

Yusra forced a pleasant smile on her face. "Of course I can. Six months, then."

Six months? If I had sixty years, I couldn't solve the problem.

She turned and headed back for her lab. After all, she needed to maintain the appearance of a dutiful scientist serving the great and powerful Caliph Hamid. Once back in her lab, she pressed the button next to the door to seal the room. Holding it down for an additional ten seconds triggered a pre-programmed course of action. The cameras were fed a recorded image of her working toward unraveling the secret of FTLC. What they had now they couldn't duplicate, and it only worked in conjunction with what made Masa unique.

Sitting down, she reached over and triggered the holocube. An image of her family appeared. Even when he was with them, her father was never really with them. As a child, she thought it was because he didn't care. As an adult who followed in his rather large footsteps, she understood. He came to the realization, much too late in life, that his work would only ever be used to kill people, not help them.

"The pursuit of science is a gift, my dear lamb. Never forget that." She heard his voice in her head as if he were there with her. After his murder she followed his study, and now she was in the same trap he had spent his life in. One of her own making.

She needed help soon. But who could she go to?

CHAPTER FOUR

President Axwell closed his eyes in frustration. He could have the brand-new Secretary of the Navy brought up on charges... but then it would make him look bad for picking the man in the first place. In fact, as far as he could tell, there wasn't a way for him to do anything but go along with Wit DeBeck's insane scheme.

"You sent a fugitive from justice"—he let that sink in—"to Caliph space on a secret mission to find the creator of this tech you say exists... tech our scientists say can't work, and in fact is nothing but gibberish, gibberish brought to us by the same spy you sent to extract the creator, if he even exists. Does that about sum it up?"

Though no longer in the Navy, Wit stood at parade rest as his commander in chief dressed him down. He'd expected this, known it would happen, but he had to do what he had to do.

"Yes sir, Mr. President."

"Don't give me that *Mr. President* crap, Wit. I fought to make you SECNAV. Hell, Noele went to bat for you, and this is how you repay us?"

"You know me, sir. I will do *whatever* I must to preserve our people. If that means crossing some political lines, then so be it. I warned you, I'm no politician."

Axwell let out a long sigh, collapsing into his chair and resting his head in his hands.

"That's for damned sure. It's not just politics, Wit. We're still navigating a minefield here. We got our war. The moment things go wrong, the other side is going to come at us with cleavers demanding a pound of flesh. Do you not see that?"

Wit held his ground, not flinching. "What I see, sir, is the chance to cripple the enemy. Possibly fatally. All I need is a ship no one is using. They sneak in, extract my asset and the package, and sneak out."

In the moment, Wit sounded so very reasonable, but Axwell knew it was a trick. Not the malicious kind, but a trick of the former admiral's personality. Wit always sounded convincing. He was, after all, a master of deception. Axwell doubted he'd ever heard one unfiltered word from the man. It was part of why he appointed him as SECNAV. He needed a man with Wit's... wit.

"Why is it that I'm the president of the United Systems Alliance, and yet I feel like you're pulling my strings?" he asked.

"I wouldn't ever *pull the president's strings,* as you say. Possibly influence them, but never pull." Wit seemed to think for a moment, looking down before continuing. "Johan, I've never come to you unless I was sure. Not once. My asset is in place, or soon will be. The system they are in is virtually undefended, but it won't be for long. Now is the time."

"You've run this by Noele?" he asked.

"She's in Zuckabar, commanding the fleet. This isn't a fleet matter."

Axwell pondered those words. *Not a fleet matter?* Did that mean she didn't know, or he didn't think she needed to know?

"What do you need?"

"A destroyer and a ground team. All of which is already in Zuckabar."

Johan glanced sharply at his SECNAV.

"Are you planning on sending who I think you are?"

Wit's steely gaze never flinched. "His record speaks for itself, sir. I'd be a fool not to."

After a long moment, President Johan Sebastian Axwell pressed his thumb down on the NavPad, officially greenlighting the mission. Sending people to their probable deaths wasn't something one campaigned on. If there was anything that would make him throw in the towel, it would be this. The screen blinked green. The orders were sent.

"Godspeed, Wit."

"To us all, Mr. President."

———

Zuck Central's frigid air bit deep into Master Sergeant Danny Cannon's bones. In his long career he'd spent time in several hell holes, but Zuck took the cake. Dirty yellow snow covered everything and the smell... he would have nightmares about the smell.

Their operation on Zuck was almost over, though. One last mission to perform, then they could use some of their leave time. One more safe house to raid. Intel suggested the target inside led the Zuckabar Resistance Army, or the ZRA. It wasn't an army so much as a bunch of smugglers, criminals, and disaffected former politicians, all who reaped the benefit of the previous governor's lax approach to law enforcement.

Working with General Remington, Danny and his men had spent the previous six months raiding stash houses and crippling their supplies. Piece by piece, his team had removed the ZRA a cell at a time.

Like a skilled surgeon, they were about to remove the last cancerous tumor.

"Nomad, Nomad, this is Kilo One-Five. You are go." Danny clicked his mic twice. In the field his team went by their call-signs; he was Nomad. They weren't regular army grunts, but the elite Special Forces. His Alpha, or A-team, comprised of himself, and four other highly trained, highly skilled, and highly motivated individuals.

"Mac, in position?" While they weren't in danger of giving away their position, he whispered all the same. Once the shooting started, they would have to shout to be heard, anyway.

"Roger. Two tangos downstream and one Phantom grounded."

Danny scanned the compound through the snow, his built-in thermal optics showing two guards Mac had tagged along with the outline of a light air vehicle parked behind the main building.

"Rico, set up on our right flank, use the hill. When we go loud, rock the hell out of that Phantom."

"Roger that, Nomad," Rico said as he heaved himself up and made his way through the knee-deep snow. All their uniforms used adaptive camouflage, if they moved slowly, they were all but invisible to sensors, or people. Their boots absorbed sounds, and they trained for stealth under all weather conditions.

"T-Bar, Bubba, on me." Every soldier in the unit trained for close combat. On top of that skill, they also had a secondary specialty. Nomad did weapons. Mac handled sniping. Rico studied engineering and explosives. T-Bar spent six months at Army medical, and Bubba handled their comms. Each soldier went through rigorous evaluations to make the unit. Less than one percent of those who applied made it through training.

"Move out," Nomad ordered.

Three snow drifts moved as one, gliding down the slope meter by meter. As they approached the first guard, he turned to look in their direction. The soft crack of a subsonic projectile echoed over the snow and his head canoed.

T-Bar leaped forward, lowering the dead man to the snow-packed ground silently.

"Good kill," Nomad whispered.

Mac used a five-millimeter coil rifle from five hundred meters away. The round was small compared to more conventional firearms, but the variable velocity allowed for greater flexibility. At its highest setting, the projectile couldn't be stopped by anything short of hardened armor.

Nomad used hand signals, directing Bubba to the right while T-Bar covered their six. Once they were clear, Nomad sidled up to the door.

He didn't need to check his 10mm LAPCR (light armor piercing caseless rifle). Danny did that long before the moment of action.

"As soon as we breach, weapons hot," he said over the team comms.

With a deep breath, he heaved his leg back and kicked the door. T-Bar went in first, pivoting to the left and stepping forward. Bubba followed, going straight, while Nomad covered their six before entering. They moved into a mudroom. Boots, coats, and discarded survival gear decorated the walls.

"Stack up," Nomad said.

This time Bubba led the way, kicking the next door. Nomad stepped in, pivoting to the left with his rifle shouldered. Two men looked up from their game and opened their mouths to shout. As Danny moved in, he fired twice, hitting the nearest man in the chest. T-Bar's rifle barked a second later, taking out the second man.

From outside, the chatter of Rico's LMG filled the air, followed a second later by a thump of overpressure as the light aircraft exploded.

"Multiple contacts, east road, east road, range two-zero-zero meters. Permission to engage?" Mac asked.

The sole door opposite the room crashed open, and two men with pistols charged in screaming. They froze upon seeing the team, their minds taking precious seconds to understand what they saw. Seconds they didn't have. The three Special Forces troopers opened fire in a hail of bullets, ripping them to shreds before they could bring their weapons to bear.

"Engage all hostiles," Nomad ordered.

The sharp crack of the sniper rifle filled the air. Drowned out a second later by Rico's coil LMG.

Nomad pointed toward the door. Bubba unclipped a grenade and tossed it into the next room. A brilliant flash and bang filled the room. They charged in, once more executing their clearing. Three more tangos went down in a hail of gunfire.

"Nomad, Nomad, this is Kilo One-Five, sending in the sweeper."

"Roger, Kilo."

Zuck's Marine battalion was minutes out, but Nomad wanted the target. "Collapse on me," he whispered. On his HUD, the dots that represented Rico and Mac moved from their current position to the compound. Within thirty seconds, the entire squad stacked up at the last door.

Mac swapped out his rifle for a sleek, fully automatic coil pistol while Rico hefted his light machine gun like a rifle.

Bubba put one hand on the door and looked back. Nomad gave him the go signal. "Breach."

The big man crashed through the door and dove to the ground. T-Bar, right behind him, pivoted to the right and opened fire. Nomad followed, pivoting left. He didn't worry about what was behind him, only in front. A broad-shouldered man with a bushy beard leaped up, firing a hand cannon. Nomad's nanite armor absorbed the impact of the first round. The second round hit like a punch. He fired simultaneously, stitching a line up from the man's belly to his throat. Nomad went down to one knee, cursing his own slowness for not shooting first.

"I surrender!" a man yelled from the center of the room. He threw his gun down and dropped to his knees. "Don't shoot!"

Nomad double-checked the man's ID to make sure they had the right package. Once confirmed, he leaned against the wall for support while Rico bagged the target.

Danny's ribs ached probably because they were broken. Who was he kidding? Everything hurt.

He opened his comms. "Kilo One-Five, Nomad, target secure."

Nomad held himself up along the wall as he limped out. His men secured the room while he stepped outside. Once clear, Danny slid down the wall, his hands shaking as numb fingers undid the strap around his armor. His heart pounded in his ears as the adrenaline pumped through him.

"You okay, boss?" Mac said as he slid down the wall next to him.

"Getting too slow." Danny clenched his gloved fists and dropped his head. "If not for the armor, you'd be in command."

"Everyone has an expiration date, boss. Maybe take some time off and get the gene mod treatment?"

Inwardly, Danny shuddered at the thought of having his age artificially changed. Something about the process felt wrong to him. At the same time, he loved his job, loved the Unit. Letting it all go because he got old also felt wrong.

Danny rested his head against the wall while he waited for the Marines to show and take custody.

His radio squawked, interrupting his reverie. "Nomad, change of plans. Transpo inbound, ETA three mikes."

Danny and Mac exchanged looks. "Say again, Kilo? Transpo?"

"Roger, Nomad. You've got new orders."

Mac stood, slapping Danny on the shoulder. "You know what they say, ours is not to question why..."

" ...just to do or die," Danny finished.

CHAPTER FIVE

KREMLIN STATION

During the long flight from the Bella Wormhole, Jacob's NavPad updated with a truly epic amount of mail. Several messages from former shipmates, one from his dad, and the one he looked most forward to: Nadia. He skipped everything else and went right to reading hers.

> *Jacob, I hope you are well. I hate writing long messages, as you can imagine. You are going to hear some things about me shortly and I wanted you to know; they are likely all true. Search your heart. If they make sense, then yes, I did it. If they don't, then it's just media lies. Know that I did what I had to do. For the Alliance, and for my own sense of justice. I will always treasure our time together; you made me whole. Because of what has happened, I must leave. I don't know if I'll ever be back. Take care of yourself and keep that ship out of trouble. All my love, -Nadia.*

Jennings' blows were softer than the one Nadia dealt to his

heart. She'd "Dear Johned" him. Nadia... not that they had a formal arrangement, but he had planned on making it formal at some point. He dearly loved the woman. Her vivacious personality and nature made her even more desirable. Not to mention she was drop-dead gorgeous.

He'd never thought in a million years she would dump him through the mail, though. There had to be more to it. He tore into the news, searching back to before his deployment began, trying to find a trace of what she hinted at.

When the Caliphate Navy made their move against Praetor, he assumed that was the reason the Alliance *finally* declared war. But no, that wasn't it at all. Wrapped up in the daily combat operations and the time it took to be an XO of TF16, Jacob hadn't stayed current on events.

The declaration of war, the shuffling of the cabinet, Admiral DeBeck's departure from ONI and subsequent assignment as SECNAV, was all due to Nadia leaking her files to the Alliance citizens.

Relief flooded through him. She hadn't *Dear Johned* him because she didn't like him, only that she thought never to see him again. Well, Jacob had beat longer odds than those. Politics were like the wind. It came and went, and mostly did nothing. Maybe it would take a year or two, or longer, but when people lived as long as they did, that wasn't much time at all.

It wasn't as if he was rushing back to Alexandria to see her. His orders were to report to Governor Beckett and proceed from there. Maybe he would see her again when he got back from whatever assignment he had next. Or maybe after that one. The life of a spacer worked like that. It could be years before he got to go home.

That thought sobered him somewhat. While the gravcoil made FTL possible, it wasn't instant. Nor were the comms... at least for now, and depending on where the Navy sent him next, he could be months or years from home.

Jacob took a moment, inhaled deep and held the breath. With his eyes closed, he let all the anxiety, stress, and fear go as he exhaled. There was just one more letter to write before things got busy. His father deserved an update.

Gunnery Sergeant Allison Jennings shouldered the old-style swinging door into the bar. Thick air, filled with sweat, alcohol, and sweet-smelling recreational smoke, assailed her. No matter if she were on MacGregor's World, or Seabring, a bar was a bar. This one, DownSpin, was a local military favorite. Navy, Marines, even the civilian police force on Kremlin frequented the place. Of course, having mixed service in one place wasn't always ideal. For the most part the other branches understood their place in the hierarchy, but tonight none of that mattered.

She didn't remember the last time she had a night off. While she loved her job, desperately loved it, two straight years aboard ship with only a few weeks' ground side between deployments was enough for anyone. She needed to cut loose in a big way. Drinking until she couldn't see would be her go-to, if she weren't from an insane planet. She could still go through the motions, though, and maybe even get herself into some trouble.

While Kremlin mimicked a human habitat, there was simply far too much open space to maintain an ideal temperature. Outside the bar, the crisp air warranted a sweater, but inside the warm air made anything more than a few layers uncomfortable. She pulled her sweater off, revealing her spaghetti strap dress that showed her figure, even if it accentuated her overdeveloped shoulder and neck muscles.

Unlike some, Allison was proud of her well-developed muscle tone. From her thick calf muscles to her taut stomach and ripped arms, there was no hiding her. MacGregor's World had the effect on everyone who lived there. Not just the one-point-four g's, but the thick atmosphere as well. By the time the Alliance had shown up to help with medical nanites, the population's adaption was genetic. While there weren't a lot of *her people* wandering off world, most citizens had at least seen a vid with someone in it.

At 150 centimeters tall, she hit the minimum height requirement for a Marine—her recruiter had fudged her height a small amount to make sure she hit the mark. He would never know how much that act of kindness meant to her, as she was desperate to leave her home planet.

She hopped up on the bar stool and slid her NavPad across to show her military ID. As short as she was, and with her youthful good looks, being mistaken for a teenager didn't surprise her, despite her age.

"What will you have?" The bartender had the thick Russian heritage accent most Kremlin people spoke with.

"Can you do a New Austin Hurricane?" she asked.

"Very much so," he said with a toothy grin.

He left to make her drink. She spun around to see who was in the packed establishment. A large man approached her. He wore civilian clothes and hadn't shaved in a few days, but his walk said military. Not Marines, that was for sure. She cocked her head to the side and decided he was Army. Unfortunately, her examination made him think she was interested, and he continued his approach. She had to look up at him when he stopped. Not as tall as *the captain,* he still towered over her.

"What's the first thing you do in the morning?" he asked by way of introduction.

It wasn't a bad opening line, but she just wasn't interested in *that* kind of company at the moment.

"You'll never know," she said coolly before turning her back to him.

Howls of laughter erupted from the other side of the bar, where his friends must have waited. She sensed him slink away and almost felt bad for shooting him down.

A second later her drink arrived, and she lost herself in the mix of flavors from the rum, vodka, and gin concoction. She knew people who drank only straight whiskey, or beer, but she liked... no, loved the fruity flavors and mix of alcohol.

Cold air rushed in as the door opened and a half dozen boisterous men entered, along with a few women they brought with them. Jennings placed them in the "civilian tourist" category and forgot them. They weren't military or police, just locals looking to impress some girls with their knowledge of hidden places to drink.

"If I can guess your drink, can I sit down next to you?" a man said behind her.

Without turning around, "You all take classes in pickup lines? Because that's not a bad one."

"Practice makes perfect," he said.

She still hadn't looked at him. "Go ahead, guess. But one guess only."

"Seabring Sunset."

Allison sipped her drink, placed it down, and shook her head. "Good initiative, bad guess."

More laughter from the same group. So, she was a target for a unit. No one saw the little smile she gave herself. Maybe she wouldn't mind some company after all.

A young man strode up and leaned against the bar, far too close for comfort. His local accent sounded more refined than the bartenders.

"My friends and I want to party. Come with me and we'll show you a good time."

Unlike the Army dogs who were hitting on her, this kid wouldn't take rejection well. She tried to think of something political to say, some way of letting him down easy. In the end, though, that just wasn't who she was.

Unfortunately, she didn't have a witty answer for him. "Negative." At least not one he would understand.

"What does this mean, negative?"

And she thought privates were stupid. "In civilianese, it means no. Go away."

He didn't like that. Looking down at her, he said something in his native language. She didn't have to understand to know it wasn't something nice.

Slowly, deliberately, she turned the stool and brought her ice-blue eyes on him. There was no give in her expression. No hint of intimidation or fear. Jennings had met the enemy and killed them with her bare hands. She had fought in desperate struggles where the victor lived and the loser died, often horribly.

Some punk from Kremlin wouldn't even begin to make her sweat.

"I don't speak your language, but I gather your meaning. Face or gut?"

Confusion filled his eyes. He glanced back at his friends, who had all stood up as the tension in the bar cranked up. After a moment he laughed at her, spittle flying from his mouth to hit her face.

"You mean to hit me? Girl, you are funny. Come." He grabbed her arm and tried to drag her with him. His body yanked up short as his arm hit extension and she didn't move, not even a centimeter.

Deliberately she reached up to his hand, placed her thumb

between his knuckles and wrapped fingers around his metacarpals, and twisted. His attempt to resist was laughable. His hand bent, followed by his wrist, then his arm, and he sank to his knees and howled.

Jennings intended to let it go at that, but then the kid's friends tentatively came at her.

"You kids need to think again," spoke an average-sized man with a beard and weather-beaten face, from the Army-guys corner. Four men behind him, including two that she recognized as the ones who had hit on her, stood up. On the other side of the room, five young Marines leapt to their feet. A pair of off-duty police officers did the same, and within seconds, everyone in the bar had risen to stand with Allison.

"Well ooh-fricking-rah," she said. With a savage twist, she wrenched the kids' arm, just shy of breaking it, then pushed him away.

The rich kids seemed to think over their chances, which made Allison let out a sharp bark of a laugh.

"You all really want an ass whooping? Then come on," she said. Now that they had started something, she itched for a fight. If she left it alone, they would realize their mistakes and move on... but she knew a few words in Russian and exactly how to make them fight.

"Petukh."

The leader of the boys turned bright red as he couldn't comprehend a girl calling him that and getting away with it.

"Oh crap," the Army guy muttered.

All hell broke loose. The offended kid charged at her while the others burst out in different directions. Charging an opponent was a rookie mistake, and she made him pay for it. She stepped into his charge, blocking his clumsy blow with her arm and slamming her very hard forehead into his chest.

He fell backward, gasping for breath that wouldn't come.

She stepped in, hooked one arm under his crotch and the other grabbed his coat. She rocked sideways, lifting him bodily up and over, slamming the poor kid down onto the floor with an audible crack. He moaned, spitting out something in Russian that was probably an apology. She pressed a knee into his chest and tapped him on the forehead so he would look at her.

"Don't start shit you can't finish, understood?"

His eyes focused on her as he managed one slurred word. "Da."

Just like that, it was over. The Army guys had downed their opponents, and the off-duty cops were swearing at the kids as they mag-cuffed them.

The bearded grunt walked up to stand beside her, a grin on his face.

"That's a hell of a move. I'm Danny Cannon," he said, holding out his hand.

She took it with a firm but polite grip. "Jennings."

"You're a Marine, I take it. Is that your first or last name?"

"Ask me next time you see me."

Having had enough, and not wanting to fill out forms with the shore patrol when they arrived, she stepped over the mewling kid she'd downed and walked out. Refreshed, she headed back to her temporary quarters with a rare smile on her face.

CHAPTER SIX

Jacob had never entered the office when Rasputin ran the station, but he was more than happy to enter with his former engineer in the position. Rod stood from behind an antique wooden desk. He held a cane in one hand, using it to aid him as he came to the side of the desk.

"Beckett, you old space dog, how are you?" Jacob asked as he slapped Rod on the arm.

"I've seen better days. Apparently the regen on my feet didn't take and they're going to have to replace them. However, thanks to you, I still have an exquisitely beautiful wife... who sends her love and apologies. If she had known you were coming, she would have made a feast. Sadly, she's off station at the moment, staying with her mother for the last trimester. I'm told it's a tradition."

"Of course," Jacob replied. "And congratulations, you'll make a great father."

Rod shook his head. "I'm too old, Jacob. If I want to keep up, I'll need the age regen and I just... well, I wasn't going to, but now I think I must."

"You'll want to run after your kids?"

"Ha, I'd settle for walking without pain."

Jacob took a seat and placed his NavPad on the wooden desk. The order lit up, and he acknowledged he'd reported.

"Needless to say, I was surprised to be ordered here. They indicated this isn't my final destination, though. Do you know what's going?"

Rod leaned against his desk, tapping the floor with the ornate cane. A smile as big as a house spread across his face.

"You know I've run this station since we annexed the system. My counterpart on the planet, General Remington, has cleaned it up pretty good. Crime has all but vanished in both places, and for the first time in a hundred years, there's actual immigration here. How remarkable is that?"

"Amazing. Having smelled the planet, I can't imagine why anyone would want to live there."

"Money," Rod said. "Lots of money. Ever since the corruption stopped and people were free to explore the surface, mining companies are finding some of the rarest minerals in the galaxy. I know the draw here is the wormhole, but that planet is worth more than any other in the whole of the Alliance." Rod reached over and pressed the call button on his desk. "Petrov, can you show Commander Grimm to the drydock?"

"Yes sir."

A tall, thin man with an impeccable suit entered and waited patiently by the door.

"I'd walk with you but—" he looked to his feet and shrugged.

Jacob stood and clasped Rod's hand. "It's always good to see you, my friend."

"You have no idea how much you're going to mean that," Rod said.

Jacob didn't understand the cryptic comments or the reason behind mentioning how valuable the planet below was. Of course, Zuckabar had value as a mining operation, but no amount of minerals would ever entice him to live on such a desolate, awful planet. The freezing temperature alone would be enough to make him leave. Add in the smell and isolation and he would be done for.

Petrov led him down the lift, into a waiting aircar.

"Where are we going?" he asked the man.

"The docks. Governor Beckett asked me to keep it a secret."

Jacob lost himself in his NavPad, scrolling through the leftover paperwork from his sudden departure from *Enterprise*. The aircar trembled, drawing his attention for a second... and he almost dropped the NavPad from shock.

"What?"

On the side of the car, the speaker squawked to life, Rod's voice came over loud and clear. "It took me all the political capitol I had, *Skipper,* but I saved her."

The aircar banked hard to the right flying into the AG zone and as she passed a pillar, *Interceptor* came into view. Her hull gleamed in the artificial sunlight. Shining silver since her armor wasn't coated yet. Jacob's mind reeled at the implication. New armor?

Rod walked him through the changes as the car circled the old boat. "We did as much of a full refit as I could manage. The MKIII reactor ended up being the bottleneck. She just wasn't designed for the power load of modern systems. We had to pick and choose which could be replaced since putting a strain on the reactor was our only restriction. She's got seven centimeters of the new ablative nano-armor, the same kind on the Griffin-class ships."

As they came around, the stencil for her shark nose stood out. Above that were open hull plates showing the forward torpedo rooms.

"Where are tubes three and four?"

"Yeah, we had to sacrifice some of her forward armament for a new fusion battery and computer node. We had to put in the node to handle the new weapons."

Then he saw the turrets. They were still single barrel 20mm coilguns; however, a wide, flat-nosed weapon rested on the top of each turret, almost flush against the armor.

"What are those?" Jacob asked.

"I'm glad you asked. They're the reason I pushed the refit through. The Terraforming Guild's protocols had the crew destroy every physical piece of technology they could. However, their point-defense weapons were on the *outside* of the ship. I spent some time tinkering and taking them apart. What you have is the first giga-pulse laser point defense weapon system. The range is only fifty thousand klicks under ideal conditions, but they can fire at one hundred pulses per second for almost a full minute. Their tracking and detection systems are why we needed two more computer nodes, a fusion battery, and an extra supercapacitor ring."

Jacob's jaw dropped. "*Only* fifty thousand klicks? That's a game changer. When are you deploying them to the rest of the fleet?"

Rod coughed over the speaker. His voice took on a nervous quality. "You're field testing them. When you return from your next mission, we'll go over the data and see how they do. If they work the way I expect them to, then every ship will have them mounted on top of their turrets."

"And if not?"

"You probably won't have returned, then," Rod said with a chuckle.

More of the ship came into view and all four turrets were mounted with giga-pulse lasers. They weren't the only change. New armor covered the ship all the way down to her gravcoil curtain. Yard dogs worked fervently to coat her in thermal absorbing paint and finish the rest of the exterior before she had to launch.

"The ship's stern has mesh armor installed on top of the regular ablative armor. What we found after you kept getting hit in the aft was that destroyers tended to be in less traditional engagements and the stern needed more protection."

"Rod, I don't know what to say. She's beautiful."

"I'm glad you think so, because as soon as you retake command, you've got orders."

Jacob couldn't take his eyes off his beloved ship as the aircar moved around her before coming into rest next to the open airlock leading to the mess. His door opened and he leaned over to take the side of his ship in a way he rarely got to. He looked back at the car. "You did all this... how did you know they would have a mission for her as soon as you finished?"

"I didn't," he said. "This was about righting a wrong."

Jacob said goodbye to his old friend before heaving himself out of the car into the airlock.

"Captain on deck." Private June stood at attention on the inside of the lock. He held his hand out to her and she stepped forward to help him in.

"Thank you, Yanaha," he said. Her shoulders straightened and her face practically glowed as he used her first name. "Congrats." He nodded at the PFC rank on her uniform.

"Thank you, skipper."

He moved past her and she returned to parade rest, guarding the open hatch. Jacob could hardly believe his eyes. *Interceptor* gleamed like she was brand new. A soft-serve ice cream machine even adorned the bulkhead.

"Skipper?" PO Josh Mendez asked through the galley pass-through. The New Austin native darted out, wiping his hands on the apron he wore as he approached. Surprise plain on his face. "It's good to see you, sir. Are you the CO then?"

"Josh, it's been too long." He clapped the PO on the shoulder. "I've got the orders right here. I'm glad to know we've got your food to look forward to."

"Aye sir. It's good to be back. Honestly, I never expected to serve on the old girl again. I was on my way back to HQ and my orders were rerouted here. Do you think anyone else is coming?"

Jacob didn't have to ask who he meant. *Interceptor*'s fellowship amongst her crew made them more family than mere shipmates.

"If you're here, I can only imagine we're getting some familiar faces. Carry on."

"Aye sir." Josh snapped to attention before returning to his duties in the galley.

As for Jacob, an eagerness to explore his ship overwhelmed him and he felt like a kid at Christmas. He took off immediately for the bridge. The ladder hatches were open, and it only took him a few minutes to ascend to the O-deck. Dim light greeted him of an empty bridge. *Interceptor* lacked the life of a crew. The ambient noise every living ship carried was missing. To him, it was like the world slept and only he was awake. Servos hummed as the massive hatches slid open. Soft white lights sprang to life along with the panels and controls of every station, activated by his presence.

Awestruck, he didn't move, just took it in.

"Something else, isn't it, sir?" a familiar voice, but one he hadn't heard in a while, said from behind him.

Jacob spun around and came face to face with Lieutenant (SG) Carter Fawkes.

"Carter," he said with genuine delight, reaching out to take the man's hand. The former weapons officer had grown, Jacob decided. Command school made him into a real officer. One who had the bearing and stood like a man with confidence.

There was more to leadership than bars on the uniform, and he had no doubt Carter had what it took to be a great officer.

"Good news, sir." He held up his NavPad for Jacob to inspect. "I'm your XO."

The grin on Jacob's face couldn't stretch any further. He was getting the band back together.

"That's fantastic. Are you officially reporting for duty?"

"Just as soon as you officially take command, sir. Chief Suresh and some of the other old hands are here as well. I think Bosun is still around too. We've also got some returning officers, and a couple of new ones, including our doctor, Commander Freydis."

Jacob clapped the man on the shoulder. "Good to know. Let's get this show on the road."

Despite having previously commanded the ship, Jacob still had to officially take authority from the yard. He couldn't do that until they declared their refit complete. From what he could tell, they were going to need a few more days.

Newly promoted Lieutenant (JG) Akio Kai, chief engineer of USS *Interceptor*, crawled through the service hatch leading under the MKIII reactor. "No, Chief, I need the torpedo level."

A moment later, Redfern's arm reached into the cramped crawlspace and handed him the oddly shaped tool.

"That will do it. Thanks, Chief." Kai finished the last adjustment before scooting out.

"What's next, sir?" Redfern asked.

Kai did a quick inspection around main engineering. His fusion reactor hummed efficiently, and all the panels were showing green across the board. Even the newly installed diamond anvil cell in the conversion chamber worked without flaw.

"The only thing I'm concerned about at this point, Chief, is the software running the new point-defense lasers. Have you looked at it?"

"Not really my area of expertise, sir. I could have one of the younger techs inspect it. I think Spacers Snow and Walt have software experience."

"Sounds good," Kai agreed.

The lieutenant went right to his console to open his notes and see where he needed to go next.

"Sir, you're pushing twelve hours on. You can hit the mess and we can finish up here," Chief Redfern said, gesturing to the ratings working in the large room.

"I'll have some coffee sent up, Chief. I don't want to tell the skipper his ship won't move."

"Aye sir," Redfern said.

Kai didn't see the worried look Redfern gave him or the way the lanky chief lingered before returning to duty.

CHAPTER SEVEN

TRANSIT STATION E-75 CALIPHATE SPACE

Nadia reminded herself to walk casually. After all the time she spent sitting idle on Jacob's family ranch, she wondered if her skills had atrophied. They hadn't.

Moving through a crowd without attracting attention was a whole other skill than hiding from detection. Her skill in both was superb. Where she shined, though, was the art of being ignored.

In Caliph space there were very few reasons a woman could travel unaccompanied. If she were married or enslaved. To their credit, married women were perfectly safe... as long as she stayed in the well-traveled parts of the station.

With the help of temporary nanite therapy, she added twenty years to her age. Making her less desirable to those who would take advantage.

Station E-75's cavernous interior held thousands of people pushing their way to their assigned gates. It boggled Nadia's mind that there were so many civilians doing business in the Caliphate.

They acted as if they weren't at war. Every planet, station, and ship in the Alliance stood on high alert. Ready to repel an attack at any moment. Not in the Caliphate, though.

Armed soldiers patrolled the metal-framed interior of Transit E-75. They were easy to spot, unlike the *Guidance Patrol* who wore civilian attire with a yellow armband.

At least with the soldiers they would only stop her for ID purposes. Guidance Patrol could stop anyone, for any reason, and arrest or beat them on the spot. Which was completely normal for the Caliphate. As far as she could tell, no extra security measures were in place.

She stopped at a kiosk, scanning her ID to access the map of the station.

E-75 orbited a gas giant and was her second to last stop. From there she would board a freighter heading in the right direction. A civilian freighter which resupplied the secret base once a week. It was far cheaper to outsource the resupply than have the military do it.

Something all governments had in common.

Wit had assured her before she left that it would be here.

"If not, I'm stuck behind enemy lines with an ID that's going to expire," she had said when he told her the plan.

"I wouldn't send you on a suicide mission, my dear."

"Yes you would," she said without hesitation.

The hurt in his eyes told her he wasn't upset about what she had said, but the truth of her words.

"Not lightly. How's that?"

She smiled, putting one hand on his arm. "I'm sorry, that was uncalled for."

He squeezed her hand. "It's not like you haven't had other

things to worry about these past months... being an interstellar fugitive and all."

Nadia snapped her head around, refocusing on her mission. Two of the Guidance Patrol were looking her way. She decided it was time to head for her gate.

They immediately followed her, not hiding their interest. If it came to violence she was blown. Odds were, she told herself, they just wanted to see her papers.

"You there," the taller of the two said. "Stop."

Nadia hesitated. Even if she could run from them, it was five hundred meters to her gate. They would just have the doors locked and her mission would come to a screeching halt.

They couldn't see her face, of course, only her eyes were visible. She turned, clasped her hands together and bowed her head.

"Where is your husband?" the tall one asked.

"Nabail," the shorter one said, placing his hand on his companion's arm. "Don't be rude."

"Sister, what is your name?"

Nadia gave them her cover ID, careful to act submissive and deferential to the two men as she held up her arm where the subdermal ID was implanted.

The shorter one held up the scanner and it beeped.

"Thank you, be careful.

Nadia bowed, not daring to speak as she turned and walked away. There was a dance she had to perform, one she had practiced a million times.

She wouldn't be found out because of some minor social faux pau.

———

Malik wandered the halls of the hidden base. A base he disliked immensely. However, he had a job to do and he prided himself on his thoroughness. Scanner in hand, he checked each person he passed, making sure they were in their assigned area, doing their assigned duty.

Others may shirk their duty, but not Malik. He wouldn't shirk it to himself, his wives, or his Caliph. Not for a second.

"You there." He pointed at a man in coveralls, whose slovenly appearance disgraced the base.

"Sir?"

"There are stains on your uniform. Your beard is unkempt. Who allows you to present yourself in such a state?"

Confusion clouded the man's face. "Sir? I'm a janitor... so..."

"Yes? And? Do you not take pride in your service to the Caliph?"

The Janitor blinked several times. "I just clean up the trash."

Malik stepped forward, right into the man's face. "You disgust me." Malik slapped the man on the face. The janitor jerked back in fear. "Take pride in your work. Report to your shift leader. One mark against you. I expect to see improvement immediately."

Not waiting for his response, Malik swiftly turned and marched away. He resisted the urge to mutter about the inefficiency of those around him. Didn't they realize the importance of their work?

He stopped by the picture window, showing the landscape outside and the dimming star in the sky. Regardless of his personal feelings about their location, he took his job seriously. Becoming an ISB agent required commitment and dedication.

There were no lazy Internal Security Bureau men. Those were executed during training.

Like himself, his office reflected the pride he took in his

work. A dozen holos showed security streams from around the scientific complex.

The sheer lunacy of the resources poured into this place astonished him. They could add an entire fleet to the navy with what they spent in a year to keep Shegeft Angiz running.

All for one *woman* to research her dead father's secret. A *woman!* How could Allah be so cruel as to make Dr. Hassan Abbasi's only daughter the one person capable of reproducing the great scientist's work?

They dare not collar her either, lest they risk breaking her mind and making her worthless.

He shook his head, burying his anger over her fortune deep down. Instead, he turned all the monitors to her lab.

Once again, they showed the same thing they always did: Dr. Abbasi, hard at work, using her computers to run calculations while she wrote notes on a board.

Despite her disadvantage, she did seem to work quite a lot. With the push of another button he brought up all her computer correspondence. To the galaxy at large she didn't exist, but she did have access to the largest collection of scientific papers in the known universe. She pursued them endlessly.

He saw everything she wrote, searched for, and did. Yet he still couldn't figure out how close to the secret she was.

If only they hadn't killed her father before learning the secret.

Their pairs were all on Masa—*No.* He corrected himself. Masa was what the common men called it. Shegeft Angiz was its proper name. He would not sink to their level.

As he understood it, Shegeft Angiz acted as a kind of switchboard. Many of the devices were aboard battleships, the capital, and the personal ships of the great Caliph's children.

They had lost two of the irreplaceable machines and they desperately needed more.

And more they would have.

CHAPTER EIGHT

Ensign Fionna Brennan stowed her Navy-issue bag above her rack, finishing her unpacking. The small cabin she shared with Midship Watanabe consisted of two racks, stacked, four cabinets, a single closet, and one head with a shower.

She considered it a luxury compared to the quarters she had on *Firewatch*, which, despite the destroyer's larger size, were cramped and crowded.

At least *Interceptor*'s weren't with the enlisted. Not that she looked down on them, quite the opposite, she thought they were more confident than herself and worried they would see through her.

She took a moment to make sure her copper curls were tucked carefully under her watch cap, and the pins on her uniform were in the correct order.

Of her interactions with Commander Grimm, she hadn't thought of him as a vengeful, or spiteful, officer. However, speaking to him on comms a few times hardly made her an expert on the man.

His reputation vacillated between grossly incompetent and

exaggeratedly amazing. The truth had to be somewhere in between. All she hoped for was to keep from making a fool of herself on her first tour as an actual officer.

Why had they stationed her at Astro, though? She was a comms specialist by training and her advisor at the academy assured her the first few tours would be at the relatively easy station.

With a woosh the cabin hatch slid open and a short Asian girl with a button nose, entered. Fionna suppressed her shock and focused on her bunk. The girl wore a thin dress that barely reached her thighs, high heels, and swayed as she came in.

She pointed at the bottom bunk. "That one's mine, right?" she asked with a drunken slur. Then she fell face down on the bunk and snored instantly. Fionna had no idea what to do.

Fionna bent down to rouse her bunkmate and the distinct smell of alcohol wafted off the sleeping woman.

Did she say something? Call someone? Or just let her sleep it off?

Ensign Fionna Brennan wanted to help, but her watch started in twenty minutes and the last thing she wanted was to be late for her first duty on a new ship.

"Sorry," she muttered as she turned the light off, then secured the hatch as she exited.

Interceptor was his again. Jacob ran his hand down the worn leather of the captain's chair. While the yard had replaced much, they'd only upgraded systems. He liked his chair. The last thing he wanted was for one of the new ones that felt like he sat on a cloud.

Bells rang throughout the ship, signaling the watch change. He hardly looked up, the grin on his face evident. He wore his typical black slacks, sweater, and high-necked white shirt underneath, finishing it with his boots and blood-red watch cap. Only he was authorized to wear the red one. The color of command. It denoted him as captain. Unlike the stripes on his right leg that ran from hip to boot. Those were combat stripes. Though he'd certainly seen more than two actions. They only denoted two. It allowed crew to know, at a glance, who had seen combat and who hadn't.

Most every returning crew member, and almost all the new ones, had at least one stripe. Which was a stark difference than the first time he took command where he was virtually the only person with combat action.

As the war progressed, more and more spacers experienced combat for themselves. Some for the first time... and some for the *last* time.

Jacob did his best to remember the fallen, placing a marker in his own psyche for them.

As was his duty.

The chair still squeaked when he rocked back and forth, and he wouldn't have it any other way.

Around him the bridge crew shuffled out. Collins and Suresh murmured details of the watch to each other. Oliv turned over the headphones to PO Tefiti with a smile.

There were new people and returning crew. Lieutenant Brown, whom he thought a competent officer, held his previous position on weapons. Of course, Carter was his XO now, something he was grateful for.

His big surprise came in the form of Ensign—no, he reminded himself—Lieutenant (JG) Roy Hössbacher, returned to the fold and took on Ops. It was a big assignment for a junior officer and showed tremendous confidence from HQ to give it to him. As skipper, he could override the assignment if he felt the particular officer wasn't up to snuff, but in this case there was no doubt in his mind how qualified Roy was for the job.

Carter appeared beside him with NavPad in hand, holding it out for Jacob to inspect.

"Final crew count sir, 130 souls."

Jacob pressed his thumb to acknowledge the receipt. "Thank you, XO."

"Sir, we've got a mix of old and new aboard. A solid crew to be sure. Any idea where we're headed?" he asked.

"Not yet, but as soon as I know, you will know."

Spacer McCall, who had held the comms duty station most of the night, swiveled nervously back and forth.

"Mac," Jacob asked, standing up to move next to him. "Everything okay?"

McCall glanced nervously at Hössbacher, who had settled into the Ops station.

"No sir, I mean yes sir, everything's fine."

Jacob knew a line when he heard one. The young man was trying not to cause trouble.

"Okay, Mac, spill. You've served with me for too long to pull the innocent act."

McCall looked down sheepishly. "Aye sir, sorry sir, it's just that... my relief is late."

"Is that all?" Jacob was about to call over to Carter to have a new rating sent up when Mac finished.

"According to the schedule it's Midship Watanabe, skipper. I didn't want to say anything because—"

"She's an officer. No worries, Mac. Sometimes even the officers are late." He clapped the young man on the shoulder. "Go get some grub, we'll call in the backup."

"Aye sir, thank you sir."

As Mac departed, Jacob pointed to Lieutenant Hössbacher. "Roy, it's good to have you back. Can you have the relief for comms sent up, then have the Bosun track down our missing midship?"

"Aye sir. It's good to be back too," Roy said.

Jacob finished his tour of the diminutive bridge, putting the midship out of his mind.

All the stations, with the exception of his MFD and The Pit were brand new. He was thankful to see they still had a mix of manual, touch, and holographic controls. The manual controls were necessary for combat, even if they weren't the easiest to manipulate. Equipment failure was all too common in battle and the last thing they needed was a failed holo circuit when seconds could mean the difference between winning and death.

He stopped at Astro, noting the officer with the coppery red hair peeking out from under her watch cap. She sat at her station; shoulders hunched in an attempt to go unnoticed.

"Ensign Brennan... Fionna, right?" he asked.

"Aye sir," she squeaked."

"Glad to have you aboard. Learn everything you can from PO Oliv and Tefiti, they're the best in the fleet."

"Yes sir."

Jacob waved for his XO.

"Walk with me, Carter." He headed for the briefing room, pausing at the entrance to the hatch. "Roy, you have the con."

"Aye sir, Ops has the con."

When Jacob entered the bridge earlier, Gunny Jennings manned the entrance. Now Corporal Naki snapped to attention.

Jacob pounded the young Marine in the shoulder.

"Good to see you," Jacob said with sincere emotion.

"You too, skipper. Glad to be back," Naki replied.

He would always have a special place in his heart for the Marines of Bravo-Two-Five. They'd seen some stuff together for sure.

The hatch to the briefing room stood open. Seeing the

broken hatch filled him with an odd kind of joy. He expected it to be fixed after every trip to the yard. Then he realized someone was likely disabling the hatch. Maybe as a good luck charm, he thought.

Inside, the freshly painted table with its smiling cartoon shark greeted him like an old friend. Jacob dragged his fingers down the rim as he took his seat at the far end.

"Okay, we've got a lot to do and not a lot of time to do it in."

"Have we got our orders yet, skipper?" Carter asked.

Jacob shook his head in the negative. "But if I know the admiralty, they wouldn't have put me on *Interceptor* for just any mission. We need to get moving on integration of the new crew, not to mention training on the new weapon systems."

Carter grumbled. "I'm jealous of Brown. I'd love to be on tactical with the new PDWs."

"I can always demote you...?"

"That's fine, sir. I'll stay as your XO if that's okay."

"Good." The next three hours went by in a flash as Jacob and Carter went to work organizing the ship and laying out a plan of action for the crew's training.

Bosun Sandivol stood outside Midship Watanabe's quarters with the hatch open, letting light from the passageway in, but he stayed dutifully outside.

Laid out on her rack, the midship snored peacefully, so blackout drunk he could smell the vodka five meters away. It wasn't like he hadn't had his share of benders back in the day, but they were always on weekends, never before watch... or at least never so bad he couldn't perform his duty.

Juan held up his NavPad. He paused to decide what he should do. Regs prohibited him from entering her cabin unless it was an emergency. He wanted to avoid problems, which was why he needed a couple of females to assist in moving her to sickbay.

"Bridge, this is the Bosun on deck six, frame eighty. Can you have Gunny Jennings and PO Desper come down and join me."

"Is everything okay, Bosun?" Lieutenant Hössbacher's voice crackled over the comms.

"Not sure yet, sir. I'll keep you in the loop."

"They're on the way, Bosun."

Eight minutes later, Desper and Jennings slid down the ladder one after the other. Desper wore duty scrubs she clearly worked in. Jennings, on the other hand, was squared away as humanly possible.

Part of Sandivol wished the Marine would have joined the Navy. She would have made an outstanding spacer.

"Bosun, what's the problem?" Desper asked as she approached.

Sandivol stepped back and gestured into the cabin.

Desper wrinkled her nose as she came to a stop. "Who spilled the vodka?"

The two women entered the cabin, leaving Bosun outside.

"She's the new midship, right?" Desper asked.

Bosun Sandivol held up his NavPad. "Yua Watanabe, midship. Class of '37. She's top of her grades according to the list." Looking at her passed out on the rack made him doubt the official record.

Usually, when Juan found crew in a drunken stupor it was after a liberty or too long in port. Virtually everyone in the Navy drank... except the captain, Juan realized. Commander Grimm never drank, not even at sanctioned events.

He shook his head. Regardless, having a midship show up one day after reporting for duty as blitzed as she was, made him think she wasn't long for the Navy.

"Is she okay?" Bosun asked.

Desper took out her own NavPad and started running it up and down the midships body. Jennings knelt beside her and opened one eye with her thick fingers. She shined her mini flashlight into her eyes and grunted.

"Pupils are dilated," she said.

"I don't think she's in danger," Desper said, "but her blood alcohol is—well look." PO Desper showed Bosun Sandivol the readings. He let out a low whistle.

"Alrighty then. Gunny, can you help me carry her to sickbay?" Bosun Sandivol asked.

Jennings heaved the midship bodily over her shoulders. "She don't weigh much, Bosun. I got it."

"Let's get her to sickbay and cleaned up."

CHAPTER NINE

Kremlin Station's transit line beeped as the maglev train came to a halt at the central axis of the station, a large tube, five meters wide that ran the length of the station.

The Special Forces troopers stood up, shouldering their bags. Each man carried two large duffels and a hard case containing their long arms strapped to their backs. They each wore a coil pistol strapped to their civilian pants in well-worn holsters. They weren't dressed like military, but anyone with sense would know they were.

Danny reached the end of the tube first, placing his hand on the security pad. The door whooshed open revealing the short gangplank to the Interceptor. Two Marines stood guard outside the long tube that connected the station to the Navy ship.

"May I help you, sir?" the redheaded Marine asked.

Danny held up his pad and showed it to the Marine, a lance corporal whose name tag read Owens.

Owens scrutinized the message. "This says you're to come aboard—"

"And so we will," Danny said as he moved to cross the gangplank.

Owens held up his hand against Danny's chest.

"No sir. I need to check with my Gunny first."

Frustration built in Danny. He wasn't used to having someone who was essentially a private, telling him what to do.

"Marines," Mac muttered.

"First of all, *Lance*, it's Master Sergeant, not *sir*. Dammit, I work for a living. Second of all, you will step aside, or we will make you step aside."

Danny didn't normally get so worked up. He knew the rawness of his emotions were a mix of fatigue and too much time spent in holes fighting insurgents and not enough downtime.

The Marine, to his credit, didn't back down.

"Master Sergeant," Owens said, "be that as it may, this is the *Interceptor*. There is one rule we all abide by here: Don't disappoint the captain. When Gunny Jennings gives you the all-clear, then you can come on board. Until then, how about I have PFC June here get you and your boys some coffee? Our man Mendez makes it good and strong."

The sudden change in the Marine's tone, along with his olive branch, deflated Danny's irritation. He respected a man who stood by his principles and didn't back down. He couldn't help but grin.

"Well played, Marine. Sounds good. Stand down, fellas."

His squad dropped their rucks on the deck and sacked out in an instant.

"June, go get them some of Mendez's special brew, will you?" Owens asked.

"Aye, aye, Corporal. On it." The dark-haired PFC pivoted with parade-ground perfection and entered the ship.

"Don't disappoint the captain?" Rico muttered. "Crazy asteroid munchers sure love their officers."

His men laughed as they waited. That was good, Danny thought. They had all braved hell the last six months. Zuckabar's insurgency was far more deeply rooted than any of the politicians back home had believed. Since his team was first on the ground, they were utilized more than anyone else.

Without warning, they were picked up and plopped down in front of the Navy.

He shook his head again. Cursing their luck. They trained and fought hard; it was no wonder his team was constantly tasked with the hardest nuts to crack.

"Boss," Mac said, tapping him on the shoulder.

"This day is looking up," Danny said with a smile.

A ramrod-straight Marine, with blonde hair held in a tight bun, marched down the gangplank. She wore the gray camo the Marines favored along with an MP-17 strapped to her thigh.

Danny hadn't realized the Navy carried sidearms aboard ship. He hopped up, dusting himself off in the process. Jennings, which he now knew was her last name, consulted Owens before turning to him.

"Master Sergeant Cannon?" she asked.

Was she playing with him, pretending not to recognize him, or just being all business?

"That's me, Gunnery Sergeant..." He purposely made her introduce herself.

"You can call me, Gunny. I'm the top Marine aboard *Interceptor*. Follow me." Without waiting for them to actually follow her, she spun on her heel and headed back into the ship.

"She doesn't talk a lot, huh?" Danny asked the redheaded Marine.

"You've no idea, Master Sergeant."

"You can just call me, Sergeant, son."

Regardless, Danny let out a sharp whistle for his boys to follow and they did.

Even though they were Army, they had travelled on their fair share of ships. Usually, larger cruisers or civilian ships transported them to their next assignment.

This *thing*, though, was something else.

"Lipstick on a pigsaur," Mac whispered to him. Danny agreed. Despite obvious signs of recent repairs and upgrades, the ship was held together with chewing gum and spacer-tape.

Jennings led them through the chow hall, out the door, and to the right, passing the lift.

"Your lifts don't work?" Mac asked.

Jennings wrapped her hands around the ladder and started climbing without answering him.

"I guess we're going up," Bubba said as he brushed passed Mac.

"Don't get too excited," Danny said. "This ship isn't the smallest we've ever traveled on, but not by much."

"I hope this 'captain' they keep talking about isn't some kind of hard ass," Rico said.

Jacob tapped a key on his NavPad, rotating the map of the local area ninety degrees. No orders had arrived. Rod certainly seemed to expect them to ship out immediately, but Jacob wasn't so sure. Either the admiralty was taking their time, or the orders were lost in the shuffle.

Regardless, he examined the map of Zuckabar and the three lanes connecting the mining system to Praxis, Minsk, and Wonderland. If he had to guess, their mission would take them back to the verdant world. For reasons only known to Department of Colonial Affairs, colonization of the lush planet hadn't yet commenced.

If Jacob were a betting man, and he wasn't, he would put money on the reason being the satellite network. While the ability to light a planet was nothing short of spectacular, if those lights ever went out, then the planet would die. He counted it among the other miracles of science the Guild produced in secret, and hid from the galaxy at large. It also meant they couldn't rely on the tech enough to start the colonization process.

Knuckles wrapped on the open hatch, interrupting him. "Skipper," Jennings said.

"Gunny, what is it?"

"We've got company for the trip, sir. While the Bosun squares away their living space they need a place to rack out."

Company? There were no visitors on the schedule. Hell, *Interceptor* had only returned to him a few days before.

"Bring them in," he ordered. Jacob stood, curious to see who it was.

Five men trudged in, each carrying a pair of army-green duffel bags and a hard case strapped to their back. They were dirty, not in uniform, and all of them had at least a month's worth of facial hair. They were all armed, Jacob noted, with *coil pistols*. If there were a worse ship-board weapon, Jacob didn't know it. The little guns could punch a hole through equipment that didn't respond well to holes, like the fusion reactor.

Five of them lined up in a parade rest against the far bulkhead. One of them, the leader, Jacob presumed, approached. Jacob's height always gave him, what felt like, an unfair advantage. However, looking in the man's eyes, he saw two things. Burnout and death.

Whoever these men were, they were dangerous and Jacob wanted to know why they were on his ship.

"Master Sergeant Danny Cannon, ODA Five-three-three-three." He held out his hand.

Jacob, not sure what ODA was, shook the man's hand. "Commander Jacob T. Grimm, USS *Interceptor*. Forgive me, Sergeant, but what does ODA mean?" he asked.

Two of the men against the wall chuckled and Jacob noticed Cannon stiffen.

"Operational Detachment Alpha, sir. 5th Special Forces Group, 3rd Battalion, 3rd Company. Uh, weren't you briefed about us?"

Now it was Jacob's turn to chuckle, and he did. "You have a high opinion of the military if you think orders routinely arrive before spacers—or grunts, as the case may be."

Cannon seemed to relax a little, returning to parade rest, then at ease. Jacob waived for the grunts to have a seat.

"I'm afraid *Interceptor* is running with a full complement, for once. However, we have the best Bosun in the fleet and I'm sure he can secure you men a rack."

Special Forces? Jacob had next to no information about Alliance Special Forces. He knew they existed, but that was about it. Once, long ago, all the branches had their own special warfare operations. However, as the branches further specialized, and the Army became less and less necessary, it divided into two camps. Garrison troops, like the ones manning Fort Icarus on Alexandria, and special ops. Neither made the Navy Times often, and he'd never interacted with spec ops before.

"That's all right, sir. We're used to hunkering down anywhere we can. We just came off a thing on Zuck Central. If it's okay with you, we'd like to get some kip before chow."

Despite having spent most of his adult life... in fact, all his adult life in the military, he wasn't quite sure what the sergeant was referring to.

"Yes, of course. I'll clear out."

Jacob gathered up his NavPad and kept an eye on the strange men as he exited the briefing room. It felt distinctly odd for him to be kicked out of his own briefing room aboard his ship.

Jennings tarried behind, poking her head in for a parting message.

"Master Sergeant, the hatch here is tricky, you have to open and close it manually." Jennings' arm's bunched and she slid the hatch shut without issue.

Jacob waited for her at the entrance to the bridge. "Interesting fellows," he said.

"As the captain says."

"You don't have an opinion on them?"

"Not unless you want me to, skipper."

Jacob smiled. All was right in the universe. "Very good, Gunny. Dismissed."

Now he needed to figure out where he would get his paperwork done.

———

Bosun Sandivol scowled as the request came across his desk. He would never show it, but the situation on the ship pushed his department to the limits. His department being himself, the two spacers in the fabricator, and his assistant, a spacer's apprentice. He liked the lad, but he was all but useless. Currently, Juan had him off buying some items from the station shops. They could fabricate most everything they needed with ease. However, there were a few luxury items he liked to keep in stock on the off chance they were needed. He also had to use civilian stores to restock the ship's retail store outside the mess. His NavPad beeped with an incoming call.

"Bosun, this is PO Write, we need five racks for a squad of

ground pounders. The captain has them racked in the briefing room for now, but he'd like them out ASAP."

"Thanks, Paul. I'm on it. Tell the grunts not to get too comfortable. I'll have them a place to stay by 1800 ship's time."

Sandivol closed the connection and pulled up his interactive hologram of the ship, filtering for available racks. There were none, other than sickbay, and the long-term recovery cabins. That would do it, then. It would crimp the sickbay overflow, but it wasn't used often to begin with.

He tapped up a quick set of orders and sent them off. Spacer's Apprentice Mizaka would run down to the fabricator and make sure the men had fresh linen, then up to the briefing room to let them know where they would be bunking.

Checking that off his mental list, Juan got to work on the hundred other things he needed to do before they were clear to depart.

CHAPTER TEN

Alarms wailed as the Richman field snapped into place around the boat bay doors. With the atmosphere shield in place, they opened like a clamshell, revealing the floating Corsair beneath. Yellow lights flashed their warning of an impending docking.

"Stand clear, Corsair docking. Stand clear, Corsair docking," Spacer Cooper announced over the loudspeaker.

Jacob stood back, toes inching the yellow-and-black checkered mark on the floor denoting the official line where the ship began. Technically, anyone stepping off the Corsair was on his ship, but for tradition's sake, the line represented the start of his command.

Boudreaux nodded at him from behind the bulbous cockpit as the nose came into view.

A bitter pit burned in his stomach and he did his best to push it down. He hoped, desperately, that her billet at OCS wasn't denied because of him. He'd quietly inquired with an old friend to see if they really were full, or if Jacob was the actual obstacle.

The Corsair hovered above the floor, her wings and tail

folded down and tucked in, to fit inside the bay. *Interceptor*'s Mudcat was hung flat against the bulkhead like a prized trophy. There wasn't enough room to have both the Corsair and the Mudcat out in the bay at the same time unless the 'Cat was hooked up in its carry-all position underneath the Corsair's tail.

Slowly, like a clock ticking down, the massive doors sealed up. Seconds later, the yellow lights shut off, and the soft white light of the bay brightened.

"All hands," Spacer Cooper announced. "Fleet Admiral Villanueva is aboard."

She stepped down from the Corsair before the large bulkhead door finished opening. Her immaculate dress whites were something to behold with their rows of ribbons and decorations.

"Chief," Jacob said.

"Company," Chief Suresh shouted, "atten-shun!"

Bosun Sandivol brought the pipe to his lips and blew the ancient tune welcoming the admiral aboard.

She stopped at the line, executed a left face, saluted the cartoon grinning shark flag painted on the port bulkhead, then turned to him.

"Permission to come aboard, Commander?"

"Permission granted, ma'am. It's a pleasure to have you on our little ship."

She smiled, and Jacob realized in that moment how much older she appeared than the last time he'd seen her. As if the war had drained her very life.

"I wish I had time for a tour, Jacob. However, I must return to the *Alexander* with all haste. We're breaking for home in a few hours and the president has reiterated that I am to be on her."

"Aye ma'am, this way, then," he said with a gesture to the hatch.

"Will *Alexander* be taking the battle group with her?" he asked.

As they walked out of the double hatch, she headed for the ladder, not the lift. Jacob already respected the admiral, but it grew more still when she climbed the ladder over taking the lift.

"Subtle, Commander." Her demeanor robbed the sarcasm of any offense. For years Jacob had noted in his log that Zuckabar needed a full fleet to defend the colony and patrol the outlying systems.

"I will tell you this, for your ears only. Only *Alexander* will return. The other sixteen ships that came with her are staying. Both to defend Zuck, *and other connected systems*"—she meant Wonderland of course—"and to act as reinforcements for Admiral Spencer's Task Force 16 as needed."

"Excellent, ma'am. Whoever decided on that clearly has a good head on their shoulders." She shot him a warning glance. He reminded himself that despite her help in the past, she was still the fleet admiral.

He couldn't recall her ever having boarded his ship. He had always gone to her in the past. For a spacer who hadn't ever stepped foot aboard and one who hadn't served on any destroyer in over two decades, Villanueva knew her way like she'd made the trek every day.

"Make a hole," PO Ignatius hollered as they approached the mess. Spacers lined up to eat, and while they didn't have to snap to attention while she walked the decks, they all did.

Jacob caught Ignatius' eye as he moved past and gave the man a nod.

Two decks later she emerged on O-deck, with Jennings offering her hand to help her up the last little bit.

"Thank you, Gunny."

"Aye ma'am."

Jennings waited by the ladder to help Jacob up as well.

"Have the grunts moved out of the briefing room yet?" he asked.

Villanueva raised an eyebrow.

"Aye sir. Sergeant Cannon is in there right now per the admiral's request."

"Thanks, Gunny. Get with the Bosun, and make sure he knows he can use your Marines to move things around as needed," Jacob said.

She snapped to, executing a perfect about-face to go stand by the bridge hatch.

"Aye, aye, sir."

"If you will, Admiral," he said, gesturing to the briefing room hatchway.

Inside, Sergeant Cannon dozed, his booted feet up on the table, covering the USS part of the *Interceptor* logo.

"Sergeant," Jacob said keeping his voice even.

Danny looked up, eyes clear and bright. Casually, as if not bothered in the least by the appearance of the fleet admiral, he pulled his boots down and stood.

"Ma'am," he said with a nod.

"Have a seat," she said with a bemused expression.

Jacob took up his usual position at the head of the table and the admiral dropped into the one between the two of them. A lot of little things bugged Jacob about Sergeant Cannon. He didn't appreciate the man's lackadaisical attitude toward officers, nor the disrespect of having his feet on the table.

Jacob's table.

Interceptor's table.

"You've got us here, ma'am. How can *Interceptor* help you."

She glanced at the hatch and jerked a thumb toward it.

Jacob coughed. "Sorry, ma'am, it's broken. I can have my Gunny close it."

"I got it," Sergeant Cannon said. Pulling, the hatch scraped with a squeal. His face turned red from exertion, leaving him breathing hard as he returned to the table.

Jacob looked on with a perfectly neutral face, but couldn't help but laugh inwardly. Allison had closed that same hatch without any effort at all.

Villanueva placed her NavPad in front of her. "Thank you, Sergeant. I'll dispense with the pleasantries and get right to it. Danny, Jacob," she said, "for purposes of this briefing, I'm raising your clearance to Top Secret. Everything I'm about to tell you is protected. Understood?"

They both agreed without hesitation.

"Good. When *Interceptor* raided Medial, Jacob, you garnered more than just a PR win. We captured a piece of technology we didn't know existed. Faster-than-light communications. Instantaneous, actually. The Caliphate have the technology and we want it."

Danny sucked in a breath. "Surely not."

Jacob, with a little help from Boudreaux, suspected this was the case. If not, then his maneuver in Medial would never have worked.

"You knew already?" she asked him.

"Suspected, ma'am. Only suspected. I take it Naval R&D couldn't reverse engineer it?" Jacob asked.

"I wish it were that simple. Not only can they not duplicate the tech, but they also don't understand how it works in the first place. I won't bore you with the science, but it's basically an impossible thing."

Danny, still stunned at the revelation, shook his head. "How can they have this and still be getting their butts kicked?"

"That's the real million-dollar question. What do they have, how does it work, and more importantly, how do we get it? That's your mission, in a nutshell. Thanks to HumInt we've located the planet the lead scientist is on, not to mention where the receivers are. I want *Interceptor* to go there, fight your way in, and then"—she gestured at Danny—"his team will go down on the planet and recover both our asset on the ground and the package. Once secured, your pilot will pick them up and off you will go. Hightailing it back here."

Jacob let the words wash over him. She made it sound so simple, so easy. Like running down to the corner store for a midnight snack.

"The last time we went into Caliphate space we almost didn't make it out. If you know where the planet is, why not just"—Jacob made a shooting motion with this hand—"go right for it? With the damage we inflicted in Medial, I can't imagine they're in a position to stop a full-on frontal assault."

To Jacob's surprise, the admiral deflated somewhat. "Normally I would agree with you. However, we're stretched thin. There are... indications... that the Caliphate won't be alone in this war for much longer."

Her disclosure of that intel shocked Jacob. Who would be entering the war to *defend* the Caliphate? Certainly not the Iron Empire. The realization they were going to have an ally combined with his knowledge of interstellar politics, left only one answer: The Terraforming Guild.

She continued on, though, and he had to refocus on her words to keep up. "Therefore, we can't in good conscious spread ourselves out any further. Not until we can either communicate with FTL, tap into their system, or stop them from using it. That's the outcome we're hoping to achieve."

There was something else, he could tell. The nagging gut feeling that helped so often dug at him.

"Ma'am, there's more to this, isn't there?"

"Yes." She activated her holo and a desert like planet sprang to life. It had no moons, no standing bodies of water. To Jacob, it looked like a chewed-up ball. The image zoomed in, showing a base built into the side of a deep, jagged ravine. Jacob spotted the power generator, a small landing pad, and what looked like a barracks, all nestled between two cavernous canyon walls. "This is Zephyr base. It is the only installation on the planet, built at the absolute lowest depth. Our scientists think that it might have been an ocean, but that was before."

"Before what?" Danny asked.

The image zoomed out and Jacob gasped.

A normal, G-type star shone on the display. Maybe the planet was closer than it should be, but scale was hard to tell in an image without reference. The absolutely massive black hole on the other side, though? That was wrong. While they watched, the feed sped up, showing hours, then days, then *months* passing, and the planet didn't move. It didn't orbit the sun, just sat there, in a pocket of space-time while the two stellar forces fought over it like dogs with a bone. The planet wobbled a bit, but for the most part didn't move.

"The planet is stuck in two gravity wells so perfect that it's motionless?" Jacob asked.

"Yes. Our experts break it down farther, but essentially you are correct."

Danny leaned forward on his elbows. "Why put a base there of all places?"

"We don't know. What we do know is that the only person in the galaxy who understands FTLC tech is on that planet. We either need them dead, captured, or turned. The only way to do that... is to send a ship."

"What kind of space-based defenses do they have? I imagine a whole fleet would be dedicated to protecting it." Jacob asked.

While shaking her head, Noelle explained, "This is the best part. In order for a ship to approach the planet, and not get pulled into the long agonizing death of a black hole, they have to exceed five hundred gravities of acceleration. In order to resupply the base, Caliphate logistics has deployed some specially constructed freighters that can make 500 g's. As for their military ships, only a handful of special purpose destroyers fit the bill. Our intel on their location is solid, and they are nowhere near Zephyr. Combine her unusual astrophysics with remote location and you have a base that isn't protected nearly as heavily as it should be for the simple fact that no one can approach her without ending up in the black hole."

Jacob let that sink in for a moment. A black hole. The single most dreaded stellar phenomenon in the universe and she wanted him to purposely fly toward one.

Danny grimaced looking at the holo. "You want us to go down there and extract the asset? We're a five-man team and they have a barracks. There're probably thirty or forty soldiers down there at any given moment. What do you want us to do, demand their surrender?"

Villanueva adjusted the holo and an image of Nadia Dagher appeared. "We have an agent onsite. She infiltrated the planet a few weeks ago... as far as we know. Her codename is India. There is a window you have to rescue her and extract the scientist. If you make it to Zephyr base in that time, then she will have disabled their main power generator."

Jacob had questions and many mixed emotions. All of which he kept, hopefully, hidden. He should have figured she would find a way back into the fight.

He wasn't a shining knight riding to the rescue on horseback. Nadia was in her element infiltrating the enemy, it was her specialty. She wasn't in any *extra* danger... but damn if he didn't want to launch immediately.

"I can get your people there, Sergeant, if you can do the rest."

Danny looked at the map, the spy, and finally Jacob. "If you can provide transpo commander, then yes: can do, ma'am."

Villanueva kept her stoic expression, but Jacob thought he could tell she was relieved. Having FTL comms would change everything. This mission risked much, but the reward would be worth it.

"Now, getting there might be a bit tricky," Jacob said. "It's twenty systems deep into Caliph territory. Did ONI have a suggestion for how to do this?" he asked. While she hadn't mentioned the military spy agency, the mission had SECNAV DeBeck's fingerprints all over it. It was bold, audacious, and damn near suicidal.

"Despite your track record of success, there is another reason for using *Interceptor* for this mission. I can assure you, Commander, you're not going to like it."

CHAPTER ELEVEN

Orbital entry and landing were the trickiest, and most dangerous, part of any journey. From her seat in the passenger compartment she could see out the display port as space turned hazy and white. Nadia had performed the procedure hundreds of times when she commanded *Dagher*.

A pang of regret filled her at the thought of her little tramp freighter. She loved that little ship, but it was also the home of the worst experience of her life. But, she wasn't willing to part with it. Unwilling to sell it, or have it scrapped, Nadia paid for the speedy little cargo ship to collect dust in a hanger on Providence, her adopted home world.

Turbulence hit the ship, shaking the crew and knocking numerous little objects loose. Nadia clung to the strap above her, praying the ship held together for the arduous landing. Supposedly, the Caliphate had these ships specially made for the system, but Nadia knew the truth. They had outfitted a dozen subpar freighters with military-grade gravcoils. For the Caliphate losing a freighter crew was considered acceptable losses.

She knew the war wasn't going in their favor. Word had reached her of Task Force 16's—Jacob's—stunning victory in Medial. *Jacob...* she thought, pushing his smiling visage to the back of her mind. It was harder than it used to be, to focus on only the mission and not think about the life she could have. A husband, children, a future. If she didn't succeed at this mission, though, there would be no Alliance to have a family in.

One more mission. DeBeck thinks I want back in... and I did, once upon a time. Now, though, I just want out with my life and freedom intact.

Before she'd met Jacob, she was happy, or so she thought. After meeting the dashing spacer, she realized there was a hole in her life. A hole no job could fill, no matter how important.

The ship banked and there was a loud bang as something hit the hull.

Nadia closed her eyes, willing the ship to the ground. Which made her smile. That part was pretty much going to happen no matter what.

"We're through," the pilot said over the comms. "Landing in five minutes. Laborers aren't to leave the ship's immediate area. All transfer personnel make sure you have your ID and orders ready or you will be shot. Trust me, I've seen them do it."

A bolt of terror ran through her. This is where the ship hit the space. If her fake ID wasn't perfect, it would be the end of the line.

Deep, throbbing, rumbles shook the hull as the engines went full reverse. Gravity pressed down on her, causing her vision to tunnel as the cheap gravity compensators failed to counteract the excess g's.

Sweat broke out on her as she exerted herself, trying to keep from banging around in the seat. Her arm ached from the strain. The ship shook hard for ten solid seconds before the nose lifted and the g's eased. Nadia breathed in deeply. So did the other passengers.

Ten minutes later the ship's engines roared as it came to settle on a small landing pad at the bottom of a deep canyon. Deep enough that the pad, the small squat building, and the entrance to the lab were cast in shadow.

Why would they build a base here? It makes no sense. Not only did any ship coming in have to contend with the black hole, but they couldn't defend the place, and it needed constant resupply. It was a logistical nightmare.

There had to be some other reason why they would pick such an out-of-the-way location to build a secret research lab.

Lights flashed as the ship came to a rest on the rocky ground.

"Don't forget to have your ID ready," the announcement said again. "I'm serious."

Nadia made sure to have the electronic ID out along with her backup. She'd paid her entire exit plan, a million untraceable Alliance dollars, to the best black-market smuggler in the entire Caliphate.

Six fully armed soldiers, with respirators, waited for them at the bottom of the gangplank. Five men stood in front of her, all with their ID out. The first soldier scanned each ID with a handheld device. A green light flashed on the soldier's scanner and he nodded the first passenger by.

Nadia bit down on her tongue, keeping her eyes down, and her demeanor relaxed. She huddled in on herself, giving the appearance that she was smaller than she really was.

Her turn came and she held up the electronic ID. His hand waivered as he held up the scanner but paid no attention to it, instead looking at her eyes.

"You're a woman."

Nadia didn't think it a question, so she kept her eyes lowered and head down.

"What's the problem?" the man behind him said as he moved forward, raising his rifle slightly.

"She's a woman, sir," he said.

Nadia frowned. She wore all the right clothing, had the right papers. Why was the guy freaking out?

"Why are you here?" the one in charge asked. "You may speak."

"Sir, I'm here to assist Doctor Yusra Abbasi, that is all I was told," she said. Hopefully they won't look too deep into her backstory. Even with the astonishing amount of money she'd paid for the ID, she wasn't sure it would stand sustained scrutiny.

"Do her credentials checkout?"

"Yes sir, but..."

"Then let her through and quit wasting time."

The first soldier motioned her through. She tucked her ID away and scurried toward the base entrance. Once inside she had to pass another security check, this one making sure she wasn't carrying any weapons.

"You have a cybernetic arm," the guard behind the counter said.

"Yes, sir. My husband gave it to me."

Her backstory included marriage, since that would be the only way to stay safe and be authorized to travel in the Caliphate. On paper, her husband was a mid-level member of the Ministry of Science.

The guard nodded. "Go in there," he pointed at a red door.

Nadia bowed and moved quickly to the door. She brought no weapons or gear. Other than her ID and a small bag with personal items, she traveled light. Besides, bringing a weapon to the overly secure facility would be suicide.

Inside the room, Nadia took a seat, acting exactly as they would expect her to.

An ISB agent, not like the soldiers on security, entered, his crisp uniform snapped as he moved. From his shiny boots to his well-groomed beard, the man screamed *methodical*.

Fooling him wouldn't be easy.

"Place your ID on the table," he said.

Nadia did as he instructed. Keeping her eyes down.

"You're the first woman to arrive here that wasn't collared. Can you clarify as to why?"

She said nothing.

"You may speak."

Was he trying to trap her? Get her to behave in a way that wasn't appropriate? Unlucky for him, Nadia slipped into roles the way others did with clothes.

"Thank you, sir. My husband sent me to assist Doctor Abbasi. That is all he told me."

"Your husband—Assistant Director of Research with the Ministry of Science?"

Nadia simply nodded, not speaking unless he specifically commanded her. She pushed her feelings about the Caliphate and the government down into a deep, dark box, and focused on her job. One mistake and they would kill her... if she were lucky.

"My name is Agent Malik. You will follow the rules here or you will suffer. I don't care who your husband is, do you understand?"

CHAPTER TWELVE

"What do you mean, we can't get under way?" Jacob asked his chief engineer.

Lieutenant Kai squirmed in his chair. He struggled to look Jacob in the eye but didn't break contact with him.

"I'm sorry, sir, no engineer wants to tell his captain that the ship won't run... but the ship won't run."

Jacob felt a familiar headache brewing, starting right behind his eyes. His muscles ached from the intense workout Gunny Jennings put him through that morning. It left him wondering if she were mad at him or trying to prove something.

"Break it down for me, Akio, and remember, use small words. I'm just the captain." Jacob used humor to take the sting out of the comment. Akio Kai's brilliance as an engineer, and his placement as the number one student at the academy, wasn't in question.

"Aye sir. The new gravcoil and housing are in perfect condition. To be honest with you, we might even break our own acceleration record... which is the problem. By *The Book*, we can't use full power if it hasn't passed the simulations. Right now, as it stands, we don't pass. The housing fails every time. The new composite nanite armor is lighter than the old nano-steel. We need to add some mass, about three tons worth."

The briefing room stood silent as the gathered officers processed what the engineer said.

"Wait," Carter interrupted. "You're saying we need more armor?"

Jacob marveled at how quickly Carter leapt into the role of XO. In a lot of ways he reminded him of Kim. Perhaps that wasn't an accident.

"Yes. Essentially. Or find a way to increase the ships weight by three nonperishable tons. Captain Beckett is on the comms listening, you can confirm it with him."

Jacob leaned over the pickup. "Rod, are you catching this?"

"Yeah, skipper. And I have to say, I should have figured this out before. Good find, Lieutenant. Next time you're on the station, come see me and we'll talk. I can probably scrounge up another ton of the composite armor."

Kai tapped his NavPad bringing up a holo of the ship's prow. "Captain Beckett, if you have any of the original nano-steel armor we can reinforce the bow, as well skipper. We lost a lot of rigidity when they took out tubes three and four, not to mention the associated mass of the coils."

"I never thought finally receiving the upgrades we've asked for would make us worse for wear. Okay, sounds like a plan. Carter," Jacob said, pointing at the young man. "I want you to personally oversee the armor add-ons. Get Redfern on the plating for the turrets. Kai, you keep working on the simulations, I don't want the ship falling apart just when we got her back together."

A round of "aye, aye" met him.

"You have your assignments, execute them."

The officers all stood, departing one by one through the

broken hatch. Once Carter left, a knock on the hatch caught Jacob's attention.

"Come in."

Bosun Sandivol entered and stood at attention. "Permission to converse with the skipper?" he asked.

"Always, Juan. At ease."

The Bosun relaxed, coming to sit next to Jacob.

"Sir, I'm running into a crew problem and I think it might end up needing your attention."

Bosun Sandivol needing help with the crew shocked Jacob. There wasn't a finer Bosun in the entire fleet as far as he was concerned.

"Tell me."

"For the first time since I've served aboard *Interceptor*, we've got a full complement. However, there are some disadvantages to that."

Jacob understood all too well the severe problems having less than a full crew had created in their last several missions. There were no magic bullets, however. With every change came new and interesting issues for him and his command to solve.

"Am I not keeping them busy, Bosun?"

Sandivol gave him a fatherly smile. "That's more our job, skipper. Since we're out in space for long periods of time, we tend to let the crew swap shifts or fill in for others as needed. It keeps morale up and as long as there is a qualified body in the slot when the bells ring, we're all good."

An unease twisted its way up Jacob's spine. The same informal system existed for officers as well. A stop gap, to allow crew leeway to navigate their lives while deployed for months, sometimes years, at a time. There were always one or two enlisted that were masters of taking advantage of the system.

"Have you spoken to the COB about the issue? I'm sure she can straighten out whoever... it... what?"

Sandivol, despite his many years in the Navy, glanced nervously at the open hatch. "Sir, if it were one of the enlisted, or even an NCO, do you think I would be here talking to you?" he asked in a hushed whisper.

Jacob's ears heated and he felt like a spacer on his first cruise. Of course the Bosun wouldn't be talking to him if it were a spacer, which meant it was an officer... but who?

"You got me, Juan." He rubbed his face, trying to shake the embarrassment. "Sorry, I should have seen that quicker. Who is it?"

"Midship Watanabe, sir. The other day when she wasn't on the bridge, I went to her cabin and found her passed out drunk."

Drunk on duty was no laughing matter. However, it was actually preferable to miss one's watch than to show up inebriated. "I had Gunny take her to the new doc and see if she were okay. We figured she just had one too many shots of the local Vodka. No harm, no foul."

"But?" Jacob prompted.

"Well sir, to be honest, I'm kind of impressed with this middie. She hasn't had a single shift of duty since. Ratings and even a few POs keep showing up for her watch. I went to speak to her about it and she can be... persuasive. As uncomfortable as I am to admit it, I ended up *apologizing* to her, and I'm not even sure how that happened."

Jacob leaned back, tapping his fingers in rhythm on the shark-painted table. He'd met a few people with a high degree of persuasive charm in his life. Nadia could speak circles around most people, himself included. While he certainly considered himself to be a raging extrovert who enjoyed public speaking, it wasn't the same as someone who could hit those notes in a one-on-one conversation. Then, something Sandivol had said hit him.

"Wait, not one shift? No watches? Juan, when did she come aboard?"

"Two weeks ago, skipper."

He let out a long whistle. "I don't know whether to give her a Captain's Mast or promote her? That's dammed impressive."

"Aye, skipper. That was my thinking. It's also why I came to you and not the XO. She has... charms, I don't think will work on you since... you know."

Jacob cocked his head to the side. "Since what?"

"Pardon me, sir, I presumed you were spoken for."

He let out a sharp laugh. "I am, Bosun. I am. Let's nip this in the bud right now." Jacob pressed the comms stud down. "Bridge, Captain, have Midship Watanabe join me in the briefing room."

McCall's voice came back, "Aye, aye, sir. Have Midship Watanabe join you."

Jacob glanced at the Bosun and thought better of meeting her with just the two men. "Mac, have Gunny Jennings and Ensign Brennan join us as well."

"Roger that, skipper."

"Midship Watanabe, Ensign Brennan, Gunnery Sergeant Jennings, please report to the briefing room," Spacer McCall said over the ship-wide. The spacer's accent reminded Fionna Brennan of home. They were both from Glenanne, and it was rare to meet anyone from her home in the Navy. Not that they had any prohibition about leaving the rainy world, just that the population was tiny in comparison to places like Seabring and Alexandria.

She hurried out the hatch to the nearest ladder, almost double-timing it. Fionna had worried since she came aboard that Commander Grimm would be upset with her. After all, Captain Hatwal had used her to answer the comms every time Grimm had called *Firewatch* during their patrol together.

Fionna glanced down at the blood-red stripe on her uniform leg and shuddered. If she never saw combat again, it would be too soon. She froze on the ladder for a moment, the memory of the horrific bombardment *Firewatch* sustained during the battle of Praetor. Sweat broke out under her armpits as she relived the abject terror of the hits coming in. She wanted to move her hands, unclasp them and climb up, but all she could think of was the battle. Blast after blast shook the ship, and Fionna squeezed her eyes shut, desperate to block out the memory.

"Ma'am, are you okay?" a soft voice said from beneath her.

"Yes," she said, not moving.

"Take your time, ma'am, the ladders can be tricky. A while back I was trying to repair one and fell right down. I thought PO Desper was gonna tan my hide for busting up my hand. Makes it hard to cook when all the little bones in your wrist are broken."

Fionna managed to open her eyes, and the warm, smiling face of the PO who made breakfast stared up at her. She glanced down and saw, not one but two, blood-red stripes on his uniform. Her eyes went to his and she saw the truth in them. He knew why she clung to the ladder like a life preserver, why her legs wouldn't—couldn't—move.

"It's okay, ma'am, *Interceptor* will take care of you," he whispered.

"Thanks, PO... I'm sorry I don't know your name." How was this kid, who couldn't be more than twenty, able to look and sound far older?

"Mendez, ma'am, Josh Mendez, Galley and gun crew."

Fionna's strength returned and she climbed up. The PO

right behind her, balancing a bag in one hand while climbing. At first, she thought maybe he followed her to make sure she was okay, but when she got to the O-deck, he was right behind her.

"I'm okay, really PO." She glanced at the Marine, a young woman with black hair and who looked hardly older than a kid as she stood guard at the bridge hatchway.

"I'm sure you are, ma'am, but I'm actually heading for the briefing room. I take it you are too?" He handed her the sack before ascending the last few rungs.

"I... well, yes."

He hopped up on the deck and took the sack back from her. Just then she noticed the heavenly aroma coming from the bag.

She followed him in and stood at attention, about to announce reporting for duty. Astonishingly, the PO walked right up to the captain and placed the bag in front of him.

"I think the skipper's alarm might be broken, sir. I'll talk to engineering about getting it fixed if you like?" Josh said with a grin. He opened the bag and proceeded to place a meal in front of Commander Grimm. Eggs, bacon, toast, and a large cup of the Navy's finest orange drink. Fionna couldn't imagine anyone, not even Commander Ban, acting as familiar with Captain Hatwal as the PO did with Commander Grimm.

"No need, Josh. I think the error lies between the NavPad and the conn."

"Not to worry, sir, I've got your six."

Josh brushed passed her as he left, making eye contact for a moment in an oddly reassuring way. "Ma'am," he said.

Then she remembered where she was. "Ensign Brennan reporting as ordered, sir."

Commander Grimm and Bosun Sandivol exchanged amused glances and she felt her neck heating up.

"As you were, Ensign. Have a seat, we're still waiting on two—"

Gunny Jennings stormed in, pulling up short lest she collide with Ensign Brennan who stood almost in front of the hatchway. A light bead of sweat collected on Jennings' brow.

"Where do you want me, skipper?" she asked.

"I needed a couple of female crew to witness, Gunny. Since June is on duty, you and Fionna here, are it."

"Aye sir."

Fionna frowned. If he needed witnesses that meant there was a reprimand coming. If it were for a formal mast or an informal one to a crew member, any of the dozen female enlisted would have suited fine. That meant it was for—

She groaned. While *Interceptor*'s crew numbered at 130, there weren't that many female officers. Besides herself, there was Chief Boudreaux… and Midship Watanabe, Fionna's roommate, and Dr. Freydis.

"Sorry, you two," Commander Grimm said. "We're just waiting on Midship Watanabe, and we can get this under way."

Minutes passed in silence, uncomfortable silence as the captain ate his meal. PO Mendez returned with coffee for everyone else, including a cup for the Midship who still hadn't shown.

"You know," Commander Grimm finally said after he finished his meal, "I could have crawled from the rec room to here by now."

Bosun Sandivol chuckled. "Aye sir. Let me see what the holdup is."

Sandivol stood up and exited the room, pulling out his NavPad as he did so.

"Sir," Gunny Jennings said. "If it's all the same, I can come back later."

"Sorry, Gunny. I need you here. What's the hurry?"

"Training, sir. We're staging some mock boarding actions while we have the ship tethered to Kremlin. I'll tell them we'll be a bit." She stepped out as well, leaving Fionna with the captain.

She had no idea what to say or if she should say anything.

"You like Cúchulainn?" he asked suddenly, finishing up his breakfast and putting the waste in the bag.

No one had ever asked her about her hometown. Not ever. How did he even know where she was from? With her accent, red hair, and generous amount of freckles, it was easy to guess Glenanne, but to know the actual city meant he'd taken the time to read her file.

"Sir? Yes sir. Very much." His friendly demeanor made her think maybe he wasn't mad at her for what happened on *Firewatch*. She held out hope that was the case.

"Did I say the name right? The language is a bit tricky,"

"As well as anyone, sir."

Jennings returned a moment later, and Fionna recoiled from the anger on the Marine's face.

"Sir, permission to throw Lance Corporal Owens out the airlock without a suit?"

Grimm frowned, clearly surprised by the Gunny's outburst. "What happened?"

"I relayed to Owens the holdup and he told me that Midship Watanabe left the boat around midnight. She told him some sob story about seeing her mom who was in system for a few hours. He agreed not to log it if she promised to make it back before his watch was over."

"I take it she didn't?" he asked.

"No. Sir." The chill in Jennings' voice made Fionna shiver. *Please never let her be mad at me like that.*

Commander Grimm stood, knuckles on the table as he debated what to do. "Okay," he said after a long moment.

"Looks like we're going on a shore excursion. Ensign Brennan, sorry to waste your time. Carry on normal duties and let your OIC know that I held you up."

"Aye sir," she said. Fionna deliberately took measured, even steps, as she walked out. There wasn't any force in the galaxy that would make her want to be in Watanabe's shoes at the moment.

CHAPTER THIRTEEN

Jacob strapped on the brown leather gun belt. He popped the mag to make sure the MP-17, locked into pistol mode, was fully loaded. He trusted the spacer's down in the armory, but it never hurt to check twice. The indicator on the mag read five hundred. A full load.

"Sir, I can find her on my own. You should stay behind," Gunny Jennings told him for the second time.

"Gunny," Jacob replied with a smile, "I know you like to think I'm constantly in danger. But really, we'll take every precaution. Besides, she's in the tourist district, not the docks or old town. We'll be fine."

Jennings scowled at him.

In a way she was right, and he knew it. Jennings saved his life twice on Kremlin, preventing an assassination the last time. Surely, though, they would be safe in the tourist district. Kremlin had come a long way in the years since he first arrived on the station.

"I'm going, Allison. She's one of my officers and my responsibility." He held up his hand to stop her from arguing. "However, I'm willing to concede to your expertise in this area.

How can we proceed in a way that would make you comfortable?"

Gunnery Sergeant Allison Jennings grinned at him like a mad woman.

This is ridiculous, Jacob thought. They were piled in the Mudcat, with PO Mendez in the turret. *The turret.* He couldn't believe it when she rolled the big truck out of the bay with the ten-millimeter coilgun mounted on top. All her Marines were decked out in soft armor and wore full kits.

They weren't messing around. Jacob sat in the middle of the back bench, flanked by Naki and June. He sighed, knowing any complaints at this point would fall on deaf ears. Chief Boudreaux drove the beast and had a grin on her from ear to ear. Jennings had shotgun, carrying a full-sized battle rifle version of the MP-17 and slung with a bandolier of extra mags.

"Every time the skipper leaves the ship, something gets blown up," she said. "I don't want to take the chance."

"It's a good call," Naki said. "You never know if there is an entire army waiting in the fake hedges."

Naki turned to Owens to high-five him, but the normally chipper redhead sat somberly, staring out the window.

"I'll remember that next time you get skewered, Naki," Jennings said.

Jacob felt for Owens, the gloomy Marine wasn't his usual chipper self. He certainly looked like a man with deep regrets. He decided to put the kid out of his misery, bumping him to get his attention.

"Sir?" Owens asked.

"Clyde, it's okay. Don't beat yourself up about it. I've heard she's quite persuasive."

"Thank you, sir. Still, I'm better than that."

Jacob took a moment to compose his thoughts. "Let me tell you, young man, it doesn't matter how old you are, how wise you are, how in control you *think* you are. A pair of pretty eyes bats their lashes your way and your judgement is skewed. Add in how charismatic and charming she seems to be and you are at a definitive disadvantage. Accept the mistake, learn from it, and move on. Beating yourself up over it is Jennings' job," he said with a hooked thumb pointing at the Gunny.

"Semper Fi, sir. Thank you," Owens said.

Five minutes later they pulled up to the Miners' Luck Casino and Hotel. As they climbed out of the Mudcat, Jennings gave instructions to Boudreaux to stay local and keep Mendez frosty.

"This is where her signal leads, sir," Boudreaux said.

It was a helluva thing. Here they were, trying to get *Interceptor* ready to depart, and he's wasting time tracking down a midship who couldn't be bothered to report for duty on time.

Four sour Marines and Jacob entered the casino. Civilians scattered, giving them a wide birth.

"May I help you?" a stout doorman asked.

Jacob held up his hand to stave off the man for a moment.

"Owens, where is she?" he asked.

"One hundred meters." Owens pointed toward the back of the casino.

Jacob turned back to the doorman. "I'm looking for a missing spacer. She's here, we're retrieving her."

The doorman raised an eyebrow and stepped from behind his podium. "Not with weapons you're not. No one comes in with—"

"Jennings." Jacob didn't even need to tell her what to do. The Marine lunged forward, slamming the man in the gut and then helped him down to a sitting position as he struggled to breathe.

"Stay calm," she said. "It will pass."

The entourage moved through the doors like they were on a combat mission. Each Marine swiveling their heads back and forth. Jennings and Owens led the way while Naki and June guarded their six.

Jacob's comms squawked. "Skipper, XO here. Bosun tells me you're off ship?"

"Sorry, Carter, I didn't have time to fill you in. We have a missing crew member and I wanted to oversee it personally."

"Missing? Bosun said she's UA."

"If she does have an unauthorized absence, then her career is pretty much toast, don't you think?" Jacob asked.

"I see your point, sir. I'll log it as a missing crew, then. Good luck."

Jacob hoped Midship Watanabe proved to be worth the effort. Regardless of what she wanted out of her life, starting it off with a dishonorable discharge from the military probably wasn't it. In his experience, young officers and newly enlisted didn't quite grasp how important showing up to your post on time ended up being. He'd participated in several Captain's Mast where the kids were shocked at their punishment. Anything from forfeiture of pay to thirty days confined to quarters.

UA wasn't a joke. Officers were held to a much higher standard than enlisted, since they also had greater responsibilities. At the very least, she would end up with a general officer memorandum of reprimand, and at most, court martial and prison.

He would like to avoid that, if at all possible. Not only would it end her career, it would make him feel as if he'd failed. Not even having met the officer before being forced by the system to prosecute her.

Midship Yua Watanabe shook the dice in her hand, praying to her ancestors this would be the one.

It must be the one.

She rolled...

"Seven," the dealer yelled. The crowd roared around her, jostling the slight woman. She grabbed the dice again, doubling down and throwing them without a second thought.

"Winner!"

For an hour she gambled, won, and gambled some more. Her civilian clothes were sticky with sweat and alcohol as she won, and kept winning.

She moved from craps to roulette to blackjack, until the small amount of money she could win at those games wasn't enough to satisfy her urges. In the early hours of the morning, she found herself in a private room, playing cards with large men in expensive suits.

"Call," she said, laying down her cards. She had a classic hand, a full house.

One by one the men threw their cards down until she faced Grigori, a brooding man with a large beard and a sour demeanor, across the velvet table from her.

"Nyet," he said, placing his cards down.

Her spirit crumpled. She'd bet everything on the hand. It was the last of her winnings and all her money. She needed a chance to win it back, but she didn't have anything to bet.

"Ante," the dealer said.

She had nothing to put in.

"Ante?" he repeated as the other men threw in chips.

"Let me play one more hand," she said. Desperate to get back in the game. Her mind filled with all the reasons she should keep playing, all the ways she could win.

"No ante, no cards," the dealer said.

"Wait," Grigori said. "Do you know what *ante* means, little shlyukha?"

Yua didn't know what shlyukha meant. Japanese and standard English were the only languages she spoke. Still, she could tell from the lecherous looks of the other men that it wasn't anything good.

"It's what you put up when you gamble," she said.

"Nyet. It's your stake. What you are willing to lose. What are you willing to lose?"

Yua bit her lip. She could feel the tension rising in the room like a cloud. She'd gotten into the table with her massive winnings and wanted to try and triple it. Instead, she lost it all.

She took another swallow of vodka, using the burn to give her courage.

"What do you want? You have all my money."

Grigori thought about it for a moment, pretending to take his time as if he didn't already know what he wanted. "You come work for me. I know you're in the Navy, but that's easy to fix. You are, how you say, exotic? I think you can make a lot of money."

Yua gulped, the situation escalating by the second. She wasn't an idiot, he was talking about making her a whore… but with the money sitting in the pot, she could walk away and have a tidy little nest egg when she got out of the Navy.

"One more hand is all I want. That sounds like a lot for thousand-dollar ante."

Two of the other men pulled out ten-thousand-dollar chips and slid them across the table to her. She gulped. Her neck tightened and she resisted the urge to rub it. They were trapping her. Getting her to commit over her head. The alcohol made it hard to see until just then.

So, of course, she took another drink, grabbed the chips, and agreed.

"Good. If you fold, or quit, it's the same as losing. Don't start unless you're prepared for the results."

Yua responded by throwing the borrowed chip into the pile. The dealer picked up his deck, a nasty smile on his face as he flicked the cards out.

Two, four, eight, three, seven...

She had nothing. Her throat tightened and pressure grew behind her eyes, a pressure like she was underwater. Looking at each of the men, she realized they all knew she had nothing... they cheated.

A muffled thump came from the door and the faux wood paneling shook. A scream sounded, then cut off sharply.

"What is going on?" Grigori pointed at the door. "Pavel, Yuri." Two burly security men Yua hadn't even known were there stepped out of the shadows and headed for the door.

The door's faux wood paneling slid aside and a short, thick female Marine in full combat gear stormed in. Yuri jutted forward to stop her. She only came up to his stomach. His long arms reached out and—Yuri flew across the room to slam upside down into the wall. Pavel swung at her, but he misjudged her height and swung high. He had to punch down, and she stepped inside his reach and planted her fist squarely on the underside of his jaw. He lifted bodily into the air and collapsed unconscious.

Two more Marines rushed into the room, hands empty, but Yua imagined that really didn't make a difference.

Then the events caught up to her alcohol-addled mind. *Marines... Here?*

A naval officer walked in after them. He was tall, by far the tallest man in the room, but not thin, his broad shoulders brushed the edges of the door as he entered. GRIMM and NAVY adorned his black uniform jacket. A blood-red watch cap on his head and matching stripes on his black pants.

Yua blinked several times before it all came together.
Oh fu—

Jacob surveyed the room and stunned expressions on the men, and one woman, sitting at the card table. Foul smelling smoke hovered at the top and the sickly sweet scent of strong alcohol lingered with it.

Despite having sparred with Jennings, and witnessed her strength first hand, the sheer speed and power she brought to an engagement astonished him. He knew that if anyone were sharp, they would see how dangerous she was and approach her more carefully. However, her size and gender made her opponents underestimate her. If she ever had to fight anyone more than once, they might prove a challenge for her.

She wasn't a boxer, though. When she ended a fight, her foes tended not to be conscious... or alive.

"Secure them," she said pointing at the two men. Naki moved opposite her, kneeling to zip-tie the man on the far side of the room while Owen tied up the other guy. June had their back, and despite how nervous Jacob could tell she was, she didn't waiver.

"Sorry to interrupt, gentlemen. However, your door man wouldn't let me in, and I don't take no for an answer. Midship Watanabe?" Jacob asked as if he didn't know it was her.

Yua Watanabe had a frame slight enough she could almost be mistaken for a child. Except her generous curves and the fact that she wore a too-revealing white top and short skirt. He frowned. While it was entirely up to an individual how they dressed off duty, he believed officers should hold themselves to a higher standard. Like an older sibling, the crew tended to behave as the officers did.

Midship Watanabe pushed herself up precariously, as if she weren't sure the floor would hold her.

"Here, sir," she said.

"I see..." Jacob said looking at the pot and then back to her. Whatever she was up to was no good. He knew dangerous men when he saw them, and these men were dangerous. Not to him, per se. But in general. "Gentlemen, on behalf of the Systems Alliance Navy, I would ask you not to gamble with any of my crew again. If she owes you money, I'm afraid that debt is forfeit. We'll be going."

"Wait," a bearded man said. "She doesn't owe us money, but she does owe us. The hand started. If she leaves now, she forfeits and we collect our *winnings*."

Jacob wasn't sure what he meant by *winnings*, but he could guess.

"I'm afraid you misunderstand, Mr....?"

"Dagovich, Grigori Dagovich." He spoke his name like Jacob should know who he was.

"Right. Mr. Dagovich. She's coming with me and back to the *Interceptor*. If you have a claim, you can file it with our Bosun through official naval channels." Jacob gave the line with a tilt of his head, trying to lighten the mood.

That didn't seem to satisfy the man. He stood up sharply, hand hovering over the side of his jacket. An unnatural stillness filled the room.

"I said she owes us, she stays," he growled.

Mirth fled Jacob and he looked at each of the men at the table, fear plain on their faces.

"Gentlemen, maybe you don't understand the situation you're in. I have four Alliance Marines with me. Each one is a lifetaker and heartbreaker. They eat razor wire and piss plasma and can put a round through a flea's eye at three hundred meters. If you think *any of you* will make it out of this room alive if Mr. Dagovich reaches for his gun, you're as stupid as he looks."

The men around the table very carefully raised their hands. "Don't be an imbecile, Grigori," the one closest to him said.

Grigori swept the room with his gaze, his brain finally catching up to his ego or maybe he noticed the Marines had surreptitiously drawn knives and were looking at him like wolves at prey. Whatever ego the man had, it didn't override his good sense. Though it pained him to do so, he moved his hand away from his side.

"I... misspoke. Miss Watanabe is free to go and should she ever return, I will refuse her entry."

"On behalf of the United Systems Alliance Navy, I thank you, and have a nice day."

Jacob turned his back on the men. Not something he would do if he were by himself, or in real danger, but he needed them to understand he gave them no further thought.

Jennings, he knew, would not. She backed out of the room, ready to kill everyone in it on his order. An idea that both thrilled and terrified him.

"Commander Grimm, thank goodness you're here. Those men kidnapped me and—"

Jacob held up his hand for her to be quiet as they made their way back to the Mudcat. The big vehicle waited for them outside, Mendez smiling as he sat in the turret.

Once the Marines were in, except for Jennings who wouldn't enter until he did, he spoke. "Midship Watanabe, you are returning to *Interceptor* so you can work. The only reason you're not in cuffs right now and awaiting a general court martial for abandoning your duty is that I dislike pushing my problems off on other people. You will resume your duties. You will report to the sickbay before and after your shift to make sure you're not drinking. You will spend your off time in the galley and your downtime in engineering. You will have six hours to sleep every night. You will do all of this, or you will spend the next four years in prison on Blackrock, wishing you had. Do you understand?"

She blinked, tears welling in her eyes as they went wide. Jacob had to admit, if Bosun hadn't prepared him for it, he might have fallen to her persuasion. There was something about her that just made him want to help.

"Sir, you don't understand they threatened—"

"Midship Watanabe." His voice, like his resolve, was full of steel. "You will answer with a 'yes sir' or 'no sir' and nothing else. Do you understand?"

Her visage waivered. "Yes sir," she said with a spiteful glare.

CHAPTER FOURTEEN

Something about the bridge smelled different than normal. Maybe the new computers, or the updated controls, something... it smelled off. Not bad, but not the same.

Jacob rocked gently back in his squeaky command chair and the sense of familiarity came to him. He was home. That was one thing he knew. His time on *Enterprise* had opened his eyes to how the larger ships ran. They were an order of magnitude more powerful, and influential to any battle in space. However, for pure command authority, his Hellcat destroyer beat them every time.

The crew scurried around, making the last-minute checks before they sealed the ship for departure. Jacob basked in the cacophony of controlled chaos. To an outsider it would appear unorganized, even inefficient, but to his skilled eye he knew they were working.

Chief Suresh verified the controls in The Pit worked, making sure each and every one responded correctly. With the computer switched to "sim" mode, she coordinated with engineering testing the thrusters and gravcoil.

Lieutenant Hössbacher spoke fervently with POs throughout the ship as they made sure the stores were full, fuel was topped off, and all the crew were present and accounted for.

Lieutenant Brown communicated with his gun crews, testing the turrets, the four remaining torpedo rooms and the new PDWs. Jacob had warmed to the young man from MacGregor's world. He had a single-minded focus that reminded him of Jennings. Once he figured out how to be a little more verbose, he would do well.

"Sir," Ensign Brennan said from astro to get his attention. PO Oliv sat in the chair next to her, headphones around her neck. POs were often paired with inexperienced officers to teach them the systems and procedures.

"Yes, Fionna?"

"I... uh, never mind, sir." She flushed deeply and turned around to face her console.

He looked to Oliv who shrugged. Whatever bothered the young woman would eventually come out. From all accounts she worked hard and knew her stuff, but when he was around her, she seemed to expect him to yell at her and toss her out the airlock. If there was a crewmember, he was likely to yell at, it wasn't the mild-mannered ensign.

Which of course, brought him to Midship Watanabe. Spacer McCall sat next to her, patiently working with her to answer the numerous calls the ship dealt with at any given moment. He didn't envy comms. Most people thought it was an easy post, just pass along occasional communications.

However, when they were in port, the comms officers worked harder than anyone aboard and juggled a hundred requests in the air. Watanabe's scores were excellent, but her work ethic left a lot to be desired. As he watched, she pushed as much of the actual work off on McCall.

That was a problem. He tossed it in the back of his mind, letting his subconscious work on it. There were no easy solutions to problem crew members. If it were easy, it was almost always the wrong answer. No, to understand how to fix the problem, he needed to understand the problem. The only way to do that would be to understand her.

A captain's job was never done.

"Skipper," Lieutenant Fawkes said, handing him his NavPad.

Jacob looked over the list of requests and reports, skimming each one before placing his thumb on the reader to acknowledge receipt. "Very good, XO. How long until we're ready to depart?"

Carter nodded to ops. "Roy's doing the final confirmations now, sir. Call it an hour? Lieutenant Kai says the new hull plating is good to go, which solves our mass problem."

Jacob leaned to the side, away from Carter as he detected something reticent about him. "What is it?" he asked.

"Well, sir, to be honest I'm a little concerned about how smooth everything has gone. We haven't had a single request for parts, ammunition, or supplies turned down. I'm not sure what to do when my department heads actually get the personnel and equipment they need."

Jacob let out a short laugh, a grin splitting his face from ear to ear. "You and me both, XO. I keep waiting for the other shoe to drop. However, if there's one ship in the fleet that deserves the fanfare, it's *Interceptor*."

"Aye sir, couldn't agree more."

"Let's set our departure time to 1800, then. We've got a long journey ahead of us, we might as well get started."

"Eighteen hundred, very good, sir."

After Carter exited the bridge, Jacob went back to observing his officers and crew as they worked. A lot could be learned by a commander who watched and listened.

Eighteen hundred hours came quick. Once the department heads signaled their readiness, Jacob had the ship put into Condition Yankee, ready for departure. All 130 crew, along with their five passengers, were strapped in and ready to depart.

"Chief Suresh, give us some breathing room with the thrusters," he ordered.

"Aye sir, thrusters engaged."

Reaction thrusters expelled gas to push the ship away from Kremlin Station. The slight thrust "pulled" the crew to the port side of the ship. Despite their secondary gravcoil operating, there were always slight gravitic forces acting on the inside of the ship. Because of that, like the crew, every piece of equipment, item, and spoon were either magnetically secured or stowed in a container. It wouldn't do to have a coffee cup flying across the room and hitting a crew member in the head during a crucial maneuver.

"Five hundred meters, skipper. We're clear to engage the gravcoil," PO Oliv said.

Jacob leaned forward, eyeing the vast empty starfield on the forward screen. He liked to keep it set to an actual forward view. Most of the time it was a tactical screen used to show distances and status, but he enjoyed looking at the stars through the lenses mounted on the bow.

"Ensign Brennan, plot a course for Wonderland," he ordered.

"Aye sir, course plotted. Helm come to, two-seven-five mark zero-four-one. Accelerate at five zero gravities for one-zero-zero minutes."

Jacob appreciated that she had anticipated the possible

destinations and had courses ready. It was the mark of a good officer and he intended to make sure she knew that.

Barring an emergency, ships weren't allowed to use acceleration greater than twenty-five g's in the harbor. Which was the area of space around a planet or space station where other ships were parked. Jacob glanced at PO Oliv, wanting her to correct the ensign so he didn't have to.

Which she did. Oliv leaned over and whispered into Brennan's ear.

"Correction," she said, her voice going up an octave. "Set acceleration at two-five gravities."

"Correction acknowledged," Chief Suresh said as she repeated the course back. Of course, Brennan could just send the course to the chief's computer, and then the automated systems could take over and they might even shave a few seconds off the whole ordeal. However, the Navy liked her traditions. Computers wouldn't always be available, automated flight wouldn't always work, and sometimes, it was just better to hear the voice of the person manning the controls.

Jacob didn't mind at all. He *enjoyed* naval traditions. They connected him to his mother, and all the men and women who had ever served throughout history creating an unbroken chain that went back to the earliest days of man when plotting courses on maps involved sections labeled, "Here there be monsters."

While Earth's oceans were fully explored and devoid of monsters, sailing through space had the same sense of the unknown. As a boy, Jacob dreamed of joining the Navy and exploring the galaxy. Back when the Navy still did that. Yet, here he was, present for not one but two historic discoveries. He may not have made the discoveries, but his ship and last name were indelibly linked to them.

He prayed, nightly in fact, that his mom smiled down on

him from heaven, watching over *Interceptor* and her crew like a guardian angel. A sudden wave of regret washed over him. She'd died when he was barely a teen. His memories of her were sharp, but few.

Jacob shook his head, focusing on the present. He couldn't go back and change anything, nor would he want to.

"Course laid in, sir," Chief Suresh said, her dark eyes on him through the little mirror they shared.

Jacob raised his hand dramatically. "Execute," he said, bringing his hand down at the same time.

Chief Suresh, whose smile mirrored his own, placed her hand on the manual throttle and eased it forward. The mechanical device clicked as it passed each increment.

"That's new," Jacob muttered.

Interceptor hummed as power transferred to the mass intensive gravcoil housed in a spiral beneath the ship. Energy built for a moment, then the ship shot away from Kremlin Station toward Zuckabar Central. Jacob double-checked the course on his MFD and the math was solid. They would pass Zuck Central in a few minutes and put the entire complex of orbital structures behind them. After that they could let the shark off the leash. Heading directly for the Wonderland starlane, they would arrive in roughly four days. The mission would only get more interesting from there.

Ensign Fionna Brennan kicked herself for the mistake. Why had she said fifty? It's not like there were any ports that allowed ships to go fifty g's on departure, or any other time. She wanted to bang her head against the console.

"Really, ma'am, it's okay. The skipper knows you misspoke. Trust me. It happens," PO Oliv said from beside her.

"You don't understand," Fionna whispered. "He already hates me. This is just one more thing." She clapped her jaw shut, forgetting how the small bridge made it easy for her words to be heard.

Oliv sat back, a bemused expression on her sharp features. "Ma'am? The skipper... hate... where did you get that idea?" she asked.

"It's nothing. I shouldn't have said anything." Fionna focused on her controls. As the astrogator, her job was to make sure the ship stayed on course and any stellar phenomena were charted and observed. Under her were the gravity sensors. PO Oliv wore the bulky headset that completely cut off sound, even vibrations from the hull, when she wore them. They allowed her to interpret (with the computer's help) the gravity "noise" the ships sensitive laser detection systems picked up.

In a harbor like Zuck, there was a lot to do for everyone. She had a few hundred ships to keep an eye on, not just the ones in orbit, but also any that were departing or arriving. Not only did she have to keep track of where they were, but also where they were going to be. It required her full attention and she couldn't afford to make another mistake.

"Bear in mind, ma'am, I know things can seem tough since you're new to the Navy and *Interceptor*. The skipper, though, he doesn't hate anyone. Not a soul."

Fionna heard what the PO said, but she didn't believe it. Captain Hatwal had made it very clear that Grimm was a loose cannon, then he made her answer the comms every time he called. She knew, not believed, knew the man had to be furious with her.

She just had to work hard and not make any more mistakes, then maybe she would escape the ship with a passable FITREP.

As the ops officer, Lieutenant Roy Hössbacher was responsible for the largest part of the ship's crew. Eighty percent of them were under his direct command. If he were on a station, he would be called the deck officer, but on a ship, ops or *operations officer* worked just fine.

His first assignment on *Interceptor* had him at comms. Then the captain somehow pulled strings and Roy went to Fleet Electronics Warfare School. There were plenty of schools to attend in the Navy. Most were for specializations, but a few, like Fleet Electronic Warfare, were reserved for officers and enlisted the Navy considered "high value." Roy had just never considered himself like that. Now, though, serving back aboard *Interceptor* with the captain again, he understood.

The way he saw things, he had two problems to deal with. One, and the most obvious, Midship Watanabe. Comms, like most of the departments, fell under ops. She was a problem. Pretty enough to avoid scrutiny and charismatic enough to escape trouble. Roy wasn't exactly much older than her, either. Maybe two years? He'd looked at her file and not found a single complaint or reprimand. Nothing else, either.

His second problem involved Ensign Brennan. His station was two meters from her. There was no whisper that he didn't hear. Odds were the skipper heard it too. He was going to have to talk to Carter about how to deal with both. The skipper would likely resolve them himself, but Roy wanted to be on top of things as ops. If he could fix it before the captain had to, all the better.

CHAPTER FIFTEEN

Master Sergeant Danny Cannon lunged forward, catching Mac off guard with a quick jab followed by a powerful right hook. The man went down with a grunt, slamming onto the mat.

Interceptor's gym wasn't much, ten meters by five, enough to squeeze in a sparring area, weights, and a few treadmills. An unused rowing machine sat forgotten in the corner—no one liked to row.

His men occupied the gym at least twice a day. And he meant occupied. They gave any spacers the evil eye if they intruded. It wasn't that his boys weren't sociable, but in his experience it was best to stay focused and not get involved with the hired help.

"Damn boss, pull your punch sometimes," Mac said as he got to his knees.

"Train like you fight—" Danny started.

"—Fight like you train," Mac finished.

It was an old axiom. Older than the Alliance, dating back thousands of years. But, it was still true. Just because it was old didn't mean it wasn't worth listening to. If he pulled his punches in training, then he would pull his punches when his life depended on it. Which was every mission they went on. The brass didn't send his boys to water the flowers or hold up walls.

Danny helped Mac up and they bumped gloves, ready to go again.

"Five days since we left port, how long do you think we'll be out?" Mac asked, punching cautiously toward Danny.

"A month, if not more. All the more reason we need to stay sharp." Danny swung furiously, two jabs and an uppercut.

Mac recoiled, leaping back on his feet and batting away the jabs while narrowly dodging the uppercut. Mac grinned, pointing at him like he'd caught the sergeant doing something sneaky.

"Not that easy," he said.

The door opened, and two Marines walked in chatting. A dark-haired woman and a redheaded man. Danny pulled up the imaginary crew roster he kept in his head. Other than being Marines he didn't recall their names.

Mac took advantage of the distraction and launched a cavalcade of blows, the final one landing hard against Danny's jaw, spinning him to the ground.

"Ouch," Danny said.

To his team's dismay, the two Marines seemed completely ignorant, or impervious to their glares. Every other spacer who'd come in while they were there left within five minutes. These two climbed on to the treadmills and started running like they were on a date in the park.

Rico and Bubba walked over and stood in front of the machines, talking loudly about some tango they had popped in the last mission. Going into great detail of the way his guts splashed around the room.

Mac helped him up. "Doesn't look like it's working," he said with a grin.

"No, it doesn't."

Danny didn't particularly dislike Marines any more than he disliked everyone not in the Army... or *in* the Army. They just happened to annoy him more than most because of their almost snobbish desire to be better than everyone else; even if they weren't, they acted like they were.

The redhead seemed to take it all in stride. He could tell the dark-haired woman was queasy. She was young, probably under twenty and new to the Marines. If it weren't for the fact that almost everyone aboard wore combat stripes, he would have thought she was straight out of boot.

Once he was back up, Mac came at him again. This time, Danny deftly retreated, once... twice, three times. When Mac lunged forward a fourth time, Danny stepped in, catching the punch on his shoulder, capturing the arm, and twisting savagely until Mac hollered as he flew up and over, landing on the mat with a crunch.

One of the treadmills stopped, and Danny looked up from where he pinned Mac. The woman rushed out of the gym, hand over her mouth as she headed for the bathroom.

"One down," Mac said.

"I don't think the other is going to be as easy," Danny said.

The remaining Marine shut off his treadmill and looked at Bubba accusingly. "That wasn't very polite," he said.

"What are you going to do about it, cry?" Bubba asked before bursting out laughing.

"Nah. I figure I take you over to that mat and wipe the deck with your face. I'll need to clean the ugly off when I'm done, though. Otherwise, the COB will be on me for messing up her ship."

Bubba shut up. Rico laughed hard, though.

"Okay, string bean, you're on."

A minute later, Bubba and the redhead, whose name Danny

now remembered was Owens, lined up on the mat. While Bubba wasn't the most proficient fighter on his team, he had the most mass at 125 kilograms. The Marine, while fit, was outclassed and didn't realize it yet. He would soon, though.

The two raised their gloved fists and banged them together.

"Fight," Mac yelled from the side.

Bubba decided against anything clever. He waded in, heading right for Owens to overwhelm him with powerful blows. Owens ducked the first one, blocked the second, and took the third on the jaw knocking him down. Bubba stepped on him for good measure.

"Ha. You lose," Bubba said.

Owens shook his head, getting his feet under him. "I lose when I'm unconscious or dead," he said.

That surprised Danny. One punch from Bubba convinced opponents to quit while they were ahead.

"Have it your way, string bean."

"Fight," Mac yelled.

Once again Bubba waded in, big arms pumping as he swung and jabbed. This time Owens lasted a little longer before taking one to the face and going down. A thick red welt formed on his cheek from the two blows. Danny hesitated to give the green light when the kid stood up, albeit slower this time.

"Come on," Owens said.

Bubba glanced at Danny who simply shrugged.

"It's your funeral, kid," Bubba said.

"Fight."

Bubba, some of his excitement diminished after stomping the poor kid, came in over confidently. He figured he would do the same thing again.

Owens ducked the first swing, blocked the second. However, instead of the third swing taking him to the face,

Owens dropped to his knee and slammed his fist into Bubba's balls as hard as he could.

The SF trooper howled as he went down, clasping his privates in both hands as he rolled on the mat.

"Worth the bruises," Owens said as he tossed his gloves down and walked out.

Danny whistled. The Marine had taken the punches deliberately in order to set Bubba up.

"That's against the rules," Mac said to the kid's back.

Owens turned to look over his shoulder, the red welt growing by the second. "I'm a Marine, winning is the only rule." The kid disappeared into the shower, leaving the troopers grinning.

It was a fair lesson and Danny was happy to have Bubba learn it and not him. "Get up off the mat, you big baby," he said to the groaning man.

Heat rose off the ovens as PO Josh Mendez wiped the sweat from his brow. Working in the galley was equal parts thrilling and tedious. When he first started, he'd learned everything he could about it. Including the art of meal planning. It wasn't just about what meals were good, or what the crew liked. How could the leftovers from breakfast help lunch, and then dinner? What could they open and in what order to maximize their inventory? The new recyclers helped immensely, increasing their deployment window by three to four weeks depending on how much was used up.

His newly issued NavPad beeped at him. He stepped back from the grill, motioning for Spacer Zack to take over. He had the NavPad setup to tell him when the skipper was on the bridge, or in the briefing room, for more than two hours. His captain worked harder than anyone realized, except for Josh. It was his job to make sure the skipper had meals and stayed hydrated. Something both the COB and Bosun had told him upon becoming the master of the galley.

The captain liked very specific meals, which made it easy to prepare them ahead of time. At any given moment, the cooler held a full day's worth of ham and cheese sandwiches made the captain's favorite way. Along with a reserve of orange drink that he liked so much.

Josh stopped at the cooler, glancing down at the deck for a moment. It was the very spot Ensign Lopez had died during the galley fire on the last tour. He closed his eyes for a moment, saying a prayer for the dead before moving inside the cooler.

The sandwiches and drinks were stacked neatly on their own rack, making them easy to grab. A large note marked them for the skipper only. He didn't want anyone eating them in the off hours. There was always someone on shift in the galley, but almost always spacers—and they were notorious for eating anything not nailed down.

Food in hand, he made his way out of the galley and into the mess. Dinner was an hour away, but there was a half dozen POs and officers scattered around the tables. Josh looped his way through, nodding to PO Ignatius who cradled a cup of coffee.

However, just as he was about to exit, he spotted Ensign Brennan alone in the far corner, her back to the hatch, shoulders shaking. Josh glanced down at the food and figured the captain would understand. He'd seen her once before on the ladder and knew she was having a hard time of it. Not everyone handled the trauma of combat the same way. He felt that one personally.

"Ma'am, you okay?" he said quietly after approaching her.

She looked up, eyes red from crying. Trying to hide it, she dragged her uniform sleeve over them.

"I'm fine PO, just something in my eye."

"Aye, ma'am. It can get dusty in here." From anyone else that could be construed as condescending, but Josh had an earnestness about him that belied such a thought.

"Can I sit down for a minute, ma'am? I'm just about off shift and my feet are killing me."

Fionna nodded for him to sit. She tried to hide her head in her hands, pretending to rub her eyes. Crying was embarrassing enough she didn't need to have a PO see as well.

"Do you like being an officer, ma'am?" he asked.

The question took her by surprise. "Do you like being enlisted?" she retorted.

"Very much. I see all the work you officers do and I cringe. Sure, you don't work with your hands as much, but I know the managing aspect of command weighs on you. I'd rather put my head down and work through a shift in the galley than fill out requisition forms or plot courses." He gave a little exaggerated shudder. "No thank you."

"I guess I hadn't really thought about it that way. My parents are both in the Navy. Going to the Academy was always my future."

Josh sat the bag full of food he carried, on the table. "My folks were thrilled to see me go. I'm the youngest of seven and all my siblings have good, respectable jobs back on New Austin... well, except Rodrigo. He doesn't do anything but live at home and mooch off my folks."

Despite the unrelenting sadness she always felt, and the fear of screwing up, Fionna laughed. "Yeah, I have a sister like that. All she does is go on dates looking for Mr. Right. For some reason she was never expected to join the Navy, I don't know why."

"Who knows why families are the way they are." He paused for a moment, his eyes losing focus as he glanced at the galley.

"Everything okay?" Fionna asked.

Josh replied with a "mmhmm," then froze. "Sorry, ma'am, I forgot who I was talking to for a moment."

She laughed again at the earnest young man's apology. "No worries, PO. You do get to be human."

"Josh, ma'am, or Mendez, if you prefer. I was just thinking about something the skipper said a few tours back."

Fionna froze up at the thought of Commander Grimm. Everyone on the ship seemed to worship the deck the man walked on, but she knew, *knew*, he hated her. How could he not?

As if he sensed her train of thought, Josh gave her an easy smile. "He's not like what you think, ma'am. I know *some* officers in the Navy are overly critical of little things, demanding, even arrogant, but the captain isn't like that. You'll see."

She wanted to believe him, but how could she? Captain Hatwal had criticized her every decision and then put her on comms duty with the job of essentially ignoring Commander Grimm. There was no way that didn't rub off on her, even if it was only subconscious. If she returned to port with a bad FITREP her parents would be disappointed.

Then there was the other thing. The overwhelming sadness, the hollow feeling in her stomach. The fear at night and the terror when the alert klaxon sounded.

Terror that never went away. Always hovering there in the back of her mind, like a tiger waiting to pounce.

"What did he tell you?" she asked, trying to focus her mind on something, anything.

"We were on a mission and saw some action. I had a close call, and it was the scariest thing that I'd ever experienced in my life. I thought I was dead. Not just a little, like a lot. After we were safe and on our way home, I was having the shakes, you know?"

Fionna did indeed understand. Was it coincidence Josh talked to her about this, or did he know? She hadn't thought the incident on the ladder very telling, but maybe it was. Or maybe, PO Josh Mendez was just that perceptive.

"I know what you mean," she said.

"The captain, and just so you know, when anyone on *Interceptor* says, 'the captain' they only mean Commander Grimm. Anyway, he told me to just breathe."

Fionna didn't mean to laugh, but she did, an awkward cackle that was far louder than she intended.

Josh frowned.

"I'm sorry," she said, horrified. "I didn't mean to. I just thought... well that pretty much happens naturally."

"Aye ma'am, it does. But what he said was to focus on my breathing. Slow things down, in and out. Focus on the fear as I breathed in and focus on letting it go as I breathed out." Josh paused for a moment, looking at her. It struck her how handsome he was. The kind of guy her mom would love if she brought home. But, with her being an officer and him a PO, both on shipboard duty, that would never happen.

"Not that I think you need any advice, ma'am, you're pretty squared away as far as I can tell."

"Thank you... Josh, I appreciate that." She lifted her coffee up to hide the obvious blush on her fair skin.

CHAPTER SIXTEEN

PLANET WONDERLAND

Aboard *Interceptor*'s bridge, with the cold making his breath fog, and the tea in his hands keeping him warm, Jacob watched as Wonderland's space elevator vanished from view.

It was only the second time he'd ever seen the station and it had grown since the last time. The Navy moved into Wonderland, salvaging what they could. It was just too amazing of a planet to let it go uninhabited. Until the Alliance could reliably repair and maintain the satellite lighting system, they couldn't colonize it, but there was plenty of research to be done, that was for sure.

Interceptor had made a quick stop, long enough to top off their supplies. They were barely there for six hours before shoving off. Any longer and the crew would want shore leave, and they were in a time crunch.

Jacob pushed down on the all-hands button. "All officers, chiefs, and Bosun: please join me in the mess at 1400 hours. Master Sergeant Cannon and Gunnery Sergeant Jennings as well. PO Mendez, please have refreshments available. That is all, captain out."

Lieutenant Hössbacher glanced his way, an eyebrow raised. Jacob hadn't told anyone of the meeting, this would be a surprise to everyone involved. While the general mission briefing was common knowledge, how they were going to get there wasn't. Admiral Villanueva had said he would hate it, but she couldn't have been more wrong. He loved it. Which was also a problem.

Part of him longed to explore the unknown and he was going to get that very opportunity. He just wished it didn't come at the expense of missing months of the war. Not that *Interceptor* would make a difference in a fleet wide battle. One more destroyer, give or take, would hardly alter the outcome of two fleets pounding away at each other.

In this, though, secret missions and covert operations, she could make a huge difference. *Interceptor* could be instrumental in turning the tide of the war—and this time he wouldn't face the threat of a court martial when he returned.

"Skipper," Josh Mendez said from beside him. He knelt, handing Jacob a prepackaged lunch and drink in a vacuum container.

"How do you always know when I skip lunch, Josh?"

"Magic, skipper," he said with a grin.

Something wavered in the young man's face, a worry that Jacob saw for a split second. "What is it?" he asked softly.

Still kneeling, Josh leaned in and whispered as quietly as he could. "Sir, you might want to check on Ensign Brennan."

Then, as if he said nothing, Josh took the empty teacup and went back to work, checking with each member of the bridge crew if they needed anything before departing. He didn't bother asking the Marine on watch; they never ate or drank while working.

Jacob leaned back, resting his head on one hand while he sipped the stimulant-laden orange drink. PO Mendez wasn't the first person to say something about Brennan. He would keep an eye on her. Midship Watanabe as well. Brennan worked hard and didn't complain, which made him think she was good to go. Whereas, Watanabe complained to everyone who would listen, even spacers, which was not a good look for an officer.

The MFD attached to Jacob's chair flashed. Carter's face appeared and he pointed to his ear. Private comms. Jacob placed the earpiece in and hit the button. "What's going on Carter?"

"Sir, is there a reason you didn't want me to plan the meeting?"

"Believe me, Carter. I wanted to inform you, but then I would be violating the secret orders of our secret mission. No one was to know until now what we're doing. Now that you do know there is a meeting, though, I want you to take point and make sure it runs smoothly."

Carter frowned; confusion evident on his face. "You want me to take point on a meeting about something that you can't tell me until the meeting?"

"Sounds about right." Jacob smiled and killed the comms. He liked Carter, and he made an excellent XO, but he did need to learn to think on his feet a little better.

At 1400 hours exactly, Jacob leaned against the exterior bulkhead. Chairs were lined up for the officers, chiefs, and Bosun. Everyone was in attendance. He'd left PO Collins with the conn, and one of her subordinates in The Pit. They were a couple of hours from entering the starlane that led to the unexplored space beyond Wonderland. PO Mendez and Spacer Perch circulated the room, handing out coffee, tea, or orange drink to those who requested it. Jacob noted that Midship Watanabe was present, her uniform somewhat in shambles.

Jennings, as always, stood guard on the inside of the hatch. Naki was on the other side just in case. He wasn't sure who she thought would sneak aboard and infiltrate the meeting, but he admired her dedication. Unfortunately, Master Sergeant Cannon was nowhere to be found. He would have to speak to him later. The man seemed to think Navy regulations were more like suggestions than actual rules.

"Call to order," Carter said. "The captain is going to give us a briefing on what we're actually doing out here, then we'll take questions. For those of you who are new, this isn't a free-for-all, or a discussion about why we're doing what we do. Our sole job is to come up with the best plan possible to give our mission the highest probability of success." Carter looked around for questions and when there were none, he pointed at Jacob. "Skipper, the floor is yours."

Jacob pushed off the bulkhead, taking a deep breath and letting it out slowly. It was rare to have the full complement of officers and chiefs attending the same meeting. Just with Chief Suresh, Redfern, Pierre, and Sandivol, they had over a hundred years of naval experience in one room.

"Thank you all for coming," he started. Light chuckles rippled through the group. It was his customary opening line, since no one was there because they felt like attending. "Once again the Navy has called on our girl to do the impossible. I won't sugar coat it. For those who were with us when we went into Caliphate space last time, this mission will be *slightly* more difficult."

"So just mostly impossible," Chief Suresh said to a chorus of chuckles.

"You know it, COB. Before I share this intel," Jacob said, taking on a much sterner look, "I need to reiterate this is TOP

SECRET. You do not share this information with anyone. You may discuss it among yourselves, but once we are back in Alliance space that ends. For some of you this is old news, for others it will seem weird. Trust me when I say, it will make sense. Don't tell your family, wives, husbands, best friend, your diary, nothing. Any breach of this information won't just get you thrown out of the Navy, you'll go to jail until you're old and gray. Then they will rejuve you and let you rot all over again. Understood?"

There were a few muttered "yes sir" here and there. Carter snapped to. "I want to hear everyone say it."

"Aye, aye, sir," they all shouted. With the notable exception of Watanabe, Jacob realized. Her lips moved but she barely said anything.

"Good enough. Now, here is the mission. Please hold your questions for the end." Jacob placed his NavPad on the table and activated the holographic feature. A map of the galaxy sprang to life. It zoomed in on the Orion Spur and circled Wonderland.

"As some of you are aware the Guild had secret starlanes charted throughout known space. We used them before and we're going to use them again."

A red line formed at Wonderland and headed toward the edge of the galaxy. Each time it stopped the line was at the limit of starlane travel. Six lanes, three weeks, all leading to Caliphate space. Not the border, but deep within the heart of their systems.

Several gasped when the line stopped. The fact that they had a direct route to Caliphate space, and that it was only three weeks long, stunned the attendees. Right in the middle of the three week journey, a single planet blinked in bright yellow script: Midway.

"I know it's a lot to take in, but please, hold the questions. I don't know how the Guild did this, but these lanes are artificially enhanced. Some kind of gate mechanism at either end of the lane allows for starlane travel that allows the lanes to go twice as far. The briefing I'm giving you was given to me before we departed and I'm still shocked. There is a downside, though. To avoid detection, the mechanism draws power from the ships using them. Because of that, we will have to refuel at the halfway point. More on that later."

"Sir, I've got to ask, if we have a direct route to the Caliph, why not send a battle group?" Chief Redfern piped up.

"I suppose it's too good for me to make you wait. Okay, only this question, then you wait, understood?"

"Aye sir, sorry, sir," Redfern said.

"It's a fair question. The devices the Guild installed on the starlanes act as mass accelerators. According to Admiral Villanueva who briefed me, they are highly power dependent and must be installed on both sides. They also can only accelerate mass up to a certain limit. One that makes it impossible to send anything heavier than a destroyer. If you look at the ships the Guild fielded, small tramp freighters, then it makes sense. While we could certainly raid them this way, if they knew about it, then the reverse would also be true. Which brings us to our mission..." Jacob leveled his gaze at them. One lane from our destination is a secret research base. On it we have an agent embedded who is prepping for our arrival. Once there we will establish orbit, drop our passengers who will secure our agent and the asset. After the ground mission is complete, we destroy the surface target. On our return trip we are to make sure the lane devices are destroyed, guaranteeing they won't be used against us."

"That's not quite accurate, sir," Sergeant Cannon said from the galley hatch. He wore Army fatigues but with no insignia, nor had he shaved. Leaning against the hatchway, he sipped his coffee and then used the cup to gesture to the hologram. "My orders are to secure the asset at all costs. They don't say anything about the agent. We'll get her if we can, but the asset is the priority."

For one, Jacob refused to leave anyone behind. He would risk his entire ship if it meant rescuing every single allied person on the planet. Two, there was no way in hell he would abandon Nadia on the planet, not when he also had to strike the facility from orbit.

"We don't leave people behind, Sergeant. Everybody comes home. Understood?"

Cannon shrugged as if to say, "Whatever you want."

Continuing, Jacob zoomed in the hologram. "There's more bad news and good news," he said. "The system is home to a supergiant black hole and a supergiant G-type star. The planet we're going to"—he pressed a button on the controls, and the image zoomed in to show the planet and the two competing bodies of mass—"is caught in between their pull. While it still rotates, it doesn't orbit the sun anymore. The gravity forces of the black hole are such that any ship entering the system must be able to exert five hundred gravities of acceleration in order to escape the orbit of the planet. Which means, once we're in orbit, we can't leave until the mission is complete. Otherwise, we would have to fly hours out, stop, then go back. It's a good thing they're sending the fastest ship in the fleet. Now, with that out of the way, questions?"

Almost every hand in the room went up. There were a lot of questions, that was okay. Jacob had prepared for it.

"How many ships will be defending the system?" Lieutenant Kai asked.

"None that intelligence is aware of. They use secrecy and the local black hole as security. They've outfitted some special cargo ships to resupply the base, but as far as intel knows, they don't have any fleet ships that can push five hundred g's."

"What is on the planet that is so important?" Chief Pierre asked.

"That's a good question, Chief." Jacob took a deep breath, letting it out slowly. "The Caliphate have developed faster-than-light communications. The scientist who did so is on this planet and we believe all their research is too. If we take them, destroy the facility, and escape, we'll set back their program and hopefully create our own."

"I knew it," Redfern said enthusiastically. "Do we know how?"

Jacob shook his head. Not that the admiral had shared any of the suspected science behind the discovery. Even if she had, he would be the last person to understand any of it.

"Sir," Ensign Brennan spoke up with a timber to her voice that worried Jacob. "If the discovery is so important, why don't they guard the systems leading up to it?"

"That, Fionna, is a very good question. Any takers?" he asked. Part of his job as captain was building up the crew's confidence. Ensign Brennan had, what he would consider a problem in that area. Not to mention, it really was an excellent question.

"Is it like *Madrigal*?" Carter asked. Everyone, Fionna included, who wasn't present on Jacob's original tour with *Interceptor*, looked confused.

"Exactly. If they were to deploy units to guard the route, then we would know there was something worth protecting. As it is, ISB, that's Cali state security, keeps a tight lid on things. I don't know how ONI pried this piece of intel out of them, but they deserve a raise. Not to mention this is deep within Cali territory, and as far as they know, there's no way to it without going through half their fleet. Which is not to say we can be lazy or let our guard down. If anything, we need to be more alert to avoid carelessness. To that end, we're going to have a rigorous drill schedule until we get to Midway—"

"Midway, sir?" Carter asked.

"Sorry, that's what HQ is calling the planet at the halfway point. Original, I know."

A scattering of chuckles filled the room.

"It's as good as anything," Carter added. "I'm sure the locals have a name for it."

"I'm sure. According to Guild records it's a penal colony. That doesn't concern us. One of the planet's three moons has a dense, hydrogen-rich atmosphere. We will use the gravcoil as a scoop and refuel there." A serious countenance overtook Jacob. "This is an important mission; one we mustn't fail. Report any problems with the crew and keep your mind on your jobs. A single mistake from anyone aboard could be the difference between success and failure. Understood?"

"Yes sir!" they all shouted. With the notable exception of Midship Watanabe, which had Jacob worried.

Yua Watanabe stormed around her quarters. Too tired to do any of her usual games but not tired enough to sleep. Anger fueled her legs. She had a good thing going at the Academy. All the instructors ate out of her fingers, and the ones she couldn't manipulate, she either avoided or used more persuasive measures.

She hated the Navy. Why her father made her join was beyond her. Enough was enough, though. When the midship cruise assignments came out, she was assigned to *Alexander*. Unlike the rest of her classmates, she knew where she was headed before they announced it. Her father's connections guaranteed she would be kept out of any real danger. A nice cushy tour on a battleship. But for some reason, either luck or design, she was rerouted to *Interceptor* at the last minute. She'd gone out on Kremlin and got absolutely hammered the night before only to find out that morning she had to go to this bucket of bolts.

All of that could have been tolerable if not for them heading to certain death. Not only was the Alliance in a shooting war with the Caliphate, her *idiot* captain, was going to get them all killed on a suicide mission.

Well, not her. What would it matter anyway? *Interceptor* would be lost with all hands. If Yua showed up in *Alliance* space in six months, she could make up whatever story she wanted. Probably even get a medal for surviving.

An idea formed in her mind. It had risks, but all great plans did. She just needed to make it to Midway and then she could set everything right.

Jacob held his breath as *Interceptor* approached the technological marvel. Floating not far from the Guild platform was a smaller civilian vessel with a bright white hull, with the name *Arcanum Explorator* on the side.

"That's a University of Alexandria ship, right?" Carter asked from next to the captain's chair. He held onto the grab bar above his head.

"I think so," Jacob replied. "Dr. Bellaits has his own department, both at the university and with the science division. I don't think they're doing any exploring at this point, though. As cool as that would be. They've got their hands full with the tech we commandeered."

"Is that what we're calling it?" Chief Suresh interjected.

"Sir," Watanabe said from comms. "Message from Arcanum. They're ready for the fuel transfer when we are."

"Thank you, Midship, give them my compliments and inform them we will start immediately." Jacob jerked his thumb toward the stern. "Carter, get to it. Just like the manual, no shortcuts."

"Aye, aye, sir. No shortcuts." Carter headed for the ladder, already calling engineering to organize the fuel transfer.

The tech really was a mystery to Jacob. How they had the ability to seed a series of lanes to speed ships through was beyond him.

"Tefiti," Jacob turned to his trusted gravtech. "Make sure we record everything. I'm not sure if we're the first to go through, but it won't hurt."

"Aye sir, recording."

"Good man."

Over the next hour, Jacob's ship disgorged nearly a third of her slush deuterium reserve to the platform. It really was a platform, too. Ships hovered over a large landing pad–looking protrusion. On the side there was a ridge six meters tall, like the ships were loaded onto a sliding walk. Once fueled they would proceed as normal, activating the gravcoil, lining up with their target sun and locating the starlane. Then boom, they were off.

This was step one, he reminded himself. Nadia counted on him, even if she didn't know it would be him, to pick her up with the package. Whatever he had to do to get to her in time, he would.

Even if it wasn't her, he still would. No one would admit it, but unless they crippled or destroyed the Caliph's FTLC capability, then there was no way the Alliance would ever win the war. Every engagement would go down like the last, except instead of an Alliance victory, it would be the Caliph Navy. Surprise attacks and perfectly timed ambushes. Jacob knew, firsthand, how effective an ambush could be. If not for playing his hunch, *Enterprise* and her entire task force would have ended up as so much space junk.

"Arcanum says the tanks are full," Watanabe said.

"Tell them thank you. Chief Suresh, let's take a stroll down the lane."

"Aye, aye," Suresh said. "Finding the lane."

While the COB did her job, Jacob used his MFD to examine the platform. The science behind it was clearly beyond him, not to mention at this point, highly classified. He hoped the Alliance could figure out a way to create their own someday, but that seemed unlikely. The only advance that had come from capturing the guild ships were Rod Beckett's point-defense lasers. The space elevator was unusable, and only sheer luck had kept it from crashing down on Wonderland before the Alliance arrived. One day they would crack some of the secret tech The Guild had developed and that would be a good day.

"Starlane located," Chief Suresh said.

"Ops, helmets on, drain the can."

"Aye sir, helmets on." Roy's voice echoed throughout the ship, ordering helmets on three times. They wouldn't proceed until they had confirmation from every crew, spacer to captain, that all helmets were on. Once they did, air hissed out of the passageways into storage tanks until the ship's internal spaces were a vacuum.

Roy turned to Jacob and gave him a thumbs up.

"Coxswain, you may proceed with starlane egress," Jacob said.

Chief Deviyanee Suresh handled the ship like a ballet dancer. Nimble fingers gliding over controls as she aligned the ship exactly as it needed to go with near perfect precision.

"Starlane in three..."

At one the ship shot forward, running down the long line of

gravity extending from Wonderland to the next star. Jacob braced his hands, gripping the armrest tight trying desperately to ignore the feeling of falling that always came with starlane entrance. Thankfully it only lasted half a minute and then gravity returned to normal.

"We are in the lane, 98.7 percent alignment with the destination," Ensign Brennan said, awe in her voice. Ninety-eight was stellar flying. Anything over seventy would work, over eighty was considered exceptional. Ninety and above was practically unheard of, yet Chief Suresh took it in stride, leaning back and cracking her knuckles.

"All part of the job, ma'am," she said over the bridge comms.

Jacob chuckled at her casual demeanor. Leave it to the COB to dismiss her own excellence.

"Well done, everyone. Travelling a new starlane can be nerve-racking. Station heads, please pass my compliments to your departments. I think a four-day liberty is in order when we return."

While Jacob didn't hear the cheers of the crew, he knew they were real. Nothing was more precious to a spacer than liberty. While he was always liberal with his praise, he held the reward of liberty for occasions like this to make it special.

CHAPTER SEVENTEEN

Nadia settled into her routine well enough. Wake up at 0445, prepare the doctor's meals, do her laundry, and general housekeeping. It had surprised her to find out the asset was the daughter of the doctor DeBeck had sent her to rescue. He must have handed his work down to her before he died.

Nadia worked tirelessly to blend in, disappear, day after day, week after week. Dr. Abbasi hardly noticed her and Malik not at all. Nadia made sure to vanish when the ISB agent made a presence. He was smart; more dangerous, though, he was clever. He acted like a pedantic manager, but she saw through his veneer. Beneath the perfectly groomed beard and crisply ironed uniform was the heart of a killer. The less he thought about her the better.

For her plan to work she didn't need to do much. There couldn't be many moving parts with an extraction mission. Too many and things would fail. She'd kept this one simple. Wait for the window of retrieval, shut down the base, grab the doctor, light off a beacon for a Corsair to find. Simple.

She completed step one, infiltrate and integrate. With her

routines and daily workload both for the doctor and others, she managed to make herself indispensable and give herself access to just about every level of the base.

Except for the one place she needed access: the security center.

The base's security room that controlled all the cameras, doors, and alarms was inaccessible from the main area. The only way in or out was through a single lift that was guarded around the clock by base security. The lift had motion sensors, lasers, and magnetic detectors. Even if she could get past the guards, she would never make it down the primary shaft. With her Blackout Suit it would be a piece of cake, but she didn't have it.

Which left her with her less straightforward and far more risky option. Masa, as the people stationed at the base called it when the ISB wasn't around, had the unique fortune of falling into a gravity well trap. Pulled by both a black hole and the star, it hovered between the two. It still rotated, but in place. Surface conditions were tolerable during the eighteen hours of light. The eighteen hours of darkness, a darkness so black only electronic enhanced vision would allow her to see, was less tolerable.

A moon once orbited, controlling the tides. There were small traces of it still in orbit where it broke up before falling into the black hole. The planet would share the same fate one day, but not for a long time... or at least she hoped. Even a tiny variance in her orbit, as little as a one-percent change could send her falling forever into the intergalactic jaws of hell.

At night the temperature fell to a bone-chilling fifty degrees below. Anyone caught out in the cold, unprotected, wouldn't survive until morning. As the sun dipped below the horizon, the entire base locked down. Shutters closed around the windows and the doors magnetically sealed. The fusion reactor at the heart of the base went into overdrive powering the immense heaters installed everywhere there were people.

She had no desire to be caught out after dark, but the only way to complete her mission, was to leave the base just before dark, enter the reactor's exhaust shaft, climb down to the bottom level, crack the code to get in, make the changes she needed, then get out before dawn. At the same time, making sure to avoid detection, and not freeze to death. The plan was simplicity itself.

To complete her mission she needed was some climbing gear, thermal clothing, lockpicks, electronic countermeasures, rope, and about six months to plan.

She had none of that. All she had were her wits and will to persevere. Which was just going to have to be enough.

Malik walked the halls of the research base, making sure there were no unauthorized personnel about. He liked being seen, intimidating whomever he could just to make sure they all understood their place. It was important in keeping the base running smoothly and efficiently. Oh, he would overlook some indiscretions. Not too many, though.

What worried him were the two females. Dr. Abbasi was a known quantity. She didn't fraternize with anyone as far as he could tell, and since he had the entire base wired for sound, including the bathrooms, he could always tell. The other one seemed harmless enough. Submissive and subservient as a woman should be. It was unfortunate she wasn't single and younger... or even just single, they could use a distraction. However, he wouldn't dishonor another man like that.

There were two entrances to the research outpost, he checked them both just as he did every night and morning. At

0500, the only staff members up were the cooks preparing the morning meals, his security people, and the servant woman. He checked his messages; no word had come back from central command yet on her. He'd run her ID and information through his databases and they all came back clear. He was intending to be thorough, though. After all, one could not be too vigilant in the service of the Caliph, especially when trying to get off the hellhole he currently served on.

CHAPTER EIGHTEEN

PLANET MIDWAY (LOCAL NAME: SIGEN)

Bijan stepped into the shadows, avoiding the patrol as it moved through the town. The local gang's men were out in force, and he wanted nothing to do with them. Once they were beyond his hearing, he took off at a jog. Overgrown and cracked paved roads from a time when the city actually functioned guided him. No ground car had operated on Sigen in twenty years. Long before he'd arrived. Brutal gangs controlled the city, and pirates raided the rest of the planet on a regular basis. To survive he had to be careful, quick, and clever.

He doubted his Caliph expected him to survive exile for as long as he had. A convenient place to throw the trash of society no one wanted to keep around. Like Bijan and his ward, he clamped down on the pangs of regret and sorrow building in his heart and mind. There was no time for recriminations tonight.

His life was three things now. Survive, hunt, and Sarina. He had to take care of her. Stopping for just a second, he adjusted the deer-like animal strapped to his back. He had no idea what they were actually called, the locals referred to them as *al-lahm*. A slang for *little meats*.

The one he had weighed only five kilos, but it was enough to feed him and Sarina for two days easy.

A high-pitched whine of discharging energy weapons filled the air, followed by the loud, sharp crack of chemical propellants. Screams echoed a second later with metal on metal and the moans of the dying.

The gangs were clashing again.

He bolted, running hard. His breaths came in gulps. Clashes like the one he fled tended to spill over into outright battles, consuming entire neighborhoods.

Bijan leaped up and surged away from the conflict. He couldn't afford to be delayed. Every day on Sigen was a struggle for life. Sarina kept him going, kept his mind focused. He desperately needed a way to move from day-to-day survival to long term. A way to escape the planet.

Escape. How?

A man couldn't think of escape when it was all he could do to feed himself and his own. He cleared his mind, extending his senses and focused on running. Fifteen minutes to cross the most dangerous part of the abandoned city, past the crumpling fire station, and to the burned-out remains that used to be apartment buildings and businesses.

They didn't live in a house, for that would be too obvious. They would never be able to cook anything or even move during the day for fear of being seen. Instead, they lived on the eighth floor of a partially collapsed apartment building. Everything above the third floor was inaccessible without either a skimmer, or better climbing gear than anyone on Sigen had.

Circling around to the north side, he looked for signs of intruders, and finding none, he let out a sharp whistle. In response, a rope flew out of the eighth floor in a lazy arc and landed at his feet. The end was tied in a loop, so he inserted his foot, held on tight, and yanked twice. A large chunk of debris, weighing a few kilos more than he did, slid off the eighth floor and lifted him. Despite their circumstance, he loved this part. As he rose, he could see the city and imagine what it once had been. A magnificent edifice, a tribute to the greatness of his people. That was before they abandoned it and moved on, using it only as a prison, a penal colony for the refuse of society.

The pulley ended and he stepped off. Sarina waited for him. Despite the harsh conditions and the minimal food, she endured beyond his expectations.

"Bijan, thank you once again for braving the night for our food."

Every day was the same, he told her she didn't have to thank him, as her protector it was his duty. She never listened. He was exhausted though, and he needed his sleep.

Bijan gazed up at the stars, wondering if there were any ships in orbit. Sarina slept next to him, curled up against him like a stray dog. How quickly things changed, he thought. Ten years ago, they lived in luxury. Her every whim attended to. Now she slept in rags, completely reliant on him to protect her.

He desperately wanted to escape. Wanted to free her from the unjust prison.

Sarina hugged him for warmth, and resisted the urge to move away. Something bothered him though, something he'd forgotten...

The rope!

Bijan jerked awake in time to see a man with a long, sharp blade at the entrance to the room. The facade of the building had fallen away long ago, leaving half the building open to the night sky. Bijan had no real weapons, no sword, or rifle, but he had prepared for such an eventuality. Grabbing a fist-sized chunk of concrete, he hurled it at the man with all his strength. It struck him in the head, and he fell backward, stumbling.

Bijan leaped out of bed in an instant and ran across the room, hitting the man full throttle and shoving him off the side of the building to fall eight stories to his death.

Two more men stared at him from where the rope led to their home. Bijan swore at himself for leaving the rope down, for letting himself forget, even for a second, the dangerous life he lived.

They charged at him, thinking to overwhelm him with their sheer physicality. However, Bijan had the home-ground advantage. He sidestepped the first one, drawing the second toward him. The man screamed as the floor gave way, dropping him three stories onto a pile of rebar and broken wood. The gurgles of his death echoed in the night.

The last man, more cautious now that he was alone, looked frantically around like a trapped rat. Bijan knew that expression well, he saw it in himself on more than one occasion.

"You shouldn't have come up here," Bijan said. "And I'm sorry you have to die."

Bijan skipped forward, picked up a hidden rebar, and swiped it across, smacking the man in the head with it. He didn't die, stumbling around, blubbering. Bijan felt bad, having to kill to survive. He hesitated.

Sarina appeared at the door, with her tattered blanket held around her for warmth. "Bijan?"

The man charged for her, seeing his one chance to escape. Bijan lifted the rebar over his head and threw it hand over hand. It struck the man in the head, sending him reeling and right off the edge into the dark. He screamed all the way down.

"Bijan?" Sarina called to him again, her voice quivering with fear.

"It's okay, my lady," he rushed to her. Holding her tight. "I won't let anyone hurt you."

She looked up at him, the moon shining in her pale, sightless eyes. "I'm so afraid, Bijan. All the time, so afraid. Please, make it stop."

He swore to himself he would get her off the hellhole if it was the last thing he did.

CHAPTER NINETEEN

"Captain on deck," Gunny Jennings announced over her shoulder. Grimm marched by with a nod and a smile, like he always did. Part of her missed when the crew sucked at their jobs and she got to yell at them. More than part of her. Most of her.

Naki appeared a moment later, a cup of coffee in hand.

"Gunny, I'm here to relieve you."

"Where's Owens?" she asked.

"We traded. He's running a repair routine on the Raptors and didn't want to stop." She raised an eyebrow at that. "Between you, me, and the bulkhead, Gunny, I think he's trying to make up for the snafu with the midship."

"Right. Very well, I stand relieved." Jennings took the coffee as they traded places.

"Hey, that was for me."

"No drinking on duty," she said with a wicked grin.

Jennings downed the entirety of the hot coffee in seconds, tossing the cup into the recycler by the ladder as she headed toward the gym.

The Navy changed shift at 0700, but the Marines waited

until 0800, when the captain usually came to the bridge. Having all the crew change at the same time was a recipe for disaster, especially if there was something going on that needed her attention. Too many new faces at once and she started asking questions.

Two decks down, she considered hitting the mess and seeing what Mendez had left over but decided better of it. Her time on *Enterprise* had left her a few kilos heavy and she needed to eat less and run more.

Four more decks down, opposite the rec room, she entered the gym only to find it empty. She hardly noticed, since the gym wasn't heavily used by the Navy-types to begin with, but there were a few die-hards who lifted weights and ran a lot. Usually one or two would be present.

The locker rooms connected to the gym were hardly big enough to walk in. Eight lockers crowded into a space made for half that many. Jennings had to turn sideways just to get undressed and changed into her workout attire. A formfitting unitard that covered her from thigh to neck.

Once out in the gym, she immediately dropped and started her push-up routine. Knocking out fifty, she leaped up and charged right onto the treadmill. The machine whined as she sprinted for the first twenty minutes before easing off into an even run, sweat dripping off her.

The hatch opened and the five-man Army team came in.

She tried to block them out as they joked loudly and made rude comments. Running for exercise required focus and discipline. Out of the corner of her eye, she watched as Master Sergeant Cannon made an excuse to walk by her machine. He stopped and observed her run.

If he thought it would bother her, or the silence would make her talk, he was wrong. After a few minutes, he frowned.

"Aren't you going to say anything?"

Jennings looked him dead in the eye as she ran faster, surging into another sprint.

"You told me I would get your name the next time I saw you, and here I am."

"That I did," she said between gulps of air. "Allison."

The one they called Rico came to the machine next to her and started jogging.

"You're pretty out of breath for a light run, Gunny. Maybe you should slow your roll," Rico said. He looked over and his face blanched. Without missing a beat, he turned off his treadmill and walked back over to where the other men were milling around the free weights.

"What is it?" Danny asked.

"Nuh-uh," he said without turning back.

Danny came around to the side of her machine. She could tell he was looking over her shoulder to see. He let out a sharp whistle. "How long have you been on here?"

"Forty-five minutes." She kept going, sprinting harder to finish with everything she had. The machine whined and shook with strain as she pushed herself to the very limit.

"Thirty klicks an hour… I didn't know people ran that fast," he said, looking at her face.

"People don't. Marines do." Jennings hit the cooldown cycle and the treadmill immediately slowed, going from sprint, to run, to jog, and finally a brisk walk.

"You know, every Marine I've ever met felt that way. Do they put something in the food or—"

"Let me stop you right there, Sergeant. If you disparage the Corps in any way, I'll beat you down and tell the captain it was an accident. He'll understand."

That was more words than Jennings spoke in a day, but she felt her hackles rise as the grunt was about to insult her Marine Corps. She wouldn't stand for it.

He backed off, hands up. "Okay, *Allison,* if you can't handle it, that's fine." The grin on his face invited her to rebuke him, almost as if he were trying to get a rise. Was he? Was she going to let him?

The machine beeped and shut off. Jennings swiped her towel from the rack and dried her face before drinking a large gulp of water. While she did so, she contemplated what the sergeant was getting at.

"I'll play, Sergeant—"

"Danny. Call me Danny," he said.

"Fine. Call me Jennings."

"You know you should have joined the Army. We could always use more cooks," Danny said.

One of his men snickered.

She stopped, eyes leveling at him. He *was* trying to get a rise out of her. Jennings took a moment to think through what was going on. She'd heard reports that they were chasing crew out of the gym. Were they trying to do that to her, or was it something else?

"If you want a beating so bad—" she pointed at the mat.

Danny's average height still had him over thirty centimeters taller than her. Reach for Jennings was always the problem in hand to hand. When she trained the captain, it was his biggest advantage, but he didn't have the skill to take advantage of it. The army grunt wouldn't have that problem.

"Now we're talking," Danny said. Hopping on the balls of his feet he bounced over to the mat, shadow boxing to limber up.

Jennings strode over to one side and stood there. She needed him to come to her. Normally, Marines solved problems with aggression, the bigger the problem, the more aggressive they needed to be. However, he had seen her fight before, he knew he had reach on her. Her biggest advantage would be to make him come to her.

"Say when," she said.

His men gathered around to watch, their confidence in his skill evident on their faces.

Jennings' stoic nature made it easy for her to stay neutral and maintain her calm. Slow was smooth and smooth was fast. She didn't need to charge in and go all out.

Danny hesitated, as if he expected her to attack right out of the gate. When she didn't, he gingerly shuffled forward. Jennings stood there, hands at her sides, knees slightly bent.

"You gonna fight?" Danny asked as he approached.

"I don't fight girls."

Her inflection was so flat it took the grunt's watching a second to catch and then they howled with laughter. Danny, however, didn't seem amused.

He lunged forward, using his superior reach to jab at her from a safe distance. Jennings sidestepped, leaped forward, and slammed her fist into his gut.

The soldier soaked her blow, though, and brought his elbow down on her shoulder with a meaty thunk. Jennings changed tactics and slipped around behind him, grabbing his waist and heaving him up, and over, to slam down on the mat.

They both hit with a grunt. Danny flipping over backward to land on his knees. Jennings kip-upped to regain her feet instantly.

With Danny on his knees, she pressed the advantage. Her feet shuffled across the mat with a swishing sound as she moved with lightning speed and absolute precision.

She feinted a kick, and when he leaned back to dodge it, she skipped forward, spun, and landed a perfect roundhouse with her heel to his temple... At least that's how it should have gone. Danny caught her foot and savagely pushed and twisted her leg at the same time. Jennings flipped over, landing on her back. He was on her in a second, thighs around her waist as he whaled on her.

In a fight, panic was the enemy. He landed the first two blows against her up-held arms. The third time he reared back to hit her, she bucked her hips, sending him falling forward. She latched on to his waist, trapped his arm with hers, and rolled him over. Suddenly, her one hundred kilos landed on top, with his legs trapped between hers.

"What?" Rico said in disbelief.

Jennings slammed her full weight behind a punch to his stomach, and Danny groaned. The next blow hit his solar plexus. He tried to fend her off, but she trapped one arm with her shoulder, moved inside, and started rapidly punching his stomach.

He desperately tapped the mat with his free hand.

"I'm out," he said breathing hard.

Jennings stood up, sweat beading on her and chest rising from the exertion. "Good fight," she said.

"Maybe next time you'll let me take you out to dinner first," Danny said.

Of everything that had happened, that one line stunned her the most. Jennings grunted and beelined for the shower, not even stopping to pick up her towel. She had to leave before he saw her crimson face.

Chief Redfern lay on his stomach, half buried in the crawlspace between deck six and the gravcoil, above life pod number three, next to a heat converter. Sensors for the last three days were detecting higher heat levels than normal passing through the system. It had already resulted in one automated heat dump at an inopportune time. It was his job to find out what was going on. So far, nothing.

There were days he regretted convincing Beech to apply for OCS. The kid's troubleshooting skills were second to none. Which made sense, with him growing up on freighters and all.

Old Chief Redfern would just have to make do with the new kids.

"Tyree, can you get me the thermal sensor?"

He reached up and felt the housing for the thin carbon filament used to transfer the heat throughout the ship. He snapped his hand back, banging his elbow on an outcropping. Biting down on a swear word, he scooted himself out from under.

"Tyree, dammit, where is that—"

Tyree stood three meters away, leaning up against the bulkhead while a sweet looking Midship Watanabe practically twirled around in front of him. She'd somehow managed to have her uniform open enough to reveal the tops of her breasts and was doing her level best to mesmerize his poor spacer.

In Echo Redfern's experience, eighteen-year-old boys lost all reasoning when a pretty girl paid attention to them.

"Tyree!" he shouted.

The spacer leapt up, slamming his head against the bulkhead. "Yes, Chief?" He turned and marched toward him, hand rubbing his head. He looked back to say something but Watanabe was gone.

"What did she want?" Redfern asked.

"Who, Yua?"

Redfern narrowed his eyes at the kid. Young or not, he needed to learn discipline.

"First of all, *Spacer's Apprentice* Tyree, midships are officers. You do not address them by their first name."

The ice in Redfern's voice made Tyree spring to parade rest.

"Yes, Chief," he practically shouted as if he were back in boot camp.

"Second of all, when you're assisting someone, you do not abandon your post. Do you get me?"

"I get you, Chief."

"Good. Now, what did she want?"

Tyree looked confused for a moment, like he wasn't sure what to say.

"You don't remember, do you?"

"No, Chief."

Redfern shook his head. Some things never changed.

To be that young and stupid again.

"Get back to work and don't let me see you do that again."

Redfern would report this to the lieutenant and let him sort it out. Officer business was officer business.

CHAPTER TWENTY

Carter Fawkes growled as he went over the log. He knew he worked in a privileged position. Hell, the first time the skipper had command he hadn't even attended command school yet. Carter had graduated sixteenth from fleet command school. Lieutenant Kimiko had taken the entire class and come in number one, even setting a record in the final exam.

The sheer amount of paperwork he had to fill out on top of his other responsibilities was simply overwhelming. Some of it made sense, like engineering asking for more spacer's apprentices to help cover fourth watch. Others didn't. PO Mendez had to ask permission, in writing, every day to turn on the soft serve ice cream machine. Apparently, there was a rule that once a crew hit a certain caloric intake for the day, the galley needed permission to turn the machine on. It made sense, on paper, since HQ didn't want the crew getting fat while on long deployments. Only on paper, though. In truth, the machine's built-in timer wouldn't allow for it to be on before 1600 ship's time and then only for four hours. Which meant ninety percent of the ship had already eaten and the days caloric intake was maxed by 1800 hours. Leaving anyone covering dog-watch unable to eat ice cream without written permission like some kind of school kid.

Carter leaned back, rubbing his eyes. They were sent into space with millions of dollars in ordnance and equipment, charged with the safety and survival of the Alliance, possibly at the cost of their own lives... and they needed written permission to turn the damned ice cream machine on.

A knock on the computer node hatch interrupted him.

"Come in," he said.

Roy Hössbacher entered carefully, as if he were afraid of intruding.

"Do you have a minute, sir?" he asked.

Carter leaned back and smiled at the young man, which was ironic since Roy was about two years younger than himself. Roy had served his midship cruise on *Interceptor* when Carter was the weapons officer. They'd known each other for too long to stand on formality in private.

"Of course, Roy. When it's just us, you know you can call me Carter."

"Yes sir, I mean, thank you, Carter." Roy looked around, a ghost of a smile playing on his face. "This is where the XO, uh, I mean Lieutenant Yumi would come to work."

Carter grinned and pointed to the seat opposite him. The chairs were new. Carter spent most of his off time in his makeshift office, so he had the Bosun scrounge up a magnetic chair for him. Roy took the seat, still acting as if he were intruding.

"Talk to me, Roy, what's going?"

"Well sir—Carter—it's about Midship Watanabe. I don't know how to say this but... she's acting weird."

Carter leaned back, examining the ops officer. Roy was a smart fella, a stand-up officer, and one of the best comm techs in the fleet without a doubt. However, none of that prepared him to handle a female officer who, as he put it, was acting weird.

"Tell me what she's doing?" he asked.

"For one, she's showing up to her post on time." He held up his hand. "I know that doesn't sound weird. She's also doing her job. But, the hard stuff, like taking maintenance reports or filing outgoing communications, she pawns off on Gouger and McCall."

"That's her job, though. The comms officer shouldn't do all the work. It's why there are spacers and apprentices there."

"Aye sir, I understand, but... something feels off. Maybe it's because I know she doesn't want to be here, or maybe..." He threw his hands in the air. "I just don't know."

Carter thought about it for a long moment, tapping his fingers on the desk in a repetitive pattern that helped him organize thoughts.

"I'll talk to the captain and see what we can do. Don't let my doubts make you second guess your gut. You know how the captain feels about going with your instinct, so do it."

"Aye sir, thank you, sir."

PO Desper wiped away the sweat from her brows as she took a step back to look at the medicine cabinet. *Interceptor* was clearly running hot, and everyone on five and six felt it first since that was where the heat exchangers were.

"Prisca," Chief Pierre said from the main room. The medicine cabinet took up the three-square meters inset into the starboard section of the hull next to the chief medical officer's office. Desper stepped back at hearing her name, closed the cabinet, and sealed it with her NavPad.

"Yes, Chief?"

"Spacer Blachowicz here had himself a header down the ladder. Can you grab me the skin spray?"

Desper crossed the sickbay, grabbed the tool and tossed it to him. Rob deftly caught it out of the air and started spraying Blachowicz's scalp to seal the wound.

"Do we need a team to go clean up the ladder you bloodied up?" she asked.

"Yes, PO, I bled a lot getting here."

Desper sighed, shaking her head. "Spacer, not only did you bleed all over one of the ladders, instead of calling for help from the ladder, you left a trail of blood all the way down here?" she asked.

Blachowicz had the decency to look embarrassed. "Yes, PO. I uh, didn't know what else to do."

"Where?" she asked.

"Deck three, aft of the electronics workstation, PO."

"You're an electronics mate?" she asked.

"Aye, PO."

By distance, that was the farthest ladder from sickbay. Annoyed, Desper slammed the call button on the bulkhead. "Bridge, PO Desper-sickbay, can you shut off access to the deck three ladder, aft. We've got a biologic to clean up. Then notify Whips to meet me there with a disinfectant kit?"

"Aye, aye, PO," Spacer McCall came back. "Right away."

An hour later Desper returned to sickbay, her uniform soaked in sweat from climbing the ladders in the heat and then scrubbing the deck clean of contaminant. The amount of blood on the ladder and deck shocked her. She was surprised the kid was conscious when he came in.

Shouting from sickbay surprised her as she stepped off the ladder onto deck five.

"This is unacceptable, Chief Pierre. Call the Bosun and man-at-arms this instant," Commander Freydis said.

Desper poked her head inside to see what the stir was before going in. Freydis held one finger out at Chief Pierre, accusingly, and both stood next to the open medicine cabinet.

Open?

"Ma'am, what seems to be the problem?" Desper asked.

Freydis turned her cold eyes on Desper. "Don't play innocent with me, PO. I'm not sure what your game is, but I assure you, I do not tolerate this kind of behavior in my sickbay."

Chief Pierre gave Desper a stern look, as if telling her to keep her mouth shut. "Ma'am," he said, "whatever happened, I can assure you it's not what it looks like."

Desper frowned. She really didn't know what Commander Freydis spoke of. "I'm sure it's just a misunderstanding, ma'am. What seems to be the issue?"

"Chief Pierre, call the man-at-arms or I will, that is an order."

CHAPTER TWENTY-ONE

Chief Suresh looked at the doctor like she was stupid. No, not stupid, *insane*. Had she heard her correctly?

"Ma'am, let me get this straight," the COB said, trying to articulate the medical officer's argument. "You think PO Desper, who has served honorably in the Navy for over a decade, just suddenly decided to start stealing nanite painkillers... and did so while we're underway on a secret mission?"

Devi interviewed the officer in the briefing room, the only spare room they could maintain for private communications. Devi, who was the COB and in charge and responsible for the enlisted and NCOs on the boat. Technically, PO Cartwright was the assistant man-at-arms, but this was her duty to get to the bottom of.

"I don't see what the issue is, *Chief* Suresh." Commander Freydis said her name with the extra emphasis on rank as to remind her of her place. That was fine; Devi knew her place quite well. Liked it even. She made the skipper swear to keep her from promotion to senior chief because of how much she liked her place.

And she had dealt with officers like Commander Freydis before. They rolled into a new command, with no knowledge of the crew or the ship, and tried to insert their authority as if all it took to command were shiny rank insignia.

"No, ma'am, I suppose you don't. Do you know how many drug-related crimes there are on an Alliance destroyer in a given year?"

"I hardly see how that's relevant."

"Oh, it is, ma'am. Five. That's the fleet average. It isn't because the crews serving are so noble, or that we don't investigate 'em. No, ma'am, it's because there's a certain kind of person that seeks drugs. Once we identify them, they're out of the Navy. PO Desper has served a long time and you're saying, out of the blue, she's stealing narcotics?"

"I'm not sure what the fleet average or her own record has to do with the evidence. It's right here. Her NavPad was used to open the medicine cabinet and five liters of nanite painkillers were removed. Do you know how much that's worth on the black market?"

Devi thought about what the commander had said, but it didn't make any sense. She might as well have said that Prisca Desper rounded up a bunch of children and forced them into the airlock.

"I understand, ma'am. I do. Believe me, this is a serious crime. The kind that, during a war, can lead to execution. So before I move forward with this investigation, I'm just trying to figure out the why. Why would she do it?"

Commander Freydis looked thoughtfully up and then back at Chief Suresh. She took a deep breath and let it out.

"I see what you're saying, COB. I do. However, all I can go on are the facts. No one can use a NavPad other than the person it's assigned to. PO Desper's NavPad accessed the medicine cabinet during the time the painkillers were removed. That's all I have.

If you have some glaring piece of evidence that says otherwise, I'm all ears. Until then, I'm afraid she needs to stay locked up in the brig."

"Aye ma'am, that she will do."

Freydis left and Chief Suresh looked at the situation. The video feed in sickbay was conveniently disabled for twenty minutes around the time Desper allegedly accessed the medicine cabinet. Regardless, though, medicine was missing, and the evidence pointed at PO Prisca Desper.

There were three possibilities. One: Human error in the logging of the medicine resulted in the mistake. In that case the meds were never there, and Commander Freydis' inventory was based on false information. Two: A third party changed the data as well as cloned Prisca's NavPad and stole the medicine. Three: She didn't know Prisca nearly as well as she thought she did and the PO was a lying, manipulative thief.

She literally laughed out loud and mentally checked number three off her list. That left two things and she needed to work through them until she could either prove or check them off the list as well.

Jacob forced his eyes open and his breathing steadied. In through his mouth, out through his nose. Exiting a starlane felt like being yanked up a rope at high speed. He wanted to vomit but wouldn't allow himself.

"Is it me, skipper, or was that worse than usual?" Chief Suresh asked.

This was their third exit using the Guild's gateway devices.

"I do—" he bit down on his own words, desperate to keep his breakfast down. After a moment it passed. "I do believe so." Jacob leaned back as the nausea passed. "All stations, report."

Inside his helmet, the light blinked as atmosphere returned to the ship.

His helmet unlatched with a hiss of escaping air and he sat it down on his lap.

"Weapons—check," Brown said.

"Conn—check," Suresh followed.

One by one the bridge crew notified of their stations and their crew's readiness. Brown didn't just tell him that the weapons panel was ready, but all his turret and Long 9 crew were accounted for.

"Ensign Brennan, anything on the scope?" he asked.

She glanced at Oliv who had her helmet off and headphones on already.

"Nothing yet, sir. Astro reports the sun is a G-type star, and there are five planets on this side of the orbital plane. Sending the ecliptic bearing to the conn."

"Ecliptic bearing received. Permission to engage, skipper?" Chief Suresh asked.

He met her eyes in the mirror. There wasn't always time to see her face when he gave an order, but he found it helped with understanding if the officer giving the order and the coxswain could see one another's expression.

"Execute," he said.

"Aye, aye, sir."

Chief Suresh deftly engaged the ship's thrusters, moving her down before activating the gravcoil and piling on the real acceleration.

Gravity pulled him into his chair, like a hand pressing against his chest. A spike of irrational fear bolted through him, but he reminded himself it was perfectly normal.

"Ecliptic will be achieved in three-zero-point-five mikes," Chief Suresh informed him.

"Understood."

Once the gravity normalized, he leaned forward and pulled up the system information on his screen. Alliance astrography had precious little information about Caliphate planets. Almost all of it came from before the Great War. When the two nations were at least on speaking terms.

According to the pilfered Guild database, Midway was one of the original Caliphate colonies they turned into a sort of prison. The kind where the only walls were the atmosphere. They literally dumped their prisoners on the planet, then departed. From what their records showed, the Caliphate only had a presence in the system when they were dumping prisoners. Though, Jacob had to wonder why with the collars they would even need a prison. He supposed there might be a need to keep people alive, or accessible. Still, it seemed odd to run a penal colony in the middle of nowhere when they had the most efficient system to punish prisoners ever devised.

Perhaps it was tradition? After all, they had exiled Captain Rashid Al-Alami rather than kill him. Albeit, after executing his family members and selling his sister into slavery. Perhaps he was applying logic to a problem where the goal wasn't a logical solution? If punishment were more important than simply stopping the crime from happening again, then he could see why penal colonies and banishment would still be popular.

"Once we're on the ecliptic, Astro," he said, "set a course for Midway and execute."

"Aye sir, set course for Midway once current course is achieved," Ensign Brennan replied.

"Excellent." Jacob turned his chair to examine the rest of the bridge, finding them all working hard at their posts. The hour after entering a new system was full of work and procedures. He wouldn't interrupt them. He had his own work to do. A few things nagged at him, things he didn't like happening on his ship.

PO Desper's status weighed on him. He couldn't quite wrap his mind around the idea of her stealing medicine. Not that she couldn't, but that she would do it in such an idiotic manner—while they were so far from an Alliance system. Who could she possibly sell it to? And if it wasn't to sell it, then why?

"Comms," he said aloud.

"Aye sir," Midship Watanabe's sweet voice came back.

"Could you have Chief Redfern meet me in the briefing room?"

"Have Chief Redfern meet the captain in the briefing room, aye, aye sir."

Jacob paused for a moment watching her work. She seemed to have turned things around. There were a few behaviors he wasn't fond of. *Baby steps*, he reminded himself.

Jacob checked the time on his NavPad, and if he knew Chief Redfern, the man was either in engineering or somewhere below decks working. He wouldn't at all be surprised if he took a few minutes to arrive.

Once in the conference room, he went about going to work. There was never enough time to do the paperwork, and while they were nominally in an enemy system, he still had a ship to run.

"You wanted to see me, skip?" Redfern said from the perpetually open hatch.

"Come in, Chief, have a seat." Jacob leaned back, hands clasped over his waist. Once Redfern had taken a seat across from him, he continued. "I know when we went to Medial, you were instrumental in finding the ship some needed supplies. I was wondering, if I may, ask you some questions about how a spacer might procure supplies not available to the Navy?"

Redfern chuckled as he leaned forward. "Are you asking me how to buy on the black market, sir?"

Jacob shook his head. "More, how would you sell? You've probably heard about PO Desper?"

Redfern sat up straight, all traces of humor gone in an instant. "Sir, I don't know what happened there, but I know Prisca Desper and she didn't do this. If it weren't for the security regs, I could promise you that she wouldn't. I'd bet a year's wages she's innocent."

Jacob noted Redfern's response in his log. He was the third person to say some variation of "she's innocent." He didn't think for one second that PO Desper had actually stolen the medical supplies, but until he had evidence that she hadn't, his hands were tied. The COB ran down her leads, but Jacob wanted to ask a few questions himself.

He raised his hand to stave off Redfern's defense of his shipmate.

"Close the outer doors, Chief. I'm on your side. What do you mean if regs didn't prevent it?"

"It has to do with how we got our medical supplies for our mission to Medial, sir. That's all I can say.

Jacob accepted that. There was much about that mission that stayed classified and he couldn't risk bringing it up in an official capacity, lest people outside the immediate chain of command face charges. The crew was protected. The people who helped them, like Lieutenant Bonds transferring the Raptors over, were not.

"Prisca is innocent, I know that—hell, everyone knows it, including the CMO. What I need to do is find out the how and why. Someone disabled sickbays camera feed for twenty minutes. That same someone managed to hide Prisca's movements on the ship, robbing her of an alibi. I believe, that if we can answer the why, we will discover the who."

Redfern relaxed, leaning back in his chair and folding his lanky legs over one another. "That's a smart move, skipper.

Normally I would say they were going to sell it, but as you've already surmised, that makes no sense."

"Exactly. Who would they sell it to? What does something like that go for, anyway?"

"To answer correctly, sir, I would have to know what was stolen."

Smart, Jacob thought. Redfern certainly wasn't under suspicion, at least no more than the rest of the crew, but he certainly knew how to cover his own butt.

"Five liters of nanite-infused pain killers."

Redfern let out a long whistle. "That's money in the bank, sir. We're talking thousands per liter, more since its military grade. I wouldn't know for sure without being involved in the black market, which for the record—I am not. If I had to guess, though, fifty thousand easy."

"Fifty thousand... dollars?"

Redfern grinned. "Yes sir, Alliance dollars to be precise. Depending on the exchange rate at any given time, more or less in other nations."

Jacob let that sink in for a minute. His annual salary was a little less than that and it boggled his mind that someone could steal that much from his destroyer.

"Okay, so let's assume whoever took it plans to sell. Where would they sell it?"

"That's the part that doesn't make any sense, skipper. Normally you would wait until the night before port, or even the day after. Not while you were underway and going in the wrong direction." He shook his head. "It just doesn't make any sense at all to steal it now. There's no way we won't find it before we get back."

Jacob agreed with him. What possible use could it be? Perhaps to cripple the *Interceptor*'s ability to treat injuries? Yes. But beyond that, who knew?

CHAPTER TWENTY-TWO

Interceptor approached the second moon with its dark-blue atmosphere and violent electrical storms. The shark-nosed ship pierced the upper layers of the small gaseous planet before the aperture on the gravcoil opened fully and hydrogen flooded in through specially designed grooves. Once inside the ship, the gas was compressed and chilled until it converted to slush in a process that would take forty-eight hours to complete. While she did, *Interceptor* couldn't maneuver or fire her weapons.

Ensign Brennan lay in her bunk, unable to sleep since she crashed at 2100. She had duty at 0700 and should really be asleep, but guilt nagged at her. Had she hurt her roommate's career by speaking to the Bosun about her? It wasn't as if she were the first midship to show up intoxicated for duty.

Unable to sleep, she rolled out of her bunk and hit the floor. Midship Watanabe's bunk was empty and still made. Which was weird because the midship was in the cabin getting ready for bed when Fionna was.

"Yua? You in the head?" she called out.

Nothing.

Not wanting to interrupt her bunkmate doing anything private, she waited a few minutes, then called out again. When there was still no response, she opened the hatch and the head was empty.

While Midship Watanabe's punishment wasn't common knowledge, Fionna knew. Shift, sickbay, galley, and engineering. That was it.

Fionna donned her uniform as fast as she could, grabbing her field jacket to protect against the cold *Interceptor* nights. While the ship orbited the moon refilling the slush tanks, cold was the order of the day. Hydrogen didn't react well to heat or sparks.

She walked out of her cabin and looked down the hatchway. Aft was Marine country, which her quarters bordered. Fore was the rest of the enlisted quarters and some of the POs. Directly above her on deck five was main engineering, the fabricator, and armory. Above that was the CPO and Officer Quarters.

Glancing forward again, the only thing Fionna could think of was the rec room. That was all the way at the bow, which was the only logical place for Watanabe to go. Anywhere else and she risked being seen by one of the officers. Fionna debated with herself whether she should call the ships Bosun or inform Lieutenant Hössbacher.

No, she told herself. That would just cause more problems for Watanabe. Fionna wanted to help her, not doom her career because she got cabin fever and ran off to the rec room to stargaze.

Deciding, Fionna followed her roommate, hoping to bring her back before any more harm was done. What the CO didn't know wouldn't hurt him.

Except she wasn't in the rec room. No one was. Ship's time was subjective, of course. The middle of the night was nothing more than the ship dimming lights. Still, it was eerie to be out in the hatchway when the lights were dim and no one was about. From midnight to six, the watch was minimal, giving most everyone a chance to sleep under *normal* circumstances. Of course, the ship could go to alert at a moment's notice.

Metal on metal echoed down the hatchway, and Fionna thought she caught a glimpse of a head disappearing into the bowels of the ship. Technically, the space between deck six and the gravcoil wasn't a deck, more like a half-deck. A maintenance access way used for repairs on the gravcoil, heatsink, and, in emergencies, the life pods.

Her gut tightened as she walked toward the closed hatch. Life pods were the absolute last resort for a failing ship and there was still time to abandon. They could survive in space for a full week or transport the crew to a planet if there was one nearby.

"Oh no," she said aloud.

Fionna hurried to the hatch built into the deck and punched in her code. The hatch slid aside revealing a narrow ladder. Below was the life pod hatch. Squeezed into it were two spacers she didn't recognize and Midship Watanabe.

"What the hell?" Fionna shouted her surprise.

"Who invited her?" the larger of the two spacers asked.

"Quiet, Blachowicz," Watanabe said. "This isn't what it looks like, Fionna. We're running a diagnostics and—"

"Oh, please. I'm not some wet-behind-the-ears noob. I know exactly what you're doing. I'll let the skipper sort this out." Ironically, it was the first time she'd felt comfortable calling the captain by that.

Blachowicz meaty hand seized her forearm with an iron grip. She pulled back by instinct, but he didn't budge.

"I don't think so. Yua's worth a lot of money and she's promised her father will pay us handsomely to get her off the ship. We're too committed to turn back now."

Fionna opened her mouth to scream when he yanked her down into the pod. Her head hit the bulkhead as she fell, whipping her body around like a doll. Everything went blurry, and she tasted blood.

"Tyree, strap her in," Blachowicz said.

She had to warn them. Her mind fell into darkness like quicksand, but she had to warn them.

"Don't... hydrogen... explosive..."

Watanabe gave a short laugh. "That's the plan; if the ship's damaged, they won't be worried about coming and looking for me. I never wanted to join the Navy; it was all my dumb father's idea. Now that there's a real war, you better believe I'm not staying in."

"I don't know about this," Tyree said. "She's an officer. Are we kidnapping her? I'm pretty sure that comes with a death sentence."

"Only if you get caught. She'll be fine. We'll leave her with the life pod, and they will pick her up in a day or two. By then, we'll be long gone."

As Fionna struggled to remain conscious, she watched helplessly as the hatch closed and sealed. An automated voice announced a countdown, and when it reached one, gravity slammed down on her like an iron blanket.

CHAPTER TWENTY-THREE

Jacob flopped over, falling onto the deck as the ship bucked. The secondary gravcoil did its best to compensate for the sudden acceleration, but there was only so much it could do. Training kicked in and he covered his head with his arms. He was yanked up by an invisible hand and slammed into the overhead before falling back onto his bunk.

He could almost pass it off as a dream, except for the agony of multiple blunt force traumas inflicted against him. Either his nose bled, or he had a severe cut on his forehead. Either one was bad.

Through the haze of pain and red-tinged vision, he managed to find the call button.

"Bridge, Captain, what's going on?" His voice sounded rough to his own ears.

"Sir, uh," Spacer Gouger's voice slurred as he responded.

Everyone on the ship had to be feeling the effects. Jacob prayed that no one had died. He didn't have time to figure out what was going on from his cabin, he was needed on the bridge.

"Felix, Condition Zulu: Action stations."

"Aye sir!"

A second later, as Jacob scrambled for his ELS suit, the klaxon warbled to life throughout the ship. Jacob was fairly sure that no one aboard needed to be told there was an emergency, but in times of crisis and confusion, relying on training tended to cut down on the response time.

Five minutes after he first slammed into the overhead, Jacob strode onto the bridge and racked his helmet on the back of his chair.

"I have the conn."

"Aye sir," Spacer Gouger noted, "Captain has the conn."

"Ops, status?"

PO Tefiti manned the ops station. "Not good, sir. Either something hit us, or a part of the ship exploded. Deck six is open to space—"

Oh God, no! Deck six housed the majority of the crew. If they were hit with explosive decompression in the middle of the night, he didn't want to imagine the death toll.

"Casualties?" he had to ask, even though he didn't want to know.

"Emergency bulkheads and hatches operated as they were supposed to, sealing off the crew in their quarters and the head. I don't have the numbers yet, but so far, no casualties."

Jacob let out a visible sigh of relief. While not prone to emotional outbursts, he certainly didn't mind the crew knowing how much he cared about them.

"I want engineering to prioritize getting atmo back to six. We need our people free."

"Aye sir. As for the ship, we have no power to the primary gravcoil and we experienced eight g's of burst acceleration. Collins, where are we at with the helm?" Tefiti asked.

"Sluggish, PO. Very sluggish. Because of the moon's atmosphere we can't use reaction thrusters. Without power to the gravcoil, I can slow us down in about a week."

Great. Two-thirds of their crew were stuck in their quarters, no power to propel, and they couldn't use reaction thrusters. This wasn't the refueling stop he wanted. While replenishing hydrogen from a thick atmosphere wasn't routine, it certainly wasn't unheard of. They had followed all the procedures laid out for them. What had gone wrong?

Other than Murphy.

Redfern clawed around the edge of the gravcoil, the simian-looking Gorilla suit giving him power and mass a regular space-suited man wouldn't have. They were perfect for field repairs and external damage assessments while under way. Like he was doing now.

It was sheer luck he'd taken a shift from Spacer Tyree who wasn't feeling well. He used that time to perform maintenance on the suits. They only had two of them, and they took up a third of the space Raptors did. Which he always thought was odd. The Marines used the Raptor's once a year, and that was for training. The Gorilla suits were used weekly.

Responding to his actions, the four fingered hand reached out and grabbed the de-powered gravcoil. Using it for balance, he pushed off the hull and swung around. His feet magnetized on impact, and he immediately spotted the problem.

From an outside perspective, if the gravcoil were teeth, and the hull the roof of the mouth, then Chief Petty Officer Redfern stood upside down on the roof of the mouth of the ship. A part of the ship one didn't see often but was unmistakable, since there were supposed to be twenty-five life pods. At six spacers per pod, there were enough to carry everyone aboard, plus twenty. The extra was because the Navy liked redundancy. They weren't fancy, just no-frills life support pods that could survive re-entry if needed.

One of them was missing.

"Lieutenant Kai, tell the skipper I figured out why we bucked, and it isn't good news."

CHAPTER TWENTY-FOUR

Eighteen hours had passed since the explosion. It took a tremendous amount of blood, sweat, and tears, but they had managed to return power to the gravcoil and free the crew. Only to find there were some missing.

Jacob found himself in the unenviable position of wishing they were dead from the explosive decompression. He certainly didn't want to be the captain who had deserters aboard his ship. Though it happened. Not everyone was cut out for Navy life, and no matter how hard they tried to weed those people out, some always managed to come through. In this case, it was Spacer's Apprentice Tyree and Spacer Blachowicz. He didn't know either of them very well; they were new transfers from fleet, but he wouldn't be surprised to find they tested on the very edge of compatibility. Midship Watanabe didn't surprise him, either. She seemed to genuinely dislike the Navy. Though she'd put on a good act the last few weeks of performing her duty.

What truly surprised him, though, shocked even, was Ensign Brennan going with them. True, she was Watanabe's cabin mate, but still she seemed dedicated to her duty, even if she was a bit shy and unsure of herself.

But to jump ship? That was a stretch.

"Six hours, skipper," Carter said. "That's how much longer we need to finish the repairs and refuel."

Jacob looked around at the gathered officers. Every single one of them was beyond tired. No one slept when the ship was in a state of constant peril as it was.

"Very good, XO. I'm sorry this happened, but I'm pleased at the results. Each of your departments have handled themselves well. Working above and beyond."

"Sir," Lieutenant Hössbacher said, "I'm afraid this is all my fault. I should have known of her plans."

Jacob shook his head. "Nonsense, Roy. From my understanding, they were very well thought out. From the food missing from the stores to the stolen medicine, she planned every step of the way. It's a shame, really."

"What is, sir?" Lieutenant Austin Brown asked.

"Someone capable of making that good of a plan would have made a fantastic officer."

Heads nodded in agreement. Roy seemed distant and Jacob made a mental note to talk to the young man. Not everything could be foreseen or dealt with.

Carter continued with the briefing. "In six hours, we'll continue the mission and head for the starlane exiting—"

"What?" Jacob's head snapped around. "No. We're not leaving them behind, Carter."

"Sir, the mission is time sensitive. We can't afford to linger looking for crew who don't want to be found."

While he never spoke up in the meetings, Master Sergeant Danny Cannon always attended them, and at the sound of a possible delay, his head snapped up.

"Carter, of course I'm aware of the time constraints on the mission, but I don't leave people behind. You know this. Not one person. We know exactly where the life pod is, and when we're done refueling, I intend to go get them."

Carter's eyes opened wide and he blinked several times. "You, sir? You personally?"

"My crew, my responsibility, Carter. The buck stops here." He planted one finger on the table in front of him. "Either I'm responsible or no one is."

Danny frowned at Grimm's declaration. Ever since his team came aboard all they heard was, "the captain this" and "the captain that." It was enough to make a grown man vomit. However, Grimm declaring his responsibility and intention to retrieve his missing crew intrigued Danny. Oh, he had no love for the Navy or how they operated. Too impersonal, too distant. Shooting each other from tens of thousands of klicks away wasn't a battle, it was a game of darts.

A man willing to brave danger to retrieve missing crew, that was admirable. Maybe he would like to see a little more.

"Captain, if it's okay with you, I can bring my team along. We have experience in this sort of thing."

Grimm smiled reassuringly at him. "Thank you, Master Sergeant, thank you very much. Your team would be more than welcome."

Danny wasn't sure what he'd gotten into with the man, but he was certainly interested to find out where it led. Grimm was many things, but predictable and boring he wasn't.

Jacob hid his surprise at the grunt's offer of help. In truth, he wasn't sure he could take them down to the surface along with the Marines. He would need to find out. Once the meeting was adjourned, he made his way to Jennings who was securing ammo and backup grenades in the Mudcat.

"I want you to prep a rescue mission," he told her.

"Rescue, sir? I thought they deserted."

"That's for a court martial to decide. Not me. They are my crew, and they will be on my ship when we leave the system. The grunts have offered to come along if it helps. I can tell them no—"

"No sir, I mean..." Alison turned her head away from him in an uncharacteristic move. "Their help would be welcome."

"Good. As soon as the ship is ready, we'll depart and—"

Jennings turned to him, looking at him like she already knew his plans. "Sir. You're not going."

"Gunny, I appreciate the concern, really. I also know I'm outside the regs on this. However, they're my crew. Mine. If I don't do this, then what is all my talk of responsibility worth?"

He faced her down, which was rather difficult. Allison Jennings was the only person he'd ever met in his life who was almost a meter shorter than him yet made him feel small and want to fall back whenever she leveled her gaze at him.

"Sir, if you go down there and get yourself killed doing something heroic, you know it's my ass in the sling, right?"

Her vehemence caught him off guard. Jacob resisted the urge to take a step back and retreat from the Marine.

"I promise I will stay in the Mudcat. However, I have to go down with you. I need to be seen doing this for my people. Understood?"

Jennings tossed the idea around for a moment, finally making her decision. "Okay, sir, have it your way. But do not leave the safety of the 'Cat, understood?"

"Yes, Gunny, understood."

Gunny Jennings strode back and forth in front of the holographic display of Midway as she briefed the ground team.

"What we have here is a SAR op. We may encounter non-military enemy combatants. These skinnies will likely be armed and unarmored. From what the captain has told me, this is a penal colony. No prison guards, they just dump people on the planet and leave 'em to fend for themselves."

Her three Marines and the five Army grunts were crowded into the armory as she gave the briefing.

"Gunny?" Naki held up his hand.

"You don't have to hold up your hand, Naki. Just ask."

"We have the location of the pod, can we use the nose-cam to give us a peek?"

Jennings shook her head. It was a good idea and the first thing she had asked as well. "Cloud cover is preventing us from any kind of aerial reconnaissance. We will have access to the Corsair and her sensors, but that's it."

"No drones?" Rico asked.

"We don't carry them. Our groundside assignments are few and far between."

Rico fiddled with something in his pack. "I've got a RSI MKIII Raven we can use. With a twenty-klick range and a top speed of one hundred MPS, it can cover a wide area."

Jennings wanted to say no, but she would be foolish to do so. It bothered her, and it shouldn't, that the Army grunts had better equipment. Her Marines were one squad of thousands, while the Army boys were the elite, top-tier Special Forces. Of course they had better gear.

"Thank you, Sergeant. That will be great." Technically, she equaled Mac and outranked Rico, T-Bar, and Bubba, which she knew were not their real names, but they all used callsigns. Which she thought was stupid. Though while under the skipper's command, she had the authority to issue orders to anyone, even officers, if they were also under the skipper's command.

In the case of their rescue op, that meant she was in charge.

"We will infiltrate here," she said pointing at a plateau a few hundred meters from the pod. "Use the Mudcat to travel to our location while the Corsair provides CAS."

"Can your aviator handle that?" Danny asked.

"Yes. Any other dumbass questions?" Jennings deadpanned.

Mac and Rico snickered at their leader as Jennings glared. "From this moment on, assume that *Interceptor*'s people know what the hell they're doing. If you spend your time trying to do our job, you won't be doing yours."

Danny's stone expression gave Jennings a run for her money, but in the end he capitulated. "Yes, Gunny."

"Once we arrive onsite, Naki, Owens, Bubba and T-Bar will provide security. Rico, my understanding is that you're an engineer?"

His back went straight at the mention of his specialty. "Yes, Gunny."

"Excellent. I want you with me on the pod. June, you're driving and you stay in the 'Cat. Mac, use your sniper rifle for overwatch. The skipper will cover us with the turret and will not be leaving the vehicle under any normal circumstances."

"What's our loadout?" Owens asked.

"Standard medium tactical. Light body over ELS, grenades, the usual."

Owens looked disappointed. "I was hoping to take the Raptor for a spin."

"Maybe next time. Right now we have too many unknown

hostiles and friendlies mixed together for that kind of firepower. Any other questions?"

When none were forthcoming, she dismissed the group to get ready for the drop. She needed the extra time to make a few preparations herself.

CHAPTER TWENTY-FIVE

MIDWAY ORBIT

Interceptor skirted the thicker atmosphere of Midway, leaving a burning ion trail behind her of glowing red embers and sparks of blue lightning.

Boudreaux looked down through the transparent hull of the Corsair through the open boat bay doors and marveled at the sight.

"Thirty seconds to zone," Spacer McCall said over her radio.

She could drop from anywhere, but to minimize the time in the air, they were going to drop over the target, or close to it. She didn't expect any resistance, but it never hurt to practice a full combat drop.

"Stawarski, you ready?" she asked her back seater.

"Ready, Chief. All systems are green."

"Cooper?"

"Electronics are green, Chief."

Boudreaux pushed the pedals in while pulling the stick back. "All control surfaces are responding." She switched her radio to the Marine channel. "Jennings, are your people secure?"

The radio clicked, "Roger, Chief. We're strapped in."

"*Interceptor*, Charlie-One-One-Actual, we are ready for drop."

"Charlie-One-One-Actual, this is *Interceptor*, you are clear to drop."

Boudreaux hit the button releasing the clamps and her Corsair lurched down. Gravity from the planet grabbed her and yanked hard. She dove into the pull, pointing the nose down at a forty-five-degree angle and letting nature run its course. Lights dimmed as the transparent hull polarized to protect the pilot.

"Three hundred and twenty meters per second," Stawarski announced.

"Roger."

As the Corsair burned its way through the atmosphere, they were essentially blind for a terrifying few minutes. Heat from the re-entry built up on the belly of the ship wrapping her in a plasma sheath that prevented the radio from working.

"Looks like hydrogen dense atmosphere, Chief. We're blind for six minutes," Cooper said from below.

Great.

Six minutes where their threat detection radar and ECM wouldn't operate. She could slow their descent, enough that the heat buildup would be mitigated, but if she did that, they would be sitting ducks for any surface-to-air missiles. She went over the mission brief in her head again. The captain had said this was a penal colony, no spacecraft, no advanced technology. It was a gamble, but she would rather see a threat coming than head into it blind.

"Fire the plasma turbines on three—" her fingers deftly flew over the startup procedures for the air breathing plasma engines. Stawarski did his part fast and efficiently and when Boudreaux reached one, the engines fired to life.

They slammed forward in their harnesses as the engines screamed to slow them down. After ten seconds, the red haze cleared and blue-green light filtered through the cockpit window. Down below the long winding rivers of a vast continent looked like noodles on a dark plate.

"Rolling, hang on to your breakfast."

She pushed the stick over while mimicking the movements with her feet. The Corsair rolled on its axis and nose-dived, piling g's on the crew and passengers.

"No threats detected," Cooper said from the EW station below her.

The Corsair shook and rumbled as it smashed through pockets of heated air.

"Who needs a space elevator," she said through gritted teeth.

"One hundred klicks," Stawarski announced.

The chop started to slack off. Boudreaux spun the craft around and pulled out of the dive, bringing the nose to twenty degrees down, slowing their descent.

She triggered the radio to the passengers. "This is your captain speaking, if you look below, you will see our landing destination. ETA three minutes. Please make sure you take all firearms and ammunition with you as you exit the vehicle. Thank you for flying Air-Boudreaux."

Tucked into the passenger seat of the Mudcat, Jennings muttered about pilots.

"Everyone's a comedian, Gunny," June said from the driver seat. They were strapped in hard, with their safety harnesses pulled as tight as the motors could get them and still let them breathe. The Marines were decked out in their "space armor" while the grunts wore soft armor under their camouflaged uniforms.

Jennings had to admit, though she was loathe to do so, the gray-and-white pattern the space armor came in wasn't going to be very effective on a green planet like Midway.

"Gunny," Grimm called over their private channel, "You have tactical command."

"Aye, sir, I have tactical command." Jennings used the controls built into her suit's gloves to pull up a holographic map of the area where the pod impacted. From what she could see, there were a few half-destroyed buildings in the area, not a lot for cover, but a sniper could hide in them.

"What's the play if things go south?" Sergeant Cannon asked.

"Stay together, improvise as needed."

"Not much of a plan," Danny said.

"My plan is to follow my training and come back alive. Anything else requires adaptability."

She couldn't see him behind her, but she sensed a sort of understanding. How could she plan for something on a planet they'd never seen with no recon? All she could do was follow general SAR guidelines for hostile extraction. The guidelines were there for a reason. She didn't need a specific plan for every instance of failure, she had her training for that.

TWENTY HOURS EARLIER

Fionna Brennan's head felt like someone had used her skull to play soccer, then put it back in when they were done. She rolled over, instantly regretting her decision to move, and vomited. Luckily, she did so on the ground and not on her uniform.

The ground?

Fionna jerked up. Her hands sunk in dark dirt, and her knees were wet. The soft pitter-patter of rain hitting a shelter filled the air around her.

"Oh, thank god, you're awake. They wouldn't let me use any of the medicine on you," Spacer's Apprentice Tyree said.

She resisted the urge to shake her head, instead, pushing herself to a sitting position and taking in what was around her. Hidden under a large green tarp. Her breath fogged up in front of her and she was only warm enough because of the nanites working in her uniform. That wouldn't last forever though.

"Tyree, what happened?" she asked after a moment.

"We argued after we hit. They wanted to kill or leave you, and I couldn't do that. It was one thing to help Yua, but you—well, I'm not a murderer. Yua and Blachowicz took off for a settlement nearby. She thinks there's a ship she can hire to take her off the planet..."

Fionna sank her head into her hands. No ships. There were no ships allowed on the planet. Wasn't she listening in the briefing? Or did she think her money and influence would be enough?

"Weapons?" she asked. Her voice came out rough, like she needed to drink several liters of water just to clear it up.

"No. They took everything. I managed to rig this tarp I found. Nothing around here is dry, though, so no fires."

She nodded. That idiot had killed them all. Midway's population were criminals and exiles. There was no escape. *Interceptor* would count itself lucky to be rid of troublemakers and move on. No one was coming for them. She wanted to curl up around her knees and cry. She knew, though, if she allowed herself that luxury, then she wouldn't ever come back.

"Okay, Tyree, I have one question for you. Are you with me?"

"Aye, aye, ma'am. I'm sorry I ever got into this. I don't know what I was thinking, and by the time I realized what was going on... well, Blachowicz is a big man."

"Don't I know it," she said as she massaged the back of her head. "Listen, we can't worry about who did what until we're out of here. This isn't a normal planet, and if she had paid attention in the briefings, she would know that."

"Yes, ma'am, I kind of figured that out on my own. We're in trouble."

At least she had an ally in the mess. "Right. Our uniforms will protect us from the cold for twelve more hours; after that, we either recharge them or find a source of heat. Before that, we need water and a more permanent place to shelter. Suggestions?"

Tyree pointed into the distance. The moonless night made it impossible to see.

"While we were crashing, I saw a series of burned out and half-fallen buildings about two klicks that way."

There wasn't much light, no moon to speak of, and no city lights to navigate on. "Did they leave the emergency kits?" she asked.

"No ma'am. I was worried the pod crash would attract attention. I dragged you away as fast as I could after Yua left."

Fionna carefully got to her feet, hands wide apart for balance. "I'm still a little wobbly. You did the right thing, Tyree. I can't imagine the people here are into talking."

As if the inhabitants of the world heard her, sporadic gunfire filled the night air. Louder than the rain and irregular.

"I can't tell if that's close or not?" Tyree said.

"I think it's close. Let's head for those buildings, if you're sure about the direction."

"I think I am, ma'am."

Fionna huddled in on herself as they set out. Her uniform resisted the rain, and steam drifted gently off her like she stood in the sunlight during the morning. Her hands and ears though, were cold. She'd lost her watch cap during the scuffle, and she promised herself from that moment on she would carry a spare.

Light far above the ground flared to life and died as quick. Maybe it was a trick of the night, or her overtired eyes, or the fact that she had taken a blow to the head, but she was sure it was there. High enough up that it had to be the partially collapsed building.

"You've got a good sense of direction," she told Tyree.

"Thank you, ma'am I—" gunfire erupted around them and Tyree dove into Fionna, knocking them both to the ground and down a small bank into a ditch. She wanted to scream from the roar of death firing above her.

Strobe light flashes of return fire lit up the night. She hit something soft, squishy, and wet. She grabbed Tyree and pushed him to the north, away from the gunfire. Tyree splashed mud and water as he crawled away using the ditch as cover.

Fionna didn't speak, she didn't dare make a sound. More gunfire roared around her, projectiles whipped by her so close she felt the air move. She wasn't trained for this. Marines belonged up to their elbows in muck, crawling to save their lives without even a weapon to defend themselves. Not her. She crept forward through the mud-filled trench, her body low to the ground as she tried to make herself as small a target as possible. The gunfire echoed all around her, the sound of bullets whizzing past, her head sending shivers down her spine. Her heart pounded in her chest, fear threatening to overwhelm her as she struggled to control her breathing. She heard PO Mendez's voice in her head.

Focus on your breathing. In, and out, letting the fear go with it.

Despite the danger, Fionna was determined to reach her

destination, knowing that every inch she gained brought her closer to safety. She could feel the cold, wet mud clinging to her skin, weighing her down as she crawled forward on her hands and knees. Her uniform was muddy, her hair matted with sweat and grime.

With no weapon to defend herself, Fionna was vulnerable and exposed, and the thought of being shot or captured filled her with dread. She couldn't shake the feeling that she was being watched, that at any moment an enemy could appear from the shadows and end her life.

Fionna tried to push the thoughts from her mind, focusing on the task at hand. But as a spacer, she had never been trained for this kind of combat. She had no experience with guns or hand-to-hand fighting, and the thought of facing an enemy soldier made her stomach churn.

She was completely out of her depth, that she was in over her head and had no idea what she was doing. She had never been in a situation like this before, and the fear of the unknown was almost too much to bear.

Focus on your breathing. In, and out, letting the fear go with it.

But despite her lack of training and experience, Fionna knew that she had to keep going. She had to find a way to get through this and make it out alive. With fierce determination, she pushed herself forward, fighting to reach some kind of safety where she could stop and think about how to fix this.

Through sheer force of will, Fionna kept moving forward, her eyes fixed on the distant horizon as she struggled to reach the end of the trench. She prayed that she would find her way out, that she would be able to make it back to the safety of her ship. As the gunfire raged on, and the ditch never seemed to end, her fear grew, threatening to consume her completely.

Focus on your breathing. In, and out, letting the fear go with it.

Once she got back to the ship, regs or no, she was going to find PO Mendez and give him the hug of his life.

Fionna and Tyree crouched in the shadows, their breath coming in short gasps as they tried to catch their bearings. They had managed to escape the trench and make their way to the relative safety of a burned-out building, but they knew that they weren't out of danger yet. Enemy soldiers were still hunting for them, and they had to find a way to get to safety before it was too late.

Tyree looked over at Fionna, his eyes wide with fear. "We have to get out of here," he whispered urgently. "They're going to find us if we don't move."

Fionna nodded, trying to steady her nerves. She knew that Tyree was right. She looked around at their surroundings and she realized that their options were limited.

"We have to get to the top of this building," she said, pointing up at the charred remains of the structure. "I think I saw a light up there when we first looked. Maybe we can find a way to signal the ship." It sounded weak, even to her, but at this point she was grasping for hope.

Tyree looked up at the building dubiously. "How are we going to do that?" he asked. "There's no rope, and the walls are too sheer to climb."

Fionna thought for a moment, trying to come up with a plan. She knew that they couldn't stay where they were, but she also knew that they couldn't just walk out into the open. They had to find a way to get to the top of the building without being seen.

Suddenly, she had an idea. "Come on," she said, grabbing Tyree's hand. "I might know a way." A destroyed building like this was bound to have debris that they could climb up, at least partially.

She led him to the back of the building, where a pile of

debris had accumulated against the wall. Carefully, she began to climb, using the rubble to help her make her way up. Tyree followed close behind, his face pale with fear as he struggled to keep up.

As they climbed, the sounds of gunfire and shouting grew louder, and Fionna knew that they didn't have much time. She could feel her muscles burning with the effort of the climb, but she refused to give up. She had to make it to the top, no matter what.

Tyree had no idea how to climb, and she had to point to every handhold, every safe place for him to use. Lucky for her, where she grew up climbing was second nature.

Handhold by handhold, she strained to climb each floor. Her arms shook with fatigue as she and Tyree made it up the last section and onto the eighth floor.

"Stop," a man said.

She looked up and saw him. Strong shouldered, with sharp features and a beard. He held a long piece of rebar in one hand to hit with. His gaze was hard, like a man who had seen much.

"Help us," she pleaded.

From the shadows a stunning young woman, with delicate features and a radiant, almost ethereal beauty emerged. "Bijan, help them," she pleaded.

The man looked down at her, and though Fionna saw caution in his eyes, she also sensed fatigue.

"If you try to hurt us, I will kill you," he said as he knelt and held out a hand.

CHAPTER TWENTY-SIX

Gunnery Sergeant Jennings sat in the front passenger seat. Blue eyes focused as she searched the rocky terrain through the Mudcat's narrow windshield.

PFC June drove the armored vehicle over the rough ground, following Jennings' instructions to the letter. Despite only having completed the basic Mudcat course on Blackrock, June did a decent job of driving.

"Anything?" Commander Grimm asked for the third time.

"Sir, if I saw something, do you think I would keep it to myself?"

"Sorry, Gunny."

At least he had the decency to use her rank in the field. She'd spent the better part of her time on the *Interceptor* trying to get the captain to stop calling her by her first name. Without much success.

Corporal Naki and Lance Corporal Owens were behind Jennings, their MP-17 rifles resting butt down between their legs. The other four men filling up the passenger compartment, Master Sergeant Danny Cannon's Special Forces troopers, cradled their unique weapons in a relaxed, almost lazy manner.

Where the Marines were vigilant, Danny, Mac, Rico, and T-Bar were dozing. Bubba had drawn the short stick and stayed back on *Interceptor*. There was no way she was leaving any of her Marines behind, but the Mudcat had finite space.

The tension in the air was palpable as Jennings scanned the area, alert for any dangers that might lie ahead. In the turret above her, Commander Grimm manned the powerful 10mm coilgun, his sharp eyes scanning the horizon for any threats. They were two hours into the search. She knew the captain was determined to find the missing crew, but they couldn't look forever. At least she made him sit in the turret and not out on foot. She was glad he didn't join the Marines, since he was crap as a foot soldier.

"Bravo-Two-Five, Charlie-One-One. I'm two klicks above you and I see several obstacles up ahead. No movement."

"Roger, Charlie-One-One," Jennings replied. Instinctively she leaned forward and looked up for the Corsair. Between the sun, and the clouds, she couldn't find it.

As they reached the area where the life pod was believed to be, Jennings signaled for June to slow down.

"Jennings," Cannon asked out loud. "Don't you guys have trackers on the life pod?"

"Yes, Sergeant. One of the crew who took it disabled the tracker."

Mac opened one eye. "How do we know where it is, then?"

Jennings slapped Owens on the shoulder. The redhead spoke instantly. "Math. The most dangerous knowledge in the universe."

"Math?" Mac's bemused expression spoke volumes.

"Yes, Sergeant. Math. I understand you ground types use pictures to communicate, but in space all we have is math. We know the location of *Interceptor* when the pod ejected, and we know where it hit the atmosphere. Lieutenant Kai did the math and gave us a few square kilometers where it could have landed."

Mac seemed satisfied with the answer and leaned his head back and closed his eyes.

As the minutes ticked by, the tension only seemed to increase. They had been searching for hours, and there was still no sign of the pod. Jennings couldn't shake the feeling that something was off. She just couldn't put her finger on what it was.

She checked the map again, superimposing it over her vision. "June, turn left around those trees and let's check the ruins on the outskirts of that bombed-out city we saw."

"Oorah, Gunny."

The front wheels of the 'Cat swiveled in the wet dirt, piling up mud in furrows as its fusion battery powered engine growled. It had clearly rained the night before, but at least they had sunshine for the search.

"Jennings—" the skipper started.

"I still haven't seen anything, sir."

"No, I've got something, I think. Twenty degrees to the left. Five hundred meters."

Jennings used the 'Cats cameras to find the spot and zoom in. Sure enough, the stark white fin of a life pod's stabilizer stuck out of the mud.

Then she frowned. The area around it was beaten down. Two bodies lay face down in the mud, stripped of their clothes and riddled with holes.

"Sir, do they have weapons on this penal colony?" Jennings asked.

"They would almost have to. There are no guards, no warden, the only thing they don't have is space travel and power," Grimm told her.

Jennings cursed under her breath, her frustration mounting.

"June, come to a stop here." She pointed at a spot on the north side of the downed pod. "Skipper, keep that gun pointed to the north. Cannon, you"—she turned to waive her gloved hand at the four troopers—"provide security. Focus on the south side."

"Roger, Gunny," Sergeant Cannon said.

The 'Cat came to a stop and the doors scissored open. Troopers piled out, hitting the mud with a grunt, rifles shouldered. They moved out, heading south, bypassing the pod to keep the area on lockdown.

Behind them, the Marines in space armor, bulkier and harder to move in, climbed out. The three of them stomped to the pod, MP-17's locked and loaded pointing at the life pod. Jennings used hand signals to stop them as she knelt next to one of the bodies.

"Not ours," she said. She stood, scanning the horizon, the feeling in her gut growing with each second.

Three hundred meters away, a lone man with a rifle and powerful scope, watched the Marines. The vehicle they arrived in would be worth a fortune. His finger hovered over the trigger. He wondered who they were and why they had come. He didn't recognize the uniform, and they didn't look like Caliphate regulars. Inwardly, he shrugged. It didn't matter. They weren't going to be leaving—ever.

With his crosshairs resting above the head of who he suspected the leader was, he breathed out and squeezed the trigger.

. . .

A bullet hit Jennings square in the head. Her powerful space armor deflected the majority of the energy, but enough remained to ring her bell.

"Contact west, sniper," Naki yelled.

Owens turned, taking a knee and raising his rifle up to use the scope. Before he could fire, Mac acquired the target and squeezed off a round. A plume of red showed in the distance, signaling a good hit.

"Nice shot," Naki said.

"Practice makes perfect. You boys wanna run out there and confirm it for me?"

"Negative," Jennings said from where she knelt in the mud. "If he signaled our location we need to bug out."

As Jennings regained her feet, she spotted something in the mud. Leaning forward, she squinted and saw what appeared to be boot tracks—Navy-issue boots.

"Skipper, I've got something. Looks like two sets of tracks, one large and one small, going off to the west. Toward where that shot came from."

Danny waived at her. "Gunny, I've got one heading south, looks deep, like they were carrying something heavy. You want us to go on foot and track it down?"

Jennings weighed the choice. Four crew missing but only three tracks? Moving in opposite directions, and she only had one armored fighting vehicle.

"You'll be exposed on foot," Grimm said. "They may not have spacecraft, but they clearly have weapons. We'll have to run them both down one at a time."

Danny and his team knelt, minimizing their profile and—they vanished. No, not vanished, blended.

Blackout suits.

"They'll be fine, sir. Do it," Jennings ordered.

The four men turned, the air shimmering around them. As

they shifted, they were easier to spot, but only because she knew where they started. After a moment, she couldn't see them at all.

"All right, Marines, mount up, outside. MK I's pealed."

The three Marines stood on the running board of the Mudcat, two on the left and Jennings on the right. It was a risk, but their armor would most likely stop anything the locals carried.

Her line clicked over to Grimm's private channel. "Gunny, you sure about that? There could be a lot more hostiles than we know of."

"Aye sir, but those men train for this. Infiltration and reconnaissance is what they do. Besides, if they get in real trouble, they can call for CAS or EVAC from Charlie."

"Which way?" PFC June asked.

"Follow the yellow brick road, PFC." Jennings used her computer to plot out a route in yellow that appeared on the Mudcat's HUD.

Danny and his men jogged off at a leisurely six klicks an hour. Heads swiveling to keep aware of their surroundings and also spot the tracks. They went over a hill, down into a small culver, and followed that for a klick.

"What do you think happened back there, Danny?" Mac asked.

"Looked like there was a fight over the remains of the pod."

Rico broke in, "What makes you think that?"

"The tracks we're following were underneath all the others. The life pod crashed and the occupants abandoned it fast. What I don't know, is why they split up."

They moved in silence after that. The culvert grew wider,

and soon the bottom filled with mud and slowly running water. As one, the four men skipped up the side and came to a crouch just below the crest, scanning the horizon.

"Nomad, four o'clock, half a klick," Rico murmured.

Danny turned, searching for what Rico saw.

Five hundred meters away, the burned-out edge of a city began. A once prominent eight story building had half its I crumbled and the roof collapsed.

"Good eye, Rico." It wasn't so much Rico spotting it, since it wasn't hidden, but identifying it as the only place a refugee would go. If he were on the run, that would be where he went.

"Fan out, stay low, eyes up."

The four-man team spread out, putting ten meters between them as they formed a line and advanced on the building.

"Movement," Mac said. "Eleven o'clock, three tangos."

As one, they froze, hunkering down until their Blackout suits made them invisible in the tall grass.

Danny eyed the direction, noting several gray-clad men marching in a line, only the tops of their head visible from where he crouched.

"Militia, it looks like," Rico said.

"Mac, reconnoiter."

"Roger."

Already invisible, Mac took off slithering through the tall grass like a snake. Danny only knew where he was from the contact symbol on his HUD provided by th' suit's goggles. They could "see" designated friendlies in any light conditions. It made avoiding friendly fire a lot simpler.

Two minutes later Mac's voice, pitched to a whisper, popped over the radio. "Twenty-five loosely organized militia of some kind. They have an officer in charge, wearing a red bandana. Looks like a hodgepodge of small arms and makeshift melee gear and a long arm I don't recognize."

Dany waited for more. They were used to working together, and he knew Mac well enough to not have to ask questions.

"Looks like they're interested in the same building we are. They're setting up camp and a three-man team is trying to ascend the building from the front."

Frag, Danny thought. *Of all the rotten luck.*

"Collapse on me. Team, form a line on their flank."

Mac met them halfway. The tall grass ended twenty meters from the building, and five meters from where the armed militia were setting up their camp. Bed rolls were put down, small tents constructed, a fire in progress.

Using a mix of hand signals and shared knowledge, the team spread out. Anchoring them, Rico converted his heavy coil rifle into an LMG with the touch of a button.

Mac flanked to his right, while Danny and T-Bar moved out to the left ultimately forming a shallow semicircle. Lying on the ground, covered by the long grass, the men were invisible to the naked eye.

They aren't overtly hostile, other than being prisoners. Danny debated inwardly, since he wouldn't have the conversation with his men about the morality of shooting these guys. They were morally right when he said they were, and that meant killing the enemy. However, the reality of the kind of life they led wasn't lost on him. A man could only kill so many before something in him snapped or died. The more unnecessary the killing, the faster they reached that point.

These militia were armed and dangerous. Not civilians, certainly not noncombatants. Could he risk trying to talk to them?

"Hold," he whispered. He slung his rifle tight to his back, leaving his hands free.

Danny crept up, moving a centimeter at a time. He angled to the far side where the man with the red bandana stood, gazing up at the building. He had two men with him; they argued animatedly about reaching the top while the officer listened. Danny wondered if they were arguing about using it as a lookout or if there was something on the top of the building they wanted?

Bits and pieces of their language came through, but not enough he could understand. When they started talking about the sungod... he was sure he mistranslated it.

The argument grew more heated. Danny slipped his coil pistol out and his combat knife in his off hand.

"Boss, they're about done setting up camp. If they pull security they will walk right on top of us," Rico said.

Danny had hoped the other would leave and he could take the leader without alerting the camp. The officer shook his head and threw up his hands as if he'd had enough. Leaving the two men to argue, he walked a few meters toward Danny.

Excellent. If his goal was to avoid unnecessary casualties, he couldn't start off by killing two men just to capture and threaten the third.

Danny, still invisible, swept around the officer and placed the pistol to his head and the knife to his throat while using him as a shield.

Men in the camp started to yell as they grabbed their rifles. "Tell them to stand down," he whispered in a broken Caliph dialect.

"No. I would die rather than surrender to a vile infidel."

"Tell them to drop their weapons or they all die," he said again.

"My men, too, would rather die."

Twenty-two men in ragtag uniforms with makeshift weapons were crouched in camp, not sure what they should do when faced with a situation they weren't trained for. Their leader seemingly held hostage by a disembodied gun. One thing

Danny knew for sure, they weren't hardened Caliph regulars. He was almost positive they weren't as committed as the officer seemed to think.

"Mac, explain it to them."

Mac picked a target on the far side of them, where the campfire smoked to life, and fired. A can exploded. All the men jerked to the feet in fear.

Danny yelled in his best Caliphate, "Drop your weapons and run."

His skills weren't so bad they didn't understand him. Rifles clattered to the ground, and they ran. Inwardly, he let out a sigh of relief. Killing locals who had no real chance didn't sit well with him. He would if he had to, but he wouldn't just for expedience. The officer tensed as his men ran away.

"Who are you?"

"Go to hell."

"You really want to die, protecting whoever sent you out here? I'm not interested in killing you. Don't make me. Last chance, who are you?"

The officer seemed to think it over. Danny knew what he had decided as he felt the man's body relax somewhat.

"Yusuf, Yusuf Omar Ali."

"Was that so hard?" Danny holstered his pistol, then reached around and deprived Yusuf of his crude pistol and knife. Once completely disarmed, Danny pushed him forward while stepping back.

As the last of the fleeing militia disappeared, the rest of the team emerged from the tall grass, pulling off their hoods as they did so. Danny removed his as well.

"There are only four of you?" Yusuf scowled, clearly angry at being tricked.

"Four is all we need. Why did you stop here?" Danny asked.

"Are you from the infidel ship, the *Interceptor*?"

"You know who we are, how?"

Yusuf hesitated, then looked to the building. "An escape pod crashed last night. My commander captured two of them, a man and woman. Subsequent questioning revealed there were two more. The man tried to escape and we killed him. The woman, on the other hand, was quite talkative, especially this morning," he said with a lecherous grin before he remembered who he was talking to. Mac's rifle butt struck the man on the shoulder blade with an audible crack of a broken bone. Yusef dropped to his knees, howling in pain.

Mac snapped his rifle back around and pressed the still warm barrel against Yusuf's forehead. "Be very careful with your next words or I will turn your head into a canoe. Is she still alive?"

Yusuf's eyes were wide with fear. It was one thing to be afraid for his life during combat, a general, constant nagging fear. Quite another to stare death in the eyes and realize he's a coward.

"Yes, yes, she is. Women are valuable for trade; we don't kill them. That's why we're here. The female said there was another woman who went in this direction. We tried to follow last night before, but the faction that controls this area attacked us in an ambush like cowardly dogs."

Mac pushed the gun harder, eliciting a whimper from Yusuf, who couldn't take his eyes off the weapon pointed at his face.

"Let me smoke him, Boss," Mac said, all the while looking directly at Yusuf.

"No. Just incap him."

Mac pulled back, shifting his rifle to his right hand while drawing his pistol.

"What, wait—" Yusuf started to say when Mac shot him in the knee. His joint exploded, shredded by the coil pistol. He sobbed and whimpered in pain.

"Better get a tourniquet on that," Mac said as he walked by.

Danny signaled for them to move out. That wasn't quite what he had in mind, but then again, Mac's sister had disappeared on a trip to Zuckabar five years earlier. He couldn't exactly hold it against him when they now knew the most likely outcome was slavery.

"Rico, T-Bar, go find those other three and either take them out or convince them to leave."

The two soldiers donned their hoods and ran off to the building.

Danny and Mac followed, staying low and moving away from the incoherent wailing of the downed officer.

"Bravo-Two-Five, this is Nomad, do you copy?"

"Go ahead, Nomad," Jennings garbled voice came back.

"We've located two of the crew and are moving in to secure them. Be advised the local militia has taken two hostages, one is possibly KIA."

"Roger that, Nomad. Two-Five out."

CHAPTER TWENTY-SEVEN

As penal colonies went, Jacob decided, this one needed some work. He and Jennings examined the image Charlie-One-One broadcasted to them. Boudreaux had the Corsair up at ten thousand meters, to avoid any possibility of her being seen or shot at. The fact that the FLIR could see as well as it did at the distance blew Jacob away.

They had an excellent fix on the camp from a top-down view. People showed up as white masses, moving around, working, and sleeping. There were dozens of buildings that could be considered part of the "fort." He suspected it was once a shopping center or school.

"We're looking at only forty-seven, sir," Jennings said.

"Roger that, Gunny. We're just slightly outnumbered."

She nodded to him as if he had told her something she didn't know.

"The way I see it, we need eyes on the package. Once we know where she is, we can move in."

Jacob's radio squawked and Nomad's voice filled his ear.

"Bravo-Two-Five, this is Nomad, do you copy?"

"Go ahead, Nomad," Jennings replied.

"We've located two of the crew and are moving in to secure them. Be advised the local militia has taken two hostages, one is possibly KIA."

"Roger that, Nomad. Two-Five out."

"We know who they are now, militia."

"That don't mean much, sir." Jennings zoomed the map out and used her finger to point a path. "Once we know the package, we can follow this route in with the 'Cat. You'll lay down suppressing fire while we extract her from whatever building she's in."

Her plan was solid, as always, the only thing worrying him was the sheer number. "That's an awful lot of weapons. They may not penetrate your armor or hurt the 'Cat, but they could always get a lucky hit."

"Always true, sir." She looked around. "Owens!" she shouted.

"Gunny?"

"Locate the missing crew member."

"Roger, Gunny." Owens went around to the back of the 'Cat and opened the hatch. He heaved out a large black case.

"What's that," Jacob asked.

"Raven drone, sir," Owens said. "Those grunts decided to play nice and let us use some of their toys. It has a simple AI that will scan faces, body type, and a host of other things, and report back to us once the target is found."

The case opened, and true to the drone's name, it did look like a raven. The remarkable bird that had somehow managed to stow away on the first colony ship to Alexandria and, despite all probability, still thrived today. In the past, people suspected that rats or mice would make it over from earth, but no, it was ravens. How, he had no idea. It was a mystery to this day if they did it on their own, or if one of the colonists had pets.

Owens set the drone on top of the Mudcat before programming in the information they needed.

"Shouldn't take long. Go find her," Owens said.

The little bird squawked, sounding just like a raven, before taking flight and heading for the camp. The case it came in converted to a viewing station, allowing them to see everything around the bird as well as hear anything it did. Of course, the drone wasn't a bird and packed more sensors than an ELS suit.

"Switch to ultrasound," Jennings ordered.

"Aye ma'am." Owens did as he was told. The view switched from a color picture to a wire frame of the camp. Fuzzy, indistinct blobs were people, but a more accurate picture of the buildings came into view.

"Watch this," Owens said gleefully. Tapping a series of keys on the console, the image reshaped, showing not only the people in the compound but the insides of the buildings as well.

"Is that accurate?" Jacob asked.

On the screen a number in the bottom right corner read 88%.

"Pretty close, sir."

The Raven drone circled the fort several times until the number rose to above ninety-five. Then it found a perch on the tallest building and went to work watching for its target.

"This might take a while," Jennings said.

Danny watched the three men run away, keeping his rifle in their vicinity in case any of them thought about returning.

"Now what?" Mac asked.

"Bust out the line, we're going up."

Rico dropped to a knee, taking his small pack off and digging out their micro-grapple gun. Bracing against his shoulder, he fired the line. It flew true, straight up and attached to the first thing it hit using nanites to bond the surface.

Danny slung his rifle, grabbed the line, and started climbing hand over hand, using his legs to propel him. Once he got to the bottom of the eighth floor, he peaked over the rim.

"Got 'em," he said to the team. "Alliance Special Forces," he said aloud as he climbed up. Two men, one clearly a local and the other was Spacer Tyree, held makeshift weapons in both hands, ready to defend themselves. Behind them he spotted Ensign Brennan and a young woman who was obviously blind, since she had a strip of cloth tied over her eyes.

"Don't hurt them," Ensign Brennan said.

Danny got to his feet, keeping his hands away from his weapons. "I'm not here to hurt anyone, just retrieve you two," he said.

A second later Mac made it up the line, his eyes flickering between the two men with weapons.

Spacer Tyree and Ensign Brennan, right?" Danny asked.

"Yes," Brennan said. "Are you really from *Interceptor?*" she asked.

"Yes, ma'am, your damn fool captain refused to leave the system without all his crew accounted for."

Brennan shook, head dropping as she came to the realization they were saved. To Danny, they looked rough. Tyree had a massive swollen bruise over one eye and his nose looked broken, and he couldn't tell where the mud stopped and Brennan started.

"Thank you, sir." Tyree slumped against the wall.

"Charlie-One-One, this is Nomad, we need evac for two missing crew at my location."

"Nomad, Charlie-One-One, ETA five mikes."

"Wait," Brennan said, wiping her eyes as she stood. "They

need to come with us. We wouldn't have made it without their help."

"That's above my paygrade, ma'am. You'll have to ask. Rico, give her comms. Mac, clear the area for me."

Boudreaux sighed in relief to hear that at least two of them were found. "Stawarski, plot me a course," she ordered.

"Aye, Chief, on it."

A second later a beacon lit for her to follow. Boudreaux gently rolled the dropship on its side, then pulled up on the stick, bringing it down and into a shallow loop before leveling out with the beacon fifty meters above the deck.

"Cooper, keep your eyes glued, the last thing we need is a surprise," she ordered.

"Yes, Chief," he yelled from below.

Stawarski tapped her shoulder and pointed at the lone tower sticking up, surrounded by much smaller ruins, burned buildings, and a veritable forest of trees.

"Roger. I'm going to do a pass, just to be—"

BANG. Something with tremendous kinetic force hit the ship, jerking it to the side. Alarms wailed and Boudreaux instantly applied power. Plasma engines whined with strain as she pulled up on the stick and roared away at three times the speed of sound.

"What the hell was that?" Stawarski asked franticly.

"Coop, you with me?" Boudreaux asked. The ship shook like she flew a roller coaster. Something was clearly wrong. The aerodynamics were off and some of her control surfaces weren't responding.

"Chief, Cooper's life signs are low, he's not dead but low."

"Roger, we're going orbital, hold on to your lunch."

If the Corsair crashed on the surface, they were done for. It was the only vehicle capable of making orbit, and if it were downed, then everyone currently on the planet would be stuck for who knew how long. Not to mention their entire mission would be scrubbed.

Boudreaux pushed the throttle all the way to the end, rocketing the ship up.

"We're losing power on the starboard engine, seventy percent... sixty five..."

"Reroute it. Helmets on and dump the can."

She hated giving that order. Cooper's helmet wouldn't be on, but if she didn't and they crashed on the planet, then it was game over for all of them.

"Aye, helmet on." Atmo hissed out of the dropship as Stawarski pulled the plug.

Boudreaux took one hand off the stick long enough to reach up and slide her faceplate down, sealing her helmet. The ship surged as the atmosphere drained, and power briefly returned to the number two engine.

"Come on, baby, just a little faster... *Tu peux le faire*," she muttered in her native tongue.

"We're not going to make it," Stawarski shouted.

The hell they weren't. She could feel the orbital pull of the planet behind them as the horizon turned white, then blue, and finally black. "Switch to gravcoil now," she ordered.

"We're too deep in the gravity well," Stawarski replied.

"PO, switch now!"

She couldn't take her hands off the controls to make the switch, not when the ship bucked and shook as much as it did.

"Five seconds—starboard wing won't retract."

"Override!" she shouted. Stawarski smashed the override button.

"Clear."

Chief Warrant Officer Boudreaux prayed for some of her captain's luck, and activated the gravcoil.

Danny watched in stunned disbelief as a boulder the size of a tank flew through the air and smashed into the right side of the Corsair. It instantly vomited debris and black smoke. He had to hand it to the pilot, she didn't hesitate, pointing the nose up and going full throttle, disappearing into the sky spewing a trail of black smoke.

"Was that your only way off?" Bijan asked.

Danny glanced at the man, annoyance flickering across his face before he locked it down.

"Charlie, this is Nomad, how copy?"

Danny snapped his fingers at Mac and pointed in the direction the boulder came from. Mac instantly went to the edge of the building and dropped to a knee, raising his rifle to look through the scope.

"Charlie, this is Nomad, how copy?" Danny repeated.

Nothing but static.

"Indigo-Actual, this is Nomad, we have a problem."

"Go ahead, Nomad," Commander Grimm said.

"Charlie's taken damage and headed for orbit. She's not responding on comms." Danny did his best to keep the anger out of his voice. He'd felt like this entire side mission to rescue his crew was a waste of time and risked the real mission. But this captain wouldn't listen to good sense, and for some reason, the Navy wouldn't let him override an idiotic officer who didn't know what was good for him. His after-action reports would reflect the captain's risky behavior in endangering the mission for a deserter.

"Do we know by what?"

"Wait one." Danny muted his mic.

"Nomad, you're not going to believe this," Mac said. "They have a damned catapult. Looks like they were rolling it this way when they saw Charlie and took a pot shot. They just got stupid lucky."

Danny muttered a string of curses under his breath. The blind woman blushed from their vulgarity, but he didn't care.

"Are you telling me a stone age weapon just took out our Corsair?"

"No," Mac said. "Looks more Roman constructed. They're using ropes for tension, so certainly not stone age."

Danny clenched his jaw and wanted to hit his number two in the back of the head.

"Funny, Mac. Funny." He returned to the radio. "Indigo actual, it looks like the locals got lucky with a *catapult* of all things."

"Nomad, you're breaking up. Say again?" Grimm sounded as disbelieving as Danny felt.

"A catapult. A stone—two-thousand-year-old rock thrower."

The line stayed open but there was no reply for several seconds.

"Roger that, the locals have access to rocks, good to know. Are you in a fortified position?"

Danny glanced around. If they took out the catapult, they could hold the building as long as their ammo held out.

"Roger, bear in mind we have two crew, plus two civilians requesting evac."

"Affirmative. If you hear from Charlie, or if the situation changes, call. Otherwise, hang tight and we'll get there when we can. Indigo-Actual out."

Despite Danny's misgivings, he had to hand it to the space-squid, the guy knew his stuff and wasn't easily rattled.

They had a problem. The catapult was easily taken out now that they knew it was here, but they wouldn't have sent it without a lot of troops as well, which meant they were here for the crew.

"Man, those guys must have broken records getting back to their camp," Rico said. He and T-Bar knelt in the center of the building's floorplan, making sure to keep their bodies in defilade from enemy ground fire. There were only a handful of interior walls, but no exterior ones. How the hell a blind girl walked around up here was beyond him. However, it was a pretty genius spot to hole up in. He could see the terrain and enemy for miles, and without a rope, only a skilled and strong climber could make it up.

He glanced at Brennan who had stopped crying and sat with her back to the interior wall. "How did you guys get up here?" he asked her.

"I'm from Cúchulainn on Glenanne, we learn to climb mountains before we can walk." She stopped, glanced around, and looked at her hands. "That and fear, it's a strong motivator," she said with her eyes downcast.

Danny glanced at Mac and used his fingers to tell him to keep an eye on things. He then went over and knelt next to Brennan.

"Listen, ma'am," he said, almost forgetting her rank for a moment; after all, she was just a kid. "You did good. From what I can tell, you're the reason you're both alive. I take it you didn't intend to desert?"

Her eyes went wide as she looked up at him. "Is that what they think?"

"We don't know what to think, only that a life pod ejected and we're here to rescue you."

"Excuse me, Sergeant?" Tyree interjected.

"Yeah?" he replied using the voice reserved for particularly annoying privates, which is what Spacers Apprentice Tyree was.

"The ensign, Sergeant, they kidnapped her. Midship Watanabe and Spacer Blachowicz forced her into the pod and then ejected it before I could stop them."

Danny noted that Spacer Tyree didn't include himself in the "kidnapping" even though he was clearly involved in the desertion.

"Well, that's good, ma'am. Regardless, though, you're safe now. Hang tight, get some water in you, and you'll be fine." Danny turned to his other men. "T-Bar, get them some rations. Rico, I want a recon of the surrounding area. Five hundred meters, set screamers at likely avenues of approach. Mac, overwatch."

"On it," they all replied in unison. T-Bar dropped to a knee, unslinging his pack to dig out food and water.

Rico went to the edge and down the rope while Mac covered him with his sniper rifle.

Once they had a picture of the area, he could form a plan. He just hoped that Corsair made it out in one piece.

CHAPTER TWENTY-EIGHT

Jennings knelt next to the screen where the drone finally identified their target. Midship Yua Watanabe. A woman, probably in her fifties, led her by a *leash* attached to a collar at her neck, to a place to relieve herself at the edge of the river that ran along the north side.

"These guys are worse than Medial," Owens muttered.

"Any sign of Blachowicz?" Commander Grimm asked.

Owens took manual control of the Raven and had it circle the camp. There were several buildings, most looking like repurposed housing from a hundred years before. From what Jennings could tell, the outer buildings were nothing more than a city wall, designed to slow the enemy down. The east side of the camp bordered a crevice and the north a river. West, which was the direction they would enter from, had a loose road and pikes with what looked like scarecrows...

They weren't scarecrows.

"June, check the back of the Mudcat. How much spare ammo do we have?" Jennings ordered.

"Yes, Gunny," the PFC said.

After she left, Grimm glanced her way with a raised eyebrow.

"Owens, check those scarecrows."

"Aye, Gunny," he said.

The raven dipped down, flying passed and Jennings realized she was right to send the PFC away. June was a good kid and a helluva Marine, but not everyone needed to see the awful things men did to men.

There were twelve pikes, loosely placed on either side of the road, six to a side. Each one impaled a man or woman, from their midsection out through their mouths. From the expression on their dead faces, Jennings had to guess they were alive when they began. They were naked, of course, since any clothing would be too valuable to lose. The freshest one, closest to the camp, held Spacer Blachowicz.

Owens swore as he realized what they were. Naki just closed his eyes and dropped his head.

"Safeties off, kill any tangos you see. Don't wait for them to shoot first," Jennings ordered.

"Aye, aye, gunny." Her Marines declared in unison.

"Let's get this done, people," Commander Grimm said. The sorrow in his voice dang near killed her. He was a man who hated to lose people, but that was part of what made him such a great captain.

"All right, Marines, who are we?"

They shouted back as one, "Killers!"

"Damn skippy. Mount up. June, drive us into the middle of that village, don't stop for anything. Pop smoke and CS as soon as we stop. Switch vision to thermal."

Back in the turret, Jacob rubbed his palms dry. He only wore his white ELS suit with red stripes, unlike the Marines who were dressed in space armor. The turret, however, was enclosed and as armored as the rest of the 'Cat. That wasn't why he sweated. Engaging in close combat was vastly different than the cold, calculated battles of space warfare. Yes, he had shot people before, several times, but this was different. Those other times he was defending himself, this time he was the aggressor.

He didn't know how he felt about that and was suddenly regretting coming along. It was important, though, for the crew to see their captain willing to sacrifice for them, even those who were trying to jump ship. He could do no less for the least of them than he did for the most of them.

Flexing his hands, he wrapped them around the butterfly trigger, testing the elevation while simultaneously swiveling the mount back and forth. There were multiple options for the ammo, he chose subsonic rounds, to keep them from over penetrating. Coil rounds would kill a man even with a non-vital shot, and he didn't need to kill anyone he absolutely didn't have to.

"Ready," he said.

"Roger that. June, hit it."

Mudcats were fusion battery–powered beasts with six wheels as tall as Jennings, each one with its own suspension. The armored vehicle had its own atmosphere and could exist in the vacuum of space (it had to since Corsairs transported them on the outside). Their angled windows and armor were resistant to AP rounds and deflected radar giving her a minimal signature. The Marine Corps versions were painted a nonreflective flat black.

The first sound the garrison heard was the crashing of a building as June powered the vehicle through a two-story house, shattering the frame. The house collapsed behind them. True to its name, the Mudcat tore through the mud, spraying it everywhere.

The drone had identified the low structure to the west of the square as where they kept their prisoners. There were more than just Watanabe, and Jacob longed to rescue them all, but he couldn't save everyone.

June slid the beast to a halt in the fresh mud. Panels opened on the roof, and a second later, the thump of compressed air sounded as chlorine sulfate grenades detonated ten meters up, followed by smoke pouring out of side panels. Anyone not in a sealed environment would choke on the gas and be blinded by the smoke.

Jennings, Naki, and Owens, leapt off the runners, weapons up. They disappeared into the building.

Jacob hated this, having no control over how the battle went or if his troops lived or died. All he could do was cover their exit.

Gunny Jennings rushed to the wooden framed door and slammed it with her foot. Wood splinters exploded in every direction. Naki lobbed a screamer into the doorway and the three Marines took cover behind the walls. A deafening, high pitch wail echoed with enough force to stun any unprotected person.

Owens went in first, his MP-17 at the ready, Naki next, and Jennings took up the rear. They cleared the room, expertly sweeping their rifles at every corner.

"Clear," Owens said.

"Go," Jennings barked.

A man stumbled out of the far door wearing a mix of fur, leather, and rags. He had a hatchet in one hand and a slug thrower in the other. Naki surged forward, butt-stroking the man in the face. His nose flattened and his right eye popped out of the socket. He stumbled back, blubbering something when Naki finished him off with two shots to the chest, and a third to the head for good measure.

The next room contained screaming prisoners, sobbing and stunned by the grenade. An old woman, the one they had seen leading Watanabe on a leash charged at them. Jennings fired, drilling her in the face, killing her instantly.

Dammit. Jennings looked around the room. There were six women, two of them were obviously pregnant. All were malnourished, beaten and abused, including Midship Watanabe.

"Charlie, clear our six. June, we're coming out."

"Roger," Owens said. He spun, heading back the way they came.

"Gunny," Naki said when they were alone.

"I know," she growled. "Get them moving. Midship first."

Jacob heard the whine of the MP-17 and prayed to God his people were okay. He focused on his own situation, though. He had figured the camp would be flooded with tangos, but so far none had appeared, that couldn't last, could it?

Glass shattered as a bottle smashed against the Mudcat, igniting the side of the armored transport in a gout of blue-and-yellow flame.

He spun the turret until he saw two men with primitive projectile weapons slung on their backs, lighting another bottle. Jacob hesitated; he knew what he had to do, but he still wished there was another way. The one holding the bottle lifted to throw. Jacob depressed the butterfly trigger, sending a four round burst that obliterated the man like he had swallowed explosives. His partner screamed as the Molotov cocktail ruptured, lighting him on fire.

"Contact left," he said into the internal mic.

June pushed her way out, lifting her MP-17 pistol, and fired at the flaming man, dropping him. She crouched at the door, scanning the area.

Owens came out of the building just then, opening the Mudcat door, then swinging around to the stern and dropping to a knee, using the armored rear of the truck as cover.

"Check front, sir," he said.

Jacob swiveled the turret to the front.

Naki came out next, a sobbing, broken Watanabe in hand as he shoved her in the Mudcat none too gently. She repeated, "I'm sorry," over and over again as Naki placed her in the seat and buckled her in.

"Sir," he said. "There's more. You're going to need to drive." Naki went to the front of the 'Cat and mimicked Owens. "Delta, we're hoofing it to Romeo-Foxtrot."

June immediately hefted a grenade from her side and hurled it at the farthest building. The thermite exploded, setting the wooden structure ablaze, adding to the enemy's confusion.

Jennings hauled two women out of the building and shoved them into the Mudcat. Then Jacob understood. Unbuckling, he dropped down, climbed over the chair, and slid into the driver's seat. It had been a minute since he took the combat driving course at the academy, but it came back to him as he buckled in and checked the Mudcat's panels.

"Power, heat, check. No threats," he muttered as he pointed his fingers at each of the readouts.

A moment later, Jennings shoved three more women in. They were practically crammed in like sardines.

"Go, sir, we'll catch up," Jennings said.

Jacob pushed the throttle all the way down, tires spinning in the mud for a heartbeat. Once they caught, the transport surged forward, almost out of his control. He fought back, pulling it into a turn. Tires spinning, he slid around the courtyard before charging out the way they came in.

"Don't take long," he said to Jennings as he passed her by. Jacob drove the 'Cat back the way they came, crashing through the same building. A man came charging out in front of him fifty meters ahead. He held a long tube over one shoulder as a second man stood behind him, trying to shove ammo in.

A rudimentary rocket, probably made from basic black powder and a hard local substance, like granite, as a warhead. The calm analytical part of him who read too many history books analyzed the device.

The space captain in him jammed the throttle down, not wanting to find out how well they mimicked the ancient Chinese weapon. Fusion power flowed to the wheels and she leaped forward hitting a hundred klicks an hour. The armored wedge at the front slammed into the man with the rocket, hurtling him away. The 'Cat's tires barely registered the other man as he ran over him.

Jacob's stomach lurched at what they forced him to do, but he didn't stop to ponder it. He regained some control as he hit the road leading through the spiked prisoners. Jacob slammed on the brakes with both feet. Giant wheels locked up and the truck slid five meters before stopping.

"What are you doing?" Watanabe screamed.

"I don't leave people behind, Midship."

Jacob opened the hatch, drawing his pistol as he did so. Jennings would rip him a new one once she found out what he did. Some things were more important than his safety. He wasn't leaving this hellhole without all his people, alive or otherwise. He didn't know Karl Blachowicz well, but regardless, the man was a member of his crew. Jacob aimed the pistol at the base of the pike and fired. The first round missed. The next three cut through the simple wooden pole with ease. Blachowicz fell into the mud and Jacob went to work removing as much of the pole as he could. He growled as it took more time than he hoped. A sharp crack filled the air and the dirt next to him exploded.

Ignoring it, Jacob grabbed the big spacer by his feet and pulled him through the mud to the rear. Repeated sharp cracks filled the air and more mud and dirt exploded around him. A single round slammed into the Mudcat, scratching the armor. Watanabe and the other women screamed.

If they were using modern rifles, he would be dead, but they sounded like black powder muskets.

The trunk opened and Jacob heaved the body up. Pain lanced through his back and he nearly collapsed. Taking a deep breath, he heaved Blachowicz up and over.

Watanabe huddled in on herself, much like the other women the Marines had rescued. They weren't fresh enough to still be in hysterics like her. One night with those maniacs had her wishing she'd never been born. Then the Marines busted in and suddenly she could be free. Now the captain had stopped the Mudcat for some reason and—

Blachowicz body tumbled into the back, his face hitting the headrest next to her, his dead eyes open, staring accusingly at her. He was dead. He was dead and it was her fault.

No, he made his choice. He didn't have to come with me.

She could lie to herself, but deep down she knew the truth. While she hadn't pulled the trigger, she had killed him. If Brennan and Tyree were dead, and how could they not be, she had killed them too.

"Bravo-Two-Five, weapons free and move out."

Naki yelped as something hit him in the back, forcing him

down on one knee in the mud. Three Marines turned as one and opened fire. A man screamed as hyper-accelerated silicate ripped him to shreds.

"I'm fine," Naki said as he regained his feet.

Trained for just such a situation, and pushed to their physical limit daily, the Marines of Bravo-Two-Five moved out, using cover and tactical awareness as they retreated.

Jennings frowned as they passed the perimeter of the camp.

"There should have been a lot more resistance," she said.

"Agreed," Naki told her. "Maybe they were out on a raid or something."

"Wherever they are," Owens chimed in, "let's just take the win and get off this crap show."

Jennings agreed wholeheartedly. She only hoped Charlie-One-One was in a position to retrieve them.

CHAPTER TWENTY-NINE

Chief Boudreaux's eyes refused to open. No, that wasn't true, she realized. She *didn't* want to open them. If she did, she would have to face the awful reality that awaited her.

"PO, you with me?" The stillness of vacuum along with the unnatural quiet suffocated her.

Stawarski coughed over the comms. "I'm with you, Chief. My chest hurts something awful."

"Check on Cooper." Boudreaux dreaded the answer, but she had to know for sure. While Stawarski unbuckled, she went about checking the status of the Corsair.

Glancing out the window, she cringed at the cloud of debris floating around them.

"Whatever hit us damaged the starboard flight controls and engine." Checking the self-diagnostics, she breathed a sigh of relief that the gravcoil ready light burned green.

"Chief... I think Coop's dead," Stawarski said.

Boudreaux silently cursed. He was a good kid.

"Seal him up, PO. If we don't get this ship fixed, we're going to be following him."

"Aye, aye, Chief."

She pulled out *The Book* and placed it on her lap as she started going through the self-check procedures. The laminated pages had short, easy instructions for finding and isolating faulty components and circuits. She bit her lip as she realized the hardest part would be finding what still worked.

"PO, when you're done down there, get on the horn and see if *Interceptor* can get us. We could do this a lot easier with help."

Carter had a much better appreciation for what the captain handled daily. Left behind to command the ship, the feeling of helplessness clutched at him. In a word, it sucked.

"Felix, anything?" he asked Spacer Gouger. Almost unconsciously, the officers mimicked the captain's mannerisms and style of command. Calling crew by their first name and remembering to thank everyone for their hard work were just a few of the things Commander Grimm did effortlessly.

"No sir. I'm on all frequencies, though. If they say anything, I'll pick it up."

"Understood. Thanks, Gouger, for putting up with my demands," Carter said with a lopsided grin.

"It's not a problem, sir."

Carter went back to staring at the plot on the captain's chair. Midway's bulk took up most of their regional space, cutting them off from seeing the exit lane or the approach vectors. The good news, of course, was the tanks were full and the fuel processed. When it came time to leave, they wouldn't have a problem fueling the gate, or their own reactor.

Sudden movement by Gouger caught Carter's attention. The spacer held one hand to his ear as if he were making sure he could hear.

"Sir, Charlie-One-One on the emergency channel. They made it to orbit, but they've lost power and need immediate pickup."

Carter didn't waste a second. "Helm, lay in that course and execute best speed."

"Aye, aye," PO Collins said. "Course received. Zero-seven-three mark zero-eight-four."

Interceptor surged forward at a fraction of her top acceleration. Orbital distances were small compared to the vast reaches of a solar system.

"Oliv, go active on all sensors."

"Aye, aye, sir, active on all sensors." Radar and lidar sprang to life, illuminating the immediate area with their powerful beams.

Carter counted in his mind, trying to focus on the time it would take to find them rather than what they might find when they did.

"Got them," Oliv said. "Ten klicks, dead ahead. I'm reading a debris field and sporadic thermal blooms."

"On screen," Carter ordered. On the nose of *Interceptor*, a powerful telescope zoomed in, transmitting the image to the main viewer.

Someone gasped, Carter didn't know who. The Corsair was lammed, one of her wings crumpled and the entire starboard side looked like it had slammed into a wall. He let out a long whistle.

"Action stations, prepare for emergency recovery," Carter ordered. The klaxon wailed instantly, alerting the crew as Hössbacher's voice sounded throughout the ship.

"Bridge, engineering. Do you want Chief Redfern outside with a Gorilla suit? I think we might have better luck repairing her in the absence of gravity," Lieutenant Kai said.

Carter thought about it for a moment. There was serious

structural damage to the Corsair. If they lashed her to the top deck of *Interceptor* between the turrets, then they could repair her easier.

"Good call, Kai. Let's use the top deck, frame thirty-five to fifty-five and lash her in place. From there you should be able to work on her with ELS and Gorilla."

"Aye, aye, sir, we'll make it happen."

"Sir, Chief Boudreaux for you," Gouger said.

Carter, not wanting anyone to overhear her in case the news was bad, tapped his ear and Gouger routed the call to him privately.

"Go ahead, Chief," Carter said.

"Sir, it's not as bad as it looks. Starboard plasma is down, and the wing is damaged too, but the gravcoil is functional."

"Good to hear. Casualties?" Carter asked with as much steel in his voice as he could.

Boudreaux let out a sigh. "Just one, sir. Spacer Cooper didn't make it. Also, sir, our people were signaling for pickup. We need to get back down there ASAP."

Carter rubbed the back of his neck, trying to ease the tension and the building headache. "Roger that, Chief. We'll have you turned around as fast as possible. Redfern is coming out in a Gorilla, he will tie you to the deck and we can get repairs started. Come in through the top hatch and get some chow before you go back out."

He could tell she wanted to argue with him, but they had been down there for six hours, and then did an emergency orbital egress. She had to be exhausted.

"Aye, aye, sir. Will do, Boudreaux out."

Carter looked up at the screen, showing the slowly tumbling, broken Corsair and the planet beyond, and suddenly realized why the captain prayed so much. When all hope was lost, and there wasn't anything he could do to impact the outcome, anything that gave him the strength to keep moving forward was welcome.

Jacob wheeled the Mudcat around the rocky terrain, avoiding a giant slate outcropping. The left front tire hit, knocking the truck up on three wheels for a second and eliciting screams from her passengers.

"Hang on," he said through gritted teeth. Forcing his leg to relax, he eased off the throttle. No one chased them, there wasn't a reason to risk crashing in order to escape. Quickly, he tapped the central navigation system and brought up rally point foxtrot. A pip appeared on the armored windshield, showing him where to navigate, two klicks to go. His suit flashed a warning at him that he ignored. He'd already had to override the pain killers once.

"Sir, I'm so sorry, sir," Watanabe said again.

"Midship, there are spare jackets in the back, can you hand them out please?" he said while trying not to lose focus on the road.

"Y—yes sir," she said.

As she climbed around in the back, the other women started to talk; he picked up a few words here and there. He'd studied the Caliphate dialect for months, ever since he'd surrendered the *Interceptor*. However, what they were speaking sounded even more broken.

"You're safe," he said in Alliance standard. "Do you understand, 'safe'?" he asked.

One of the pregnant women nodded to him, then started rapid-fire speaking to the others. Watanabe found the compartment with the shore coats and handed them out. They weren't ELS, but they would keep them warm, dry, and relatively safe.

You have arrived at your destination, the computer informed him.

"Midship, out," he ordered.

She did as he bid without complaint. Jacob slid the door up like a scissor and spun slowly in his seat to face the outside. He feared if he tried to stand, his back would give out on him.

"Why did you come after me?"

With the overly large shore jacket, and her tear-streaked face, she looked so much like a lost little girl it hurt his heart. She was filthy, covered in bruises and welts, and the broken look in her eyes spoke volumes, but she still had enough wherewithal left to realize the enormity of what she had done.

"I don't operate that way. I don't leave anyone behind. Ever. It's our duty, my duty to see everyone I ship out with, return."

Watanabe looked to the muddy ground, her bare feet squishing it back and forth.

"You don't understand, I never wanted to be in the military. My father made me and—"

As soon as she started to cry Jacob tuned her out. This was the same Watanabe, making excuses trying to shift the blame. He wished he had gotten to her sooner, had more time to shape her into the officer she could have been. It was a waste, to him, to take a cadet and throw her away.

"Are you through?" he asked when she paused. They might be real tears this time, but they were the same words as always. "Until you accept responsibility for yourself, and your actions, it won't matter where you are. In the Navy... or in prison, you won't be happy. You won't ever find something worth living for. You'll just keep living like a robot, hoping that life will happen one day and then... then you'll wake up and realize your life is almost over and it's too late."

Jacob liked to think he could get through to her, and maybe he would. Maybe now she understood something she hadn't before. How her actions have consequences, not just to her but to everyone around her.

"Sir?" She sniffled as she asked, "Am I going to prison?"

Jacob looked at her dead in the eyes. "Midship, if we get through this alive, prison will be the least of your concern. For right now, at least pretend like you're still in the Navy. Understood?"

"Y—yes sir. Understood. It's just... nothing I have ever done in my whole life, good or bad, none of it mattered. I didn't think... I didn't think this would either."

Part of him sympathized with her. There was an entire generation of kids who joined the Navy as a job or something to do, never expecting to go to war, and here they were, in a shooting war with the most powerful nation in the galaxy.

"What we do, Yua, how we behave, it matters. It always matters."

CHAPTER THIRTY

Danny wanted to mutter the most foul curse he could think of. A string of them really. One on top of another. However, the blind woman had him on his best verbal behavior. She heard everything, and the last time he'd sworn, she turned bright red and somehow that embarrassed him.

"Dammit," he whispered. "Mac, what's the situation?"

"FUBAR, boss. Nothing but FUBAR without lube," he said back over the comms.

"RTB ASAP," he ordered.

Mac had gone out on a patrol with Rico, and they encountered the same thing in both directions. A few thousand men in some kind of ragtag militia. At first, he thought the catapult was from the group they encountered trying to climb the building, but no, it would seem that Bijan picked the spot in the exact middle between two warring factions.

"T-Bar, what's that catapult doing?"

"They're still setting up," he said. T-Bar lay on his stomach on the far side of the platform, nearly invisible thanks to his blackout suit, using his combat rifle scope to keep an eye on them. He could easily take them out, but Danny wanted to hold off until they had positioned and set it up. He didn't want them realizing they had put it in plain view of modern weapons and then moving it where he couldn't just shoot the operators.

"Coming up," Mac said.

The line shook as Mac and Rico used handheld motorized ascenders to scale the building in a few seconds. Once they were back on top, Danny assigned them each a corner.

"We might have to hold up here a bit. I haven't heard back from Charlie. Are the explosives set?" Danny asked.

Mac and Rico nodded.

"It won't stop them," Mac said. "But it will surely break their hearts."

"Ten-four. Take your positions, conserve ammo, and don't open fire until we have to."

Danny took the north side, lying down in the rubble, he squirmed trying to find a comfortable position.

"Sergeant, is there anything I can do to help?" Ensign Brennan asked from behind him. He turned to look over his shoulder, admiring her courage. She was so out of her element. It would be like if asked to command a ship. He pulled his pistol, spun it around butt first.

"Leave the rope down, if anyone peeks, blow their head off."

She gulped audibly, but she took the pistol and retreated to the side with the rope.

Danny turned back to the battlefield, pulling up his hood to disappear. A second later, the first explosions of their traps echoed through the woods and fields, followed by the screams of the dying.

It's not funny, he told himself, but he still chuckled.

More explosions, more screams.

"They're slowing their advance," Mac said.

"I bet."

From his vantage he could turn in either direction and see the approaching armies. They weren't small. Thousands of men, with what looked like long-barreled iron pipes. Not accurate, he imagined, but dangerous all the same. They were a thousand meters from each other, and he was right in the middle.

"Identify the leaders and make them priority targets," he ordered.

"Boss, the catapult is winding up," T-Bar said.

"Mac, deal with it."

A second later, the subdued crack of Mac's sniper rifle echoed. Danny used his goggles to zoom in on the catapult. The rope snapped, launching the projectile when it was only halfway pulled back. One of the enemy soldiers held onto the rope pulling the cup back. He launched with it, flying a hundred meters through the air to land with a crunch on the hard ground.

"Ouch," T-Bar said.

"Do you think they'll buy it was a malfunction?" Rico asked.

A volley of loud cracks filled the air and their shelter turned into ground zero as hundreds of rounds impacted the walls and floors beneath them. Danny ducked his head instinctively. Even though they were invisible, or close to it, volley fire didn't need to aim, just shoot in the general direction.

"Return fire?" Mac asked.

"Negative. If they shoot again, yes. But I think they are guessing we're up here. Let's not prove it."

"Bubba is going to be pissed he missed this," T-Bar said.

Long seconds passed as the soldiers focused on their breathing, watching the men below scurry around.

"Damn," Mac said. "They're getting a new rope on the catapult fast."

Danny swiveled to look at the other army. He decided to

call them Red team and Blue team, just to make it easy for him to keep them straight. Red team had the catapult and seemed far more organized than Blue. However, as Blue approached, they did take advantage of cover, and while they were armed with the same long iron rifles, they also had wide, wooden or bamboo tubes on the backs of one out of ten soldiers.

"Rico, what do you make of that," he said, highlighting one of the tubes. The goggles they wore shared information, and as Danny highlighted something, everyone on the team could see it.

"Uh, if I had to guess, some kind of rocket or large projectile. Given the length of the tube, I'd say they could do some serious damage."

As they watched, the lead element of Blue team activated a trap. Three metal canisters leapt five meters into the air, turned to face the army, and exploded. Hundreds of five-millimeter ball bearings shot out, shredding the leading edge and downing at least twenty men.

"Ha," Rico said. "They walked right down the most obvious lane."

At this point, both Red and Blue had to know there were other players on the field. What he wouldn't give for air support.

"With all due respect, what the hell, sir?" Jennings fumed back and forth. Owens had Commander Grimm leaning over the hood of the Mudcat as he examined the injury. ELS nanites had extracted the massive round, but there was still a gaping hole in Jacob's lower back, and enough blood loss that the commander felt it.

"We don't leave people behind, *Allison,* even ones who jumped ship," he said.

"Fragging hell, sir. You could have radioed me, and I would have grabbed the body. When I tell you to stay in the car, you stay in the car. Damn fool officer, you act like a private."

June glanced up, frowning.

"Point taken, Gunny," Grimm said.

"I refilled your nanites, sir. They should be able to stop the rest of the bleeding and close the skin, but not enough to fully repair it. We'll have to get you to sickbay for that."

"Understood, can I get dressed now?" In order for Owens to examine the wound, Jacob had pulled the suit down to his waist. He was by no means shy, but he also wasn't a fan of standing around half naked in a combat zone.

"Go ahead, just try not to swivel your back for a bit. If you hadn't worn your ELS, we wouldn't be having this conversation and you would be dead."

Jacob grunted as he gingerly pulled the rubberlike suit up and over his shoulders.

"What about them, sir? You planning on taking them back to the ship?" Jennings asked, pointing at the women huddled next to the 'Cat while they greedily ate emergency rations. Jacob didn't want to think about how hungry they must be the way they were devouring the E-rats.

"I don't see that I have much choice."

"Sir, we can't save this entire planet. There have to be thousands of people in need of our help. We have to stay on mission," Jennings said.

"Gunny, I'm no idealistic fool. I know that. There is a difference, though, between staving off help and ignoring those in front of us. There may come a time when we have to turn our backs on those in need, but that isn't today."

"Aye sir," she said, shoulders slumping in defeat.

Jacob finished sealing up his suit and activated his comms. "Nomad, this is Indigo-Actual, how copy?"

"Indigo, a little busy. I don't suppose"—there was a pause as a machine gun rattled away in the background, followed by the crack of high-powered rifles— "there's air support coming our way?"

"Negative, Nomad, none that I know of. We'll head to your location and provide mobile fire support."

Nomad's radio activated but a deafening boom filled the comms and Jacob's earpiece had to cut off to avoid damaging his hearing. After a few seconds it returned to normal.

"Be advised, Indigo, bad guys have rudimentary rockets. They pack a helluva punch."

"Roger, Nomad, hang tight, we're on our way." Jacob twirled his finger in the air. "Mount up," he said. With the rescued women packed into the back, along with Watanabe, the 'Cat was packed and only two Marines could fit. June drove and Owens rode shotgun while Jennings and Naki secured themselves to the running boards. Their armor magnetized to the 'Cat, so they could point out and shoot with both hands.

In the turret, Jacob closed his eyes and took a deep breath. This wasn't the kind of combat he trained for, but he was ready.

"I've got a thousand rounds on the turret, Gunny," he said.

"Short, controlled bursts, sir. Aim for maximum damage."

"Aye, aye, Gunny," he said with forced calm.

"You're one lucky flyer, Chief," Redfern said as he placed the last hull strip and ran the molecular bonder built into the Gorilla suit's hand.

"Oui, that's what they say. I don't think Coop would agree with you."

Boudreaux kicked herself the moment she said it. Losing people was part of the job, it didn't mean she had to like it. Baxter, Kennedy, now Cooper. Why did they die and she live? Sure, she had suffered. Only one of her legs was the one she was born with. She'd spent months recovering after Wonderland, but she was alive.

"That's just the way it is sometimes, Chief. When it's your time, it's your time, doesn't matter how fast you're running."

She nodded in understanding. Turning, she took in the starscape around her. The Corsair's landing gear held her tight against the top deck of *Interceptor* while Chief Redfern completed her repairs. She stood by, in case he needed help. Standing on the top deck like it was a ship at sea, she could almost imagine what it must have felt like to her ancestors, sailing the high seas. With nothing but their wits and reflexes.

"That's the last piece." Redfern stepped back, admiring his handiwork.

"Thanks, Redfern. You do good work." She clapped him on his oversized metal shoulders. "Stawarski, let's go. Move it or lose it. We have a package to pick up."

CHAPTER THIRTY-ONE

More Red team members fell as they charged through the bush trying to get to the tower. Danny picked them off one after another. They were so thick, he could almost shoot without aiming.

"Okay, what the hell," Danny muttered. "Brennan, what did you and Tyree do to piss these guys off?" he asked.

Rico's light machine gun chattered a long stream of bullets tearing up a line of Blue team.

"I have no idea, Sergeant. I don't even know how they know we're here, let alone why they would want us so bad."

Danny kept a rough count in his head; all in all, they had killed at least a hundred at this point. Something was going on, something that wasn't about the Navy pukes who crashed. He glanced back at the two natives, who were being suspiciously quiet. Bijan held Sarina close, keeping her protected with his body. Danny respected the man for that, but it also didn't mean he was being honest.

"Bijan, do you know what has these guys riled up like murder hornets?"

The man only shook his head in response. Why didn't he speak?

"Tell him," Sarina said. She "looked" at her man in a way, cocking her head to the side and turning her face to him. Bijan let out a sigh.

"What if they hand us over?" Bijan asked.

"Would you rather die a liar?" she countered.

Bijan jolted at her tough remark. Danny grinned at the woman's sharp tongue. In his mind, she was the whole package. Pretty, tough, and quick witted.

"You're right, of course." Bijan turned to Danny. The Special Forces trooper expected the man to come clean. After all, if they weren't after the space-squids, then they were after Bijan.

"This is Sarina Bint Hamid, the Caliph's only daughter. She was born blind and cannot take regen or cybernetics. She is my charge, and I will die defending her if required."

Danny's mouth hung open. As he was about to respond, a massive boom shook the building, sending dust and debris flying.

"Uh, boss," Mac said. "The building is moving."

Danny activated his comms. "Indigo-Actual, Nomad. We have a priority VIP for evac. I say again—priority VIP for evac." Without waiting for a response, he turned and shouldered his rifle, firing at full auto. "Weapons free, light these bastards up."

Jacob replied to the message, but there was nothing more forthcoming. The gunfire and explosions were loud enough he could hear them even though they were still a klick out.

"PFC, can you make this thing go any faster?" he asked.

"Aye, aye, sir," June replied. The engine whined as the

vehicle shot up to higher speeds. Small bumps became harsh jostles as the team were thrown against their harnesses.

"Well get on it, PFC," Owens shouted. The grin in his voice was unmistakable. Jacob marveled at the Marine's ability to stay positive even as they were chasing death headlong.

"Who are we, Marines?" Gunny asked.

"Killers," they shouted back.

June steered the Mudcat into a thicket and blasted right through it, revealing dozens of men with crude weapons and armor guarding a... catapult.

"Fire!" Jennings shouted. Both her and Naki opened up with their rifles, ripping flesh apart with sprays of hyper-accelerated silicate. Owens stuck his rifle out the partially rolled down window, firing at full auto.

Shocked by the sudden appearance of the armored beast, the men they ambushed were too stunned to react. Dozens fell as they were torn to pieces. Jacob swiveled the turret and pointed the reticle at the catapult and depressed the butterfly trigger. Ten millimeters of destruction spat out as the turret vomited flame. Not from a chemical reaction but as the nano-steel-wrapped tungsten projectiles ignited the air.

His aim was true.

The catapult exploded into shards of death as the rounds shredded wood, rope, and the men working on it.

"Good hit, sir," Owens said.

The Mudcat hit bounced hard and Jacob realized they hit a man as the body flew over the turret.

"Keep, going," Jennings said. A loud whoomph of air exploded behind them as one of the primitive rockets came close to hitting them.

"Go left—LEFT," Naki shouted. June started to go right, then violently turned the wheels. The Mudcat skittered into a turn, slamming into two men who were trying to set up another rocket.

"Good driving," Gunny Jennings said.

Jacob barely had time to find another target before they had moved on, leaving the burning catapult and the dead behind. His mind replayed the battle and he realized how little he had done with the turret, while the Marines with their rifles had accomplished so much more. The chaos of space battles was one thing, even the hectic nature of close combat, but the sheer bedlam of those thirty seconds left him breathing hard and full of adrenaline.

Danny heaved his last grenade off the roof. Death rolled out from where it exploded, killing a half dozen men who were trying to attach ropes to help pull down their already precarious structure.

"I'm running low, boss," Rico said.

"Grenades," he ordered. His three men pulled the last of their grenades and threw as hard as they could. Explosions ripped around the base of the tower, leveling men like tall grass in a strong wind.

"Indigo-Actual, if you're close, we could use some backup."

"Out," Mac said as he slid his rifle around to his back and pulled his coil pistol. Using both hands, he aimed carefully and started picking off Red team members who ventured too close.

"Nomad, Indigo-Actual. Look to your east."

Sure enough, a second later the Mudcat came flying over a small hill, weaving its way through trees and gullies. The turret lit up, firing short bursts into Blue team. Two Marines hung from the side, firing their rifles while another sprayed automatic fire from the passenger window.

"That's good to see, Actual, but that's the weak side."

A hail of bullets hit the roof top, pinging around in ricochets. One hit Mac in the side, dropping him like a stone.

"Mac," Rico yelled. He slung his machine gun and crawled over to the second-in-command.

Danny didn't have time to worry about his friend, they had bigger problems. The building was seconds away from collapsing.

"Actual, north side. Now. Cover our descent." Danny pointed at the rope. "Bijan, go."

The man hesitated. "I cannot leave her."

"I've got the princess. You go on the rope or at the end of my foot."

Bijan ran for the rope, grabbing it and leaping over with practiced ease.

"T-Bar, go."

The trooper didn't hesitate; he followed Bijan down.

More auto fire from the Mudcat's turret filled the air and militia died by the dozens.

With Rico's help, Mac got to his feet and limped over to the rope.

"Go," Danny ordered. Both men went down, one after another.

"Why am I last?" Sarina asked over the tumult.

"I want boots on the ground covering you, princess. You're the most important person on this mudball. Brennan, Tyree, go."

Tyree went first, followed by Brennan who wisely kept her pistol hand free as she descended.

"Nomad, this is Actual, I see your descent, almost—"

A massive explosion lit up the air. Not anything like he had heard before. Danny ran to the edge, diving to the floor, keeping himself low. The Mudcat tumbled through the air, its back half on fire and landing with a crunch of broken metal. Two hundred meters away, he spied what did it. A modern shoulder mounted plasma launcher. Danny knew instantly their mistake. They had gotten complacent with the low-tech, it didn't occur to them someone could have smuggled a more hi-tech weapon on the planet.

Jennings hit the ground with a grunt, rolling multiple times as the flaming Mudcat flew overhead. She came up on her knee, facing back the way they'd come and spotted the tango immediately. Two hundred meters and change to the south, a man with a shoulder-fired plasma launcher lowered the weapon he'd just used. Without hesitating she raised her rifle, aimed and fired. The plasma launcher jerked out of the man's hands. Her second shot split his skull.

"Bravo-Two-Five, sitrep?" she said over the team freq.

"Bravo, good." Though Naki sounded shaky, she could see him standing.

"Charlie, good." Owen climbed out of the overturned Mudcat, holding his weapon in one hand.

"Delta good," June said as she pulled herself out of the window. "For the record, I would like to request no more crashes on this mission."

"Skipper, you with me?" she asked.

"Still here, Gunny. Upside down, but here."

"Contact front," Naki yelled. His rifle whined as he fired, moving toward the Mudcat for cover. Massive slugs the size of her thumb struck the ground kicking up mud and dirt.

"What the hell are they firing?" Owens asked as he returned fire.

"Fifty-caliber ball rounds, if I'm right. Unrifled, not accurate but they pack a mean punch," Grimm said.

Jennings fell back toward the Mudcat, shooting any targets that presented. Without the turret on the vehicle, they were in trouble. Their ammo, while plentiful, wouldn't last forever.

"Skipper, stay in the 'Cat. It's still armored. How are the passengers?"

"Shaken but unhurt."

Two more targets appeared. She dropped one, but the other fired, smacking her right in the helmet. To her amazement, the ball round skipped off the slanted helmet without jarring her. The shot she fired was far more effective, blowing his head to pieces.

"Nomad, Mudcat is down. Where are you?" she asked.

"On your six," came the reply. She looked toward the tower, and his men congregated at the bottom along with the two missing Navy types. They charged across twenty meters of open field to huddle behind the armored remains of the truck. There just wasn't anywhere for them to go, certainly not on foot.

"Star formation, shoot as they present," she ordered.

Boudreaux guided the Corsair down through the atmosphere, heat bleeding off the ship as she pulled back on the stick. The ride shook and jostled, randomly slamming her against the harness.

"This the best they could do?" PO Stawarski asked.

"Let's be thankful they could repair her at all," Boudreaux replied. The stick jerked and wobbled, and there certainly was a looseness about her. As if her motions weren't precisely translated to the flight control surfaces.

She wiggled her feet, cajoling the rudder to run the spacecraft in a straight line.

"Coming up on the beacon," Stawarski said.

"Indigo-Actual, this is Charlie-One-One, how copy?"

Static filled the line. Her brow creased as she repeated her query.

"Charlie-One-One, good to hear your voice. Danger close, my position."

"Say again, sir? Danger close?"

"Yes. Danger close, we're being overrun."

Boudreaux flipped the switch on her stick, deploying the ten-millimeter chain coilgun on the nose followed by dropping her visor to activate the forward looking infrared.

"Combat mode, PO," she ordered. Her hand slammed the throttle forward and the plasma engines screamed in response. The airframe shook as they broke the sound barrier. Boudreaux aimed the ship right for the ground.

"Uh, Chief, the ground is coming up awful fast."

Boudreaux pulled up, feeling the craft lag through the air even as she fought to change direction. She timed it perfectly, Corsair skimming the treetops.

"Take the gun, PO," she said. With the way the ship waddled, she couldn't fly and fire. "Weapons free. And PO?"

"Yes, Chief?"

"Don't hit the captain."

"Dammit sir, I said stay in the 'Cat!" Jennings yelled at him as Jacob climbed out.

"It's not exactly safe in there, either. I've got a gun and I know how to use it," he said waving his rifle for emphasis. He ushered the rescued women out to the center of the crater.

The spec forces had deployed around the crater the tumbling Mudcat had made as it came to rest. The civilians and Midship Watanabe huddled together in the center of the crater while the combat forces used the small depression as cover to return fire. They were running low on ammo and time.

"Contact left," Owens yelled. Musket fire peppered the ground, sending chunks of dirt flying.

Jacob couldn't see beyond the rim of the crater, but he could still attack without exposing himself. He pulled his only grenade. "Proximity detonation, concussive," he said as he chucked it as hard as he could. Three seconds later the ground shook and debris and men vomited into the air. Much closer than he expected.

"They're crawling up," Jennings yelled. "Fix bayonets!" The ancient battle cry wasn't one she'd thought she would ever use. In five seconds flat, the four Marines had their knives attached to their rifle barrels.

Just then, six men popped up over the small crest, muskets out and firing. The Marines fired at the same time, ripping them to shreds in a spray of arterial blood.

They weren't fast enough. One of the rescued women screamed as she went down in a heap, a hole blown through her chest.

Several more rushed over the artificial ridge and they were suddenly in it, fighting hand to hand. Jacob switched his carbine to pistol and fired as fast as he could. Desperate to avoid CQB.

Jennings charged the closest man, slipping inside his range before he could fire his musket. She jammed her rifle in his gut, sinking the nano-steel combat knife twenty-centimeters into his flesh, before she yanked it out and fired at point blank range.

Naki downed one with a sharp crack of his rifle-butt against an unprotected skull. The man crumpled, and Naki fired three rounds into his head.

Plasma turbines roared overhead, followed by the whine of coilgun fire. The Corsair stitched a line of death in her wake. Nothing stopped the 10mm rounds hitting the ground like small grenades. Men shrieked as they exploded and were dismembered from the weapon.

Jacob ducked as the Corsair flashed overhead. He raised his head once the dirt stopped falling only to see a man climbing over the remains of the Mudcat to get to the girls. He fired from two meters away, hitting his arm. The man screamed. Jacob took a step closer and shot again, this time killing the man.

Despite the chaos and death, he swore he was going to spend more time at the range.

"Indigo-Actual, Charlie-One-One, doing another pass, then I'll drop in for a pickup."

"Roger, Charlie," Jacob said. He fired again, making sure the man stayed down.

Naki batted aside a musket being used as a club, He stabbed the man in the throat before pulling the trigger and spraying those behind him with his brain.

Owens switched his MP-17 to pistol, and somewhere had picked up a coil pistol and fired with both weapons, drilling anyone stupid enough to get close to him.

While Jennings and Naki fought with knives, PFC June reached behind her and pulled a lethal nano-steel tomahawk from her back. She hollered as the militia flooded over the ridge. She threw her tomahawk hitting the first man in the heart, and she came in right behind it, pulling her ancestral weapon from his chest before he finished falling. Her MP-17 held in her off hand as a pistol, barked over and over, punctuating each chop of her tomahawk.

The Corsair's plasma engines roared again as she came for

another pass. Dirt, mud, and blood kicked up as hundreds of ten-millimeter rounds spat out of the rotating nose gun. Death's shadow passed overhead and both militias fell to its icy embrace.

Then it was over.

Jacob fell against the Mudcat, panting for breath, surrounded by the dead and dying.

CHAPTER THIRTY-TWO

Nadia kept her head down as she scrubbed the floor. They didn't even look twice at her anymore. Not only had it become clear she was off limits to the men, but she had also managed to virtually disappear among the framework of the base. They saw her, they even acknowledged her presence, but her disguise and ability to blend in was so perfect, they forgot about her the second she was out of sight.

Her entire time on the base she'd spent listening, watching, waiting for the right move. All the while keeping track of the dates. The window was approaching rapidly. When the time came, she would be ready. All she had to do was circumvent security and nab the doctor.

It had taken her time, but she identified the location of the three things she needed to succeed. Malik's assistant had the key card to the secondary armory and storage, where she could find the gear, she needed. It was a matter of stealing it from him without his awareness and then returning it before he noticed anything wrong.

Which was why she was scrubbing down the walls outside Zaid's quarters, waiting for him to fall asleep.

"You there, what are you doing?" Malik asked her.

She silently swore. He was supposed to be surveying the kitchen staff, which he almost always did after dinner.

"Cleaning, sir."

"Who told you to clean here?" he demanded. His tone wasn't quite confrontational, just short of angry.

"No one, sir," she said speaking the truth. "I was walking by on my way to Dr. Abbasi's to pick up her laundry for the next day when I noticed a smudge on the wall here." She turned and pointed at the spot she scrubbed. All of what she said was true, and if he looked up footage of the evening, he would see her stop and notice a smudge on the wall.

He raised an eyebrow. "It's too bad our janitorial staff do not have the pride you do in your work. Carry on."

She bowed, keeping her head low until he walked by. She didn't dare breathe a sigh of relief. If he went back far enough on the feed, he would see her put the smudge on the wall to have the excuse to be there. She had set up the smudge as a "just-in-case" excuse, and she was glad for it. Malik was no fool.

It had taken her precious time to steal the right ingredients to make a sedative syrup she could then add to his nightly tea. The base cook hadn't wanted to order them at all, but she convinced him he could make delicious lemon-flavored tea with a mixture of lemon balm, passionflower, and valerian root. In low doses it relaxed and calmed the drinker. In a refined syrup concentrate, like what she'd slipped Zaid earlier, it resulted in a deep sleep.

Once the sound of Malik's boots faded, she moved over to the door and punched in the code she had seen him use a dozen times. The door slid open, and the soft snores of the sleeping officer greeted her. Quick, to minimize exposure, she dashed to the bed. He'd fallen asleep shortly after disrobing and his pants hung over a chair next to him.

She felt around them, finding his security ID and SecPad. It was locked of course. Holding the SecPad steady, she placed his hand on the screen, unlocking it. So far so good. As she took a step to the door, he snorted, as if waking. Nadia froze. If she had to kill him her plans would be out the window and she would have to go to her backup.

That plan required her to kill a lot of people.

He didn't awaken. She crept out of the room, turned, and glided down the hall toward storage. The primary security room and armory were always guarded. Malik had them staffed twenty-four seven. The officer was too good in her mind. While he happened to be right, he had no way of knowing she was there. Running men ragged with generally unnecessary duty was a quick way for morale to nose-dive. As it was on the base. The only reason they did as well as they did was Malik's relentlessness in his obsession with duty.

Nadia walked by the security checkpoint, hands clasped in front of her and head down. They dismissed her without a glance, the two uniformed guards spoke in hushed whispers about the latest news on the war.

From what she had gathered by listening to the men, the war wasn't going as well as they hoped. The ISB had their *official* reports, but the truth was known. She smiled inwardly as she heard the loss of Medial and an entire battle squadron.

Good.

Medial was a slave pit. Once past them and around the corner, she stopped with her side pressed against the maintenance door. Counting, waiting for the motion-sensitive cameras to shut off. Once she was reasonably sure they had, she took out Zaid's SecPad and used it to loop the cameras and motion sensors, making her effectively invisible. If the breach was realized by Malik, he would hold his second responsible, not her.

Inside were the usual supplies required for cleaning and general maintenance along with the emergency access to the base subfloors. Something not even the janitors knew about. Thanks to the schematics she'd paid handsomely for, she did. The access hatch presented another problem, though. Once the builders completed the base, they sealed the hatch. It would take a plasma cutter to rip through it, or—

Using her cybernetic hand, she grabbed the latch and squeezed. Metal fingers that looked and felt like flesh, creased the hatch, digging in. Nadia braced her body with her other hand flat against the concrete floor. If she pulled wrong, she wouldn't open the hatch, but rip her own arm off. Not something she wanted to do.

Exhaling, she slowly pulled on the hatch, increasing force with every second. Her fingers slipped and she flew backward into the wall with a thud. Shaking her head, she knelt and tried again, making sure her fingers were secure.

The hatch squealed and relented with a bang as she ripped it off the hinges. She froze, holding the hatch over head like a weapon, waiting for the guards to rush into the room. Seconds ticked by and no one came.

Gripping the sides of the frame, she lowered herself down into the subflooring and pulled the hatch back over as she descended. She'd picked the time most of the workers were off duty or asleep. No one would be coming into the room to get supplies unless Nadia was extraordinarily unlucky. She hated relying on luck, but she would be a liar if she said she never had to.

It was a tight fit, the passage wasn't meant for people after the base construction finished. She squirmed her way through, working hard for every inch of progress. Slow progress, slower than she could afford. In her mind, the timer counted down until the tincture reliability wore off and Zaid awoke.

After crawling through dust and left over construction debris, she found the hatch she wanted, nestled in the ceiling over the door leading to the secondary armory. While the base's security was tight, tighter than some military installations she had infiltrated, it had one flaw. The same flaw every security system had. Any system could be impossible to breach, but the harder it was to breach security, the harder it was for *anyone* to access it. If people had to come and go, then she could beat the security. In this case, it was a secondary armory that needed to be accessed daily. In the result of an emergency, it had to be accessed quickly. Therefore, she could circumvent the security and sneak in.

Taking out Zaid's pad, she input his codes. Sure enough, she was able to run everything on a one-minute loop, just like she had in the hall.

The hatch opened upward and she pulled it in, hiding it in the access way. Dipping her head down, she made sure the coast was clear before unspooling like a rope and dropping to the floor. She pulled the card and held it to the reader while activating the pad. Security scanned the card and the pad, and then the door opened.

"So far so good," she whispered.

Inside was everything she would need to infiltrate the security center and prepare for her exfiltration. She checked the SecPad and set a timer. Five minutes to grab what she needed and get out.

CHAPTER THIRTY-THREE

Interceptor approached Midway's exit lane at only a few hundred KPS. Radar and lidar beams scanned the black, looking for the hidden Guild platform. The other three they had used, including Wonderland, were easy to find. They had beacons that showed their location.

According to the Guild DB they had stolen, this one was hidden. It required a challenge for the beacon to activate, a challenge they didn't have. They weren't stealth platforms, though, just small with a tiny cross section.

"Anything?" Jacob asked.

Tefiti glanced at him for a moment, holding his gaze.

Jacob shook his head. He'd gotten into the bad habit of asking for updates when he knew his crew would provide them the moment they had something.

His head was still out of the game from Midway. All in all, they had rescued three of the missing crew, and while Brennan insisted that she and Tyree weren't involved in the desertion, Watanabe said nothing at all. Tyree's own movements and access showed him as helping Watanabe, but as long as Brennan vouched for him, he would remain out of trouble.

Brennan's story made sense. She and Tyree stumbled upon Watanabe and Spacer Blachowicz accessing a life pod. They were forced into the pod and then, as soon as they crashed on Midway, abandoned.

It was fortuitus that they found Bijan and Sarina. Jacob had no way to verify her identity, but the fact that there were two armies trying to kill each other to capture her, lent credibility to her story. He'd checked the official information, Caliph Hamid had a daughter named Sarina, but it was hardly secret information. What the public information didn't have was what happened to her.

Having her aboard left him with a decision. It wasn't really a tough decision, he would charlie-mike no matter what. However, if he returned home and her identity turned out to be true, then he would have to answer why he didn't immediately turn around and RTB.

The answer was simple: he wasn't about to abandon Nadia. No matter how much help the daughter of Hamid might provide, if any at all, he wasn't about to miss the chance to cripple their FTLC systems or leave Nadia behind. He wouldn't do it, not for anything. There was a bond, legal and otherwise between an officer and his subordinates. Who was he if he left his people to die, if he left Nadia to die? She was counting on him, even if she didn't know it was *Interceptor* that was on the way to pull her out.

No. As sure as a black hole pulled in light, he would never, not ever, abandon his duty to the people who served under him and the people who counted on him. He had faith that if anything happened to him, Carter and the rest of the crew would carry on with his wishes. Charlie-Mike. Continue mission. No matter the cost.

"Found it," Tefiti said. "Two-three-three mark zero-one eight. Approximately eighteen hundred klicks."

"Well done, PO," Jacob said. "Helm, set a course."

"Aye, aye, sir," PO Collins said.

Jennings held the crow pose, even as her arms started to shake. Despite having returned from combat less than a day earlier, she was back in the gym, working herself into a sweat. The fighting on the planet had drained her; there was only so much death and destruction a person could see before they needed to clear their mind. She'd been a part of some brutal actions in her time as a Marine. Midway easily topped that list.

"All hands, we're docking with the Guild platform in five mikes. Engineering, prepare the fuel hose."

The message repeated as she held her pose. There wasn't anything for her to do during a docking maneuver, which was why she spent her off time in the gym.

Metal slid and whooshed as the hatch opened, and in came Master Sergeant Danny Cannon.

She'd dreaded this moment. He was alone. A spark of something unfamiliar ignited in her gut. An emotion she hadn't felt before. Dismissing it, she unfolded from her yoga pose and stood up.

"Leaving already?" he asked. His workout clothes fit loosely around him. An old tank top he'd obviously worked out many times in, allowed her to see the scars on his chest, ribs, and arms.

"You should try dodging," she said with a gesture toward one large scar on his rib cage. He looked down, touching the scar as he grinned.

"Couldn't. We were extracting the Alliance Ambassador from *Malia* in the former Terran Republic. It was take the hit or let the ambassador die." He shrugged. "Sometimes you can't avoid the hit."

Jennings certainly understood that. She decided that the feeling in her stomach had nothing to do with the much older operator. After all, he was almost forty, in a different branch, certainly not a Marine. She couldn't have feelings for him. Not after this short a time.

Grabbing her towel off the mat, she headed for the locker room.

"Stay, Jennings. That's your preferred address, right? Jennings or Gunny? Certainly not Allison."

She turned to look at him, suppressing the butterflies, keeping her face neutral.

"Only the captain calls me Allison." She had spent the first two years annoyed at the captain for using her first name. Suddenly, it sounded wrong out of anyone else's mouth.

Confusion crossed his face for a moment before vanishing. "You don't belong here, you know that right?"

"I belong wherever he is."

Danny took a step toward her, not unlike how a person would approach a wild animal they were afraid of spooking or being bitten by.

"What is it with your captain?" he asked.

She didn't like the way he said "captain."

"If you have to ask," she said, "then you won't know."

That answer didn't satisfy him. He took another step forward. Allison found herself having to look up at him. She frowned, taking a step back, as if he were advancing in a fight.

"I thought Marines never retreated?" he asked with a wry grin.

Retreated? She wasn't retreating, just giving herself some room to maneuver. *It's not a fight, Jennings. You don't have to move,* she told herself.

He moved again and she found herself bumping into the bulkhead, hands down at her side feeling the metal frame of the ship.

"I'll say this for him, he handles himself in a fight pretty good for a space-squid," Danny said as he took one more step forward.

She had no place to fall back. The cold metal bulkhead pressed against her from behind. The only way out was the women's locker room to the side and... suddenly he was there in front of her. She had to crane her neck to look up at him. He wasn't as tall as the captain, of course, few men were. But she wasn't tall at all. In fact, they fudged her height on her official record so she could join the Marines since she was one centimeter shy of the minimum. Whereas Danny's average height still had her face-to-chest with him.

Why was she shaking? She could kick his butt up and down the gym if she wanted.

He leaned forward, putting a hand over her shoulder against the bulkhead. She raised her hands to push him away, but he easily engulfed them and raised them above her head, pinning them to the bulkhead with one hand.

"The captain's good people," she whispered.

"I'm sure he is." He smelled of firearms and sweat mixed with a minty breath. *He'd brushed his teeth,* a distant part of her mind noted. *Why would he brush his teeth?*

"What are you doing?" she asked, finding it hard to speak as her breathing became panicked.

"Don't they teach Marines how to have fun?" he asked. He leaned down, mere centimeters from her face. His other hand gliding down the outside of her arm, past the hollow of her chest to her waist. Her stomach burned with unfamiliar feelings.

Jennings bit her lip. Terror, possibly for the first time in her whole life, froze her to the deck.

"Fun?" she whispered.

Danny engulfed her lips with his own. Panic was replaced by elation. Her whole body tingled. He pushed against her, trapping her body with his own against the bulkhead, and she found herself responding as he pressed against her.

CHAPTER THIRTY-FOUR

Malik scowled at his men. With the exception of the six security men he needed on duty, the rest stood at attention in front of him. Zaid at their head, eyes forward, knees locked straight, and hands at their sides. Each one immaculately groomed with perfect creases in their uniforms. Well-polished sidearms placed in gleaming black holsters adorned their sides.

"One of you is a thief. A liar. A traitor," he said as he stood in front of them.

"If that person doesn't step forward immediately. I will have the lot of you shot." Ripples of fear rolled through the assembled men.

"Quiet," Zaid barked.

"I know who the traitor is," Malik continued. Which was true. He had the logs left behind by the man's own SecPad. What he couldn't figure out was why? What possible motive could he have to steal what he did? It wasn't like there was a black market he could sell to. The outgoing freighters were searched, scanned, and checked multiple times on arrival and departure. This was the Caliphates most secure facility. Not even a whisper of what they did could leak.

Which was the whole reason he was there. Before he'd taken over, there were leaks. Information slipped. He'd put a stop to that shortly after taking charge from the previous security chief, whose failure had earned him a long walk on the surface of the planet.

"I will say this one more time. Step forward and only you will be punished. If not, I shall shoot every man involved, and perhaps a few who were not."

Nothing.

Ultimately, he didn't need to know why Zaid had betrayed him. Just that he did. In one swift move, Malik pulled his electrostatic-charged plasma pistol and fired. A green beam of superheated, directed gas flowed along an electrical charge and struck Zaid in the head. The sudden, massive temperature spike burned away his scalp and hair, causing the grey matter within to instantly boil and explode his skull like a ripe melon, showering the men behind him.

He hadn't even time to scream, simply falling dead with a meaty thud.

"If I find any of you were working with him, you shall wish I had only shot you." He stared them all down, daring any of them to flinch or betray a hint of fear. When they didn't, he turned on his heel. "Dismissed. Throw out the refuse."

Two men grabbed the burned, messy corpse and dragged it out, leaving a trail of blood behind.

"Disgusting," he muttered. Activating his SecPad, he called the janitorial staff down to clean it up.

He had to admit, he was shocked at Zaid's betrayal. Even more shocked that he didn't try to make some excuse or plead for his life. Malik replayed the last few minutes in his mind. Not a single trace of fear or apprehension showed on him.

Yet Malik knew no mistake had been made. The logs were clear. Zaid had used his SecPad, a foolish move on his part, to infiltrate the secondary storage and steal basic supplies. Thermal clothing, a hundred meters of rope, miscellaneous electronics, and one hold-out ECP pistol. Enough to kill an unarmored man, but hardly a threat.

Why? Why risk his life for a handful of supplies that had no obvious use? Unless he was forced to. Suddenly Malik regretted killing the man. He thought since they lived inside a sealed base with no way on or off the planet, then he was safe in summarily executing him. Only after did it occur to him that there may have been extenuating circumstances. He could have lied to Zaid, promised him life in exchange for who he worked with. He would have to look into the matter further to find the truth. Find it, he would though. He just needed a little help. Smiling as he made his way to the comm center, Malik decided they needed some military assistance. Surely there was something that could be sent his way. It might take a week, but with the FLTC, they certainly could be headed their way immediately.

Doctor Yusra Abbasi watched in shock as two of Malik's men dragged the horrifically gory body out of the base and tossed him onto the rocks under the too-hot sun.

What did the fool from ISB think would happen? There was no wildlife to deal with the body, it would remain until it rotted away on its own... *Oh,* she realized. *That* was the point. Leaving him as an example.

She had to get off the planet. Not in six months, not in six days, she needed to be gone tomorrow. But there was no way. No ships would arrive for another month.

The guards finished their tasks, their faces none too excited to be doing it, either. They had to know it could have just as easily been them. Yet, she had no allies here. If she tried to recruit one of them, then they would just betray her and that would be that. Not only would she be dead, but the secret of her dad's amazing technology would be lost forever.

She couldn't allow his genius to go unknown forever. She activated her stealth systems, shielding her from the security cameras. Under her desk she depressed a hidden button, and a drawer slid out, revealing her only weapon. A vibro-blade as long as her middle finger. It would only be useful for stealth, but when the next ship came into the system, she was leaving on it whether they liked it or not.

"I wouldn't use that if I were you," a woman's voice sounded in her ear.

She turned, shocked to see Nadia, her maid servant standing behind her. How had she entered? She also looked different in a way Yusra couldn't quantify. Gone was the subservient, barely noticeable woman. In her place was someone else, far more confident.

"What—what are you doing in here?" Yusra shut the drawer as she turned, pretending as if Nadia hadn't seen it.

"Before I answer that, I need to know, are you planning on staying here or do you want to leave?" asked the woman, who didn't at all seem like the handmaiden who had served her tirelessly.

"I'm a loyal servant of the Caliph. I don't know what you speak of," she said.

Nadia frowned. "Doc, we don't have a lot of time. I already know enough to march to Malik and turn you in. So I'll ask again, what are your intentions?"

Yusra spun, opening the secret drawer, grabbed her knife, and leaped at Nadia. The blade flickered to life in the air and— the world tumbled as she rolled over, seeing the ceiling followed by hitting the floor hard enough to chase the breath from her lungs.

Nadia knelt on her chest, cold brown eyes drilling into hers like death incarnate. "My name is Nadia Dagher, I'm with Alliance Intelligence, and I'm here to extract you," she said as she held the vibro-blade and shut it off. Flipping it around, she held the hilt out.

"You got my message?" Dr. Abbasi said, eyes welling with tears.

"That was you? I wondered how we got the location. Yes, and we have to hurry. There's a ship on the way here to pick us up. It won't be long and there are things we need to do to prepare. Can I count on you, Doc?"

Yusra held out her hand for Nadia to help her up. "You can. Get me out of hell, and I will tell you things you never dreamed of."

"I'll hold you to that."

Captain Khaled Al-Faris tapped the control panel of his screen, waiting for the information to update.

"Lieutenant Sattar, is this correct?" he asked his first officer.

The Caliph destroyers bridge layout allowed them to sit next to each other, almost in a line behind the rest of the bridge crew of the *Al-Qud*.

"Yes sir, as far as I know."

Khaled frowned. The orders were legit, then, but he failed to understand why they would have orders to go to a deserted system with a known black hole. The Navy avoided astronomical black holes like Imam's avoided married women. He chuckled inwardly at his own joke. The ministry of religion had warned him several times about his sense of humor, which was why he stopped saying jokes aloud. Instead, he just laughed at them inwardly. His crew was used to his offbeat sense of humor and sudden chuckling fits.

He scrolled back through the log, looking for who sent the orders, but they were only tagged with an ISB identifier. Which meant the orders were above his paygrade.

"Ensign Shah, set course and get us going. Can't keep the ISB waiting." In a way he was happy to have an assignment. He'd heard of the disaster 3rd Fleet had suffered and was glad not to be on the front. However, with a shiny new class of missile boat at his command, he couldn't expect his luck to run on forever. He'd been skeptical of arming a ship with missiles, which compared to torpedoes lacked the individual ship-killing power. They made up for it in volume, though, his ship could launch hundreds of them. While they didn't have the range or power of a torpedo, they could easily overwhelm a target's defenses. He just wished he hadn't had to give up all the rest of the ship's armament to do it.

He had to admit, though, it made a kind of sense. The Caliphate Navy needed a way to secure planets and a short-range missile boat, capable of obliterating anything in close orbit would do the job well.

CHAPTER THIRTY-FIVE

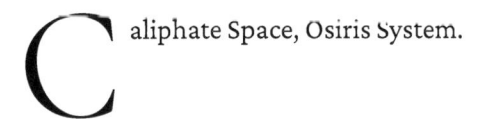

Caliphate Space, Osiris System.

Interceptor accelerated away from the Guild platform, the last in the line, toward the final starlane of their journey, and the most dangerous part of the mission.

It was the middle of the ship's night and Jacob rested on his rack, guitar cradled in his hands as he strummed a few errant strings. The notes echoed in the dim light as he tuned, turning the knobs at the head, little by little as he drew the instrument closer to harmony. His hatch was open, just in case anyone on the bridge needed him urgently.

He was supposed to be sleeping, even though they were officially in enemy territory. They were going to be in enemy territory for the next seventy-two hours, so there was no point in trying to stay awake for all of it. The open hatch helped keep the room's temperature down. They were still a few hours away from their next heat dump.

The notes finally sounded right and he started playing for real.

Lost in the darkness of deep space
Searching for love, a steady pace
Wandering alone, through the stars
Hoping to find who we are

"That's some song, skipper," Jennings said from the hatchway.

Jacob dragged his arm across his eyes, the hidden depths of his emotions catching him by surprise. It had just come out of him. He hadn't even recalled thinking about it.

"There's a bit more to it. It was my mom's favorite. She used to play it before she headed onto a deployment. I still remember the last—" Jacob paused looking up for the first time and realizing that his Gunny wasn't in uniform. There was no regulation that stopped crew from wearing civilian attire off duty. As long as the modesty standard was met, they were free to dress as they wished. It was just... he'd never seen her aboard ship in anything but Marine-standard attire.

Allison wore a pair of yoga pants, and a tank top that showed off her overdeveloped shoulders and neck, and for the first time in his memory, her long blonde hair cascaded down over her back in waves. He had to question if she had some kind of quantum gate to keep all that hair in a bun while on duty.

"Sir?" she asked.

"Jennings, everything okay?" he asked.

"Now you call me Jennings," she muttered. "Can I come in and talk to you, sir?"

"By all means."

He scooted over on his rack so she could sit at the end. As

long as the hatch was open, he wasn't worried about it seeming improper.

She took his invitation; even in her civilian getup, she moved like a predator. He couldn't help but admire her on a professional level. He'd seen those muscles in action up close, when she saved his life multiple times or when she beat the snot out of him trying to teach him hand-to-hand.

"I never asked you, but the fighting style you use, what is it?"

She cocked her head as if it hadn't occurred to her to tell him. "Mua Thai, mostly. Some Judo, Karate, and Escrima. A little bit of everything, I guess."

You guess? Jacob wanted to say aloud. If he wasn't sitting a meter from the diminutive blonde Marine, he would think she had been replaced by someone else.

"What's on your mind, Gunny?" He felt the need to reinforce her rank, and his position, with her in his cabin dressed as she was. Something was certainly wrong, and he wanted to help, but he also found himself in unknown waters.

"I met someone, and I want to take leave after this mission. I have enough saved up—"

Jacob raised his chin slightly as he thought through what she said. "Master Sergeant Cannon?"

Her piercing blue eyes widened before narrowing. "Did someone tell you?" she asked.

"It doesn't take the ship's grapevine to tell me you're interested in him, Allison." He put away the idea of playing the stern captain. She needed a friend, not a CO.

"I guess not. We talked and we would like to spend time learning if this thing between us is worth pursuing."

Typical Jennings, Jacob mused. Determine the op, execute the op.

"Not everything can be broken down so easily," Jacob warned her. "Especially relationships."

"Sir—I—" she looked away, a bright red creeping into her skin.

"Allison," Jacob said tenderly. "Have you never had a boyfriend before?"

She shook her head. "Not really, sir. I've always focused on the Corps. It's my life. Besides, look at me. I have no illusions about beauty."

Jacob frowned. He hadn't realized the level of insecurity she had about her shoulders and back. Yes, Allison was a little oddly shaped, but out of uniform she was beautiful, if a little hulking.

"I won't argue with your self-image, nor will I try to strip you of it. You're a good-looking woman, Allison. Maybe that's part of why the sergeant is attracted to you. Regardless, yes when we get back, I'll approve your leave. Though I can't promise you a spot on the ship when you return. You know how the military is..."

If she weren't able to keep her assignment to the *Interceptor*, it would suck for both of them. He'd truly come to depend on her over the years.

"Yes sir, I do. Thank you, sir," she said quietly.

"No, Allison, thank you. No matter what happens, you can always come to me."

Chief Suresh went over the logs of what happened with Midship Watanabe, and there was no doubt she had deserted in war time, an offense punishable by death. The girl sat in the brig, which was nothing more than a cleared-out supply closet. Destroyers were too small for actual brigs.

Devi hated seeing a person's potential wasted because of

one stupid decision made when they were young, and ignorant. The captain might have been able to overlook it if it weren't for the two deaths, Spacer Cooper and Spacer Blachowicz. Cooper was an innocent, killed in the line while trying to rescue the two who had not gone willingly.

One, really. No one believed Brennan when she said that Tyree wasn't in on it. The record was pretty clear, but as long as the only three people with firsthand knowledge of the situation insisted he wasn't involved, then they were legally obligated to believe Ensign Brennan. What a spot they were in. Deep in enemy territory and she was busy filing the charges against the midship.

"It's a damn shame," she muttered as she finished typing out the long list of charges.

"COB, you have a minute?" Lieutenant Hössbacher asked from the hatchway.

"For you, sir, always. Come in."

She'd known Roy Hössbacher since he was a baby Navy officer. It did her proud to see the kind of man and officer he'd turned into over the intervening years.

"I feel like it's my fault, COB. The whole thing. I should have kept a closer eye on her, given her more work to do."

"No one else sees it that way, sir. Trust me, I've been in this spacer's Navy a long time. It doesn't happen often, but when you get a kid determined to jump ship, there's not a lot you can do to stop them. In a way, I feel bad for her. Not too bad, mind you, since Spacer Cooper didn't deserve to die for her mistake."

"Bad for her, Chief? Why? She's a deserter."

Suresh picked up her mug and sipped the dark brew, letting the strong black coffee percolate her senses.

"'Cause she's a weed now, Lieutenant, instead of a flower. On Vishnu, we know a thing or two about gardening. The black soil of my home world covers almost eighty percent of the landmass. They say it's because of the ancient volcanic activity that lasted millions of years in her distant past. Regardless, we have the best gardens. Not just gardens. Farms, ranches, you name it."

She stopped to take another sip.

"I'm not sure I follow, Chief."

"I'm getting there. Every once in a while, a young farmer will think they can take a shortcut. Whether it's because of the richness of the soil, or the fact that their family had tilled the same soil for a hundred years. They make the same mistake thousands made before them. They think they know better. They don't have to follow the rules. They're *special*. Sure, it won't work for anyone else, but it will work for them because they're just that damn magical."

Devi's story wasn't just about some random farmer on Vishnu. Her father had thought that way as a young man trying to make his plot of land he'd inherited from his father. Soon, though, the once lush acreage turned from life sustaining vegetation into worthless dirt. All because he made one choice—he lost his farm and his inheritance, and so did she.

"What happened?" Roy asked.

"He let the weeds grow on the edge of the property. The problem is, the weeds grow just as well as the flowers, often better. By the time he realized his mistake, it was too late. I'm in the Navy instead of working my family's farm... She's a weed, Roy. Maybe we could have saved her, but like my father, the decision she made cannot be undone."

"Oh, I was hoping for a happier ending."

Devi shook her head. "Happy for me, I joined the Navy. Not everyone makes the choices necessary for a happy ending. It sucks, but sometimes, when we're the least able to make the right decision, we make one that ruins the rest of our life. That's where the midship finds herself."

CHAPTER THIRTY-SIX

Jacob yawned as he sipped his morning orange drink alone in the conference room. He'd maybe slept for two hours as they silently sped through the system toward their destination. Both he and Tefiti were surprised at the initial report. The only shipping they picked up on the long-range gravitics were civilian freighters. No military ships at all.

This was going to be a long mission with a bitter finale if their target wasn't on the other end of the next starlane. They relied heavily on Guild intelligence, and he hoped and prayed that wasn't a mistake.

With everything else happening, he had two important meetings in a few minutes and he needed time to clear his head and catch up on missed paperwork.

The latter of the two was the easier one. He simply forwarded virtually everything to Carter, all but two. The inquiry into Midship Watanabe's desertion and the two VIP's they picked up on Midway. If the Caliphate had used a normal planet as their de facto prison, then they would have never stumbled across them, but since Midway's only landmass was smaller than Anchorage Bay back home, it made sense.

"Mr. Bijan and Princess Sarina to see the Captain," Jennings said.

"Bring them in, Gunny."

Jacob leaned back as they entered, pleased that the two they rescued already looked healthier than before. They had a nice glow about them. The fabricator produced appropriate clothing for them, which had to be a nice change of pace from wearing rags. Bijan led the blind woman in by the arm, showing her where to stand as if he had been doing it her whole life. They were bonded by shared trust, something he could tell just by looking at them. They had survived together for a long time.

Jennings left them standing in front of the shark-nosed table, shutting the briefing room hatch as she left.

"Captain Grimm," Sarina said, "let me thank you personally for allowing us to come aboard." Her voice had a lyrical quality and he imagined she was a gifted singer.

"Commander, ma'am. I'm the captain of the ship, but you can call me Commander Grimm, or just Jacob if you prefer," he said.

"Thank you... Jacob," she said. She smiled demurely at him even while Bijan frowned from beside her.

"What are your intentions, *Commander?*" Bijan asked.

"I'm afraid I can't drop you at a Caliph-controlled planet, if that is what you're asking. We're on a... delicate mission. May I ask how long you were on Midway?"

Bijan frowned, eyes glancing at Sarina, then back to Grimm. "Is that what you call Sigen? What year is it?"

"Twenty-Nine-Thirty-Seven."

Sarina let out a gasp. Bijan however, simply nodded to himself. "Ten years."

"Ten... years? On that place? How did you survive?" Jacob asked.

"Guile, Captain, and luck," Bijan said. "Advanced tech is

limited, and if you know where to hide you can avoid it. The main city had a few skimmers with plasma weapons, but beyond that, nothing. No power, no sensors, no way of tracking. Until recently no one even knew we hid in the burned-out building. Until I..."

"It's not your fault, Bijan. It was a long time to remain vigilant, it was bound to happen," Sarina said.

"As you say, highness."

"We don't wish to be let out on a Caliph-controlled planet, Jacob. Can we return to the Alliance with you?"

He hadn't told them that was all but a certainty. While they weren't technically prisoners on his ship, the beautiful woman and her guard weren't free to go, either.

"I'm glad, because that isn't a possibility. I'm afraid you're stuck with us for the foreseeable future. We're on a mission"—he held his hand up to stop Bijan whose mouth was already open—"that I can't disclose the nature of, sorry. I can promise you food and board until we return to Alexandria. After that, I don't know."

"Thank you, Jacob," Sarina said. "The fact that you took us with you is more than enough."

Once they said their goodbyes, and Bijan guided the princess out, Jacob had another, albeit far less pleasant, task awaiting him.

"Gunny," Jacob called her, "bring in the prisoner."

Jacob hated this part.

Gunny Jennings, CPO Suresh, and her second, PO Cartwright, led in Midship Watanabe followed by Lieutenant Hössbacher who acted as her advocate. Watanabe stood at attention before the table.

"Prisoner will remove her cover," Chief Suresh said.

Watanabe did so with sharp movements. Jacob winced at seeing the bruises and welts on her. Nanite medicine took care of the worst of it, but she had still been through hell. A hell she might never recover from.

"Before we begin, Midship, you have the right to refuse any council and await our return to Alliance space for a hearing. If you choose that route, you will spend the rest of the journey confined. Do you wish it?" he asked.

"No sir, I do not."

While she might look like a beaten bag of potatoes, her voice had iron in it.

"Very well. Midship Yua Watanabe, this is the beginning of a formal process that will culminate with your court martial. While that can sound intimidating, it doesn't usually result in a severe punishment. It would have likely only resulted in your dishonorable discharge if not for the death of Spacers Cooper and Blachowicz. I apologize we weren't able to find a way to help you sooner. I don't shirk responsibility and I certainly don't pass the buck."

"As I told you on Midway, sir. This is all my fault. I'm the sole responsible party. Brennan, Tyree, and Blachowicz wanted no part of it, and I forced them."

Jacob raised an eyebrow at the obvious lie. However, he did admire that she was trying to take responsibility for her actions and shield those she either manipulated into helping her, or outright forced. Since she was a slight woman, he hardly believed she could have strong-armed Blachowicz into helping her. With his death, though, she was clear to make up any story she wanted. Her taking all the blame surprised him; he would have thought she would try to blame others, like she had initially.

"I admire your honesty, Midship, and your willingness to face the music. If it weren't for the death of two of the crew, I would clear you of the charges and let the lesson be learned. That's not the case, though. You present another problem."

Jacob punched up a series of numbers on his NavPad, showing the crew distribution by department. "Cooper and Blachowicz were part of engineering and the boat bay. I'm shorthanded. With your communications skills, you should be able to work the ECM on the Corsair if needed."

Jacob caught the shock on the faces of his crew. Well, not Jennings, for she was as impassive as ever. Hössbacher and Suresh, though, didn't hide their surprise all that well.

"Yes sir, I can," Watanabe said.

"Do I have your word you will fulfill your duty to the best of your ability?" he asked.

"Yes sir," she said, some small glimmer of hope appearing in her eyes. Jacob didn't want her to think she was off the hook. There was no doubt she would be going to prison at the very least. Perhaps, though, the hope had more to do with reclaiming some small part of her soul than her freedom.

"Very well. For the duration of the voyage, you are confined to your quarters with the exception of mealtimes. Your duty post is the boat bay, and you will report to Chief Boudreaux and do whatever tasks she sees fit. Dismissed."

"Thank you, sir," Watanabe said as she snapped to attention.

Jennings led her out, though Chief Suresh remained.

"Did you have a question, Devi?" he asked.

"Skipper, we've served together a few years now and you still surprise me," she said.

Jacob leaned back, a slow smile spreading. "Good to know. I truly wish we could have avoided this whole fiasco."

"Me too, sir. Me too. You did right by her, though, and that's more than I think she's ever had before."

He'd thought long about what she had told him, about never having to face the consequences of her actions, good or bad. What did that do to a person, never being punished for their bad behavior or praised for their good? Add in natural charm and good looks, then suddenly she was someone who achieved only selfish things. She was never taught she could achieve greatness.

That's what got him, what made him want to do something... the loss of greatness.

"Maybe with the next one, Chief. As it is, we've got our hands full."

"Aye sir."

CHAPTER THIRTY-SEVEN

"That's the plan, then?" Jacob asked the Special Forces trooper.

"It's not like they have a complicated planet to infiltrate, Commander," Danny replied.

A hologram of the planet hovered over the shark-painted conference table, showing their target nestled in a canyon that was deeper into the crust than the bottom of Alexandria's vast Novus Ocean. To Jacob, it looked like a giant had split the planet with an axe, leaving cracks and splinters running along the bedrock. The brief assessment Astro did, suggested the planet's water had boiled off once the moon had fractured and the planet was stuck in a "summer" orbit, unable to revolve around the sun.

"We use the Corsair to drop you a few klicks south of the base before their dawn. You infiltrate, extract, then retreat back to the LZ and up into orbit where we pick you up? That's it?"

Danny nodded, pointing at the map. "Of course, you're going to want to orbit the planet on the black hole side, since we don't know what kind of ground-to-space defense they have."

Jacob shrunk the image of the planet until the edge of the supermassive black hole and the dying sun were just visible. Chief Suresh, PO's Tefiti and Oliv, along with his engineering department had all gone over the math, and it came out the same. As long as they stayed in the narrow tunnel of space, leading from the starlane to the planet, and maintained an acceleration of 500g's, they wouldn't spend eternity falling into the singularity.

The spacer in him railed against the idea of going anywhere near the gaping maw of death it represented.

"Chief Boudreaux, will the Corsair be okay to make the drop?" he asked.

"If *Interceptor* is below the Hill Sphere, we should be good. Normally that would be millions of klicks, but with this wonky situation, I'm thinking no more than a low orbit. I want to go in with plasma engines, not the gravcoil."

"Devi, can we make that happen?"

"Aye, skipper. Not a problem for me. Maybe if you had a lesser coxswain, it would be an issue, but not me." She had her usual no-nonsense expression that made it hard for Jacob to tell if she was serious or sarcastic. Of course, he also thought she was the best coxswain in the fleet. Something he wasn't afraid to tell her.

"Okay then. There's one change I would like to make—"

Danny frowned, interrupting him. "All due respect sir, this is my mission, you're just the taxi driver."

Jacob stomped on the urge to jump down the man's throat. Something about him just galled him and he hoped he could get it under control. Sergeant Cannon was correct, though, this was his mission.

"I'm not debating that, *Sergeant*. I'm simply adding a safety catch. I want Gunny Jennings and my Marines in their Raptor armor on standby—just on the off-chance things go south."

Jennings, who stood at parade rest by the door, perked up at the new information.

"Blow out, Skipper?" Boudreaux asked.

"No. God forbid if something were to go wrong with the landing, I don't want all our forces on the Corsair. Gunny," he said looking at the diminutive woman, "am I correct in understanding that, under the right conditions, Raptors can make drop from orbit."

"Oorah, skipper."

"I'll take that as a yes," Jacob said with a grin. A light round of chuckles filled the conference room. "Jennings, outfit the Raptors with external jump jets for orbital drop. Is that an acceptable change to you, Sergeant?"

Danny wanted to disagree with the captain, but it was actually a good idea, one that he should have thought of. They were just used to working with no backup and no plan B. He really disliked the idea of agreeing with Grimm, though he was a big enough man to admit when he was wrong. Despite his inclination to not like the man, based only on everyone liking him too much, Danny found himself grinning. "Yes sir. I think that will work just fine."

Jennings grunted as she pushed the man-sized plasma jets into place behind RPT-001. They were self-contained, one-use jets that attached to the back of the Raptors. Not unlike the ion drives that were used for space maneuvers, the jump jets could be used for rapid ground deployment. Or in the case of an orbital drop, slow them enough not to kill the pilot when the mechanoid suits impacted.

The Marines were stripped down to their undershirts, soaked in sweat, and breathing hard. They grunted with exertion as they pushed the half-ton jets into place to make the connection. Once the engine fit to the back, couplings locked into place sealing the jets against the hull.

"Just three more," Jennings said. Her team groaned. Part of her hoped it was all for nothing, but the larger part of her yearned for the experience of dropping from orbit. There were few Marines, if any, that had done an orbital combat drop. This was what she lived for, doing things others only dreamed of. "I want this squared away before we're in-system people."

Her three Marines shrugged off the fatigue and rallied back across the morgue to the hanging jets. She was proud of them, though she wouldn't tell them that. The skipper's style of leadership wasn't hers. They would work harder than they ever had in their lives, then she would push them even farther. Marines had no limit. Soldiers with limits died and her Marines didn't die. Not if she could help it.

In his time in the Navy, Jacob had witnessed more than his fair share of stellar phenomena. Quite a bit more. The Bella wormhole and Wonderland were extraordinary and complex miracles of science and nature. No one expected them, at least no one in the mainstream of the galaxy. Black holes, though, were known. They had existed in the minds of the people of the galaxy for thousands of years, and every spacer knew exactly where they were and how to avoid them.

Yet, here he was, flying his ship right toward the largest, deadliest black hole he'd ever heard of. It was impossible to judge the size of the thing without a frame of reference, but it dwarfed the sun it ate and even from a billion klicks away showed up on visual.

"I'm glad we're not staying here," Tefiti said. "I don't know when it will happen, but the starlane isn't going to be around much longer."

Jacob turned his squeaky chair to face the gravman. "Why do you say that?"

Tefiti pointed at the screen. "It's eating the sun, pulling stellar materiel out of it. As it does so, the sun's gravity lessens. Soon the planet will fall into the black hole, and when the sun goes, so does the starlane."

"That will suck," Chief Suresh added from The Pit.

Jacob couldn't help but chuckle along with a few of the bridge crew.

"Besides the death maw there, what else can you hear?" Jacob asked.

Tefiti pressed the headphones into his ear a little harder, focusing his hearing, listening for the distinctive drumbeat of spacetime. Throughout the outer hull, a network of lasers intercepted gravity waves as they passed through the ship. The disruption fluctuated the lasers at a specific frequency, which the computer then turned into sound. The real problem, though, was distinguishing the different sounds. The computer could tell the frequency and amplitude, but only a trained spacer could guide the computer toward the correct classification of the sound. Was it a star? A black hole? A ship? How large a ship? How powerful a gravcoil?

Jacob was fortunate that he had PO Tefiti and Oliv, two of the best in the business.

"It's hard to tell, sir. With the pounding the sun is taking from the black hole, we could be right next to a battleship and not hear it," Tefiti said. "Unless we want to go active on radar/lidar there's just no knowing."

Not even the best were infallible, though. Jacob sighed, hoping to have more information before moving in from the starlane. They'd spent the last hour hovering in space, looking and listening for any sign of other ships. Intel did say the traffic in the system was scarce. He figured, though, intel was wrong.

"Let's continue running silent for now. Okay, Fionna, set a course for Zephyr. Let's make sure we don't stray too close to the black hole. I don't want to test the old girl's engines."

A three-dimensional tunnel formed on the main screen showing the path *Interceptor* would have to maintain. "What's that?" Jacob asked Ensign Brennan.

"It's complicated, sir, and a little beyond me. I'm linking in Lieutenant Kai. PO Tefiti is also helping... well, he's more, like, letting me help him," Ensign Brennan said.

A glance at Tefiti told Jacob he approved of the ensign's assessment. It was a rare officer who would remember to give credit to those under her. He was glad his instincts were right about Fionna.

"At its most basic, skipper," Tefiti said, "there is a place where we can escape the black hole's gravity, but it's narrow. We accelerate toward the planet and decelerate, as long as both are done above five hundred g's, then we will be safe. Once we're in orbit, the planet's gravity, along with our own thrusters, will keep us in orbit."

Jacob didn't understand all the technical details of the system, but he did understand safe. Then something occurred to him.

"Tefiti, when we're in orbit, can we leave without going to full acceleration?"

"That's the catch-22, sir. We can accelerate at five hundred g's, or we can't. There is no in between. Once we break orbit, the only safe place to come to a stop and turn around is right where we are now."

They would be stuck. Jacob leaned forward, contemplating the implications of the situation. Once in orbit they had to stay. Jacob prayed the reliability of their intel would hold a bit longer. The last thing he needed was a battle with a warship where neither party could engage their gravcoil without a full-on retreat.

"Understood."

"Helm, set course zero-five-one mark three-three-two. Accelerate at five-zero-zero gravities," Brennan said.

"Roger, course laid in at zero-five-one mark three-three-two. Accelerate at five-zero-zero gravities," Chief Suresh confirmed.

"Execute," Jacob ordered.

CHAPTER THIRTY-EIGHT

Danny and his men stood ready, hanging onto the grab bar next to the closed door of the Corsair. According to their info, the dark side of the planet rested at a ridiculous forty below zero. Not something he wanted to experience personally.

Mac, Rico, T-Bar, and Bubba stacked up behind him, their weapons at the ready. He would have liked more intel, despite what he had told the captain before they departed.

The captain... now Jennings had him saying it. Damn that woman. He raised his hand, feeling her on his lips as they had said goodbye that morning. She was something—special. Not in the usual way of a beautiful woman who was competent in a field normally dominated by hyper-competent men. No, she was special in the feminine way. She had something about her. A bold, fierce, uncompromising soul that made him want to follow her to hell if he had to.

Just to be with her.

He shook his head, forcing the memory of her skin out of his mind.

"You okay, boss?" Mac asked. His team had spent the last

several years together, all of them were friends, brothers. Mac was the closest thing he had to a best friend.

"Yeah, just... clearing my head. Too many nonessentials weighing on me."

"I don't see how, she's ninety-five kilos at most."

Danny whipped his head around, stunned that Mac knew only to see his team grinning at him like idiots.

"What?"

"Come on, boss," T-Bar said. "She's hot. We all thought so at the bar."

"Get your mind on the mission," he said with a scowl. That made them laugh even louder.

"Two minutes to light side. It's gonna get bumpy, so make sure you're hanging on," Chief Boudreaux said over the speaker.

"Roger that, Chief," Mac replied. "You heard the woman, strap in."

Danny's team reached up and held the grab bars above their heads with one hand, and the horizontal grip next to the hatch with the other. It wasn't the safest way to travel. However, Danny wanted them out and on the ground in a heartbeat and not trying to unbuckle from the safety harnesses in the passenger seats.

Through the digital porthole, the world went from the blackest night he'd ever seen, to a blazing daylight unlike anything he'd ever experienced. The sudden change in air temp outside was like running the Corsair into the water. It rose up, shaking before crashing violently down.

"Yeehaw," Bubba yelled. Danny just shook his head.

TEN HOURS EARLIER

"Nights coming," Nadia told the doctor. "I don't have a lot of time before Malik starts shooting everyone he suspects. Our ride will be here soon and we have to go."

"How, though?" Yusra asked.

Nadia pulled out the hard copy of the map she'd taken from her borrowed SecPad. "Here is the access shaft to the security bunker. There are only two men stationed there overnight. I will rappel down, access the room, kill them, and sabotage the reactor. While everyone freezes to death, you and I will head for a cave and hunker down until rescue arrives."

Yusra looked at Nadia like she was insane. "Malik will stop you. There are dozens of security men here. Sensors, radar, missile batteries. You can't just walk out."

Nadia cocked her head to the side, glancing at where Yusra kept the vibro-knife in her drawer. "Wasn't that your plan? Board a freighter and make them take you?"

Yusra blushed, looking down at the floor and fidgeting with her feet. "You don't understand the fear I live with. Every day. I had to do something."

Nadia did understand, a little. She, too, had lived in fear but she desperately avoided making decisions based on that fear. They were always the wrong decisions. Always.

"Fear is a powerful motivator, but it makes poor choices. You've done great, Yusra, really. You're a physicist, not a spy, yet you've managed to tap into the security feed, control the cameras in your quarters, and fool your captors. You did all of this to stay alive."

Yusra shook, wiping her eyes. "My father didn't want to die the way he did. I don't want his discoveries to vanish into nothing. I just don't know what to do."

"You're very good at your job, and so am I," Nadia said. "I'm telling you this so you know. Look at everything you achieved without my training and now imagine you had it... I'm going to get us out of here if I have to kill everyone on this base, one by one. That's my mission." Nadia didn't add that it was also the only way she would ever be free to pursue a life. Free from the crime of telling the truth.

Yusra wrapped Nadia in a surprise hug. "I just want to leave. Do what you have to."

Nadia squeezed the small woman for a moment. "I can't do it without you. Use your cameras, get me outside, and I'll do the rest."

"Okay. Here, take this." She handed Nadia the knife and small comms device for her ear.

Nadia pressed it into place, nanites embedded it into her inner ear, making it all but vanish. The knife she stuck under her cuff, with the hilt facing her hand.

"Let's go. If my people did their job, the rescue ship is either already here or will be soon."

Nadia closed the door behind her, bowing her head and resuming a subservient demeanor. She walked toward her room, passing several base personnel along the way. None of whom gave her a second look. While Zephyr was primarily a research base centered around Yusra Abbasi's work. The other facilities on the base were centered around providing for the personnel stationed there.

Her ear piece clicked to life and Yusra's voice sounded like she stood beside her. "There are two guards up ahead. They are stopping and searching everyone going to their quarters."

Crap, Nadia thought. She assumed that Malik would eventually resort to searching the entire base when the goods she stole didn't turn up in Zaid's room.

She couldn't carry it around with her, though. Stashing it in her room was her only option. The small vent under her bed she accessed fit everything nicely. Going outside without the equipment she stole would be suicidally dangerous.

Turning the corner, she saw the men frisking down one of the cooks. Nadia shuffled forward, head down and shoulders hunched. Her movements were anything but confident.

"Stop," the smaller of the two guards said. "Arms to your side."

She did as they ordered, keeping her head down.

"Zaki, look," the taller said.

The one called Zaki frowned, hands frozen where he reached for her.

"Uh, Fahd, what do I do?"

Nadia played them without even speaking. They weren't allowed to touch a married woman, unless the specific situation demanded it, which, unless they were ordered to search her, it didn't.

"Let her pass, she's just a woman," Fahd said.

"Go on," Zaki told her.

Without saying a word, Nadia bowed and scuttled past them. Once in her quarters, she moved her bed and opened the vent. Inside was everything she would need to escape the base and take Yusra with her.

"Okay, find me the shortest route to an exit."

"Are you sure? The temperature is already dropping. It will be below zero soon."

Nadia shrugged off her top and pulled on the nanite thermal shirt that would keep her core warm and by extension her extremities... she hoped.

"Yes. Let's go."

. . .

The sun set behind her with a lack of fanfare. With very little water vapor in the atmosphere, it just sank down, no hues or colors, no spread of light.

Nadia tossed the rope down the exhaust port, watching it fall until it went slack. It was trickier to secure it than she thought, since there were no trees, no vegetation to speak of. Essentially, she dug a hole and pushed a big rock on the other end. It was a good thing she didn't weigh much more than sixty-five kilos sopping wet, or she would have had to find a bigger rock.

Once she was sure the rope would hold her, she eased over the side and started her descent, hand over hand, making no jerking movements that could disturb the rock holding her rope.

As she descended, the sun vanished completely. The air froze fast enough that a breath she had just let out, froze in the air.

Ice crystals formed on her hands as she watched. The shirt she wore kicked in and the heat rose off her in waves.

"I might have underestimated how cold it's going to be," she whispered into the comms.

With numb fingers, she went hand over hand down the rope, breaths coming in short gasps as the cold seeped into her. She watched in horror as the top of the shaft frosted over and white icicles formed, following her down, encasing the shaft centimeter by centimeter.

"Faster Nadia," she muttered. Her fingers froze into hooks, not letting her open them. She futzed with them, blowing hot air on them, trying to thaw them enough to open. A glance up told her she was out of time.

She opened both her hands enough to slide down thirty meters, the line zipping by her. Once her flesh hand heated enough where she could move it, she let go of the rope and hung on with only her artificial one. Pain lanced through her as the "nerves" relayed the burns to her. Gritting her teeth, she closed her hand hard, slowing the rate of descent to a mere meter per second when she hit the bottom with a thud.

"Nadia?" Yusra asked in her ear. "Are you okay?"

The doctor sounded genuinely worried, which didn't surprise Nadia. If she didn't complete her mission, neither of them were leaving the rock alive.

"I made it to the bottom," she replied, pitching her voice as quietly as possible.

The natural rock shaft that was once a lava tube, gave way to the metal vents that led into the cooling system and the base as a whole. It only took her a second to dig out the tools she'd stolen to undo the bolts and disable the security leads. The vent came off with a tug and she could see down into the crawlspace.

Gripping the sides, she leaned in and flipped over, landing on her back. There was just enough room for her to squeeze into. With a shimmy, she moved down the vent to the T junction, straight ahead led to the reactor. Down, to the security station. Generally, she would avoid ventilation shafts leading to reactors, but in this case, it would only be a problem if there was an overload or an attack.

Bracing herself against the sides of the T junction, she dropped her feet and allowed herself to slide down. Sweat beaded, dripping down as her muscles quivered with exertion, lowering her meter by meter until her feet touched bottom.

Static filled her ear, interrupting her.

"Yusra, did you say something?"

More static. The relative proximity of the reactor blocked her signal, she hoped. After ten more minutes of wiggling, shimmying, and exertion, with her face covered in grime, she reached her destination: the vent overlooking the security control station.

Two uniformed security men manned the station below, one eyeing the feed on the vital area of the base, the other watching the exterior feeds. The sheer mind-numbing boredom of what the two men were doing made Nadia question whether they were even effective at it.

Had she managed to infiltrate their security, or was their security so lax they didn't catch her? Malik certainly handled things with an iron fist, but was it possible his men were just doing their best to make him think they were squared away?

Below, and out of view, a door whooshed shut.

"He's gone," the one on the right said.

"Finally."

The monitors flickered and changed from security views to a movie Nadia didn't recognize. Within seconds, though, a bloody violent shoot-out happened, and the two guards leaned forward in excitement.

The drop was farther than she thought it would be, almost three meters if she guessed right. She had to risk it, though. Nadia drew the pistol in one hand and the vibro-knife in the other. It hummed lightly and glowed ever so dimly. With a deep breath, she kicked in the vent and dropped three meters to the floor. Her left foot hit wrong, sliding out and she cracked her right knee on the ceracrete as it took the full brunt of her fall.

She fired the pistol at point-blank range.

A blue line reached out from the pistol in the blink of an eye and then the plasma ignited, burning a hole through the one on her right. Nadia leaped up—only to have her knee fail and she fell on her side. The remaining man sat stunned for a moment, eyes wide and slack jawed as the body of his friend twitched through death throws.

She lunged for him, but her knee refused to cooperate, and

she stabbed the chair instead of him. The knife's blade slid through the metal and fabric as if it didn't exist, sparking as it hit the hard floor.

The guard reacted, coming out of his bewildered state, and leapt up, his hand reaching for the pistol on his side.

Nadia rolled back, ditching the knife and grasping the hold-out pistol in both hands, the sights lined up on the man's chest and she fired. Time froze as the blue beam of electrically charged ions speared him in the chest followed a millisecond later by the plasma discharge. He tried to scream, but his lungs were gone. He collapsed in a heap of smoking, burned flesh that made Nadia want to vomit.

Adrenaline coursed through her, helping her overcome the agonizing pain in her knee as she pulled herself up. She didn't know how much time she had, but unless she disabled the base's defenses and shut down the reactor, she and the doctor weren't going anywhere.

CHAPTER THIRTY-NINE

Danny leaped off the hovering Corsair, hitting the rocky terrain with a crunch. He glanced at the walls of the narrow canyon Boudreaux had deposited them in and shook his head in disbelief. He'd known some crazy, talented pilots in the past, but she took the cake. Only a meter stood between them and certain death. She'd flown into the canyon just under the speed of sound, with only a meter of clearance on either side of the wings.

"You're one crazy woman," Mac said over the comms. "I like it."

"Oui, you too. Be safe. Don't die," she said back. "I'll be ready if you need extract or CAS."

"Roger Charlie-One-One, Nomad out."

Narrow granite walls made up the canyon. Normally, it was the last place Danny would lead his team, but the crevice led right to the target.

"Time to see if this works," Rico said as he held the small transmitter up to Danny.

Danny took it and depressed the transmit key. "India, this is Nomad."

Static played back.

"India, this is Nomad."

He glanced at Mac who shrugged. "Could be the walls."

"Rog. Rico take point. Mac, you got our six. Move out."

The team formed up with practiced ease as they moved toward their target. Danny pushed all thoughts, worries, and feelings out of his mind. Laser focus on his mission required him to. He couldn't spare a single thought for anything or anyone else. He ordered them to move out with a hand gesture and they stalked forward, like a spider-bear looking for prey.

Jennings, strapped in her Raptor armor with the canopy open, gazed down at the planet below. They were on the wrong side to see Zephyr base, though. Until they knew their defenses were down, *Interceptor* couldn't risk orbiting on that side of the planet. Her three Marines were beside her, canopies open, since the suits could be downright claustrophobic. Owens slept, snoring softly, head tilted to one side. Naki read a book on his MarPad. June ran diagnostics on her armor. She'd scored high on her aptitude test, but never worn the suit in actual combat. When they returned to Alliance space, she would be sure to send the PFC to Raptor school on Blackrock. For now, she would have to adapt.

"Let it go, PFC. The suit knows what to do," she said.

"Aye, Gunny. It's just that, I've only read the manual and walked the suit from the morgue to here."

Jennings recalled the first time she'd seen the suits in action, and they took her breath away. She knew the moment they had growled that was what she wanted.

"Understood, PFC. If you're worried close the canopy and

catch more sim time. Stop running diagnostics, though, the Raptor's fine."

June did just that, closing the suit to play in the sim more. It was good for her, and Gunny was glad there was at least one PFC in the Corps that followed orders.

Jennings didn't suffer the shakes before combat. As a Marine, her life revolved around training, duty, and sacrifice. If today was her day to die, she wasn't going to waste time worrying about it.

At least, that's how she wanted to feel. Something new had awakened inside her, and she couldn't help but resent its intrusion into her life.

Jennings shook her head. What would be, would be. Whether she lived or died, if Danny lived or—

Danny.

She balled her fist in outrage. Everyone, from the captain, to Bonds, to June, even herself, she thought of as their last name. But, suddenly, because of one *damned kiss*, she was swooning and calling him *Danny*. What was next, marriage, kids? Give up the Corps? Other women had relationships while on active duty. Hell, they even had families and children.

They weren't on ships, though. They served on garrisons, ground duty, and forts like Kirk above her homeworld.

What if they assigned her there? What if some well-meaning fool decided he was doing her a favor by stationing her on MacGregor's World? Was the risk worth the reward?

Nadia's hand hovered over the big, red shutdown button. The complicated procedure and security checks in place to prevent her from doing exactly what she wanted had taken her far more time to overcome than she had anticipated. Here she was, though. In the dead of night, with only three hours until dawn, ready to shut it all down. Once she hit the button the bases heaters would instantly stop. Not even the emergency backups would engage, since she planted a virus that sent them into an unending maintenance cycle.

There was no going back. If the Alliance... if Wit hadn't sent someone to come get her, then they would freeze to death with the rest of the base.

Now or nothing.

She stamped the button flat. Alarms wailed like banshees out of a nightmare. It would take a full minute of her holding the button down for the reactor to go offline. On the off chance someone like Malik could get there in time, she drew the little pistol and took a bead on the lift doors. If they opened, she would fire without hesitation.

Sixty seconds felt like an eternity. Each one passing audibly in her mind. Would the Alliance arrive in time? What if no one came? What was her backup plan?

She thought, perhaps, with the right preparation, she could survive in one of the deep caves. It would be easy enough to flee the base, and the security who guarded it. As long as they weren't able to get the reactor up and running again, and she was confident they wouldn't be able to, then everyone on Zephyr Station would freeze to death the next night. At most, it would take three days. Nadia could survive that long.

She hoped.

Once they were all dead, she could return to the base, scavenge the equipment she would need and survive until either an Alliance rescue ship came or the next shuttle arrived in five weeks. Of course, once the entire Caliph Navy's FTLC stopped functioning, they would probably send someone to investigate.

Her internal clock ticked over to sixty and the entire base went dark. Emergency lighting above the lift flickered to life, but that was the only light. Not a single panel had power. It would take time for the temp to drop, but she could already feel the cold.

Pivoting, she lit the console up with her pistol. Sparks showered as she vaporized metal and melted plastic. Once the control console was nothing more than molten remains, she turned to the lift door and fired. It was made of sterner stuff and it took the rest of the pistol's plasma ammunition to warp and distort it to prevent anyone from easily opening it. Now she just needed to return to the doctor, tune their frequency to the Alliance's, and get the hell out.

She looked up at the ventilation shaft she needed to reach to escape. Three meters separated her and freedom. She stood 1.6 meters tall and could easily leap another third of a meter straight up. That left her shy by half a meter.

"Quit procrastinating," she told herself, to get moving.

Of course, all that math was predicated on a working knee, and in the several hours since she'd fallen, her knee throbbed even more.

Bending down, she instantly realized it wasn't going to work. She tried anyway, leaping straight up with her good leg but she came woefully short and ended up falling on her butt when her hurt knee refused to support her weight.

"Great," she muttered. There wasn't much to climb on, and with the lights off, she could barely see. Toxic fumes filled the room. The smell of burning plastic assaulted her nose and forced her to cough.

She grabbed the only working chair and placed it under the vent. It wasn't stable enough for her to climb, though. What could she use to stabilize it? The only thing in the room were—

Five minutes of exertion later, she had the remains of both bodies piled up against the chair, holding it perfectly still as she climbed up. With the added boost, she could just reach the lip with her cybernetic hand, which could easily pull her out.

"Thanks for the hand, boys," she said to the dead men. Her metal fingers grasped the lip and she pulled. A dull throbbing ache emanated from her ribcage as the parts of the cyber that were anchored to her body took the brunt of the force.

Two hours later, Nadia pulled herself up out of the exhaust shaft, grunting from the exertion, covered in grime and dirt. It was too cold to sweat, though. The little beads froze even as they formed, leaving her hair frosted and a layer of ice on her exposed skin.

The nanites in her shirt worked overtime pumping heat into her body, but they were never designed for sixty below. She needed a full thermal suit like she used on Zuckabar. That, however, was impossible to hide, as the only reason one would need it on Zephyr would be to go outside at night. Not something anyone stationed there was supposed to do.

She didn't have much longer before the cold won and she died. Forcing herself up, she limped to the exit of the cave, keeping her hands tucked under her arms and her head down.

"Doc, you there?" she asked.

Nothing.

That worried her more than the cold.

CHAPTER FORTY

Khaled looked out at the maw of the black hole and shivered. Even his renowned sense of humor escaped him at that moment.

"Death is not the end, but a separation," he muttered.

"Sir?" Lieutenant Sattar asked from beside him.

"It's an old quote from an ancient philosopher. *Ibn Arabi*. It's supposed to bring comfort when faced with death, to know it isn't the end of all things but the beginning of something new," he explained.

"Ah," his XO said. Though Khaled wasn't sure the man understood.

The black hole dominated the system, even at the distance they'd arrived in, it was still visible of sorts. Distorting the sun it ravaged, slowly and surely killing the system.

More than ever, he wanted to know why the ISB had ordered him to come. They couldn't possibly have a base here, and no fleet would be foolish enough to wander too close to such a hungry beast.

"Let's crack open those coordinates in the sealed packet," Khaled ordered. Unsealing the file required both him and his first officer to sign off on. They held their hands steady as the computer compared their biodata to the record. Once confirmed, the remaining orders were revealed.

Khaled looked at the screen like it was made of poison.

"Surely not," he muttered.

"Orders are orders, sir," Sattar said.

Khaled frowned inwardly. His XO acted as if he wouldn't obey every order given to him, as if the man were waiting for the chance to pounce and send him to the stocks.

"Of course, that's not what I mean. What are the odds a lone planet would survive, trapped between a black hole and a dying star? And why would anyone be there?"

Sattar simply shrugged. "It matters not, sir. Should I set a course?"

The weight of command pressed down on Khaled. He had two hundred men on his ship, and he didn't want to risk them needlessly. However, Sattar was correct about their ability to disregard orders. Khaled had none.

"Yes, follow the instructions exactly. I don't want to spend a thousand years falling into the maw of hell."

Yusra checked the clock again. Barely a minute had passed since the last time she looked and over an hour since their comms went down. She'd spent the first ten minutes just repeating the spy's name. When that didn't work, she started on plan B.

Malik would kill her the moment he thought something was wrong. She knew that. She read the man's correspondence. He had orders to kill her rather than allow her to escape or give any information to their enemies. Even without knowing the secret of FTLC they would rather she be dead than allow it in the hands of the enemy.

However, her plan B involved using the next cargo ship to escape hell. Not waiting around to freeze to death. The next ship was weeks away. Only in that moment did she realize how much she had counted on being rescued instead of rescuing herself. It was foolish and shortsighted. How could an Alliance agent, a woman to boot, free her from captivity.

"I'm going to die and my father's work will be for nothing."

Her only option was to hide. Yusra grabbed her pad, a ration bar, and a hairbrush, not sure what she was doing just that she had to leave.

As she headed for the door, the lights flickered and died. Emergency lighting clicked on. Yusra hesitated at the door. This was the plan, after all. Nadia would disable or destroy the reactor, eventually killing everyone on the base.

It was just... Yusra was no murderer. Yet... she couldn't let her father's work be used the way it was. She glanced at the door, wondering exactly what she could do if she didn't want to follow either plan.

Absolutely nothing was her silent response.

Malik leaped out of bed, coming up with his pistol in an instant. Pitch blackness greeted him. Cold air swirled around him, filling his heart with dread. He kept his SecPad beside the small bed he occupied and flipped it on. Light shed in the room, and the device functioned correctly; however, there was no connection to the central computer.

This was no malfunction; he could feel it. The equipment stolen was too specific for cold weather survival and climbing. Whoever did it, and it was now clear Zaid wasn't directly involved, had just sabotaged the reactor.

Malik swore, mostly at himself for letting his anger at the

betrayal get the better of him. He should have interrogated Zaid *before* killing him.

Out of bed and alert, he went to his closet and dressed in his cold-weather gear and armor. It wouldn't be enough to keep him alive for more than a day or two. With any luck he could get to the reactor room, find the source of the problem, and restart the device to keep them all alive.

He shrugged on his coat, zipped it all the way up and then grabbed the short-barreled plasma carbine he stored in a secure safe. The pistol would be sufficient for almost any situation, but he wanted more firepower. If there was sabotage, they were either there to kill or extract Dr. Yusra Abbasi or destroy the equipment that handled the FTLC for the Caliphate. Neither of which he could allow. He double-checked his armor, making sure it fit securely. Took a deep breath, and readied himself for his duty.

Nadia made it back into the base, hands frozen into claws as she pushed on the door with her shoulder. It only took her three attempts.

Pitch black, interrupted only by dim, red emergency lighting, greeted her from the interior. There were no windows looking out. No moon to cast light and no starlight came through the blackhole. Windows were a security risk, so they used advanced artificial reality displays that simulated images of the outside, giving people the illusion of an exterior.

She collapsed into the corner, her breath coming in ragged gasps and filling the air in front of her with steam. The base's internal temperature had already dropped ten degrees. In a few more hours, it would be below freezing. Probably just before the sun rose and warmed the place up.

With a silent growl, she pushed up, willing her body to move through the pain and cold. Her hands in particular hurt with a dull, throbbing ache. All she needed to do was reach the doctor's quarters and she could signal whatever ship the Alliance had sent. Her internal clock told her that she was two days into the five-day window. She hoped and prayed the ship was actually there.

From where she was to Abbasi's quarters was ten minutes of twists and turns, and three floors down. All she had to do was get there.

Which proved fairly easy. With main power down, the doors failed-secure, yet another difference between Caliph and Alliance. With the doors all electronically locked, there were very few people wandering the base. Those she came across were busy trying to find the problem, or warmer clothes.

Her hands finally thawed enough to use and the nanites in her vest even settled down to the point where sweat started to form. A painful tingling crept into her hands as she descended the emergency ladder down to Dr. Abbasi's level.

When she returned to the room, she could use Yusra's communications device to signal any ship in orbit, and then they would be on a Corsair within an hour and out of Caliphate space soon after.

"You will tell me who's helping you," Malik said from around the corner. Nadia froze. The blubbering response of Yusra came back, almost unintelligible. Nadia felt the fear from the woman.

She didn't want to get in close to Malik who out massed her by a good twenty kilos. He was dangerous and smart. She had to be careful. If he had the upper hand, he'd take her out without hesitation.

Nadia poked her head around the corner and pulled it back

instantly. Malik's back was to her, and he had a plasma carbine pressed up against Yusra's head.

Taking a deep breath and letting it out slowly to steady herself, she counted down from five. At one, she leaped out of the corner on her side. Malik spun, firing as he did so. Superheated plasma sizzled above her, striking the wall with an explosive clap. His instincts and speed were remarkable; had she not dived low, she'd be dead.

Nadia slid to a halt. Her barrel hovered over his chest and she squeezed the firing stud. Electrostatic charge leapt forward, striking him in the torso followed by the plasma. The impact knocked him back into Dr. Abbasi's room.

Yusra jumped up and pulled the exposed lever that opened and closed the door manually, slamming it shut.

"Why did you do that?" Nadia demanded as she stood up. "The communications gear we need is in there."

"He's not dead, that's why. Come. We can call your ship from the Hub."

Nadia followed Yusra back the way she had come to the emergency access stairs.

"What's the hub? That's not on any of the blueprints."

Yusra stopped, turning toward Nadia, hesitation clear in her eyes. A creeping sensation crawled up Nadia's spine. It felt like she was being lied to.

"I... I didn't say anything in my call for help because I feared you wouldn't come if I told the truth. But..."

"I saved your life, Yusra. I came into the worse possible place, parsecs from my home, into the proverbial lion's den to extract you. To be honest, at this point, you're coming with me whether you want to or not."

She thought on that for a minute, reaching a decision. "Can you bypass a blast door?"

"In my sleep. Lead the way."

Yusra led her down a hallway that Nadia had cleaned a hundred times. At the end of a seemingly blank wall, she pressed her hand against an unassuming spot and an audible click sounded. The wall thunked, unlatching but not moving.

"With the power down we'll have to push."

The two women lined up and heaved. Nadia's enhanced strength kicked in and her side throbbed where the anchor points attached the cybernetic arm. Centimeter by centimeter, the wall moved until it gave and swung freely. The door, which should have swung closed automatically behind them hung open on its hinges as they passed.

"Is this the Hub?" Fusion batteries lined the wall, their readouts glowing as they continued to power... something, not the base, not even the heat.

"No. This is the emergency backup power to the Hub. Enough to run the machines for months if needed."

"I killed the backup power."

"This is on its own system, completely independent of the base."

A lone lift door at the end of the hall was the only other way out.

"Is this where you store the quantum entanglement devices?"

Yusra shot her a furtive glance. There was definitely something the doctor wasn't telling her, beyond her own self-admitted lie.

"How do you know about that?" she asked. "I only told them I had the knowledge of how FTLC worked... not what it was."

"I've seen one up close before."

The lift binged and they entered. Nadia instinctively moved to the side, using the wall as cover. Yusra keyed in her code. The doors shut and the magnetic lift hummed to life, descending rapidly.

Nadia guided Yusra to the side, keeping her from exposing herself when the doors opened.

"No one is down here," Yusra said in response.

"Maybe, but why take the chance?" Nadia replied.

The sense of motion came to a halt as the lift slowed to a stop. The doors opened and Nadia grabbed Yusra to keep her from blindly charging out. She peeked, just to make sure.

A short hallway with workstations jutting out of the wall at regular intervals led to a pressure door. Windows in the door revealed a massive computer network beyond.

"Wow," Nadia whispered.

"It's not what you think," Yusra said. "I wish it was. Come, the comms are just beyond the door."

CHAPTER FORTY-ONE

PO Oliv pressed the headset hard against her ears. It was mostly a meaningless, emotional gesture she did to focus her mind. The headphones were perfect in their ability to cancel out noise and pressure around her. Even though she knew this, she still found herself holding them tightly to her head. Maybe it was instinct or maybe it was just a bad habit.

Regardless, she did it and, while doing so, focused on the sounds with all her might. There was something out there. She felt it in her bones. Maybe another ship, but something other than the black hole's gravitic pounding was at the edge of her ability to sense.

She glanced around the bridge for a second, taking her eyes off the panel. Everyone stationed in the command center was at ease, relaxed even. The gaping maw of the blackhole, visible on the forward viewer, dominated the bridge's attention.

It would her, too, if not for the slight ping she heard every few seconds. Maybe if she came at it from a different angle... Delicate fingers danced along the panel, zeroing out frequencies that were too far from what she heard to impact the signal, cleaning it up as she attacked the noise from an oblique angle.

"PO, you have something?" Ensign Brennan asked over their private comms.

Her interruption startled Oliv, making her jump a little.

"Aye, ma'am. I think so, at least. Here—" Oliv handed the ensign a pair of headphones from under the console and plugged them in. While it would make some sense for everything to be wireless aboard ship, and on the civilian vessels that was absolutely the case, aboard a warship, an errant signal would get them killed. The fewer electronic emanations the better, even if it meant having to deal with optical cables and physical controls.

Brennan slipped the headset on and listened. To her credit, she didn't jump to a conclusion, simply listened.

Oliv went back to work, filtering through the heavy metal drum beat of the black hole, the rapid fire of the dying star, and even the low bass of the planet below. All were sounds she couldn't remove because of how close and powerful they presented. What she needed was the one single percussion she heard every now and again. It would fade in and out, almost fast enough that she might have imagined it.

"Is that it?" Brennan asked.

Oliv cocked an eye at the young officer. She might make something of herself after all.

"Aye, ma'am, good ear."

Brennan nodded, keeping her lips shut as she listened some more. Another notch in her favor, Oliv decided.

"PO Collins, can you adjust course to heading two-seven-five, lateral, no acceleration," Oliv said. These kinds of attitude adjustments were common enough she didn't have to clear it with her boss Lieutenant Hössbacher, who was also the officer of the watch. He would have approved it even if she had. Hössbacher was good people.

"Aye, aye, attitude adjustment. Two-seven-five, lateral," Collins replied.

"PO, anything I need to know?" Lieutenant Hössbacher asked.

"Not yet, sir. As soon as I have something you will be the first to know."

"Sir!" Spacer McCall practically shouted. "Message from the surface. Call sign India."

"Get the captain!" Hössbacher replied instantly.

"I say again, any Alliance vessel on this frequency, this is India. Please respond."

Jacob wanted to shout for joy upon hearing Nadia's voice crackle over the radio.

"India, this is Indigo-One-Five-Actual, go ahead."

When the call came in, Jacob was in the conference room going over gravity maps of the system they were in. It wasn't often they had a chance to get up close and personal with a black hole, and he wasn't going to waste the scientific possibility.

"Indigo... I should have known," she said with obvious relief. "I need immediate extract. At least twenty hostiles are still active. Power to the base is mostly cut off. Over."

Jacob smiled at her professionalism. Who knew how long ago she'd infiltrated the enemy base, yet here she was, all business. The woman had a mind like a steel trap. Something he very much admired.

"Roger, India. Indigo-One-Five-Actual copies Lima Charlie. Extraction on the way." Jacob paused for a moment, checking the ground map. "Head South one-seven-seven three klicks to rally point alpha. Ground forces are in play, call-sign Nomad. Charlie-One-One will extract."

"Understood. India out."

No goodbye, nothing emotional—exactly what he expected from her. He breathed a sigh of relief. It would be good to see her again. Jacob closed out the holo of the maps, tossed his refuse in the recycler and headed for the bridge. When Jennings wasn't on station, the door to the briefing room stood continually open. He grinned, passing it by, sure now that one of the crew made it inoperable.

PO Cartwright manned the bridge hatch. The Marines were down in the boat bay ready to drop on a moment's notice.

"Sam, you know you don't have to be here, right?"

Cartwright was the ship's man-at-arms, and he served directly under the COB.

"Skipper, if Gunny Jennings finds out I left you unsecured, she'll beat me black and blue... sir."

Jacob grinned, patted the man on the shoulder. "Having been on the receiving end, I think you made the right call. Well done."

"Captain on the bridge," Cartwright said in a slightly louder-than-normal voice.

"Lieutenant Hössbacher, notify Nomad that our ground team is ready to go and give them their coordinates. Move the ship so we can drop the Marines as needed."

Roy spun in the chair and stood, gesturing for the captain to take it, then turned to Ensign Brennan. "Fionna, make the call."

The curly haired, fresh-faced ensign blushed at the use of her first name. "Aye, aye, sir. Notify Nomad of extraction."

Proud of the way his people handled their stations, Jacob took a moment to walk by each one and hover for just a moment, before clapping them on the shoulder and telling them so. He chose to praise in public as often as it was warranted.

"Lieutenant Brown, any problems with the fire controls for the new point defense lasers?" he asked.

"Captain Becket gave me thirty pages of tests to run, skipper. So far, they've passed with flying colors." Jacob turned to move to the next station when Brown waved at the monitor to his right. "I would like to point out, sir, that the new nodes run extremely hot during testing. Three times as hot as the ones running the rest of the ship. That's just during the testing. If we actually have to use them, it could be more."

Concern crossed Jacob's countenance. One of the most challenging problems ships faced was what to do with the waste heat generated by equipment and people. They had radiators, of course, fins that vented heat into space. In a last-ditch emergency situation, they also had the option of draining the can, which took a good bit of heat with it. However, as it turned out, the two most dangerous situations for heat buildup were during battle or when running silent. The latter could mitigate the problem by ejecting the heatsink at the right time, or out of view from the enemy. The former, well, the can was already drained at that point. They would risk total system shutdown at the most crucial, critical junction.

"Keep an eye on it and let the XO know if you come up with any thoughts on how to mitigate the problem."

"Aye, aye skipper."

From there he stopped at the Pit, but he left Collins alone to do her job. She was in the middle of a helm change for astro he didn't want to interfere with.

"Did you want the conn, sir?" Hössbacher asked.

"Negative, Roy. I'm on my way to engineering to see Chief Redfern. I just wanted to make sure everything is running smooth." Despite his worry about the ground operation, Jacob long since discovered he couldn't control everything. The best thing he could do was carry on as if the world would keep spinning.

Interceptor was in orbit, there were no enemy ships in detectable range, and the ground team was under the capable stewardship of Master Sergeant Cannon. Yes, he could sit in the center seat, tapping his fingers until they hurt, but it would prove worthless. All it would do was show the crew his worry.

Captain Khaled Al-Faris rubbed his bearded face, trying to wake himself up as he stared in the mirror. The once dashing young man had seen a few better days. *Too many years spent on a ship and not enough at home.*

A place he would much rather be than chasing ISB ghosts in a system the navigational charts showed as too dangerous to travel through.

He slapped the button on the bulkhead next to the hatch. "Bridge, captain. Status?" If he couldn't sleep, he might as well know where they were at.

"Bridge, Ensign Shah. Three hours to orbit, sir. We're decelerating at five-zero-zero gravities just as the instructions laid out. If it's permitted, sir, I have to say these guidelines are rather vague and disturbing."

"How so?" Khaled Al-Faris asked.

"Things move in space, sir. There's no exact coordinates. We have to stay above five hundred accelerating in and out of the system until we hit the planet's orbit. But we can't stay in orbit for more than three days? We have one specific frequency to make contact with the surface? I don't know which of these are because of the dangers of the black hole, or because of some unknown danger the ISB chose not to inform us of."

Khaled admired his officer's honesty. He knew he wouldn't get that from his XO, for the man had his nose so far up ISB's rearend he couldn't smell anything. Ensign Shah, though, took a chance and trusted his captain.

"Very well, Ensign, bring us to alert. I want the crew in their suits. Rotate out for meals and set up a schedule. Is there anything on the gravity sensors?"

"Aye sir, alert, suits, and meals. Gravity stations tell me there is too much interference. We're flying blind, sir."

"Captain out."

Blind... in space. How ironic. The ships that traveled the universe relied on the strong drum beat of space-time to guide them, like an ancient lighthouse. Yet another in the long list of reasons to avoid a black hole.

Regardless, in three hours he would find out. He had to be in orbit for the radio to work, according to the guidelines. Three more hours and they would know what was going on.

Maybe.

CHAPTER FORTY-TWO

Nadia put the mic down. Relief filled her with a calm she hadn't known in weeks. *Interceptor* was here for them... for her. *Of course, they sent Jacob.* If there was one thing her Navy man had proven over the last several years, it was he knew how to complete a mission. She just needed to follow suit.

"Rescue is on the way, Yusra. Where is the FTLC tech?"

"I told you, it's not what you think."

"You said that, but I've seen one. It's quantum entanglement and you invented it. We need a working device, not schematics, so we can duplicate it."

"Promise me you will take me away from here, give me a new life in the Alliance, no matter what?"

Nadia cocked her head to the side, trying to see beyond the visage the scientist put forth. Yes, she was a brilliant woman, obviously, but there was a tremendous amount of fear clouding her. Fear and something else... shame. Yusra's shame ran deep. It drove her every decision. Her every interaction.

"What did you do?" Nadia asked in a whisper.

"Only what they made me do. You have to understand. I

didn't invent this, my father did. He was a genius. I'm just the product of his education. It's not really quantum entanglement, not the way you think. It's much more complicated than that. It only works here," she said pointing at the floor.

"No... I've seen it on Medial. We know you have it on ships."

Yusra turned to the far door and hurried toward it, away from the lift and the rest of the base.

"You will see."

She entered a code, followed by a complicated scan. Nadia frowned as it only opened to a small room like an airlock. She trusted the doctor enough to follow her in. Once the door shut behind her, Yusra placed her eye against the scanner.

"This is a lot of independent security for a secret base," Nadia said.

"The base above is secret, this is something more. Only Malik knows the true secret."

A sinking feeling in the pit of her stomach filled her with dread. There was something more going on, something so much more and Nadia had a nagging feeling she should turn and run now, while she still could. Gripping the small pistol tightly, she continued to follow Yusra through yet another door, this time into a hallway with a half dozen consoles sticking out from the wall. Nadia made a note that she could hide behind one if needed.

"I want a straight answer, Dr. Abbasi. How do you have FTLC? If not quantum entanglement, then what?"

She looked away, then back at Nadia with eyes full of tears. "It was my father, you see. He was a great man, a great researcher. He knew there had to be a way to use quantum entanglement to have faster-than-light communications. He just couldn't find the right particle to entangle that would allow for it. He thought, maybe, if we studied the way particles interacted with black holes, then that could make it work... He had no idea, though."

The dread turned into a full-on body sweat. "Yusra..."

"It wasn't his fault." Her hand hovered over the button that opened the door. "He loved science. He just wanted to see..."

Nadia lunged forward and hit the button, not waiting for Yusra to finish whatever terrible story she was building up toward. There was no time for self-recrimination. Nadia needed the tech and they needed to get out of the base before Malik found them. The door opened and she brushed past the scientist. It wasn't like she would understand the quantum field machinery anyway and...

"What did your father do?" Nadia asked, staring at the room in disbelief.

"India, this is Nomad, how copy?" Danny said again for the third time since *Interceptor* had told them she was there.

"Anything?" Mac asked. They were huddled thirty meters south of the base, underneath an overhang that gave them a solid view of the buildings built into the crevice. The barracks was the easy one to spot. The two other ones, though, including what he thought was the main facility, were built into the walls and heavily shielded.

"If I had something, I would tell you," Danny said. These kinds of hurry-up-and-wait missions weren't his favorite. It was one thing to do a long-range reconnaissance or sit in a hole for a month listening to the enemy's radio transmissions.

They were on a hostile planet, with only hours to go before they had to bug out, in a system that would gladly kill them if their ship handler wasn't spot on.

"Sorry, Mac, I'm a little frustrated."

"This ain't going to make it better, look..." Mac pointed at the barracks as two dozen men in survival suits and plasma rifles stormed out.

"Down," Danny whispered. His men flattened against the rocky ground. Their outcropping gave them defilade against the base, but a sharp eyed soldier could ruin their ambush.

"Look at their body language," Rico suggested. "Were they locked in?"

He was right. They stretched, jumped around, and one man even stood still, looking up at the sun. All behaviors of people trapped for an extended period of time. Three of them broke off and went to what Danny suspected was the main entrance. They shouted in frustration as the door to the base didn't budge.

"What do you want to do?" Mac asked.

Their position was ideal for a firefight, ten meters up, with heavy rocks as cover. They could fire on the enemy with little danger of effective return fire. As long as they didn't have any crew-served weapons. Those changed the dance fast.

"Rico, take T-Bar and set up over there." Danny pointed to a crag ten meters to the west. It would put them out of LOS of the main entrance, but anyone trying to charge their position would be out in the open.

"Rog," Rico said. He hauled his pack and LMG with him as T-Bar followed suit, using his rifle to cover the move even while their blackout suits made them indistinguishable from the rocks.

"Us, boss?" Bubba asked in a whisper.

"I'm going to give India another half an hour, then we're going in and getting her whether she wants to come out or not."

Khaled frowned as his ship slipped into orbit around the rocky, barren planet. "Someone lives here?" he asked in disbelief.

"Could be a nice summer home, if you like dying," Lieutenant Sattar said.

Khaled turned in his chair, mouth hanging open. "My dear XO, did you just make a joke?"

"I'm afraid so, sir."

"Wonders never cease."

"I've still got nothing on gravity, sir," Ensign Shah said. "Radar is slightly more useful, but there is a lot of high-energy interactions in the atmosphere from the dying sun and the..." He pointed at the screen showing the magnificent, yet terrifying visage of the black hole.

"Are you saying there could be another ship in orbit and we wouldn't see her?" Khaled asked.

"Correct, sir. However, what other ship would be here? The radar and lidar are in constant fluctuation. We might have perfect visibility one second, and nothing the next. Between the pull of the singularity, and the radiation of the sun, I'm surprised the gravcoil even functions."

That was a sobering thought. If the gravcoil failed it would be a long, slow death. Technically, he imagined, it would be a normal-length death. However, to the rest of the universe, it would be long and slow.

"Let's not do that," he said. "Comms, open a channel. Use the codes we were provided."

"Masa base, this is the Caliph Destroyer *Al-Qud*. Come in."

Khaled expected an immediate reply, but none came. Even if they were delayed, he would think that the bases defenses would need to be stood down. He waited a full minute, watching the seconds on the main screen wind down.

"That's weird. Are we sure we're getting through?" Khaled asked.

Ensign Shah ran through a check on his console, then another. "The radio's working, and we're getting reflections off the surface. They're just not responding."

Captain Khaled Al-Faris hated to leave things as they were. How long did he sit in orbit? The restrictions in his orders didn't strictly forbid going to the surface...

"Try a few more times, and if they still don't respond, put together a landing party and take the Dhib down to the surface. If they're having equipment failure, that's why we could be here."

"Yes sir," Ensign Shah said.

CHAPTER FORTY-THREE

"Oliv, take a break," Tefiti said, holding out a cup of coffee to her. She didn't hear him, her focus so targeted on the screen in front of her. "Oliv," he said again, waving the coffee in front of her.

"Oy vey," Oliv muttered. She took the steaming hot mug. "Thank you, Tefiti."

The PO from Ohana slid into the chair next to hers. Astrogation had three stations, gravity was the one he and Oliv, along with a rotation of spacers manned daily. She lowered her headphones, rubbing her ears before leaning back.

"I heard it," she said. "Too quiet, though, for the computer to pick up. I swear, though, I heard it. A ship, not a big one, but a ship all the same, decelerating into orbit. It's gone now, though, so either I misheard or it's in orbit."

Tefiti looked over the logs for the last eight hours and scanning them with a practiced eye. He'd served a few years longer than her and some called him the best gravity man in the Navy. He could see where in the logs she thought she'd heard the ship, but he couldn't make heads or tails of it.

"Play it for me," he said.

Tefiti listened, headphones tight around his ears as the noise played. The black hole was like a hammer beating against metal. The rest of the spacetime noise was much harder to pick out... but he did hear something... like a soft thump in between the harsh sound of the black hole.

"Do you hear it?" she asked.

Tefiti nodded. "Aye, but... I can't say what it is. Has the database hit anything?"

She shook her head. "I couldn't get a clean enough read. Too much interference. If I were a betting woman, I would say it was a ship. Something small."

"A private freighter maybe? Like a resupply ship?" he asked.

Leaning back, Oliv ran a hand through her thick hair. Frizzy bits had started to stray from hours underneath the headphones.

"Could be, I just don't know."

"Get some rest. I'll make sure the captain knows."

"Thanks," she said with a smile. She stood, stretching out, before leaving the bridge. Tefiti admired the woman's skill and dedication. She spent two shifts trying to decipher the sound. Anyone else would have just logged it and moved on.

"XO," Tefiti said after he'd logged in.

"Yes, PO?"

"Sir, PO Oliv picked up a sound that might be another ship in the system. Because of the interference, it's just impossible to know for sure. I thought you and the skipper would like to know."

"Good work, Tefiti. Let PO Oliv know that's double for her," Carter said.

"Aye sir, will do."

. . .

They were blind and Carter knew it. The mission was predicated on the fact that there couldn't be any other ships in the area except for a handful of cargo freighters the Cali Navy had retrofitted for acceleration. He debated their options. With all the high-energy electrons bouncing around, radar and lidar were useless. It was a miracle they had visual reckoning.

Leaning back in the center seat, he played a game with himself. What would the captain do? Carter knew instantly what his skipper would do. What was good for the mission. What was good for the crew.

He pressed the button that opened a channel to the captain.

"Sir, I think you better get to the bridge. We have a situation up here."

"Acknowledged, I'll be right up." Jacob patted the armored hide of the Raptor Jennings wore. "ONR really outdid themselves when they came up with these beasts."

Jennings let out a sound somewhere between a growl and a laugh.

"Sir, do you know what the Office of Naval Research's grand contribution to the Raptor was?"

"I thought the designs came from ONR?" Jacob asked.

"Owens, show the skipper what came from ONR."

Owens reached up into his canopy and pulled a plastic blade from within. "In the unlikely scenario we will need to cut ourselves free of the crash webbing, ONR designed this handy plastic knife so that we can do so without hurting anyone," Lance Corporal Owens recited, like he was the poster child for a Marine recruiting station.

"No sir, these babies are pure Marines, 100% created at the Warfighting Lab on Blackrock."

"Lesson learned, Gunny. Carry on."

"Oorah, sir."

Jacob left the boat Bay, head shaking, and a large grin plastered on his face. Gunny Jennings and the Marines of Bravo-Two-Five were some of the bravest men and women he'd ever met, and they were certifiable.

It took him a few minutes to climb up to deck two, then walk forward dodging crew as they lined up for evening mess.

"Make a hole," Chief Pierre said when he saw the skipper.

"Thanks, Chief."

"We'll save you some soup, skipper."

A number of his people nodded and said, "Skipper" as he walked by. He knew them all by name and tried to greet each one when he was alone, but on his way to the bridge wasn't the time to stop and socialize.

Coming up the ladder from two, PO Desper jumped out of the way, letting him pass. "Glad to see you're out and about," he said as he started the climb.

"Me too, skipper. Thank you."

He was up and out, jogging back toward the stern to the last ladder in a few seconds. The final ladder up to the O-deck was nestled above the aft magazine storage and right before the entrances to torpedo rooms five and six. The hatches were dogged at the moment since the ship wasn't on alert. They were certainly in an elevated status of readiness, just not in action stations.

"Captain on deck," Cartwright said as he passed the double hatch that marked the bridge's boundary.

"I have the conn," he said as Carter stood up from the center seat.

"Captain has the conn, aye," Lieutenant Fawkes replied formally.

"Lay it on me, XO."

Carter turned to Tefiti who then played the audio over the bridge speakers.

"PO Oliv picked this up almost eight hours ago, sir. She's been working on it ever since. Tefiti made her take a break while he looked into it, and he thought it was worth my attention—"

"And you thought it worth mine. Fair enough. PO Tefiti, what do you think."

Tefiti clenched his jaw, lips going thin while he thought. "It could be a ship, skipper. However, I can't say for sure. Oliv thinks it is one. I'm inclined to agree. Unless we want to go active, though, I don't think we can know. With the way the black hole and sun are bouncing off the atmosphere, we might not even know then."

"What about the towed array?" Jacob asked.

Carter shook his head. "I thought of that, sir. After checking with Ensign Kai, I don't think it will work. Unless we want to go into higher orbit it won't be much good. We could even lose the array with all the high-energy particle collisions happening. The truth is, sir, if there is a ship out there, we can't know with active sensor unless we break orbit."

Jacob ran over the possibilities for a moment. If there were another ship, then it was a freighter. So far intel had called it right every step of the way. From the Guild's enhanced starlanes to the black hole. ONI hadn't known about Midway's purpose, but that wasn't part of the mission, either. Damn the limitations of the system. Too high orbit and they would have to engage the gravcoil, which meant running back to the starlane entrance and then returning. They had to stay low and slow.

"With this much electronic noise in the atmo, and the gravity interference from the black hole, would running silent do us any good?" Jacob asked his men.

Tefiti turned to his console, pulling up the ship's current emissions, along with the relative EM of the ship along with the ambient interference.

"I don't think so, sir. If we were on a planet, this would be a radar-, light-, and sound-absorbing fog. We're ninety percent obscured as is everyone else."

Jacob didn't like being blind. He certainly didn't like the possibility of another ship out there. However, they might have to spend two more days in orbit, then hours back to the starlane. Would the stress of a constant alert undermine the crew's capability? It was one thing to spend time in an ELS suit as part of a drill, but to live in it, day in and day out, for two or more days? He would like to wait until he had more than a guess to go on.

"Give me a second..." He sat in his chair, elbows on knees as he looked forward at the main screen showing the planet below. He said a silent prayer for direction, letting his mind find the words for him.

"XO, bring us to Yankee. No suits. However, I want everyone to be in arm's reach of the ELS at all times."

"Aye, aye, sir, set Condition Yankee. Suits at the ready."

Klaxons wailed throughout the ship as Spacer Gouger's voice filled every crack and crevice. "All hands, set Condition Yankee, no suits. I say again: set Condition Yankee. Keep your suits at the ready."

It wasn't often they would have such a high level of readiness without ELS suits. If anything did go down, though, they would be ready.

"Jen, when are we going to be over the outpost again?" he asked PO Collins.

"Approximately five minutes, sir. We're orbiting at a good clip."

Jacob had an idea. "PO Tefiti, can we drop an anchor?"

Tefiti's tattooed face looked grim as he shook his head. "No sir. The same energetic reactions will destroy any satellite we put out."

"Worth a shot. I guess we're just going to have to pay really close attention."

CHAPTER FORTY-FOUR

Khaled scowled. The interference on their systems was even greater than Ensign Shah had surmised. They were blind and deaf.

"Okay, that's enough, Shah. Take as many men as you can fit in a Dhib and go down there and see what is going on. If it's an equipment failure, then assist them. If they complain, don't get out, just come right back up."

"Yes sir. I'm on it."

Khaled glanced over at his XO who didn't seem to mind him giving the assignment to Shah, when technically it was an XO's job. However, Khaled didn't fully trust his second.

"Helm, put us in geosynchronous orbit above the base."

"Yes sir, geo-synch orbit."

In short order, Shah rounded up twenty ratings and armed them with plasma rifles and pistols. The experimental destroyer they served on wasn't fully crewed. No Immortal Guards or regular army types. His twenty-year-old ratings would have to do. Not that he was much older.

"Ifriti, you good to go?" Shah said as he buckled in next to the Dhib pilot.

"Yes sir. Say when."

Shah smiled as he assisted the pilot in the preflight. It wouldn't be long and they would be down on the planet, and then they could get the heck out of this Allah-forsaken system. What reason could they possibly have for building a base in a dying system?

The complex machinery humming in the room was so far above Nadia's understanding of science it might as well have been alien. Lights flickered from the one thing she did recognize: a massive fusion reactor centered inside a huge cavern, large enough to park a light cruiser inside. There was barely walking space once the blast doors closed behind her.

"Your father built all this?" Nadia asked.

Yusra shook her head enthusiastically. "It was his dream to create an FTL system that could unite the galaxy. Imagine, instantaneous communications everywhere. It would be like it was on old Earth, everyone connected. Everyone could speak to everyone."

Nadia wished the universe were that simple, that it actually worked that way.

"That's not what happened, though, is it?" Nadia asked.

A single tear ran down Yusra's cheek. She sniffed, wiping it away with her sleeve.

"No. Once he completed the machine you see here, and dozens of prototype receivers, the ISB moved in and took over. He told them he wanted this to be the contribution of Allah to the galaxy. The ISB stripped him naked and forced him onto the surface of the planet that night. He died alone, freezing in the darkness, thinking his life's work was for nothing."

The pain in Yusra's voice hit Nadia hard. Her usual steely emotional armor cracked slightly as the emotion poured out of the woman. She got it, for sure. Her mother had fled the ISB, and the reign of terror that came when Caliph Hamid murdered his father and took over the Caliphate.

Nadia struggled to push the surge of emotions and sympathy aside. Yusra's father's idiotic ideals had led to the enemy of all humanity getting the most powerful weapon ever known.

"How does it work?" Nadia asked. She looked over as the scientist opened her mouth. "And keep it simple."

Yusra nodded sheepishly. "If I could do that, I would be dead. What the ISB failed to understand, what everyone failed to understand, my dad wasn't just a genius. He was gifted. Beyond, gifted. I know what this machine is. I know what the devices he created to go with it are. I know what they do, and I know how they do it. What I can't tell you is why it works. I've spent the majority of my life confined here, reading his notes, studying his equipment, trying to decipher it. So have other scientists, but they all gave up. It was too far beyond them."

"What about you?"

Yusra placed a hand on the computer beside her. "In truth, it is too far beyond me as well."

"If you can't tell me the why, tell me the what," Nadia demanded. The scientist *seemed* to be honest, but Nadia wondered if Yusra knew more than she let on.

"This machine is like a telegraph. It can send and receive. However, the units my father created with it can only send and receive to here." She pointed at the ground. "They can't send to each other. If you destroy this... then none of them will work and they will never be able to duplicate them."

Nadia wished she had something stronger than a holdout plasma pistol. Like a nuke.

"Can you overload the reactor?" she asked.

Yusra shook her head. "There are safety mechanisms in place to stop any form of sabotage. The only option is to blow it up. I don't have any explosives though."

"How far down are we?" Nadia asked.

"Five hundred meters."

Nadia looked up at the ceiling, frowning. Could the Interceptor's Long 9 penetrate this far down?

"That's not my area of expertise," she said aloud.

"What?" Yusra asked.

"The ship in orbit, the one here to rescue us. I'll leave it up to them. Come on, we need to get out of here before Malik finds us."

Nadia took one last look at the amazing machine, more than just a wistful glance, she committed as much as she could to memory. If the doctor told the truth, and Nadia believed she had, then destroying this would end the FTLC the Caliphate had while eliminating their advantage. She led her back through the blast door.

Malik waited for them.

Nadia reacted with the trained reflexes of a combat vet, shoving Yusra aside as Malik fired his carbine. Plasma burned through the air, striking the wall next to her.

Spinning, Nadia fired her pistol blind, grabbed Yusra, and shoved her back into the room with the machine. A plasma beam seared her leg as she followed the scientist, agony blossoming as flesh and nerves burned. The blast door was still open, and Malik advanced, firing at the floor.

He doesn't want to hit the FTLC.

Pain and Nadia were old friends. She ignored it, pushing it aside. Her leg refused to function, but she was far from helpless.

Crawling as fast as she could to the wall, she reached up and slammed the emergency shut mechanism.

Malik screamed. His feet echoing on the deck as he ran for the closing door.

Air hissed as the door shut. Malik raged on the other side, shooting the blast door ineffectively.

They were trapped, but Malik wouldn't be getting through.

Nadia huddled, trying every technique she knew to block out the pain. Fear gripped her, fear that she had lost her leg, fear that her mission would fail.

"Come on," she muttered through gritted teeth. "You can do this." With extreme effort, hands shaking, she took the small comm's unit and activated the transmitter.

"Nomad, Nomad, this is India, come in."

Static.

"Boss, it's time," Mac said.

Danny swore. He'd let ten minutes go by, then ten more and still no response. Meanwhile, the soldiers fanning out from the barracks set up a security perimeter and continued to work at the door. Every minute he delayed was a minute that made his job more dangerous. If they'd attacked immediately, they could have taken them by surprise, but that ship had sailed.

"Okay. Don't miss."

There were too many to kill in one sweep. No matter how he played it, this was going to be a firefight. India wasn't responding, and even if she did, she couldn't come out in the middle of this.

Danny took a deep breath, and when he let it out, he forced out all his anxiety and stress with it. All that was left was the machine. The soldier who'd trained countless hours, performed hundreds of missions, and pulled the trigger thousands of times.

"On three."

His team had coil rifles; powerful weapons capable of defeating even the strongest light armor. There was no body armor that would protect the men below from the wrath they were about to bring down.

"Bubba, target the closest one. Mac, see the guy with no hat on, he's the leader. Take him down first. T-Bar, grenades. Rico, full auto, suppressing fire."

A chorus of "roger" came back to him. They were ready. The odds sucked, but his team had the element of surprise.

"Shoot straight," he said. "Go."

The cacophony of fire roared through the canyon. Rico fired first; his LMG spitting out rounds at a rate of three per second. Air rippled where they passed and the hot metal turned men into pincushions, blowing their insides all over the rocky ground. Mac's rifle cracked sharply, and the officer went down in a splash of crimson. T-Bar wracked the grenade launcher under his rifle like a shotgun and fired one, then another. The projectiles flew the air in a lazy arc. The first one detonated in the air, showering a twenty-meter area in superheated shrapnel. The second one sailed through, hitting far back and driving the cowering men forward.

Finally, Bubba and Danny popped up, rifles shouldered and their selector switches to auto. Fifty round boxes ran dry in seconds as they sprayed the remaining soldiers with death and destruction.

When the last round hit the dirt, not a single Caliphate soldier moved, nor had they even had the chance to fire back.

"I almost feel bad about that," Rico said. "Almost."

Danny had long ago disassociated his emotions from what he did. Taking a life was just part of the job. He didn't like it, but he didn't agonize over it, either. His men lived, that's all he cared about. Part of him wondered if he'd hit the threshold he worried about for his men. Had he lost his soul? Had he killed too much?

"Move out. Rico, door," Danny ordered.

They fanned out over the empty canyon floor, thirty meters between them and the enemy. It was no time to be lazy. They kept one eye on the bodies and any that looked like they could still be alive received a double tap.

Rico crouched in front of the blast door, LMG slung behind him as he went over the mechanism. "It's magnetically sealed, failed secure, boss. I'm gonna have to blow it."

"Are you waiting for an invitation? Fall back, take cover on the far side of the barrack." Danny stayed to cover the demo while the other three hustled to the designated position.

"I'm not sure, man. This isn't like any blast door I've ever seen. I don't know how much to put on it..." Rico said over his shoulder.

Danny glanced at the door, then at the sky. This was a problem. They were already a few hours over how long he'd planned to stay. If night fell, they would have to either stay the night in the base, or bug out to the *Interceptor*.

He keyed his mic, cocking his head to the side to bring it closer to his mouth. "India, this is Nomad. How copy?"

Static greeted him.

"They could be too far down for the handhelds to reach?" Rico suggested as he packed the explosive on the door.

"Use it all," Danny said.

"What if we need to blow another door?"

"It won't matter if we can't get through this one. Use it all."

Rico shrugged off his pack, digging out the rest of the bars, and started placing shaped bricks on the door. "This would be an excellent use of the binary molecular de-bonders I keep asking for," he noted.

"Yeah, yeah, tell it to supply." It was an old tale. While A-teams got the best gear, they didn't always get the gear they wanted or needed. He had a locker full of useless crap he planned to sell one day. It was his retirement package. Things got lost in the field all the time and more so when the S4 insisted his team carry *modular sleep systems* even while stationed on a base. Those were *lost* on an FTX a week after they were issued. A tragic accident involving a waterfall and a swarm of truck-sized *moosegers*

"Ready," Rico announced.

They backed up to the barracks making sure to cover their rear before ducking behind the building.

"Those are shape charges, right?" Mac asked.

Rico grinned. "You know, I might have forgot that part."

"Oh holy fu—"

The detonation shook the barracks and filled the air with dust. The men cowered with their ears covered as the shockwave rolled over them.

Danny shouldered his rifle, spun around the corner and charged for the door, followed by his men.

"Knock, knock," T-Bar said.

The remains of the door littered the inside hallway, pockmarks riddled the walls from where the shrapnel bounced around. Danny was glad no one was in there; it would have been an absolute mess.

"India, this is Nomad, how copy?"

"Nomad... India... down... six... blocked."

"Rico, scan it," Danny ordered.

Rico slung his weapon behind him and pulled out a scanner capable of tracking signals among other things.

"Ready."

"India, say again."

"India trapped at..." The signal jumbled into static.

"Got it. That way," Rico pointed.

Danny took point, letting Rico guide him with a hand on his shoulder. "T-Bar, Bubba, secure our six."

The base loomed before him, and as far as Danny could tell, it was a maze of corridors. The computer would show them how to get there, but could they get back?

CHAPTER FORTY-FIVE

With T-Bar and Bubba watching their six, Danny moved into the depths of the base with Rico in front, using the tracker to find their route. Mac covered their six with his pistol. The sniper rifle slung on his back was too unwieldy to use inside.

"This way," Rico said. The handheld used ultrasonics, a radio frequency tracker, and a rudimentary AI to map the base and guide them to the last known location of India's signal.

Even in a building they had never visited or seen, it was good enough to get them through almost without fail.

"Boss, you ain't gonna like this," T-Bar whispered.

"What?"

"Company. A Dhib just over flew our location, they're circling."

A Dhib? What... that would mean there was an enemy warship in orbit.

"Call *Interceptor* quick. Tell them before the Dhib jams us."

"What happened here?" Ensign Shah said from the passenger seat looking out the window. The Dhib banked slowly, keeping the base as its focus.

"Any movement?" Ifriti asked.

"Nothing. They were obviously attacked, and from the smoke still rising from the bodies, I think it was today. Activate ECM."

Ifriti flipped the switch, slamming a curtain of EMI down on the area.

"That look like a good place to land, Ensign?" Ifriti asked as he pointed to a rocky outcropping south of the base.

"Do it."

Chief Boudreaux lay back with her boots up on the console, reading a trashy romance novel she'd had on her NavPad for years. Hours had passed since they landed, and she wasn't one to do busy work. If her Corsair needed maintenance, she would attend to it. Otherwise, she was going to read or sleep. Her book was just getting to the good part when Midship Watanabe interrupted her.

"Chief, I've got a blinking EMI light down here. Can you come look?"

Boudreaux grumbled something about midships as she pocketed her NavPad. She was already unbuckled, but it took her a moment to extract herself from the comfortable position.

"Stawarski," she said to the sleeping PO in the second seat.

His eyes popped open.

"Keep an eye on the controls," she said.

"Aye, Chief." He sat up straighter, shaking out his hands.

Boudreaux could fly the Corsair one-handed. Having a pilot, gunner, and EW was the right call for this mission, though.

Watanabe manned the comm's position below the cockpit. Boudreaux climbed down the short ladder and hit the bottom deck with a crunch.

Watanabe tapped the light trying to confirm it wasn't a fault.

"That's not EMI, that's jamming," Boudreaux said, suddenly very much alert.

"Who's jamming us? The base?" Watanabe asked.

"Maybe? It's originating in that direction." She pointed toward the way the troopers had departed. "Two point three klicks."

Boudreaux swore. If the base knew they were there, then the mission was about to get very loud. If they needed CAS they were crap out of luck. As the only Corsair, if she went down, then everyone was trapped on the planet to die. It wasn't like *Interceptor* could land.

She reached past Watanabe and brought up the laser communications system, searching for *Interceptor* in orbit. The computer knew the general location of the ship, but with the jamming, she would have to look visually using the FLIR and that took precious minutes. Thermal was almost useless, with all the upper atmosphere interactions. She turned it off and refocused the laser to a wider beam. If she caught even the edge of the ship, she could narrow it down.

"Got it," she muttered as the laser picked up the ship. Within seconds she had a lock on.

"This is Charlie-One-One, come in Indigo."

"Indigo here, Charlie, go ahead." The crystal-clear voice belonged to Ensign Brennan.

"I think the ground team is under attack. We're experiencing localized jamming and I don't think it's environmental."

"Wait one, Charlie."

Seconds ticked by and Boudreaux had to fight her own

instinct to take off and go help. Her original logic stood. She was the only ticket off planet. If the troopers were in trouble, it was on them.

"Charlie, we're seeing the jamming as well. Standby. Do not depart from your location. Power down for one hour and we will call you back. I say again, power down."

Power down? Why? The only reason to do that was—

"Mon dieu. Shut it down, shut it all down. Stawarski, emergency shutdown." Boudreaux leaped for the ladder, painfully slamming her knee as she half climbed half hopped to the cockpit. He finished the procedure before she was back in her seat.

"What's going on, Chief?" Watanabe asked as she frantically went through the shutdown procedure.

Boudreaux didn't even wait to sit before she flipped up the row of red safety switches and jammed them all down with one hand, cutting power to the ship. The lights died and the temperature immediately climbed.

"The only reason for us to cut power is to avoid detection. Which means there's a ship in orbit above us."

―――――

"All hands, set Condition Zulu: battle stations. I say again, set Condition Zulu: battle stations." Brennan's Irish lilt rang throughout the ship. No corner, no place a crew could be, escaped the notification. *Interceptor* was already at Condition Zulu, but battle stations was a whole lot more. ELS suits were donned, ammo moved to the turrets, torpedoes loaded. The reactor output increased, charging all the supercapacitors in the ship for maximum readiness.

Jacob pulled on his trusty ELS suit. The red stripe up his right leg and his red helmet denoted him as not only the captain but one who had seen combat before. He wasted no time once the alarm went out. He could find out why when he arrived on the bridge.

Less than two minutes after the klaxon wailed, Jacob strode onto the bridge.

"I have the conn," he said.

"Captain has the conn, I stand relieved," Lieutenant Kai said. "I'll get to engineering, sir." He brushed past on the way out in a hurry to get to his combat station.

Jacob racked his helmet on the back of his chair. He found keeping the helmet off until the last minute relaxed the crew. Battle stations was stressful enough, he didn't need to add to their nerves by sealing his helmet at the first sign of trouble.

"Roy, fill me in?" Since Lieutenant Fawkes' battle station was DCS, that made Lieutenant Roy Hössbacher the de facto XO for a situation report on what was happening.

"Sir, several things happened at once. We received a partial message from Nomad. It was too garbled to understand, though. From there we started going over the passive sensors, but again the unique properties of the area make us blind, deaf, and partially dumb. Once we couldn't contact Nomad, we tried for Charlie One-One, no go. A few minutes later, Charlie found us, somehow, with a tight-beam laser."

Jacob raised an eyebrow, a little shocked. "Wait? Chief Boudreaux hit us with a tight-beam laser from the surface, by eyeballing it?"

Roy shared his shock along with an amused grin. "Aye, skipper. One for the books. She told us that there is localized jamming happening at the base. Which means the jig is up..."

"Except?" Jacob asked. This was always a possibility. He wished the Corsair could provide air support, but if anything happened to the ship, his ground team would be stuck on the planet. If they hadn't gotten the Mudcat blown up on Midway, they could have taken it with them. Instead, all he had were his Marines on standby.

"Except, India killed the power and Nomad reported entry into the base. The question becomes, who's doing the jamming?"

Jacob turned slowly around the bridge, taking in every monitor in a moment's glance before coming to the same realization his crew already had.

"We're not alone?"

Roy nodded with a frown. "There could be other explanations, skipper, but this would be the most likely."

"Good man," he said, clapping Roy on the shoulder.

Jacob took his seat and prepared himself. He didn't know for sure that ship-to-ship combat was imminent, but his gut told him it was.

"Gouger, put me on the ship wide."

"Aye, aye, sir. You're on."

Jacob cleared his throat and gave his most confident and direct look at the camera. Some would see, all would hear.

"Attention, *Interceptor*, this is your captain. We stand at a crossroads. Below us, our comrades fight for their lives. Our intel on this planet and the mission was spot-on. ONI outdid themselves. However, no mission, no matter how well planned, no matter how well executed, avoids Mr. Murphy.

"Because of the nature of the black hole, we are blind. We have, though, a strong reason to believe that there is another ship in orbit with us. A warship. This isn't the first time we've faced fateful odds. Some of you have been with us since the beginning, others are new. All of you have a proud history of bravery and excellence.

"If we must go to battle, our mission, our victory, our lives will depend on each and every one of you. You must dig deep.

It's all right to be afraid, there is no courage without fear. No heroism without bravery.

"*Interceptor* will not let us down. She's the fastest, strongest, toughest Hellcat in the Navy. Like the shark on her bow, she is the predator in space, not the prey.

"I have faith in you all. I know that you have what it takes to do what must be done. I have seen your bravery, I have seen your dedication, and I know that you will not let me down.

"Through faith and determination, we will be victorious. Also, when we return to Zuckabar, having completed our mission to great success… the first round's on me. Godspeed and good luck, Captain out."

He killed the comm and leaned back suddenly drained from the exertion.

"Skipper?" Chief Suresh said from the Pit.

"Yes, Devi?"

"You gave me goosebumps there," she said with a mocking grin.

"All right, COB, keep it up and I'll promote you to civilian."

"With all due respect sir, you couldn't fly this ship without me."

He laughed, lightening the mood on the bridge. "Okay, time to get to work people. Helmets on and drain the can."

"Aye sir," Roy said. "Felix, make the announcement."

"Aye, aye sir." Gouger said. He activated the ship wide and spoke clearly for all to hear. "All hands, helmets on. Helmets on. Helmets on. Contact your department heads if you cannot comply."

CHAPTER FORTY-SIX

Khaled frowned as Ensign Shah reported. The base was under attack, multiple wounded and it was all fresh.

"XO, battle stations. Just in case."

"Aye sir, battle stations."

The alarms rang throughout the ship as his people prepared the experimental destroyer for combat. They pulled on fire retardant suits and made sure their respirators were intact.

"Tactical, missile launcher status?"

"Aye sir, the computer reports all Thunderbolt batteries are responding."

"Good, good." The tactical shift of the destroyer doctrine didn't make a lot of sense to Khaled. Arming destroyers with short range, area saturation weapons for close-in combat, seemed like one of those ideas someone who had never seen combat would come up with. Not that anyone asked Khaled his opinion.

He would wait until the ship reported ready, then go on active sensors. It would be the only way to know for certain where any other ships in orbit were. Just because he couldn't think of any other reason the base was attacked didn't mean there wasn't one.

"Comms, put me through to Ensign Shah."

"Yes sir, one second."

The line clicked open, and Khaled waited for the static to subside. They could overcome their own jamming, but with the bizarre atmosphere interference their communications was messy.

"Shah, this is the captain. I want you to enter the base and assess the situation. Do not take any unnecessary risks. Do you copy?"

Static swirled around, growing louder then quieter.

"Yes sir. Assess the situation, no risk."

"Well done. Captain out."

Khaled leaned forward, running down the list of things he needed to do and found all of them were finished. His ship was ready. They just needed to know what they faced.

"Sir, orders?" his XO asked.

It wasn't that Khaled feared combat, or even dying. He feared the loss of his crew if anything were to go wrong. What if the ship out there was a cruiser? It seemed unlikely since the only reason *Al-Qud* made it was because of her acceleration. Larger, more mass-intensive ships simply couldn't accelerate as fast. So either there was a freighter out there manned by pirates or rogues, or there was a warship.

He prayed to Allah that it wasn't a warship. His destroyer's only weapon was the experimental FPMS, fast plasma missile systems. What they called Thunderbolt. He could launch hundreds in a barrage, but the weapon system was intended to enforce orbital jurisdiction. Not interstellar combat.

"XO, if we go active, at what distance can we expect to pick up an enemy ship?"

"It's hard to say, sir. Could be a few thousand klicks. Maybe less..."

Khaled didn't like not knowing. If they activated sensors, they would shine like a beacon on another ship's passives. If they didn't see anything, it would put them at a serious disadvantage.

"Stay silent for now. Let's wait and see."

"Contact front," T-Bar yelled as he opened fire with his coil rifle. Air sizzled as the five-millimeter rounds whipped out at fifteen hundred meters per second. Glowing from friction, the rounds looked like tracers as they shot through the air before impact. The first three soldiers went down in a heap, torn to shreds by concentrated fire. The others scattered diving behind the barracks building and any cover they could find.

When the shaped charge blew the blast door open, it did so like a butterfly, leaving a meter on either side for the two troopers, who used the reinforced metal as cover.

"Bubba, pop smoke," T-Bar said.

The big man pulled an all-purpose smoke grenade from his vest, activated it, and threw it out the door. Thermal and visual blocking smoke poured out of the little cylinder, instantly obfuscating the front door.

"Nomad, this is T-Bar, we are in contact. Hurry it up."

Green beams of electrostatic plasma passed through the smoke, burning holes in the walls behind them and starting a fire. The edges of the blast door absorbed a half dozen hits and started to glow around the edges.

Nomad stood in front of the open secret door they had found, revealing a lift leading down to who knows where. He was right about the place, it was a labyrinth, as if it were designed to keep people lost and confused.

"Anytime Rico," Danny said.

"Everyone's a critic." The soldier knelt in front of the panel with it cracked open. Wires connected his electronics to the lifts as he tried to override the system locally. Mac was one corner back, covering their six while Danny acted as immediate security.

"Got it," Rico said. The lift doors opened. Danny brought up his rifle to cover it, frowning as he noticed the still smoking plasma burn on the back wall.

"Looks like India's busy. Let's go."

Rico and Mac collapsed on him and they started the lift. There were only two options, up and down. He hit down. For operators, lifts were nightmare scenarios: small, compact, and anyone on the other side knew exactly where they would come out.

"Grenades?" Mac asked.

"Flashbangs," Danny agreed. They pushed themselves up against the walls as much as possible, pulled out a grenade each and thumbed them on. They didn't have the fancy voice operated ones the Marines used. Too much could go wrong in the heat of battle.

The doors opened and they side-threw them out, never even looking.

A loud, BANG, sounded at the same time a bright flash of light lit up the lift like a supernova.

Danny spun through the door, going low, while Mac covered him high. Plasma fire lit up the doorway above Danny. He fired his rifle in a full auto burst to keep whoever was shooting at them down.

A glance to his left told him that Mac was okay. The hall they were in had consoles sticking out of the walls at regular intervals. They weren't hardened, but they would do for temporary cover. Whoever fired at them was at the end of the ten-meter-long hall behind his own cover. Danny risked a peek. The door at the end was covered in scorch marks and the center of it glowed from repeated plasma hits.

"He's trying to get through, Mac. India must be on the other side."

"Roger that."

Mac pulled another grenade, this one an explosive, and thumbed the activator. He could throw it blind, but Danny knew he stood a much better chance of hitting his target if he could see where to huck it.

"On three... one..." When he hit three, Danny ducked out low from the side and sprayed the hall with a long burst from his rifle. Rounds punched through the consoles, walls, and ceiling.

Danny watched the grenade sail through the air, willing it to blow at just the right time. A man with a well kept beard and crazy eyes, leaped out from behind the console, firing his weapon, right into Danny's line of fire. He didn't hesitate. Three coil rounds popped him like a watermelon, spraying the door. Then the shrapnel grenade went off, shredding his body and showering the rest of the wall with his guts.

"Clear," Danny shouted as he stood and moved forward, never taking his rifle off the body.

"Clear," Mac shouted, following suit.

They got to the body of the man. It was hardly recognizable as a human being anymore.

"Rico, come get this door open," Mac said.

A feeling of dread came over Danny when Rico didn't respond.

"Stay here," he said. He turned and went back to the lift, rifle up just in case. He spied Rico's legs, splayed out from the left side of the lift.

Danny closed his eyes, anger flooding through him and gone with the next heartbeat. There would be time to mourn, just not yet.

"Rico?" he asked as he poked his head in.

Bad luck. That's what it was sometimes. Every soldier on his team knew it. You could make all the right decisions, but sometimes it didn't matter if you went left or right, when it was your time, it was your time.

Rico's head was gone, burned off from a direct hit by the plasma rifle. Danny reached down and dug through his tacvest and grabbed his tags, just to be on the safe side. He had no intention of leaving his friend on the planet, but that wasn't always possible.

"What about the door?" Mac asked.

Danny hustled back down the hall, shaking his head when Mac's look asked.

"Try knocking," Danny said.

Mac gave the lift a glance, saying goodbye to his friend, then wrapped his knuckles on the door. "Alliance Special Forces. We're here to rescue you," he said.

To Danny's shock, the door opened. Inside a heavyset Caliph woman sat, with a shaking, sweating, woman who matched India's image, cradled in her lap. A bad plasma burn—more than bad, ran across India's thigh.

"Ma'am, Admiral DeBeck sent us to extract you, can you move?" he asked.

"I can damn well run if I have to," Nadia said. Though the way she shivered as she spoke said that it wasn't likely.

"Mac, help the lady up."

She could stand, even hop a little, but not without hanging

on to Mac. The doctor, on the other hand, could move on her own.

"Do you have any explosives?" Nadia asked.

"Grenades. We used the heavy stuff to get in."

Nadia gestured at the vast complex of machinery below her. "Would they destroy this?"

Danny glanced at the fist-sized cylinder on his belt. "No ma'am. Not likely."

She nodded as if she already had come to that conclusion.

"Sergeant..." She paused, waiting for him to tell her his name.

"Master Sergeant Cannon, ma'am, you can call me Nomad."

"Right. Nomad, under no circumstances can we leave this base intact. Understood? If we all die, then we die, but this machine *must* be destroyed."

Danny felt the cool, calm resolve of experience wash over him. "Can do."

CHAPTER FORTY-SEVEN

Shah cradled his plasma rifle to his chest, his knees pulled up in terror. When the captain sent him down, he hadn't actually expected *ground* combat. He was no soldier, no martyr.

The whine of their death rifles filled the air as the unstoppable projectiles tore more of his shipmates to shreds. He had to do something, but his hands refused to move.

"Ensign, fire your rifle," the kid next to him yelled.

Shah looked over just in time to see his head explode and bits of blood and brains splashed across Shah's face.

He was going to die. They were all going to die and there wasn't anything he could do about it. A glance at the kid's body revealed the two grenades he carried. Maybe... maybe Shah could throw one and hit well enough to make them stop firing for a second. Then his men could retreat a little farther away.

He grabbed the grenade, fumbling the mechanism. He'd had a class—once. Adrenaline purged his fine motor skills and his training. The light turned green and he hurled it for all he was worth.

. . .

T-Bar leaned out, firing full auto until the mag ran dry. Two more dropped, including one hiding behind cover who had forgotten to put his head down.

He ejected the mag, letting it clatter to the ground as he reached behind him to pull another one out. The world slowed down as the grenade sailed perfectly through the door to land halfway between him and Bubba. He made no decision, thought nothing through, he simply acted, hurling himself onto the deadly weapon with as much speed as he could muster.

Plasma ignited, fountaining up through him at five thousand degrees, killing him instantly and burning Bubba's face and arm from two meters away.

Shah yelled for his men to run. There was an outcropping not far away that would be excellent natural cover and give them the high ground. There were twelve of them remaining. Twelve out of twenty.

He waited, waving them toward cover as they struggled themselves to get up and move. The overwhelming fear Shah felt was still there but, in the background, repressed under the need to save what remained of his people.

No fire followed them as they ran, leaping behind the rocks. Shah was the last one in, lying down and lining up his rifle with the entrance. They were at a semi-oblique angle, perfect to ambush whoever came out. A classic kill-box, he thought to himself.

"Indigo actual, this is Nomad. We need immediate fire support on our location." Despite the jamming and the planetary interference, the signal managed to reach *Interceptor* intact.

Jacob wanted to send in the Corsair to provide CAS but there was still the issue of the bird going down and leaving them all stuck on the planet. No, the Corsair had to stay tucked safely away.

However, the Corsair wasn't his only option. The manual on the Raptors said an orbital drop was possible. The external jump jets would slow them down enough to stay intact when they hit. The only trick the orbital part added was the heat. If the Raptor's heat resistant armor failed in any way, his Marines would die.

If he didn't send them, Nomad and India would surely die.

Jacob straightened up in his chair, thumbing the comms button on the armrest. "Bravo-Two-Five... drop."

Gunny Jennings' grin spread from ear to ear when the order came through.

"Canopies down," she shouted. One by one, they reached up and pulled the canopy closed. Jennings thumbed the comms button to keep the line active between them. "Marines, who are we?"

"Killers," they shouted back.

"Oorah."

As one, the four Raptor powered armored suits leaped off the ship, plunging through the Richman field and down toward the planet. Inside their suits, the computer performed the complex calculations to guide them toward Zephyr Base. Once they were lined up, the suits curled up into a ball and converted their armor to heat shielding.

"I'd like to order some pancakes for a party of four," Owens chimed in.

She didn't chide him. Despite her excitement, her *eagerness* to drop, Gunnery Sergeant Allison Jennings wasn't immune to fear. When Owens felt fear, he joked. However, for her, it was easy to push down and hide deep in her stomach. There was something she felt that trumped her fear.

Jennings had something she never would have achieved on her home planet: *she belonged*. Belonged to something greater than herself. That was something no amount of fear could ever take away from her.

Raptors hit the atmo and rocketed around like a pinball. Jennings grunted with each slam, desperately trying to keep her teeth in her mouth from the racket.

"Is it supposed to be like this?" PFC June asked.

Not knowing if it was or not, Jennings simply grunted.

Naki's voice popped on the line. "This isn't something we do PFC. You're a pioneer."

Jennings kept one eye on the altimeter and the other on the course. If they were off even a half of a percent, it could translate into hundreds of kilometers. While the Raptors were fast, they weren't fast enough to cover more than a few klicks to do the ground team any good. This was the part where she was glad the base's defenses were down. They were sitting ducks for a surface to air missile or battery.

Danny ran forward, leaving Mac to cover their six while he charged up to reinforce Bubba. The acrid smell of burnt flesh and spent plasma fuel hit him like a hammer. One more friend, a man he'd served with for years, gone on some nameless planet. At least this time, they had a solid reason. Not some political foul up or mistake.

"Bubba, you good?" Danny said as he slid into place next to the big man. Burns covered his left arm and side of his face, but he still held the rifle one handed and fired from behind cover every few seconds.

"I wasn't that pretty to begin with, boss."

"Switch sides," Danny ordered. He fired a burst out the door, then lowered his weapon for Bubba to leap over T-Bar's body and get to the other side, where he could use his right arm better. Danny took up his old position and waited.

Despite him firing out the door, there was no return fire. Had the ship's reinforcements gotten here that fast? Or was the enemy baiting him to peek and get his head blown off?

Lucky for him, he didn't need to peek. Grabbing a snapshot grenade he tossed it out the door without revealing himself. No r, waieturn fire once again meant that the enemy was either down or applying a great deal of patience.

A high-pitched whirr clicked as the grenade went off and transmitted the image back to Danny's goggles. Sure enough, exactly where his team had made their initial entry from, he could see the barrels of plasma rifles sticking up over the rocks.

They had the high ground. If anyone tried to exit the base, they would be cut to ribbons and burned to ash.

"Status?" Mac asked as he placed India against the wall. The scientist remained with her as Mac crouch-walked along the wall to stay behind cover and get up next to Danny.

"A half dozen or more tangos with the high ground. Right where we were."

Mac examined the carnage out front, the dozen dead added to the bodies that were already present. "Bubba, you gonna be okay?" he asked.

The big man grunted. Nanites were already doing their best to keep him from entering shock, but the wounds would take time to heal fully.

"What are you thinking?" Danny asked.

"Pop smoke and evac. They might get a lucky hit on the Corsair but I doubt it."

Danny hated depending on luck. Hated it. But they couldn't stay there forever, not with two wounded.

"Okay, I'll—"

A high-pitched whine filled the air. Danny had a second to react, leaping back into the base, tackling Mac as he went.

Plasma fire from a mounted gun lit up the doorway, slagging the floor, and turning the walls into rubble. Bubba screamed as a bolt melted his legs, and he went down, his cry of pain only cut off when the roof collapsed on him.

Danny closed his eyes, banging his head lightly against the tile floor. He'd lost half his damn men on this mission. Half.

"You better be worth it," he barked as he got to his feet.

India met his steely gaze with one of her own. She was a woman who had seen stuff and lived to tell.

"She is. We get her, and destroy this base, then they have no more FTLC. It's that simple."

CHAPTER FORTY-EIGHT

"Sir! Thermal bloom, two-five degrees port... range, three hundred klicks..." Lieutenant Sattar yelled.

Three hundred? It was closer than Khaled would have imagined. However, if the enemy ship orbited the planet and was above the base, there were only so many places they could be. Since they had to keep a low orbit to avoid the black hole's pull, they were bound to be somewhat close.

"Can we see them?" he asked.

"No sir. There was a brief thermal flare like something hit the atmosphere at high speed and our aft passives got a solid look."

At such a distance he dare not move the ship. If the enemy had seen him, they would already be dead. The only explanation was the interference ran both ways. Not only could they not see the other ship, they also couldn't be seen.

This is like fighting in pea soup with a blindfold on.

"Thrusters only, small burn. Let's line up with their estimated location. Weapons, plan a saturation burst, with a detonation at three-zero-zero klicks over an area of five cubic kilometers. At that rate, we'll hit something. If it's a pirate or one of the small raider factions, one barrage should wipe it out."

Now he understood why they sent his ship. A traditional battle this wasn't going to be. Neither ship could break orbit without having to commit to a retreat. Neither ship could use their gravcoil without having to go full power. This was an old-fashioned hunt in the dark. Through the fear and uncertainty, Khaled's confidence rose. If Allah had foreseen the need for his ship, then maybe it was for a reason.

"Missiles loaded, sir," Sattar said with glee.

Khaled waited, hoping they would get a better look through all the interference. After a few minutes of watching and waiting, he decided to risk it.

"Fire."

Along the top of the ship, right down her spine, nineteen missile pods elevated, spewing forth nineteen missiles each. Without radar or lidar to guide them, they flew on a preprogrammed course. Three hundred and sixty-one missiles flushed from the pods. Each one with a five-kilogram payload of unstable plasma held in a magnetic bottle. Not as powerful as ship-killing torpedoes, but deadly enough in a volley.

PO Mendez fidgeted in the command chair of the Long 9. It was more a contoured chair lined up with the targeting computer scope. From his position, his right hand firmly gripped the firing stud as a backup to the computer. The two men below him, locked into harnesses were ready to load the shot at any given second. Because of the nature of the coil, and the power of the shot, they couldn't risk keeping a round loaded. The coils aligned and checked, both by computer and by manual inspection before firing.

"PO?" Spacer Zack asked. "You think the skipper's gonna get us in a fight this time?"

Perch, locked into his own harness stood across from Zach. They all had their helmets on and locked, but the comms were tied to the compartment. The two spacers always managed to be in the same duty roster regardless of how they were split up, either joking together or arguing about which graphic novel in the ship's library was better.

"You itching for another fight, Zach? The last four weren't enough for you?"

"Hell yeah I am. New Austin's got to represent. Besides, chicks dig those ribbons."

"I think you'll get your wish soon enough, Spacer Zach," Mendez said. "Now focus on the job."

Josh had to admit, it was a little weird sitting in the chair. As the PO of the Long 9, he had the responsibility to make sure the main gun worked smoothly, that the weapon was ready when the skipper needed it.

Lieutenant Brown diligently watched the passive scope connected to the weapons stations. Any sudden flair or anomaly could be the difference between life and death. The scope, though, was a mess of static and conflicting lines. The passive sensors that normally picked up thermal radiation, radar, and light were barely more than flickers of solid light in between thick lines of electronic noise. If he didn't know better, he'd believe active jamming from an EW battleship affected the area.

Then for a heartbeat, it cleared. Austin's eyes went wide with shock as the signal showed a veritable wall of missiles swarming toward them. As fast as he could, he slammed the emergency ship-wide comms. "BRACE FOR IMPACT!"

Hell came for the *Interceptor*.

Three hundred and ninety-one missiles streamed out of *Al-Qud*'s banks. Her targeting computer assigned each missile a volume of space to target and set the entire barrage to detonate simultaneously. *Al-Qud* tactical officer weighted the center of the area heaviest, spreading out the rest of the missiles as evenly as he could.

The thermal bloom Lieutenant Sattar picked up was the Raptors hitting the atmosphere as they fell from *Interceptor*'s boat bay. Putting *Interceptor* just above their initial target area. Which was the only reason the destroyer survived the firepower thrown at her.

Six missiles impacted her hull directly, another twelve detonated within maximum yield range, hitting the ship with radiation from the resulting plasma burn.

The first one failed to explode, either through fault or from physically hitting the ship before the triggering mechanism had loaded. The next two detonated against the new armor on deck two. Seven centimeters of reactive armor, the very best the Alliance had, held as sun-hot plasma burned for a brief instant against it.

The fourth hit deck one and its armor folded at frame fifty, melting the torpedo transfer assembly, emergency radio, and three spacers manning the rails.

Missiles three and four hit the mess and shower area, vaporizing armor and steel, welding the aft magazine storage hatch shut. Five and six impacted a meter apart at frame eighty on deck four, obliterating the officers' quarters and the overhead of Raptor storage.

While the damage from the missiles burned and bathed the hull in radiation, the kinetic force imparted by the direct hits, and the near misses, pushed *Interceptor* deeper into the planet's gravity, sheathing her in a thermal burn that shown brightly on the enemy's scopes.

Jacob held onto his chair for dear life as the ship shook and gravity pushed him like a gorilla sitting on his chest.

"Chief, thrusters," he said.

Suresh struggled herself, forcing her hands to work the controls despite the sudden lateral stress from the explosions. Radios filled the suits as calls for help and support flooded the bridge.

"Roy, lock those down to DCS," Jacob ordered.

"Aye sir," Hössbacher said, his voice shaking from adrenaline.

G-forces started to surrender as Devi managed to use the ships thrusters to compensate for the sudden downward force.

"Tactical, what the hell hit us?" Jacob asked.

Brown held onto his console with both hands but had the status screens already pulled up. Red lights flashed along the torpedo transfer tubes, but all weapons were green.

"Not torpedoes, that's for sure. If I had to guess, I would say short-range missiles, sir, armed with a low-yield plasma charge. The armor on deck two held but failed toward the stern."

"How did they see us well enough to hit with a handful of missiles?" Jacob asked. Missiles were fine for ground-to-orbit, or even in orbit, but capital ships didn't carry them because of their short range and lack of punch.

"I only saw them on the scope for a second, sir, but there were hundreds."

Jacob racked his brain for any information he had on a Caliphate missile boat with such capabilities.

"Tefiti?" he asked.

"Nothing, sir. I'm logging it as Uniform-Mike-Bravo, designation zero-one and starting a new file. I hadn't heard they were using missile boats, but there's a first time for everything."

Jacob would almost prefer to be out massed by a class of ship he was more familiar with. Missiles, though, weren't something he faced in combat before.

"Devi, keep us moving. Try to stay out of the thicker parts of the atmo. Comms, go full EW, deploy everything we have. Weapons, load a pair of MK XIV's into the forward tubes and set them to the lowest possible velocity."

A chorus of "aye, ayes" followed. If he could convince them to shoot one more time, maybe they could see where they're coming from.

Seconds crept by, each one possibly their last. Deaf, blind, and unable to maneuver with the gravcoil, *Interceptor* wasn't a shark, but a minnow.

"Torpedo room one reports MK XIV loaded."

"Fire," Jacob ordered.

Sattar pumped his fist in the air. "We hit them, sir. Our computer got a good look, too; she's a destroyer. Alliance for sure, what kind it doesn't know."

Khaled shook his head in stunned disbelief. *An Alliance destroyer? Here? Why? There wasn't even a colony, just a lone base.* The answer wasn't nearly as important to Khaled as the reality. He and his men were in the thick of it now. His duty was to destroy the enemy and keep his people alive.

"Do your best to keep track of them. Get those Thunderbolts reloaded."

"Yes sir," Sattar said.

They were in unknown territory here. Fighting blind and with an enemy they only read about. Surely Allah wouldn't have sent his ship to fail?

CHAPTER FORTY-NINE

Jennings focused on her screens as the Raptors passed through the ionosphere and regained contact with the ground.

"Charlie-One-One, this is Bravo-Two-Five-Alpha," she said, her voice calm to her ears even though her heart raced.

"Two-Five-Alpha," Boudreaux said, "good to hear you. I can't see you on the scope, but we're in a canyon, no surprise there. Be warned, though, they have a Dhib in the air."

A Dhib? The Caliphates all-purpose dropship and air superiority craft. She'd faced them before on Medial, and that had cost her a Marine. She bit down the bile in her throat. This wasn't Medial. Cole went down fighting; he died a Marine with his honor intact.

"A good death is its own reward," she whispered the ancient battle mantra whose author was lost to time.

She keyed her mic. "Roger, Charlie. Hostile in airspace. Time to ground is zero-two-mikes. Prepare for evac on my signal."

No response came back immediately like Jennings thought, almost to the point where she began to worry. She wouldn't risk

Charlie-One-One since Jennings had no desire to spend her life on the crappy planet they found themselves on.

"Roger that, Alpha. Good luck."

"Okay Bravo-Two-Five, wake up and get to work. System test now."

All four Raptors unfolded from their ball shape and spread their arms and legs out like a skydiver attempting to slow their inexorable progress to the ground. Bits of armor and ablative heat shielding shed behind them, leaving a trail of black smoke as if the suits hadn't ever seen the inside of a wash.

The suit shook as it hit terminal velocity down from its orbital entry speed. The altimeter beeped at six klicks, just under two minutes to impact at their current velocity. Which would change as the external jets kicked, slowing them to a survivable speed so they didn't splat on impact.

"Green across the board," Owens came back over the team frequency. As their electronics expert, his job was to make sure the equipment checked out.

"I've got a threat light," PFC June said, her voice shaking but firm.

"What?" Naki asked. "Where?"

"It says there's a threat, it doesn't tell me from where," she said.

The Dhib, Jennings realized.

"All Raptors, roll and go weapons hot."

As one, the bipedal, dinosauric, powered armor flipped on their backs, falling with their heads facing up. Sure enough, three klicks out and two thousand meters above them, Jennings' radar picked up the Dhib targeting them.

"Missile launch," Naki shouted.

Jennings flipped the shield off her turret switch. "I bet you didn't know we could do this." With her other hand she activated the slave feed, all four multi-barreled five-millimeter coilguns traversed as one, tracking the incoming missile.

Tracer fire reached out, firing hundreds of rounds from the suits until it intersected with the missile and the warhead exploded a hundred meters short of hitting them. Shrapnel pelted the suits as they continued to fall. Jennings, though, wasn't done. She locked onto the Dhib and fired a long burst at it. The little ship juked, rolled, and dove as hundreds more rounds of tungsten flashed by her.

The Marine couldn't tell if she hit, but the way it dove for the ground made her think they realized the precariousness of their position.

"Roll back," she ordered. Three of the suits external thrusters fired, rolling the powered armor over. PFC June's thrusters fired, but instead of rolling her over, it sent her whirling. She screamed over the radio as her suit went into a flat spin.

"June, stay calm," Naki said.

Jennings checked the diagnostics from her suit. Sweat beaded on her brow as the computer reported June's vitals racing, and the g's on the Raptor quickly approached tolerance.

Piece by piece the computer came back green on her suit.

"The thrusters... Owen, it's the thrusters," Jennings said. The thrusters were add-ons, tied into the computer for control but not part of the system's central diagnostics.

Owens kept one eye on the diminishing altitude and the other on the computer system as he desperately tried to override June's thrusters. As each second passed, the suit spun faster and faster. He had maybe twenty seconds to stop it before the internal g's knocked June out. Twenty seconds beyond that and none of it would matter, because she would be dead.

"Screw it. Gunny, give me control," he said.

The light on his canopy flipped from red to green as local control was established. The Raptor suits weren't air vehicles. The external jump jets slowed them before impact, so they didn't die when they hit the surface. Not to fly the suit.

Owens cracked his neck, relieving the tension, and he focused on his screens. June not only spun, but each rotation sent her farther and farther away.

"Activate jump jets," he said.

With the suit horizontal, the thrust kicked in and he felt the g's in his spine as it blasted him forward. The only way to steer was to physically lean left and bring his feet around. Owens' muscles protested as the lithe young man forced his body to obey his commands. Pain lanced through his back and thighs as tendons and muscles protested the sudden use. Owens prided himself on athleticism, even among Marines. He wasn't a weightlifter like Naki or Jennings, though. He could outrun them and had an agility index twice what they did. It made his electronics work easy.

Forcing the Raptor to *fly* used every gram of muscle fiber he had and then some. The suit fought him, air resistance fought him, and gravity absolutely tortured him.

"Owens, what in the hell are you doing?" Jennings asked.

He grunted in response, unable to speak as he finally managed to line his suit up with June's. Then he slammed the thrusters to full and raced toward her like some kind of ancient hero trying to catch the falling damsel in distress. Except the damsel weighed half a ton and spun out of control.

"Brace yourself, June," Owens said.

Metal clanged with a deafening boom as the two suits collided. Alarms wailed in Owens ear as multiple systems flashed yellow from damage.

"Ow...en...s," June tried to say. "H...el...p."

His plan was to hit her and then hit his thrusters full to slow their fall, but all he did was cling to her Raptor suit and spin as well. Owens growled, tightening his stomach muscles to keep the blood in his torso as he tried to align the thrusters with the ground, which rushed up alarmingly fast. The green dots that were Naki and Jennings were far above him as they had already engaged their jets.

"Hang on, June," he said through gritted teeth. Each time he thought he had his feet aligned, the suit would jerk wildly out and end up with them pointing up instead of down. He took a chance and switched his grip, letting go of her for a heartbeat, and then swung his legs down like he was jumping onto a slide. For a second, they lined up and he hit the gas. Jump jets roared to life, flame and exhaust spewing from the external mounts. Temperature warnings flared to life and the engines threatened to shut down from overheating.

Owens thumbed the override, ignoring the alarms.

Two hundred klicks per hour, five hundred meters to go.

One hundred and fifty klicks, three hundred meters to go.

Too fast.

If they hit at anything faster than eighty klicks, it would overload the internal musculature and flatten the two Marines.

One-twenty... one hundred meters.

Owens squeezed his eyes shut, praying to God like he hadn't since he was a child.

Save June, at least. Please.

Ninety klicks... impact.

The suit shook, hitting the ground with the force of a bomb, breaking through the thin layer of soil and collapsing an entire overhang above a canyon. The angle threw the suits into a tumble, luckily dispersing much of the impact energy, sending them careening down an eight-hundred-meter-deep crevice. They hit the bottom in a plume of dirt seconds before thousands of kilograms of soil collapsed on top of them.

CHAPTER FIFTY

"I've got them, they're running," Sattar said with glee.

Khaled smiled with pride. With the unique nature of the black hole, the enemy running was the same as victory. Too bad for them they wouldn't get far.

"Track them," he ordered.

"Solid lock, sir, their acceleration is too low to escape the black hole, and not nearly enough to get out of range. Should we fire?"

He contemplated letting the black hole do the dirty work for him. There was no honor in such a death, though. No dignity in it. No honor in allowing such a death.

"Missile status?"

"All pods are loaded."

"Fire as she bears."

―――――

Interceptor's lone MK XIV flew through space at one hundred gravities of acceleration. The lowest the micro-gravcoil could produce and still function. The EW module blared loudly into space, desperately trying to convince every sensor in range that it was, indeed, the *Interceptor*.

And it worked.

After sixty seconds, the torpedo hit three hundred- and fifty-two-kilometers distance from *Interceptor* just as *Al-Qud*'s missiles were finished reloading. She fired almost the moment she could, unsheathing another three hundred and ninety-one missiles at the torpedo as she passed by at a distance of less than one hundred klicks.

"Got her!" Ensign Brennan shouted. "Bearing, zero-four-zero relative, mark zero-two-three. Range: three-zero-four klicks."

Jacob pointed at Lieutenant Brown. "On my mark, helm descend five-zero klicks, maximum thrust. Weapons, fire all turrets once, once only. Confirm."

Hands flew across the consoles as the crew made the necessary preparations.

"Minus five-zero klicks, maximum reaction thrust, aye, aye," Chief Suresh said.

"All turrets, manual controls, track target and fire once. Aye, sir," Lieutenant Brown said.

As a commander, strategy and tactics were where he shined. His crew's performance on their equipment and their commitment to duty was something they trained for. Broader strategy, though, wasn't something he practiced much, with the exception of the books he read and the battles they fought. He only got to be wrong once.

"Brown, spin up the PDW for when they return fire. Even with the clouded sensor conditions, they should offer us some protection."

"Aye sir, computer nodes four and five online, giga-pulse laser systems are active and tracking."

The plot updated, showing a massive thermal bloom where the enemy ship was as it fired its payload of missiles that streaked toward the decoy torpedo. For a split second, he got a solid look at her. A destroyer, no doubt, but new, something they hadn't seen before. Tefiti was right. Was the Caliphate shifting tactics? Why would they build a missile boat that would be essentially useless in a fleet engagement?

Those were questions above his paygrade; for the moment, he had to focus on one thing: victory.

Flying away at a hundred g's of acceleration, the MK XIV torpedo vanished in hellfire as the entire barrage of missiles detonated around her—enough firepower to destroy *Interceptor* if he let them hit her full on.

"Execute," he said.

Down in Turret One, PO Collins eased the controls over to line up on Ensign Brennan's coordinates. Numbers flashed by as she aligned both arcs of fire until her crosshair matched the one the computer showed. Radar, lidar, and gravity were useless. The computer screen, with the large crosshairs showing her the target, filled with snow and static as the ship's systems desperately tried to see something through the mess of colliding electrons, gravity waves, and solar winds. All her time in the Navy, which Jen admitted wasn't the longest, she'd never seen such a mess before. Ships relied on their sensors, both passive and active. Space was big. Bigger than anyone could imagine. Finding an enemy ship at a distance was already difficult beyond thinking.

Here the enemy was, only three hundred klicks away, and *Interceptor* couldn't see her. Jen's head still ached from the previous hit, tossing the ship around like she was built in a kid's snow globe. Another hit might destroy them.

"All turrets, on my command, fire only once. Confirm," Lieutenant Brown's voice sounded.

"Turret One, one shot only," Jen confirmed.

"Turret Two, one shot only," PO Oliv chimed in.

"Turret Three, one shot only," PO White said.

"Turret Four..." There was a pause and Jen could almost imagine hearing PO Rodriguez knocking on the turret's armored inside for luck, "one shot only."

Seconds ticked by and a bead of sweat formed on Jen's forehead, dripping down before the ELS suit's cooling could evaporate it.

"Fire," Brown's voice jarred in her ear. Without hesitation she squeezed the trigger. One 20mm-round burst from the coil turret, the barrel assembly rocked back, absorbing the recoil.

The ship's thrusters engaged, and negative g's hit the crew as she accelerated down toward the planet. Jen breathed hard, trying not to vomit in her helmet as her vision tunneled with red light, narrowing to the point she couldn't see.

"I do not like this, PO," Spacer Alvarez said. "Not at all."

Negative g's just weren't something they had to deal with often and PO Jen Collins couldn't disagree with him one bit.

"Target destroyed..." Lieutenant Settar said.

Khaled heard the question and hesitation in the man's voice.

"What is it?"

"I would have thought there would be a bigger explosion..."

Khaled checked the screen, even with the static, the explosion was easily visible for a brief moment. Shock slapped him like an angry woman.

"Helm, full thrust—"

He didn't get to finish his order. His helmsman, to his credit, applied thrust as soon as his brain heard the order; however, it wasn't in time.

Alliance coil turrets were designed for engagements in the four- to six-hundred-thousand-kilometer range. Technically they could shoot until they hit something, but with ships maneuvering in combat, anything beyond a million klicks was almost impossible to hit.

At three hundred and fifty kilometers, the twenty-millimeter nano-hardened tungsten penetrators crossed the distance in 0.000035 seconds, or thirty-five milliseconds. Not nearly enough time for *Al-Qud* to move.

Projectile one went high, taking missile pod three along with six centimeters of the hull. The resulting explosion from the empty pod pelted the topside deck with shrapnel. Projectile two missed entirely. Three, hit at a ninety-degree angle eighteen meters down from the top deck. Megajoules of energy blasted through the armor, turning the atmosphere of the long-term stores into a conflagration from which no life could escape. Two crew were incinerated in the initial hit. The energy expended itself against the internal armor, leaving eighteen cubic meters of the ship open to space and burning until the atmosphere was exhausted.

The fourth round hit low, deflecting off the armored stern of the gravcoil, leaving a furrow of gouged nano-hardened armor in a trail down and away from the center of the ship. The imparted energy pushed the ship laterally, and into a slow spin.

CHAPTER FIFTY-ONE

Danny fired several rounds out of the hole the Dhib had blasted into the base. Thankfully, the damned bird had diverted to shoot at something else for a minute. Once it had, the remaining Caliphate had grown a spine and started firing into the base at the slightest sign of movement. Two grenades had landed woefully short, turning the ground to glass in front of the now destroyed blast door.

"Mac," Danny said. "I'm going to draw their fire, and you need to take at least one of them down." He crouched, ready to sprint, when Mac grabbed his shoulder.

"No," his sniper said. "Even if I got three, it wouldn't be enough, and you would surely get hit. If we're going to get out of here, we're going to have to rely on your Marine."

Danny growled in the back of his throat. He allowed himself to be foolish, and this was the price he paid. *His Marine.* She wasn't his Marine; he doubted she would ever be anyone's anything. The woman had a streak of independence that would make the founding citizens feel inadequate.

"I don't see any Marines here, Mac, do you?" Danny asked.

A roar of noise, like a jet breaking through the air above

them, filled the canyon. Two armored figures, larger than a human that looked like a nightmare cross between a velociraptor and a person, screamed overhead. External jump jets burned with intensity, vomiting exhaust as they fought to slow the behemoths down.

"I do now," Mac said.

Ensign Shah's blood drained from his face as the two monstrous figures screamed by overhead to crash five hundred meters deeper into the canyon.

"Ifriti, come in. We need immediate fire support. Something just fell out of the sky south of our position."

"I saw them, Ensign. We engaged in the air and they damn near shot me down. I can't get within a klick of your position without taking fire. If we lose an engine, we're never leaving this place."

Shah frowned, swallowing the profane words that begged to be released.

"Sir, what if we set an ambush? We can head back down that way," one of the navy ratings said, "and use grenades. There's no room to maneuver. If we time it right, we can hit them hard."

Shah glanced at the man's uniform. Al-Diamond was his name.

It was a good plan. He had twelve men left. Those inside the base were clearly not coming out, and with the narrow entrance, he couldn't risk going in. No, they would have to wait for the *Al-Qud* to make contact and send the Dhib back for heavier weapons.

"Take three others and do it."

"Yes sir, Allahu Akbar," Al-Diamond said before turning to

pick out three men. They ran off, staying low in case the raiders inside fired off any more shots. Maybe they could get out of this after all. A successful combat patrol would certainly look good on his service jacket. The fear that had hovered over him, infecting him since they were pinned down, faded. He had the upper hand now. Ensign Shah dictated the terms of the engagement.

Jennings' Raptor slammed into the ground with a dust-billowing boom. Three-toed feet dug trenches as the half-ton armor slid to a halt. She immediately ejected the jump jets. They clanged to the ground, nozzles glowing red from the heat, but with their fuel spent they were worthless.

"Bravo, you with me?" she asked over open comms.

"Roger that, Alpha. Two-three meters to your six. Any sign of Charlie or Delta?" Naki asked.

Their signal had vanished on impact. Between the crazy amount of interference in the atmosphere, and the lack of LOS, she wouldn't know if they were ten meters on the other side of the wall.

"Negative. Charlie-Mike."

"Roger, Charlie-Mike."

There had to be something she could do, though.

"Charlie-One-One, this is Two-Five-Alpha, how copy?"

Static crashed into her ear full of tormented sounds of interference. Through the mess, though, she thought she heard Chief Boudreaux's voice. The static at least meant someone had transmitted back. Maybe, just maybe, the chief could hear her with the more sensitive and larger antennae on the Corsair.

"Charlie-One-One, if you copy this, I have two Raptors MIA approximately..." She glanced at the computer screen about level with her chest. "Two klicks east of your position. Please assist with Sierra-Alpha-Romeo."

She waited for the line to come back, but there was nothing. Allison Jennings wasn't the praying type. If it wasn't in the Marine Field Manual, she ignored it. But the captain was, so she prayed on his behalf for her Marines.

"Okay, Naki, take point. By the numbers. Shoot, move and communicate."

"Aye, aye, Gunny." Naki shook the dust off his Raptor before stomping past her. Active camo came alive, disguising the suit's exterior to look like rocks and sand. While it didn't make a moving suit invisible, it did make them harder to see, especially in the deep shadows of the canyon.

Jennings glanced up. The lip of the canyon above her was almost five hundred meters up. She tried to ignore the voice in the back of her head that told her even if they survived when they hit the ground, five hundred meters was a long way to fall.

———

Boudreaux stared long and hard at the radio as the sound of Gunny Jennings' voice played over again amidst the background of a cacophony of static and squelch.

She'd heard it right. Two Raptors had gone down, roughly two klicks from her position. They'd powered the ship back up after an hour and hadn't heard from *Interceptor*, nor could she find them again with the laser. She certainly would not fly the Corsair around down here. Not with an enemy ship in orbit and a Dhib in the area. They didn't have to destroy her, just damage the plasma engines enough and she would never break orbit. She had already had that close call back on Midway and it cost her Cooper.

She let out an expletive string in her native French to avoid breaking regs. Stawarski just stared at her. Watanabe laughed.

"You're not the only one who speaks multiple languages, Chief. What's the problem?"

"Two Raptors went down. Gunny Jennings called in their location. Grab a rifle and come with me." Boudreaux slid down the ladder, then marched right for the cargo bay to grab her own combat gear.

"Uh, Chief?" PO Stawarski called to her. "What do you want me to do?"

"Stay here. If they call for evac, do it. Otherwise, you do not lift my bird off the ground, understood?" she asked.

"Aye, aye, Chief," Stawarski replied.

Boudreaux grabbed an MP-17, pre-configured into a rifle, along with a pair of goggles, the micro radios they used when off the ship, and a vest of soft armor.

"That won't do anything against plasma," Watanabe observed even as she equipped herself with the same gear.

"Oui, it's better than nothing, no?" Boudreaux tried to remember to push her native language down and just speak Alliance standard. She was stressed, though, and when she was stressed, French came naturally to her.

"Don't forget water," Stawarski hollered from the cockpit.

Boudreaux stopped herself just as she was about to jump out of the side door onto the dusty canyon floor. The PO had likely saved their lives. She grabbed the two-liter packs that fit snugly onto her back and handed one to Watanabe.

"We look for two hours. We don't find them, we come back," Boudreaux said.

To her credit, Watanabe didn't argue, simply followed Chief Boudreaux out into the alien world to look for two missing Marines buried under a mountain.

CHAPTER FIFTY-TWO

Jacob breathed hard, trying desperately to keep the blood from pooling in his brain as Chief Suresh descended at negative four g's.

"That's good," he said between gritted teeth.

As soon as she reversed the thrust, the g's slammed them in the other direction, but somehow the positive g's felt more natural and easier to handle after the negative ones.

Once the ship's movement came to rest relative to the planet, the extra g's vanished. He wished they could rely on the gravcoil to nullify the g-forces, but they were using thrusters to move, not the gravcoil. It would kick in if they went beyond 9 g's but not before. They were just going to have to tough it out.

"Status?" he asked.

His MFD flashed as Carter spoke from down in DCS. "Multiple casualties. We've got a hull breach on deck two and four. I've never seen this kind of weapon before, skipper. It's not a plasma gun or a torpedo."

"Brown says they're missiles. Short range, fast, and meant to overwhelm defenses with a barrage," Jacob replied. A single torpedo could destroy a ship; they were devastating in their firepower. The missiles, though, were designed to peck his ship to death.

"That makes sense, I guess. Despite the damage, our combat efficiency is undiminished, as long as we don't need to move torpedoes from the aft ammo stores. The rail is slagged."

This really wasn't a torpedo battle anyway, and while Jacob would use any weapon at his disposal if he thought it would make them victorious, he would use them in a way that was tactically sound.

"You think they'll fall for that again?" he asked his XO with a grin.

"Not a chance, sir. Would you?"

Jacob shook his head, agreeing with his XO. The MK XIV's were awesome EW tools, but once the enemy knew what to look for, they lost their usefulness. Even in the haze that was the atmosphere, they would spot the difference.

"Fionna, Tefiti, anything?" he asked his sensors.

"Nothing on passive, sir," Fionna said without looking away from the radar/lidar scope. Any errant energy waves that could be recognized as coming from an enemy ship would alert her, and she wouldn't take her eyes off it even for a second.

"Unless they fire a torpedo, if they even have them, or activate their gravcoil, I won't be able to hear them, sir." Tefiti, who Jacob considered the best gravtech in the fleet, frowned at his equipment.

"Keep an ear out regardless, and record everything. I want a decent profile on this ship. When we return to Utopia, I want them to have a report ready to send out to the fleet."

Jacob made sure to project confidence in his voice. He didn't want anyone doubting they would return to base.

"Aye, aye, sir," Tefiti said.

"Devi, do you think those missiles came in straight, or did a dog leg at the end?" Some torpedo systems would juke at the last moment to throw off defense systems. The missiles, though, were so small they were already almost impossible to see. Why use the extra fuel on such a small weapon system when space was a premium?

"From the way the ship moved after we were hit, sir, I think they came in straight at us."

Jacob leaned forward, resting an elbow on his knee and debated his next move. He could keep the ship's orientation orbital normal, which meant the deck was pointed "down" to the planet. However, if the enemy ship did the same, and as far as he knew that was standard, then the next missile barrage might hit the gravcoil. If they lost that, they might as well head for the surface and build a town, because they were never going home.

On the other hand... the only way to protect the coil would be to roll the ship, putting a constant strain on her secondary gravcoil, and exposing the bridge. A cold emotionless logic formed in his mind. Carter, if need be, could command and navigate the ship from DCS.

They absolutely couldn't take any damage to the gravcoil. He glanced at the little mirror he and Chief Suresh shared and he saw the same argument play out on her face as well.

"Coxswain, roll us to starboard, forty-five degrees," he ordered.

"Aye, aye, sir, forty-five-degree roll."

Thrusters fired and the ship rolled along her central axis. The planet's gravity pulled them down, but only a little, giving the crew the sensation they were about to fall over. Most of them unconsciously corrected by leaning to the port.

"Sir..." Carter said from DCS.

"I know, XO. But the gravcoil cannot be damaged. Until we find and destroy the enemy, we have to protect it."

"Aye sir, understood."

. . .

PO Desper struggled with a screaming Spacer Paulson. His right leg ended at the knee and third-degree burns ran up his entire side. While he still had his arm, the suit's material and the man's flesh were seared together. Not for the first time she was thankful to be in her fully sealed ELS suit. The stench of burns would take days to wash off the deck, but at least right then she didn't have to endure the sickly-sweet smell of burned human meat.

"Tyree, get your butt over here," she yelled. Tyree hustled to her side. He was assigned extra duty in sickbay as punishment, and she was glad to have him. The young man had worked hard. He grabbed Paulson's remaining leg and heaved. There was no delicate way to move him. The burns were such that the only treatment was through the nanite-infused fluorocarbon tank and a medically induced coma. No pain killer in existence would stop the insanity provoking agony of having skin and bones melted from a plasma explosion.

They didn't even need to take his suit off, just manhandled his writhing and screaming form until they could dump him in the tank. The nanites did the rest, immediately going to work disassembling his ELS suit and the small amount of clothing he wore under it. In seconds the coma took effect and Paulson slumped, his whole-body shuddering from relief.

Part of Prisca Desper's soul wondered what possessed her to *volunteer* to do this for a living. Elbow deep in other people's blood and guts, pulling pieces of their skin off her suit... and not be the least bit bothered by anything, other than those she *failed* to save.

"Desper," Chief Pierre yelled over the comms. "Get over here."

"On the way." She pounded Tyree in the shoulder to make

sure he followed her.

Khaled didn't allow his emotions to show as the damage was listed and the dead named. They were with Allah now, and there was nothing to be done about it except honor their sacrifice. The man over on the enemy ship was devious, clever, admirable. He, too, wanted to save his ship. It was a shame they were enemies.

"Maybe start by telling me what is working?" he asked Sattar.

"We lost two pods, sir, which puts our throw weight—"

"I can do basic math, Lieutenant. Are the loading mechanisms still intact? Thrusters?"

Sattar checked his board, running through a dozen different screens. Every crew member on the small bridge did the same, none of them wanting to disappoint their captain.

"All critical systems are functioning, sir. Other than the destroyed pods, they hit nothing vital," Sattar said.

Nothing vital... Khaled winced inwardly. Perhaps it was a fluke; maybe he wasn't fit for command, but he considered his crew vital. Others in the Caliph's service didn't always see things his way.

"Helm, minimal thrusters, get our orbit under control and point us in the direction those shots came from. No need to present a larger silhouette than needed."

As his crew confirmed their orders, Khaled pondered his next move and what the enemy captain would do in his place. Either one of them, or both, were incredibly lucky. The weapons of the Alliance and Caliphate were devastating in their effectiveness. One or two more hits would decide the battle.

Khaled prayed it went in his favor.

CHAPTER FIFTY-THREE

Owens groaned as consciousness returned to him. The last few seconds of the doomed planet-fall came rushing back in a blur of panic and pain. He tried to lift his torso, but he couldn't feel himself, and he certainly couldn't see in the pitch-black interior of the armor.

"Power on," he said through a thick, dry tongue.

Lights flickered to life all around him as the armor's fusion battery sprang to life, bringing the systems back online one by one. Strapped in as he was, there wasn't a lot of wiggle room inside the suit, for obvious reasons.

"June, you copy?" he said over the keyed mic.

As he waited, he eyed the report filling the screen in front of him. Right leg actuator damaged, thirty percent functionality. Right hip actuator, zero percent functionality. Maximum speed, less than ten KPH.

"Great," he muttered.

The suit still had power and life support. Owens tried again to move, using the Raptor-powered arms to push against whatever held him down. Dirt shifted as he heaved against what felt like a solid rock that pinned him to the ground.

Alarms flared as the synthetic muscles approached tolerance. Owens wasn't about to give up, though. Gritting his teeth, he surged forward.

Ground gave way and a boulder the size of an aircar rolled off him and down the newly made hill to his right. Bright sun shone from above, kicking in his polarization instantly.

Now clear of the boulder, he keyed the radio again. "Raptor Delta, how copy? Bravo-Two-Five, this is Raptor Charlie. How copy?"

Static answered him. Either his radio was busted or the tall cliffs and canyons surrounding him prevented communications.

Not one to waste time, Owens leaned forward to test the damaged actuators, and rose to his feet. He flipped the safety off the multi-barreled coilgun mounted on his shoulder and brought the targeting to life. A crosshair sprang into existence in front of him and the barrels turned. He didn't need to fire to know it worked... mostly.

Turning slowly, he scanned the area, looking for anything familiar, any topography that would give him a clue where to go.

"Hey," a feeble voice said over the radio. "You gonna help me, or just stand there and look pretty." He almost didn't recognize June's voice, so full of pain.

"You know me, PFC. I like to strike a pose." Owens kept his voice jovial, but he had genuine concerns about the rasping voice that was the private's. "Where are you?"

The computer should have tagged her the second she spoke. He wanted to smack the console in his suit, but the armor didn't work that way. His arms were in the Raptor's arms.

"I ejected just after impact. Two-four-one meters to the south of you."

Ejected? Why the hell would she do that? Ejection was the

last thing any Raptor driver did. The suit couldn't have taken that much damage, could it?

"Hang tight, PFC. I'm on my way."

"Yeah, I don't think I'm going anywhere," her voice faded as she spoke.

"June?" Owens said. "PFC June, respond," he ordered. "Dammit," he muttered. Once he felt out the knee actuator, he took a tentative step. When the whole leg didn't collapse, he pushed harder, not wanting to waste any time getting to her.

Istifan Al-Diamond clutched his plasma carbine with sweaty hands in the afternoon temperature. Despite their location almost a kilometer below the canyon surface, the heat was nearly unbearable. Their uniforms, made for normal temperature variance aboard ship, strained to keep the men cool in the overbearing intensity of Zephyr.

"There," he told the three men with him. The canyon walls narrowed into a V not far away. No more than two meters across, it was the only way to the base, and anyone on foot would have to cross through the section. Even the Alliance's vaunted armor would have to move slowly and carefully to avoid a collapsed wall.

"You two, there." He pointed to the right side where there were almost steps to an alcove five meters up. The footing looked precarious, but if they moved carefully, they could make it.

"With me," he said to the single remaining man, then went left. The bottom of the V on the left-hand side had a small hole against the wall of the canyon, just big enough for him to slide in on his belly. He could roll out and fire at point-blank range. It would be glorious.

Jennings wanted to push the suit harder, speeding up and providing fire support that much faster to Nomad but... the damn canyons were a maze and narrow as hell. Her Marine training, while normally favoring aggression and attack, cautioned her from recklessly charging forward when an ambush could be at any turn.

"Bravo-Two-Five, Nomad. Come in?" Master Sergeant Cannon said in a hushed voice.

"Go ahead, Nomad," she replied.

"The Dhib has departed for the moment. I snuck a peak out and I'm pretty sure they split up. Whether it's to flank us or intercept you, I don't know. Regardless, I've got three KIAs and one severely wounded, so the faster you get here, the better. Nomad out."

Jennings felt the pain of loss for a brief moment before compartmentalizing it. She had two of her own people MIA. They couldn't help them right then. Wasting effort worrying would only distract her from the situation at hand.

"Alpha, close quarters up ahead," Naki whispered. Despite the fact the suits were soundproof, they still acted as if they were on foot—an essential drilled into them repeatedly at Raptor school. Stealth was stealth. How they acted in the suits was how they would act outside the suits.

"Naki, fall back and cover my six," she ordered. The brown-gray camouflaged Raptor halted, hunkering down for a moment.

With the tight quarters up ahead, she wanted to make sure the suit stayed agile and didn't catch anything going through. With the touch of a button, the multi-barreled five-millimeter coilgun on her right shoulder pointed straight up before recessing into the housing. The suit only had two actual weapons, the coilgun and grenades. They also acted as mortars in a pinch, but they certainly weren't designed for close-quarters battle—other than being a half-ton armored killing machine, capable of shredding armored steel with its taloned hands and three-toed feet. She turned sideways, keeping her head pointed forward, and shuffled through the narrow passage.

Something told her it was a mistake. They had to move forward, though, and risk was part of the job. She shook her head; the suit mimicking her movement. Dust fell down against her visor and she looked up.

In an alcove above her, two men in Caliphate naval uniforms clung to the cliff for dear life, pointing their plasma carbines at her. She didn't know who was more surprised, them or her.

"Fire," a man yelled from below. The two men startled into action, firing at point-blank range. Green beams of electrostatic plasma splashed against her chest armor.

She stepped sideways, but her armored leg hit something with a meaty thunk. Another soldier had clamped on to her leg, attempting to magnetically lock grenades against the knee joint.

"Contact close," she yelled into the mic.

Naki's gun roared to life turning the two men in the alcove into memories as the five-millimeter rounds shredded their bodies. Jennings, though, had bigger problems. The carbines wouldn't hurt her suit, but the plasma grenades would melt the armor like so much wax left out in the scorching sun. She reached down and grabbed the man who clung to her leg by his back, bones cracking under her metal fingers, and she flung him violently off. He flew, smashing against the canyon wall thirty meters above, splattering blood around the point of impact.

The grenades went with him and detonated a second later.

Rocks, dirt, and debris showered her suit. She lifted her arms in reaction as shrapnel pinged off her armor.

Istifan Al-Diamond hid under the lip of the canyon as they killed his three shipmates in the blink of an eye. It wasn't fair, he thought. They had surprised the enemy. Had his companion clamped the grenades to the first suit, that would have been it. As it was, Istifan had but one plasma grenade left. He didn't want to die, but... he had a duty to do. Allah would demand no less than his very best. Better to die doing his duty to Allah and his Caliph than live as a coward.

He closed his eyes, summoning the courage to do the unthinkable. A brief image of Ariana filled his mind. Oh, how he wished he'd had the guts to ask her out before deploying. Maybe in the next life.

Istifan pulled the final plasma grenade, keyed the detonator to explode on release, and rolled out of the hole screaming, "Allahu Akbar."

The grenades above Jennings had barely detonated when another soldier appeared, rolling out of the hole below her and screaming his war cry. Jennings' instincts took over, and she stomped down hard with her taloned foot, crushing his head against the rocky canyon floor like a grape. The grenade he held detonated a second later, consuming his body in plasma fire, ironically shielding Jennings' Raptor from the worst of the conflagration.

With one eye on the passive heat sensors, she stepped back

from the still burning plasma. Those grenades, she knew from experience, were nasty business.

"Clear," she said, turning back to the base. "Thanks for the assist."

"Any time, Gunny," Naki said as he squeezed his armor through the narrow gap. "Geez, Gunny, I think I'm gonna be sick."

It wasn't like Allison Jennings enjoyed hurting and killing people, she just happened to be very, very good at it. When she was alone at night, staring up at the rack above her, the faces of the people she killed came to visit. She didn't feel guilty about it, but she did feel some kind of way that was hard to explain.

"Don't look, Corporal," she told him.

"You splattered his brains all over the canyon floor, Gunny. Kind of hard not to."

She ignored his attempt at humor, instead easing her Raptor into a quicker half run—a gait that shook the ground and filled the air around her with a cloud of dust.

"Let's go. They know we're here, so the faster we move the better."

CHAPTER FIFTY-FOUR

"Anything?" Jacob asked. There were times he wished they had some magic technology that would allow him to look at the area of space with his eyes and see the enemy. However, even the relatively short distances they faced one another at were far greater than the human eye could perceive. Their best estimate was somewhere in the neighborhood of three hundred klicks. Trying to find a ship a hundred meters long, with nothing but his MK I eyeball was the very definition of impossible.

Ensign Brennan looked at her panel in disgust, hands gripping the sides to steady herself from the cocked gravity of the ship.

"Negative, skipper. I... all I see is static and light," she said.

The damned solar radiation affecting the planet made seeing anything with electronic or gravitic instruments nearly impossible at regular ranges.

Regular ranges...

Jacob caught a glance from Chief Suresh, who gave him a look.

"You have an idea, skipper?" she said over their private comms.

Jacob found his COB invaluable. Both in her ability to understand exactly what the crew needed to succeed, and her understanding of him. They worked well together. On a destroyer, where ship handling was crucial, that mattered.

"As a matter of fact, COB, I do." He switched his comms to the XO. "Carter, can we reprogram the warheads on MK XIVs?"

Carter looked back thoughtfully. "I suppose we could, sir, but why? They mimic our signature well enough."

That wasn't what Jacob was thinking at all. He looped in Lieutenant Kai.

"Engineering, Lieutenant Kai."

"Akio, can you alter the warheads in a MK XIV?"

"Alter, sir, how so?"

This was the tricky bit. He didn't know if this would work at all, but he laid out his thinking to his XO and Chief Engineer. If there were any two people on the ship who would know, it was them.

"Damn sir," Carter muttered. "That's brilliant."

"Only if it works, XO. Get to it."

They both straightened in their seats and came back with a crisp, "Aye, aye, sir."

Jacob looked at the plot, tracing their movements and where they thought the enemy ship had been when they last fired. If he were the captain of that ship, he would move, try to change orbital angle. If only Jacob knew how their weapon system worked. Were they on turrets? Did they have to turn the ship to shoot?

"COB, I'm sending you a course."

She glanced at the plot that mirrored his own and raised an eyebrow at him. "You want us to get closer?" she asked to clarify.

"Yes. Spitting distance, Chief Suresh. Spitting distance."

"Course plotted, sir."

Jacob keyed the all-hands button. "This is the captain speaking. Prepare for g's. I say again, prepare for g's."

He gave the crew a minute to situate themselves before giving the order. "Execute." Jacob swiveled his chair through the piling g's to face tactical.

"Austin, tie the PDW into the fire control computer."

"Sir? We won't be able to hide the increased thermal output."

Jacob gave the young man a reassuring nod. "I know. It will also mean they will fire as soon as a threat is detected.

Lieutenant Carter Fawkes struggled to step through torpedo room one's hatch. Working on a live head of a weapon was hard enough, then the captain decided to put on two g's of acceleration. At twice his normal weight, a fall could break a bone.

"Kai, be careful," he said as the other officer bent down to pick up the tool needed to remove the warhead's panel.

The crew of torpedo room one watched on from their positions with a bemused smile. PO Ignatius commanded the room, and he manned the firing chair.

"XO, you sure you don't need a hand?" Ignatius asked.

"Negative, PO, don't unhook."

Carter knelt next to the torpedo, each movement calculated to keep himself safe. Kai, three years his junior and built like a swimmer, had far less problem moving.

"Okay, sir, remove the panel there," Kai pointed.

Carter took the offered tool and carefully removed the seal on the warhead panel.

"You really think this will work?" he asked Kai.

"EM is EM, sir. We're simply telling it to pulse out like a radar rather than a constant jamming signal. The real trick is tying it into the ship's systems. The only thing I could think of was the remote control unit in the back of the Mudcat. It took me a minute, but I was able to break the RC unit down and pull out the chip I needed. Then I just had the fabricator run me a few copies."

Impressed with the engineer's ingenuity, Carter made sure to note it for later. "You know Chief Boudreaux will have your hide if you leave her Mudcat disassembled."

Kai reached in and opened the EW warhead's control circuit. "All due respect, sir, she's a chief warrant officer. I don't think she can—"

PO Ignatius' laugh rolled over their channel. Kai frowned as he fused the wireless control chip in place.

"Something amusing, PO?" Kai hadn't quite mastered the art of talking to petty officers with deference he should, despite the rank difference.

"Yes sir. Chief Boudreaux won't say a word to you."

Carter knew what the PO meant, and despite the tension of the moment, and the pain in his lower back from the added g's, he couldn't help but laugh as well.

"If she won't say anything, what's the problem?" Kai said without taking his attention off the delicate work.

"She'll fly that Corsair in such a way, sir, that you will wish you were dead," Ignatius explained.

"Oh." Kai's simple word of surprise said he got it. "Better put the chip back, then."

"Aye, aye, sir. You do that. If not, just don't be on the same flight home as me."

Carter held the panel shut while Kai sealed it.

"Skipper," Carter said over the comms, "got a live one for you."

"Good man. Load it up in the queue."

Silence filled the bridge so thick, Khaled imagined he could feel his men's heartbeats. Red emergency lighting cast dark shadows on the floor. Every one of his crew gazed with intent at their screens.

He looked over Sattar's shoulder, eyeing the passive radar returns. Should he go active? Perhaps if they did, then he could fire again. Surely the enemy's luck wouldn't hold a second time. This was what they designed his ship for. Orbital control and suppression. Even down thirty-eight missiles, his salvo would be more than enough to shatter the enemy ship.

"Sir?" his junior astrogator spoke up. "I think I have something, a sudden increase in thermal radiation. Three-four-one mark three-three-nine... range..." The astrogator gulped audibly.

"What?" Khaled snapped.

"Five-seven klicks," the astrogator said. That was far too close to be the enemy ship. Surely they would try to increase the distance, not close with him.

"Go active on radar. Maybe it will tell us more."

"We won't be able to see far, sir. They'll be able to see us if we do and—" Sattar didn't finish. His screen blared, showing another torpedo rushing out into the void. Confusion overcame him, though, since the torpedo wasn't mimicking the enemy's signature. No, it was more like a flashlight, making it easy to see. Not that he would fall for that trick again.

"Sir, they fired off another EW torpedo... but it's hitting us with EM radiation. It's almost like radar except weaker."

"You clever bastard," Khaled said about his opponent. "Weapons, rough bearing on the new thermal bloom and fire."

"Yes sir, fire on bearing three-four-one mark three-three-nine."

Al-Qud shuddered as the seventeen remaining Thunderbolt missile pods flushed their payload out into space.

"Thank Allah," he said as the missiles sped away.

Ensign Brennan's eyes watered from the fierce attention she paid to the scope. She dared not take her attention from it even for a moment. Static swirled about like a wind in the desert. There was no seeing anything. Even if the enemy ship was on top of them, she doubted the radar/lidar scope would see a thing.

"Prepare for link," Lieutenant Kai told her from engineering.

"On my mark, Fionna, go active on all sensors," Commander Grimm ordered.

"Aye, aye, sir. Active on all sensors on your mark." She pushed the metal shield up and her finger posed above the activation switch.

They waited breathlessly as the torpedo sped away from them, disappearing from their screens after a few seconds, vanishing it from the interference.

"Link established, activating remote radar," Kai said over the shared comms.

Suddenly, the light on her console flared to life, and she had a near perfect radar return.

"Go active!" Commander Grimm ordered.

She slaved the ship's radar/lidar stations to the torpedoes. Under normal circumstances, the measly hundred-klick addition to a clear radar picture would be meaningless, but in the fog that was Zephyr's orbit, it meant everything.

"Got her!" she yelled. "Zero-zero-four mark zero-two-one.

Range, four-five klicks." Brennan gasped at how close the enemy ship was.

Commander Grimm turned to Lieutenant Brown. "Target and fire everything."

"Launch—" Brennan started to yell the warning, but at their extreme close range, she didn't have time to finish the customary repeated phrase.

When Rod Beckett's work crews refitted *Interceptor*, they weren't working on an Alliance ship. They worked on the ship that saved their lives, their families', and the homes of their ancestors. Every cable laid, every relay installed checked and double-checked, and confirmed working.

No shortcuts, no mistakes. Giga-pulse lasers went to work.

In engineering, Lieutenant Kai's flow control panel screamed at him as the new nodes suddenly demanded five hundred percent their usual power. Heat bloomed at the bow of the ship, pushing the control systems to their maximum failure threshold. Even suited, the crew in the torpedo room's one and two and the Long 9 felt the sudden thermal increase as the internal bulkheads absorbed the heat.

Three hundred and twenty-three ion-pulse missiles with plasma warheads sliced toward *Interceptor*'s exposed topside. Giga-pulse lasers flashed into existence, invisible beams of light carrying five mega-watts of energy. Each giga-pulse laser turret fired a hundred times a second, not exactly a giga, but it sounded better than hecto-pulse, according to Captain Beckett.

Laser beams shot out into the dark, blasting into missiles with megajoules of energy. The payloads ignited, creating a wall of plasma that the missiles behind flew through, only for them to be detonated by the laser system. Wave after wave of terrifying destruction grew ever closer to the embattled destroyer.

"Critical thermal build-up," Lieutenant Hössbacher said from Ops.

Jacob was stunned, as were the rest of the bridge crew, as the enemy's missiles exploded ever closer, each wave reaching klicks beyond the last before the giga-pulse turrets obliterated them. Lights flickered all around as consoles lost power. Alarms in his suit warbled to life, warning him of critical external heat.

"Good God," Austin Brown said. "I had no idea."

None of them had. Rod Beckett's weapons were experimental. That was the whole point of testing them in a live-fire situation.

"Drop the heat sink," Jacob bellowed the order to Hössbacher before the situation became dire.

His suit's external temperature shot to forty-eight degrees Celsius in less than ten seconds and continued to rapidly climb.

"Sink dropped!" Hössbacher said.

The increased heat stabilized, but it didn't go down. Half the ship's systems went offline from either the heat or lack of power. When Beckett told him the fusion reactor was the bottleneck, he hadn't realized he'd meant it so literally.

"Can we fire?" Jacob asked.

"Computer nodes one and two are offline, sir. But yes, I think the gun crews can aim and fire locally," Brown said.

"Good, weapons free. Fire at will," Jacob ordered.

PO Collins wanted to wipe her brow, but the suit prevented it, of course. The sudden increase in the temp had caught her crew by surprise. She half expected the deck to glow with heat. Unlike the bridge crew, who only saw space from the safety of their instruments, she got to see it up close and personal. The targeting computer built into the turret also showed a visual, and she watched in stunned silence as the wave of missiles exploded from the laser PDW systems. Alarms screamed at her as the heat shot past sixty-five Celsius. Her suit could withstand three times that, but it was still a hazard.

"All turrets, you have local control. Fire at will," Lieutenant Brown ordered over the suit comms.

That wasn't something they got to do often.

She activated the joystick, rotating the turret to the last coordinates she'd received. The targeting reticule lined up on the coordinates. Jen blinked several times. She could actually just make out the glimmer of the enemy ship's hull. The other three turrets fired at roughly the same time. Jen fired last, taking the extra second to make sure she was on target.

A half a second later, a fresh round loaded, and she pulled the trigger—nothing happened. The lights in the gun turret blinked and vanished. Only the stark-red emergency lighting remained.

"Bridge, Turret One. I've got no power. I say again, no power."

The situation Jen Collins found herself in was unlike anything she'd trained for. Everything about the battle wasn't anywhere in *The Book*. She knew, though, that if there was one captain in the entire Alliance to deal with it, his name was Jacob T. Grimm.

Forty-five kilometers in atmosphere was far beyond most ground-based weapon systems. In space combat, the distance hardly warranted a target lock.

All four of the *Interceptor*'s turrets fired one round before heat from the giga-pulse lasers shorted out power runs and supercapacitors all through the ship. Panels exploded along deck three where the primary runs were.

Twenty-millimeter tungsten penetrators had just enough time to shed their nano-reinforced steel jackets that allowed the magnetic coil to shoot the rounds at ten thousand kilometers per second.

Al-Qud bucked as the first round hit the starboard armor plating, running down half the length of the ship before deflecting into space.

The second missed entirely. The third hit the forward leading missile pod as it rotated clockwise in preparation to lower into the hull for automated reloading.

The box-shaped pod fractured into a million pieces of destructive shrapnel rippling down the top deck into six pods like heavy rain on a puddle.

All of that was devastating for *Al-Qud*, but PO Jen Collins' shot finished the fight. She'd fired a millisecond after the other three turrets and her round went low.

Ten to the ninth power megajoules in the form of a twenty-millimeter tungsten round smacked into the first gravcoil ring, demolishing the dense ring and the three behind it.

Al-Qud shuddered as the imparted kinetic energy pushed the ship deeper into Zephyr's orbit.

Khaled coughed, spitting out blood as his ship died, drifting without power, deeper into the atmosphere of the planet below. Part of Captain Khaled Al-Faris breathed a sigh of relief that they were falling into the planet and not the black hole.

"XO," he stopped to cough as smoke from burning circuits filled the bridge. "Status?"

Sattar held one hand to the side of his bleeding scalp from where he'd hit it against the console.

"Gravcoil is offline, sir. Emergency power is at thirty percent. We can manage another volley if we need to."

Khaled glanced at the engineering panel, only then realizing the young man slumped over his station with shrapnel sticking out of his neck.

He pushed the comms button. "Medical to the bridge." After he made sure they were on the way, he hefted himself up and checked the man's pulse. He lived for the moment.

Khaled pulled up the thruster diagnostics and his heart fell. A hard realization hit him. No matter what happened next, *Al-Qud* would never leave the system.

And neither would any of his people. The only thing left for him was his duty.

"Find me that enemy ship, Sattar, and we will take them to hell with us." If they were going to die, it would be a glorious death for his Caliph and for Allah.

CHAPTER FIFTY-FIVE

More plasma fire rained down on the hole that used to be the door to the base. Danny, Mac, and his packages were five meters back, well away from any stray shots. As he watched, the edges of the hole heated, glowing red, and then as the fire stopped, they cooled again.

He counted. Whoever was out there, they certainly weren't regular soldiers, or even trained civilians. They all fired together. Reloaded together. Fourteen seconds after the plasma fire stopped, it started again.

"What are you thinking?" Mac asked.

"I'm thinking the next time they stop to reload; we charge out there and find some ground. If Jennings were coming, she'd be here by now. We either get to the Corsair on our own or..." He glanced back at the two women. Mac had performed rudimentary first aid on India, sealing her leg in spray and administering enough nanites that she could function. The beads of sweat on her brow and the way her hands shook told him that she was one tough hombre.

Mac followed his look and nodded. Danny hated the idea of leaving anyone behind. It was bad enough to leave three of his men on this forsaken world. He wouldn't also lose the package. However, he had his orders. Rescue the doctor if possible. Stop the Caliphate from having FTLC at all costs. If he thought, for one second, they weren't going to make it off the planet, he'd shoot her without hesitation.

"Ready smoke," Mac said. "Any second now."

They slung their rifles behind them and pulled smoke grenades. Just as the last plasma beams hit, they hurled their grenades and ran after them.

Mac was right before, when he told Danny that going out was suicide. That was when the enemy wasn't firing, though. With predictable patterns of fire that only an amateur would do, there was a window they could make it in.

Danny cleared the hole first, diving headlong after the grenade, hitting the hardened ground and rolling over his shoulder. Shouts from the men to his left rang through the canyon. He knew where the barracks was, the only available cover. He ran full speed for it, booted feet digging in the ground for every ounce of traction.

The clatter of spare magazines and hurried reloads filled the air. The sudden appearance of the smoke and soldiers startled the enemy.

He hit the ground behind the cover. Mac passed him, sliding to a halt on loose pebbles a few meters beyond.

Green plasma fire erupted as the men using the rocks above as a fort fired their carbines as fast as they could squeeze the firing stud.

"Not exactly disciplined, are they?" Mac said.

"Everyone gets lucky, just ask the rest of the team," Danny reminded him.

Jennings' computer alerted her to weapons fire up ahead. Raptor control computers were amazing in their ability to parse a hundred different sounds and visuals to determine threats.

She slowed her roll, holding up one arm to alert Naki to do the same. Caution was the order of the day. If she had her entire squad, she could afford to be more aggressive.

"What's the play, Gunny?" Corporal Naki asked.

"Nomad, Nomad, this is Bravo-Two-Five-Alpha, how copy?" The canyons blocked the previous transmissions, but she hoped they were close enough. Nothing, though.

"I can go high, see what I can see?" Naki suggested.

Jennings scanned the sky, looking for the Dhib. Naki, exposed on the ridgeline would be easy pickings. She couldn't charge in blind, though. They needed something.

"Do it."

"Oorah, Gunny." Naki took three vaulting steps and leapt up twenty meters. Taloned feet and clawed hands slammed into the walls. He hung for a moment, defying gravity. One hand and foot at a time, the half-ton suit climbed.

Jennings, not one to wait around for something to happen, moved forward. Figuring she could close the distance and be ready once Naki sent her some useful intel.

"I'm up, Gunny," Naki said. Her external sensors picked up the rhythmic thump as he charged by above her. At full speed on unbroken ground, the Raptors could hit a hundred klicks an hour. Zephyr was anything but "unbroken" ground.

Threat detected.

Jennings scanned through her three-sixty-degree view, not seeing anything immediate.

"Naki, the Dhib is back. Get down if you have to," she ordered.

"Roger that," he replied.

Withing seconds, the roar of approaching plasma turbines

echoed off the canyon walls. Her computer couldn't triangulate where it originated because of the rebounding soundwaves.

She picked up speed, bouncing off the canyon as she took tight turns too fast. All the while the whine grew until it drowned out all sound. They came in low and fast.

"Found them," Naki said excitedly. "Looks like the grunts are pinned down. The bad guys are in a natural redoubt, twenty-five maybe thirty meters to the south of them. One sec."

Plasma cannons fired and were answered by Naki's chattering multi-barreled five-millimeter coilgun.

Rocks pinged off her suit as Naki leaped from the canyon top, one clawed hand dragging down the side to slow him down until he hit the ground three meters from her.

More plasma bursts from the Dhib's cannon flashed overhead before the ship itself disappeared.

"I don't think they like us, Gunny," Naki said.

She clanged his suit with her fist. "Don't act like a private. What's the situation?" she asked.

"Fifty meters that way." He pointed north with one clawed finger. "Eight men in an elevated position. They have a clear line of sight on every approach. I don't know how we'll get to them. All I saw were plasma carbines, but clearly, they have grenades."

Jennings thought through the options. If they charged, one or both of them could be killed without completing the mission. If they tried to go high, it would only take a single hit, at most two, from the Dhib's cannon to destroy a Raptor.

If only they could sneak up on the enemy and...

"I have an idea. Stay here. On my signal, fire every smoke mortar you have into the combat zone. Then wait for the shooting to start before you follow."

"Understood." Naki's coilgun instantly locked into place,

reconfiguring to fire forty-millimeter mortars instead of coil rounds.

Jennings jogged forward, following the canyon wall that led to the secret base. It was a good defense, she thought, having a maze of crevices shielding the doorway.

Plasma fire volume increased, and her computer indicated that the origination was around the next corner. Pressing the suit's back up against the wall, she activated adaptive camouflage. A meter appeared on her HUD, showing her the percentage of adaptability, and at one hundred she was practically invisible.

She took one slow step and the indicator dipped below eighty. Another step and she was at the corner. Slow enough to keep the adaptability above ninety, she peaked her raptor-shaped head around the corner to see the situation. It was just as Naki had described.

Fifteen meters from the wall, a natural redoubt of rocks and dirt rested five meters above the canyon floor. Eight men in Caliphate naval uniforms huddled behind rocks, firing their plasma carbines. Occasional return fire from coil rifles ricocheted off the rocks and canyon walls.

Two of the eight lay on their bellies, rifles cradled and pointed directly at her. They didn't see the suit, though, they were simply watching their six. As slow as she had moved before, she moved even slower still. The angle wasn't quite right. She could fire her coilgun and hit most of them, but not all. She wanted the fight to be over and done with as minimal engagement time as she could swing. She considered a grenade, but she couldn't see where Danny and his men were. If she missed, or if it skipped off a rock, friendly fire could be the result.

"Bravo," she whispered Naki's callsign. "Fire."

Repeated thumps rumbled down the canyon. Mortars whistled as they rained down from the long arc. Men screamed, "Incoming!" She counted down from five. On one, she took a single step out. The percentage dropped to eighty. However, the area filled with thermal- and visual-occluding smoke. Enough that even with her suit's optics she couldn't see.

She didn't need to, though, the location of the redoubt was clearly marked on her HUD. Another step. The weapons fire ceased as they tried to clear out the smoke by waving their hands. They yelled, she heard the unmistakable sound of boots shifting on dirt.

Each step brought her a meter closer.

Six steps.

Seven.

A gust of wind from the unpredictable weather rushed through the canyon, clearing some of the smoke.

Eight steps. Adaptability waivered to seventy-five as her three-taloned foot landed on a fist-sized rock. Jennings froze. A dozen scenarios played out in her head, each one ending with her suit overwhelmed by plasma fire.

Six of the men resumed sporadic fire down from their defilade onto the troopers.

Nine.

Ten.

The man lying on his belly on Jennings' right, squinted at her. As if he saw something. Taking his hand off the rifle he wiped his face, rubbing his eyes, and squinted again.

"Damn," she whispered. Five more steps and she would have taken them all.

Jennings flipped the safety up off the joystick her right hand held and pulled the trigger. The five-millimeter coilgun on her shoulder roared to life, ripping the two men to shreds as she charged forward.

Two more turned back, screaming at their companions as

they fired their carbines. Jennings leaped up into the air, coilgun firing the entire time, and landed in the middle of the redoubt. Metallic clawed fingers grabbed the first guy she could reach and flung him behind her.

Suddenly the tiny area lit up with green fire as they opened up on her at point-blank range. Her coilgun continued to roar, sending hundreds of rounds in a circle. Three more died. Another when she kicked him in the head.

Five seconds after it begun, only Jennings lived. Her armor was painted in sizzling gore from where the plasma hit and blood splashed.

She turned, making sure they were all dead.

"Alliance Marines," she said over the PA.

"You don't say?" Master Sergeant Cannon appeared from behind the very little cover he had. He looked worse for wear, dirty, and blood splotches covered his uniform.

Naki's Raptor careened around the corner, skidding to a halt in the dirt.

"All clear," Jennings said.

"Roger," Naki replied.

"Let's get you guys to the Corsair," Jennings said.

Boudreaux let out a whistle when she came upon the impact crater. The Raptor suit had hit like a bomb, leaving a hole in the ground and a collapsed canyon wall. She reconfigured the rifle, changing the selector to pistol. In seconds, the nanite reservoir within the weapon reduced the size until it fit comfortably on her hip.

"Don't," she said to Midship Watanabe who was about to change hers. "Cover me while I climb down."

"Yes, Chief." Watanabe took a knee, raising the rifle the way her instructors at the academy undoubtedly wished she had while she was there.

From the canyon wall, where they had climbed up to, she saw down into the ravine below. At least twenty meters separated her and the canyon floor. She placed a foot on the edge and pushed. The rocky soil held firm.

Looking beyond the impact crater and the collapsed canyon wall, Boudreaux saw no sign of the Raptor suits.

"Here I go," she said more to herself than Watanabe. The angle was such she half slid half jogged down. Trying desperately not to lose her footing. Her calves burned by the time she hit the bottom.

Drawing her pistol she turned a complete circle, making sure there were no surprises waiting for her.

"Okay, Midship, get down here."

Dirt and pebbles rained down as Watanabe practically ran down the hill. Boudreaux stifled a sigh at Watanabe's display of youthful energy. Her knees and ankles would remind her tomorrow that she was getting older.

"This way," Boudreaux said. "Watch our six."

A distant echo of plasma cannon fire rolled through the canyon.

"That sounds close," Watanabe said.

"Hard to say with all these twists and turns. Though I doubt that was handheld, more like the gun on a—"

Plasma turbines roared above and past them in a split second. Hot air blasted through the narrow canyon and the two spacers ducked out of reflex.

"—Dhib," Boudreaux finished. "I was really hoping the Raptors took that thing out."

She waited a minute in silence, making sure it wasn't going to swing back around and look for them. It was a good opportunity to take a few deep breaths and push down her worry.

The Corsair was well hidden. No amount of searching would find it.

"Can you shoot it down with the Corsair?" Watanabe asked once they were moving again.

"Sure. I've done it before. They could still get a lucky hit and we would end up stranded."

Fifteen meters of broken dirt and collapsed wall later, she glimpsed something. Running up ahead, she knelt when she found the tracks.

"Hard to miss these," she said. Activating her comms, she called out for the Marines. "Bravo-Two-Five-Charlie, do you read?"

Static was the only reply.

"Between the canyons and the jamming, comms isn't working well," Watanabe added.

Boudreaux sighed. Of course, it wasn't easy. Pistol out, she followed the tracks while Watanabe trailed behind her, making sure their six was clear.

Owens popped the canopy, unbuckling as the torso split open. "June, what the hell?" he asked.

PFC June had propped herself up against the canyon wall, MP-17 resting on her chest. Her Raptor, five meters away, was upside down and imbedded in a crystalline rock the size of a house. Both of June's legs lay bent in ways human legs weren't meant to bend.

"Sorry, Corporal," she said through rapid breaths.

Owens frowned. June's vitals were all over the place. Clearly, she was in shock. He jumped out, landing next to her. He reached back, grabbing his rifle before kneeling next to her. Readouts on her suit showed her vitals were bad, but they weren't pumping her system full of medicine like they should be.

He keyed into her suit and manually activated the med panel. Nothing happened. Gently, he rolled her to the side enough to see the reservoir. It was crushed. "Damn, PFC, you don't do anything half-assed, do you?" he muttered while he unhooked his nanite reservoir to replace hers.

"I try to fail as spectacularly as possible, Corporal."

The old reservoir was jammed on, and he couldn't get the quick release to actually release it. "Hang tight, this is going to hurt." Owens pulled his twenty-centimeter combat blade from his side. He wished he could do this more gently, but her condition meant he needed to hurry. She winced as he hauled her up all the way to her side, braced her body with his foot, then used the knife to pry the reservoir free. While she was still up on her side, he attached his and let her back down.

Sweat beaded on her forehead, and her breathing was far too shallow for his comfort. He knew the moment the nanites went to work, though. June's whole body heaved a sigh of relief as she relaxed.

"Th—thanks," she stuttered.

"Hang in there. How's that young man who seemed so interested in you? Tell me about him?" he asked.

"Travis?" she said, her eyes going wide. "I—I mean Lieutenant Rugger?" she said.

"Oh, he's an El-Tee now, eh? Gonna leave the Corps and go have a Navy husband to take care of you?" he said. He showed no concern on his face, but even with the near miraculous medical nanites, she was in a bad way. Maybe if he'd gotten to her immediately... but if he tried to move her now, they were in deep shi—

"Owens?" Boudreaux said from behind his suit.

"Chief? Over here, hurry."

Ten seconds later Chief Boudreaux and Midship Watanabe cleared his Raptor.

"Mon dieu, what happened?" Boudreaux asked.

"Bad luck, Chief, just bad luck. That's a galena rock, mostly made up of lead. The suit ejected her seconds before impact and well..." He gestured to her. "We need to evac immediately."

"Let's get her up. The Corsair's two klicks away. It will be rough but—" She stopped talking when Owens shook his head.

"Chief," he said, leaning in close, "her back is broken. She won't make the trip. Can't you come get us?"

Boudreaux looked away. Owens hadn't ever known the woman to mince words before. Despite her desire to make Marines puke in their helmets whenever possible, they respected her.

"I can't, not yet. They still have that Dhib up there," she said with a nod toward the barely visible sky.

Owens weighed the options in his head. He didn't want to leave June, but the success of the mission hinged on the destruction of the Dhib.

"Okay, stay here. I'll reconnect with the rest of Bravo, and once we've cleared the airspace, PO Stawarski can come collect you. Sound good?"

"Corporal, whatever you do," Boudreaux told him, "Do not lead the Dhib to the Corsair. We lose that, we become permanent residents."

CHAPTER FIFTY-SIX

Jennings led the team out of the canyon and back toward the Corsair, her eyes scanning the sky for any signs of the Dhib. She expected them to attack any minute since their ground team no longer existed.

Behind her, Danny and Mac slung the wounded Nadia Dagher between them. Jennings wasn't at all surprised the woman lived, nor that she completed her mission. The captain knew people, and he didn't put his faith in those who quit.

"Jennings," Nadia said over the comms.

"You should save your breath, Dagher," she said.

"Listen, no matter what happens, I need that base hit hard. The FTLC is a half klick deep. Conventional explosives won't be enough."

"What do you suggest?" Jennings moved between the rocks where they had triggered the ambush, stepping over the burned remains of the man who tried to take her with him.

"Long 9, from orbit. Twice on the same spot. I ran the numbers, that's the only way."

The three-sixty-degree camera caught a look of distaste on

Danny and Mac as they gingerly stepped over the remains of the dead.

"Roger that, Long 9 from orbit, twice. I'll let the captain know."

That was if they made it back to the ship. She wasn't a doomsayer, and her instincts were of the "no quit" variety, but Dhibs were powerful close air support craft. She had two working raptors and not much else.

"How far back to your ship?" the woman they identified as Dr. Yusra Abbasi asked.

"Twenty minutes of hustle," Danny said over his shoulder.

Owens skulked through the last turn of the canyon. He'd taken longer than he wanted to, especially with June in such bad shape, but he couldn't risk leading the Dhib back to the Corsair, like Boudreaux said.

"Charlie-One-One, this is Bravo-Two-Five-Charlie, come in."

There was a moment of static before the line clicked on.

"Charlie? Good to hear your voice," PO Stawarski said. "Did Boudreaux find you?"

Navy types, Owens mused. *No radio discipline.*

"Yes, One-One-Actual found us. I'm coming in, don't shoot."

He made the last corner, breathing a sigh of relief to see the hunched form of the Corsair. Her wings were swept back, and the tails folded like she was stored in the boat bay. Owens knew it minimized her ground footprint.

The canopy popped open, and Stawarski waved at him. An MP-17 rifle cradled in his arms.

Owens stopped the Raptor at the side of the ship and popped his own canopy.

"Where's the Gunny?" he asked.

Stawarski shrugged. "You're the first one to come back. The Dhib flies over every couple of minutes. The jamming's still bad and I can't raise the ship. Hell, I don't even know if the ship is still up there."

Owens put the concern over *Interceptor* away. Lieutenant Bonds drilled into them not to waste brainpower on things beyond their control. Either she was up there, or she wasn't. There was nothing to be done about it.

"PFC June is critically injured and I need to get her back to the ship. The moment the others arrive we get airborne and go pick them up."

"You got it, but that could be a while. About thirty minutes ago all hell broke loose"—he pointed toward Zephyr base—"and then nothing."

Owens didn't like the implications. There was no way on this hellscape that a pack of Navy ratings or base security would ever, in a million years, take out the gunny.

"Do the preflight all the same. We got to go as soon as they're back."

Stawarski frowned. "Not until they're back, Corporal," he said as a not-so-subtle reminder of their rank difference—which honestly wasn't much.

"Just be ready—" The scream of plasma turbines drowned him out. The Dhib flashed overhead with a sonic boom rattling the canyons.

Owens ducked in his suit out of reflex. The pilot was smart, staying low and moving fast. The Raptors would never get a bead with it moving like a bat out of hell.

Realizing the futility of arguing, there was something

Owens could do to prepare. Raptors mounted on the underside of the Corsair; he could mount his suit and stay in it, or ride inside. He opted for the latter, that way he could help June when they picked her up.

———

The Dhib's sonic boom shook them as it passed. Jennings halted, making sure they didn't move a muscle until it was gone.

"You worried it will pick us up down here?" Danny asked over the comms.

"A reckless Marine is a dead Marine," Jennings said. "Move out."

Before long, Jennings recognized the final piece of the maze that led toward the Corsair.

"Charlie-One-One, this is Bravo-Two-Five-Alpha."

"Gunny, good to hear you. Are you close?" PO Stawarski asked.

Jennings fumed as she stomped forward. "Charlie-One-One, did you just use my rank? Mind your radio discipline, understood?"

"Uh, roger that…" He paused. Jennings imagined he had to check the roster to see what he should call her.

"Roger that, Two-Five-Alpha. Uh, Two-Five-Charlie is present."

"Roger, ETA two minutes. Get the preflight started."

By the time she led her ragtag team around the final bend, the Corsair's wings were spread out and rotated with the plasma engines pointed down. The tails were out, and the rudders wiggled as Stawarski tested flight control surfaces.

Owens leaped down from the side, rifle slung on his back, as he rushed over to help the troopers.

"Where's June?" Jennings demanded as she popped her canopy.

"She's down and in a bad way, Gunny. Her suit is trashed, and I think her back is broken. Chief Boudreaux and Midship Watanabe found us and they're still with her."

Jennings kept an eye on the sky.

"Mount up."

Danny let Mac hop in first before lifting a groaning India up to him. He put his hands under her shoulders and dragged her up. The poor woman's burnt leg hit the side of the ship but she only winced. Her pain control impressed the hell out of him.

"Get her over to the first aid station."

"You got it," Mac said.

He climbed in next, turned and helped the doctor in. "Take one of those seats, buckle in, and stay quiet. Understood?" He wanted to keep his voice neutral, but three good men had died rescuing her and he wasn't at all sure she was worth it.

"Yes sir," she said and did as he instructed.

"Pilot," he yelled not remembering the man's name. "How long to dust off?"

"Two mikes," came the reply. The Corsair shuddered as it lifted a moment later but stopped two meters from the ground.

Jennings and Naki parked their armor underneath, reached up and dragged their suits to the fuselage like doing a plank pull-up.

"Locked in," Jennings said over the comms.

"Ditto," Naki said.

"Are they seriously going to ride on the *outside?*" Danny said aloud.

The carrot topped Marine, Owens, grinned. "That's where I would be if I didn't need to help with June."

"Raptor suits locked in. Everyone buckle up. That Dhib is going to come for us as soon as he spots the ship."

Danny did as he was told, but he buckled in the seat closest to the large sliding door on the side of the ship.

"Here we go," the pilot said over the internal speaker.

Boudreaux started to think she made a mistake. She hated the idea of leaving anyone to die, but she should have gone back. Stawarski was a fine pilot, fully qualified, but she had experience in air-to-air combat. Specifically against Dhibs.

"You okay?" Watanabe asked PFC June. The midship seemed overly concerned about her. Then again, June was one of the Marines that came to save her butt when she decided to jump ship.

"Fine," she said. The look in her eyes said anything but fine.

Boudreaux's ears perked up as she heard a distant rumble.

Watanabe heard it too. "The Dhib is coming back."

Boudreaux shook her head. "Turbine spin is too high for Caliphate, that's a Corsair," she said with a smile.

Less than thirty seconds later, her bird crossed the lip of the canyon and descended. Stawarski messed up the pedals and hit the tail against the wall, for which she glared at him.

Then it set down. Owens and one of the troopers rushed out to get June.

"Watanabe, back on EW. We're going to need it."

"Aye, aye, Chief," she said.

They raced back to the ship, leaping into the open side door. Boudreaux tossed her weapon at Watanabe to put away before hitting the ladder.

Stawarski was half out of the chair and climbing into the second seat by the time she got to the top.

There wasn't time for all the regulations she needed to follow. The buckle went on fast, and she barely had time to pull it tight before her other hand feathered the throttle.

Threat warnings beeped to life.

"Is she onboard yet?" Boudreaux asked over the internal comms.

"Aye, Chief, but we're not—"

Whatever Owens said next was lost in the roar of engines as she lifted the ship straight up.

She *knew* he was going to be waiting. Something in her instincts told her so. Maybe because she would have done the same.

Three klicks away and closing fast, the Dhib rushed toward them. Boudreaux flipped the wings to horizontal and jammed the throttle forward, heading right toward the Dhib.

"Uh, Chief, shouldn't we run away from it?" Stawarski asked.

"Non. If we give it a shot on our six, we're done. I need to lure it into a dogfight."

"A what?" Stawarski asked.

"Air-to-air combat, don't they teach that at flight school anymore?"

Boudreaux pushed the throttle hard forward. Starting on the deck wasn't ideal; she didn't have any time to build velocity or room to maneuver.

"Your job is to keep your eyes on him at all times, understood?" she asked.

"Yes, Chief."

"Watanabe, full ECM. I don't know if he has missiles, but I don't want to find out."

"Aye, aye, Chief."

The two craft screamed at each other, engines leaving a trail of burning atmosphere behind them. Though the Dhib had the advantage, where the designers had intended her for the role, Boudreaux had experience.

She wiggled the ship laterally as the Dhib's forward-mounted plasma cannon fired. Green bolts flashed by the cockpit close enough Stawarski screamed.

"I thought you said we didn't want to do this?" he asked in a panicked voice.

"Tell him that," she replied.

Just to keep the enemy from getting comfortable, she squeezed off a burst from the ten-millimeter chain cannon mounted under her nose. Tungsten balls shot out at fifteen hundred meters a second.

They missed.

The two birds shot past each other. Stawarski twisted in his harness trying to track the ship.

"He's going vertical," he shouted.

Boudreaux figured he would. The Dhib had the speed advantage. It would take her precious seconds to build up enough velocity to break orbit, and in that time she would be a sitting duck.

Her only real option was to lure him into a one-circle fight and bring him down to the ground.

She jerked the stick over, putting the aircraft on her side and pulled hard. The ship shook as the g's piled on. She had no pity to waste for the wounded, this was kill or be killed.

The Corsair wobbled and shook like a ground car with a flat tire.

"What the hell?" she yelled sharply. Then she realized her mistake.

"He's already coming over above us," Stawarski said.

The Raptors were mounted underneath, three of them. She'd forgotten since they'd mounted before the Corsair picked her up.

Her hand hovered for a second over the *disengage* button, that would kick the Raptors free. Without them, they stood a chance, with them...

"He's lining us up!"

Her hand went back to the throttle, no way in hell would she return to the ship and tell the captain that. No way.

She heaved the stick over opposite, pushing the rudder in the same direction. The tail shot up and the ship pointed almost at the ground as more green plasma bolts shot through where she would have been.

Boudreaux's ELS suit did its level best to keep her blood in her brain, and combined with breathing exercises, she stayed conscious as she pulled the ship through a six-g turn. Stawarski blacked out, and she imagined everyone aboard did.

Her hands flashed, slapping the wing rotation until they whirred to point down. This was a last ditch move she had used before... of course they had shot her down on Medial.

Spinning the ship, she brought the nose around to track the Dhib, which was already pulling up again into a loop.

The ten-millimeter cannon's pip appeared on her HUD showing her where to aim. When she'd first tried this, she thought it would be easy, but a target moving at six times the speed of sound wasn't easy to hit at all.

Her first burst missed by a large margin. The ammo counter ran down, racing toward zero and their death.

Another burst missed. The Dhib turned, bringing the nose back around toward them. For a brief instant, she knew where it would be and pulled the trigger, pushing the nose along the path the dropship would take.

Rounds burned the air spitting out of the Corsair's nose like pellets of fire. At range, they seemed to drift like glowing angry bees until the two merged...

The Dhib shredded, splintering and flying apart into a thousand pieces as the tungsten balls shredded it.

"Good shot, Chief. Let's go home," Jennings said.

"Aye, aye, Gunny," she replied.

CHAPTER FIFTY-SEVEN

"Clear the air," Jacob ordered over the bridge-wide. Atmosphere rushed through the ship as thousands of liters of pressurized nitrogen flowed out of storage. Once the nitrogen filled the ship, outer hatches opened, clearing the ship of smoke, toxic gases, and a tremendous amount of heat without risking fire.

Smoke whisked past Jacob as the nitrogen did the job, and he noted with a sigh of relief the temperature on his HUD decreased.

"Propulsion is green," Chief Boudreaux said.

"I'm rebooting astro, it might take a few minutes," Brennan added.

"Weapons are offline, sir. I can't get the main computer nodes back up. I need someone to go down there and put eyes on them and find out what happened."

Jacob could guess what happened. Thermal radiation fried the systems. However, guessing wasn't how a ship ran.

"Do it."

"DCS, I need an engineer down in computer node one, ASAP," Brown said.

Jacob turned his attention to the MFD attached to his chair. Passive still worked, but the static and interference continued to cause nothing but problems.

"Felix, do you think we could punch a signal through to the other ship?"

Felix checked the comms board before turning to his captain to answer. "Aye sir. If you wanted, I could stand on the hull and wave flags. At this range they would have to be blind not to see it."

"That won't be necessary, spacer. See if you can give me a tight beam on their last known bearing."

"Aye sir, tight beam on last bearing. You're on."

Jacob resisted the urge to clear his throat.

"Caliphate Navy ship. This is Commander Jacob T. Grimm, USS *Interceptor*. You've put up a good fight, but don't throw your lives away. If you can use your thrusters, head on a bearing of —" He glanced at the orbital map to make sure he had it right. "Two-six-zero. We will not pursue; we will not fire unless fired upon. Please respond."

Spacer Felix Gouger activated the message and prepared to send it. "Sir, uh, if we send this, they will have an idea where we are, won't they?"

Jacob nodded at the young man, appreciated the courage it took to ask his captain the question.

"Yes, but considering they just launched at us, they already know. Send it."

"On the chip, sir."

Jacob hoped the enemy captain could see the sense in retreating. Jacob couldn't leave the planet, not until his people were back on board. The enemy, though, could fall back and let them be. It was a risk, he knew, but he felt in his heart it was the right thing to do.

Under a more normal engagement, such a request would be

impossible. With the planet's ionized atmosphere and the black hole's interference, though, perhaps they could.

"Skipper," Gouger said. "Message coming in."

"Put him on."

The main screen flickered from the static of the plot to show the face of his opponent.

"Captain Grimm, I am Captain Khaled Al-Faris, of the Caliph Naval Ship *Al-Qud*. I appreciate your offer. It shows a respect and honor I didn't think the Alliance had."

Jacob felt a profound respect for the captain. After his last encounter with a Caliph naval officer, he'd decided to read up on his enemy and learn more about them. The Caliphate, like any group were diverse and complex. However, the condoning of slavery and the collars would prevent any peace between them.

"Captain Al-Faris, I think you will find the Alliance is very different than you have been taught."

"Be that as it may, we live in the world we live in. I cannot change who I am, or who I serve. I must take the galaxy as it is. As must you."

Jacob glanced at Ensign Brennan. She pointed at the scope to tell him sensors were back online. Though he wanted to hope they wouldn't fire on him while they were speaking. It wouldn't be beyond realistic to think they might.

Gouger turned in his seat and waved to get his attention. A text message appeared on his HUD.

Corsair inbound, ETA five mikes. Mission accomplished.

Relief flooded through Jacob. This wouldn't be all for naught.

"Captain, let me assure you, there is no victory here. My mission is already complete. Please do not throw away the lives of your crew."

For some reason, known only to God and his soul, Jacob

desperately wanted the man to surrender. He had a look around his eyes that spoke of honesty and kindness. Something more, though. Now that he'd seen him face-to-face, he didn't relish the idea of killing him.

Al-Faris looked away for a moment, consulting with a bridge crew the same way Jacob had moments before.

"I... I want to believe you, Commander. I will trust you to not be the monster my people think you are. My ship is dead, Captain. I could shoot you with another volley, but that would be all I have. My weapons officer thinks he could hit you, too, but then we would both never leave this system. If I surrender to you, will you guarantee my men be treated equitably under the treaties of war?"

Leaving a ship to die in the black hole wasn't an option for Jacob. It would be more kind to simply finish them off than to abandon them to die a long, slow death.

At the same time, could he take on a hundred prisoners?

"One moment, Captain." Jacob pressed the mute button. "Carter. Can we take them on? Do we have the life support and provisions?"

"Let me check with Bosun Sandivol, sir, but I think we can manage it. Half rats will be the order of the day until we get back, though."

It wouldn't be the first time, he thought. Unmuting himself he turned back to Captain Al-Faris.

"Captain, if you power down your reactor, and I mean completely, load all of your men into lifeboats and exit the ship, I will pick you up and you can join us for the return trip. You have my word as an officer that you and your men will not be harmed."

Captain Al-Faris deflated as he fell back into his chair.

Jacob knew what the man felt; he'd gone through it as well. Surrendering one's ship to an unknown enemy was never easy.

"Your terms are acceptable."

Jacob waited in the boat bay, wearing his ELS suit but with his helmet off. Jennings and Naki, exhausted, but unwilling to let their captain meet the enemy without them, flanked him, armed of course.

There simply was no way to do this with the Corsair. Jacob made the decision to dump it overboard. Boudreaux scowled at him the entire time.

The lifeboat passed through the Richman field, the blue line flashing across the hull. They were simple clamshell-shaped craft with limited thrusters on one end and no weapons. They were designed for short-term survival in space, or for orbital entry.

The boat hovered until the doors closed beneath her, then it came to a rest.

He was surprised there was only the one boat. Captain Al-Faris assured him every member of his crew who remained alive was on board, all sixty-three of them. Several of whom were wounded. PO Desper and her men were off to the side, ready to assist.

The hatch opened and the man who could only be Captain Al-Faris came out. He strode to the line, shoulders back, trying to be brave for his crew. Stopping short of the line, he went to attention.

"Captain Al-Faris of CNS *Al-Qud*. Officially surrendering."

Jacob stepped forward.

"Commander Jacob T. Grimm, USS *Interceptor*. I accept." His next move was a calculated risk, but he wanted the return journey to go smoothly. He wanted, well, not to be friends, but for this man to know he could trust Jacob at his word. "As-salamu alaykum, Captain Al-Faris."

Khaled's eyes went wide, as did the two men who had come to flank him. Jacob assumed they were his officers.

The man put one hand over his heart. "Wa alaykum as-salam, Commander Grimm."

Interceptor sped away from Zephyr after firing two rounds at the base, both impacting almost on top of one another. A crater several klicks deep was all that remained of the secret base.

Even with the Guild's starlane catapults, they were still weeks away from Alliance space. Between the remaining Special Forces troopers, his three uninjured Marines, and enough of his own people volunteering for guard duty, they turned the boat bay into a prisoner-of-war camp.

With any luck, the return journey would pass smoothly.

Jacob swiveled aimlessly in his chair. The main screen showed the black hole growing ever so smaller as they accelerated away.

He would have to find the time to write it all up in his report. From what Nadia told him after they stabilized her in sickbay, they weren't going to get FTLC for themselves.

The good news: the moment his weapons obliterated the base, the FTL comms died. There would be no more FTLC for them. Any ships out in the black, waiting for the call to attack en masse, would never receive it.

All that remained of his mission was to destroy the Guild platforms leading to Caliphate space, make sure the enemy aboard his ship didn't attempt a revolt, and the most difficult part, figure out how to avoid fraternizing with Nadia for the trip home. The first two were a cake-walk comparatively.

CHAPTER FIFTY-EIGHT

TWO MONTHS LATER

Jacob stood at attention in front of Admiral Villanueva and SECNAV DeBeck. When he'd shown up for the debriefing he expected a naval review board, not two of the most powerful people he knew.

"That's everything, then?" Admiral Villanueva asked.

"Yes ma'am. Upon reaching Fort Kirk, I turned the men of the *Al-Qud* over to the garrison, then proceeded here. We also turned over Bijan and Princess Sarina at the same time. Per instructions, we kept Dr. Yusra Abbasi with us until we could hand her off to ONI here at Alexandria."

Villanueva nodded as she turned through the NavPad's holographic feature with his written report along with the reports of other officers and those at Fort Kirk.

"That was quite the find," SECNAV DeBeck said. "Our Intel on his children is sporadic at best. I'm not surprised we keep running into them considering he has several dozen. Finding one he'd abandoned, though, was… fortuitus."

"How so, sir? If you don't mind my asking," Jacob added hastily.

DeBeck only smiled. "You've served the Navy and your nation, son, no need to worry about stepping on my toes. Princess Sarina is willing to try and persuade her people of the evils of slavery. She wishes to use her influence to try and convince some of their planets to rebel. Apparently, despite her disability, she was quite popular with the people. If we can get a civil war going, it will help us and hurt them."

Jacob understood the strategic benefit of finding a way to make the Caliphate implode. Though, he suppressed a shudder at the slaughter that would ensue. The Caliphate was known for putting down insurrections with orbital bombardments. Sometimes it seemed everything he did led to more death.

"Understood, sir."

Villanueva frowned as the last sheet appeared on the NavPad. Jacob saw Midship Watanabe's face through the hologram.

"You recommend against a court-martial for Midship Watanabe's egregious actions? Her decisions resulted in the death of two crew, and almost cost you the mission. Is there a reason why you wouldn't want to throw *The Book* at her?"

Jacob had prepared for the question. Reviewed the situation, the events on Midway, and everything leading up to it. He cleared his throat.

"Ma'am, while the loss of Spacer Cooper and Spacer Blachowicz is unforgivable, and as a direct result of Midship Watanabe's actions, I"—the next part would be tricky—"think the Navy failed her first."

Villanueva frowned and DeBeck sat up straighter. Had Jacob not already stood at parade rest, he would have snapped to attention from their sudden change in demeanor.

"How do you figure that, *Commander Grimm*?" Villanueva asked. Jacob did not miss the sudden cold in her voice.

"Ma'am, she floated through the academy. Either from a failure on her instructors part, or because of her family connections. She should never have made it to her midship cruise. To be honest, ma'am, she should never have made it *into* the academy. She didn't want to be in the Navy. She didn't want to be on a ship. I know it's unlikely that a court martial won't be established, but I do think the mitigating circumstances should be considered."

"I understand, Commander. I don't agree with you, but I understand," Villanueva said.

DeBeck waved his hand as if to dismiss it. "Doesn't matter. She will be tried, most likely found guilty and, since we're at war, shot."

Jacob frowned at the frankness of the SECNAV. He'd thought long and hard about his feelings on the matter. Watanabe is culpable for the deaths of two crew, and other crimes, but she wasn't the only one. Just the only one who would pay.

"Understood, sir."

DeBeck stood, moving toward the door. "I'm sorry, Commander, there is an important matter to deal with. Good job on this mission," he said as he departed.

Silence filled the room as Villanueva scrutinized the files until she read the last one.

"Any questions, Jacob?" she asked.

"Yes, ma'am, just the one... the *Interceptor*?"

"Of course. You will remain in command. I'm reassigning her to the USS *Alexander* battlegroup for the time being. Despite the war, we still must train, and I want to use the battlegroup as a training command. Help get the ships up to speed before sending them to the front. With the FTLC disabled, it might allow us to start pulling ahead."

There was something else bothering her. He could see it in her eyes, but more importantly, he felt it in the room. Call it his gut, or instincts, but something.

"Ma'am, is there something else?"

"Very astute, Jacob. Yes. The Guild is still a threat. They are making noise about our illegal seizure of their property. Considering they have no qualms about bombing our planets, and have the tech to do so, I'm concerned."

Jacob snorted. "That's hardly news, ma'am. They've complained about that since we kicked them out."

"Indeed. Our intelligence has indicated that they've purchased at least two Tzu-class battleships from the Terran Republic—"

His jaw tightened at the news. The Alliance, for all its economic power, had four. Four. The Guild bought two out of pocket.

"Why would they sell them to the Guild?" he asked. "They're our allies?"

"They were, yes. Official enquiries have fallen on deaf ears. As for now, though, we're beefing up Alexandria's defenses and I need you here, training other captains. You are dismissed."

"Aye, aye, ma'am."

Jacob snapped to attention, then did an about-face and exited the room, leaving the Admiral to her work. He made his way outside into the crisp winter air.

A thin, dark-haired woman in a winter coat and red scarf waited for him at the bottom of the stairs. She hadn't fully recovered from her ordeal, but even the cane she leaned on didn't detract from her allure.

"Why, Commander Grimm, are you beaming?" Nadia Dagher said.

"I am now. I hear that you are no longer on the top ten wanted list?"

She limped forward, grabbing him around the waist and hugging him tight.

"I hope I'm still on your top ten."

"I don't have a top ten, only a top one," he said. Jacob tilted her head up and kissed her lightly on the lips. She smelled of jasmine and vanilla. "And that slot is taken by you," he whispered.

"Oh goody. And yes, I'm free and clear. Apparently destroying the enemy's ability to communicate with FTL bought me a pardon directly from the president himself. I have a *signed* letter and everything."

He pulled her tight and headed for the aircar station. They walked at her pace, careful to keep her from slipping on the ice.

"I don't have any work, at least for a while, maybe even longer," she said.

"It looks like I'm stationed here for now," Jacob said. "I think I've got a normal assignment for once."

She giggled and it was music to his ears. "You don't do anything normal," Nadia said.

"True, very true." He stopped, turning toward her. "Nadia, I submerged my emotions that entire mission. All the way there, and all the way back. I had no idea if I would lose you in either direction and it—"

"Don't get all maudlin on me, Mister Grimm. I did what I had to do, and so do you."

His hand tightened around the small object in his pocket. It was one thing to guess the feelings of another under normal circumstances, but what he was about to do would change everything.

"I'm trying to say something here. We're a nation at war,

nothing is normal. We could die tomorrow in our sleep, but... if I'm going to die—"

Jacob took a deep breath and knelt in front of her.

"What are you doing?" she asked. She looked around with wide-eyed surprise.

He pulled the small golden ring with the single diamond, from his pocket. "Nadia Dagher, will you do me the honor of marrying me?"

"Is this a joke? Are you joking with me?" she asked.

"I love you. We spend all our available time together. Marriage is important to me, and I want to be with you forever. So no, not a joke."

She looked down at him, her brown eyes wide. "This... I'm a spy, Jacob. How did you surprise me?"

"Do you want to know, or do you want to answer?" he asked.

Nadia closed her eyes, taking a deep breath before spearing him with her gaze.

"You jerk. Yes, the answer is yes."

Commander Jacob T. Grimm and the USS *Interceptor* will return in A GRIMM DECISION, GRIMM'S WAR BOOK SIX.

THANK YOU FOR READING KNOW THY ENEMY

We hope you enjoyed it as much as we enjoyed bringing it to you. We just wanted to take a moment to encourage you to review the book. Follow this link: Know Thy Enemy to be directed to the book's Amazon product page to leave your review.

Every review helps further the author's reach and, ultimately, helps them continue writing fantastic books for us all to enjoy.

ALSO IN SERIES
AGAINST ALL ODDS
WITH GRIMM RESOLVE
ONE DECISIVE VICTORY
A GRIMM SACRIFICE
KNOW THY ENEMY
A GRIMM DECISION
TRADITIONS OF COURAGE

Check out the entire series here! (tap or scan)

You can also join our non-spam mailing list by visiting www.subscribepage.com/AethonReadersGroup and never miss out on future releases. You'll also receive three full books completely Free as our thanks to you.

Facebook | Instagram | Twitter | Website

Want to discuss our books with other readers and even the authors? Join our Discord server today and be a part of the Aethon community.

LOOKING FOR MORE GREAT SCIENCE FICTION AND FANTASY?

It's 2079. The Sleer War is over. Earth lost.

When Lt. Simon Brooks discovered an alien A.I., he made a name for himself as an officer in the Unified Earth Fleet. And while his tech skills are next level, he has a lot to learn about running a combat squadron.

After flubbing a training exercise, Brooks is set to choosing worlds for human colonization, and he thinks he has the perfect candidate: Vega. But rumors and intelligence reports make him think there's something there which the Sleer missed.

As Brooks and the crew of UES Gauntlet head to Vega to prove his theory, a Sleer science vessel is already working to claim the prize: an armored military base from a long-forgotten war. Acquiring it for the UEF would put humanity back in the fight to reclaim Earth…and Simon Brooks back in control of his career.

But events from neighboring empires threaten to destabilize the UEF, pitting Gauntlet's crew against secret police, government bureaucracy, interstellar trade negotiations, and Sleer merchant guilds. In the face of encroaching chaos, does victory in battle even matter?

Get Disjunction Now!

When the rules of war keep changing, fight for each other... *Humanity has been banished to a distant star. Left to fight over resources rationed to them by mysterious machine-overlords known as Wardens. Commander Rylan Holt labors against inter-colony arms trafficking when an informant gives him horrific news. The ruthless cartel boss, Lilith, has stockpiled outlawed weapons of mass destruction. Worse, she claims to have permission from the Wardens to unleash them upon the system. When the battleship* Audacity *speeds to investigate Rylan's discovery, operations officer Scott Carrick finds himself in a trap more deadly than he could have ever imagined. His only hope of escape may lie with their most junior crewmember, a nurse named Aila Okuma, who's never seen battle. As Rylan, Scott, and Aila struggle to survive a war where the rules keep changing, they must answer a terrible question: how do they win when it seems the Wardens intend for everyone to lose?*

Get Hellfire Now!

JEFFERY H. HASKELL

A smuggler, a spy, a brewing revolution...and a rogue agent who could destroy it all. Perrin Hightower can fly a run-down freighter through the galaxy's most dangerous wormholes blindfolded, a handy skill in her shipping business... and her smuggling enterprises. Special agent Tai Lawson dreams of leading the Ruby Confederation's spy agency. But when his partner steals a top-secret list of revolutionaries and vanishes, Tai's accused of helping his friend escape. When Tai seeks her navigation expertise, Perrin would rather jump out an airlock than help. But the missing person is her ex-boyfriend—a double agent she thought was helping the revolution. Her name's on that list, and she'll do anything to keep it secret. **Hiding their true agendas, Tai and Perrin follow the rogue spy's trail across the galaxy. Each must decide where their allegiance truly lies when they learn the spy carries more than a list of conspirators—he carries information that could shatter the fragile peace in the galaxy.**

Get Rogue Pursuit Now!

For all our Sci-Fi books, visit our website.

AUTHOR'S NOTE

During the book there is a snippet of a song. Not that I'm some great songwriter, but I ended up writing the entire song. My intention was to play it on an acoustic guitar. If you're interested in playing it, for some crazy reason, please record it and send it my way. I would, in return, send you *signed copies of the entire series.*

Here it is:

Verse 1:
C Major
Lost in the darkness of deep space
G Major
Searching for love, a steady pace
D Major
Wandering alone, through the stars
C Major
Hoping to find who we are

Chorus:
C Major

In the void, we'll find our way
G Major
With love as our guide, we'll pave the way
D Major
Together we'll fight, through the unknown
C Major
We'll make a home, far from our own

Verse 2:
C Major
Battles rage on, in the cold
G Major
But love will keep us warm, to hold
D Major
Though we're far from home
C Major
We're never truly alone

Chorus:
C Major
In the void, we'll find our way
G Major
With love as our guide, we'll pave the way
D Major
Together we'll fight, through the unknown
C Major
We'll make a home, far from our own

Bridge:
C Major
With every step, we'll grow
G Major
With love, we'll overcome

D Major
We'll find a way, to call it our own
C Major
In the darkness, love will be our guide, our home

Outro:
C Major
Lost in the darkness of deep space
G Major
With love, we'll find our place
D Major
Together we'll fight, through the unknown
C Major
We'll make a home, far from our own.

ABOUT THE AUTHOR

Join me in whatever way works for you. I love talking about my work, about how to help other's succeed, and sci-fi in general.

Mailing List: https://goo.gl/LJdYDn

Haskell's Heroes (New FB fan group): https://www.facebook.com/groups/731572934942029/

YouTube: https://www.youtube.com/c/JefferyHHaskell_Author

Twitter: https://twitter.com/jeffery_haskell

Email: jeffery.haskell@gmail.com

Website: www.jefferyhhaskell.com

Printed in Great Britain
by Amazon